Praise for

'Intelligent and pacy thriller... revenge, perseverance and the struggle against injustice.' (Paula Hawkins)

'A compelling read and refreshingly original. Beyond good and evil, with a bit of Sepp Blatter, and a grenade. So many great characters and a thundering climax on a rope bridge in the Himalayas.' (Andy Martin, *Reacher Said Nothing*)

'A detective (and author) to remember' (Ed Church, the Detective Brook Deelman series)

Also by James Ellson

The Trail

James Ellson was a police officer for 15 years, starting in London and finishing as a Detective Inspector at Moss Side in Manchester. When he left the police he started writing. His debut novel *The Trail* was published in 2020 and longlisted for the Boardman Tasker Award

James is a keen climber and mountaineer, and has visited Nepal many times. In 2004 he climbed 6,812 metre Ama Dablam, and in 2008 soloed the Matterhorn.

He lives in the Peak District with his wife, and manages their smallholding, which includes bees and an orchard.

Twitter @jamesellson3
facebook.com/james.ellson.98
www.jamesellson.com

COLD DAWN

JAMES ELLSON

Cambium

First published by Unbound in 2022
Second edition, 2023

Cambium Press

A CIP record for this book is available from the British Library

ISBN 978-1-7394421-2-5 (paperback)
ISBN 978-1-7394421-3-2 (ebook)

Printed in Great Britain by Clays Ltd, Elcograf S.p.A

1 3 5 7 9 8 6 4 2

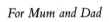

For Mum and Dad

Namaste!
Lexicon at the back

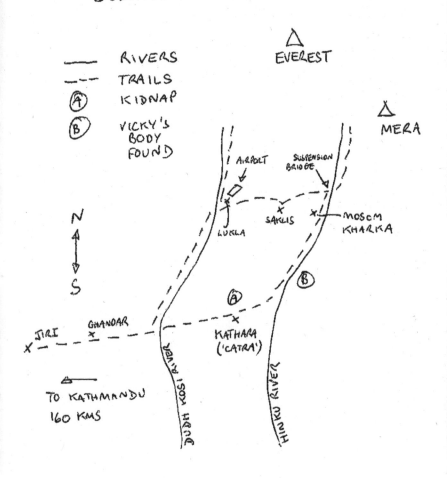

SKETCH MAP OF MERA TREKKING TRAIL

DCI Rick Castle

——— RIVERS
----- TRAILS
(A) KIDNAP
(B) VICKY'S BODY FOUND

△ EVEREST

△ MERA

AIRPORT

SUSPENSION BRIDGE

LUKLA

× SAKLIS

× MOSOM KHARKA

N ↓ S

(B)

(A)

× KATHARA ('CATRA')

JIRI ×

GHANDAR ×

TO KATHMANDU 160 KMS

DUDH KOSI RIVER

HINKU RIVER

Exhibit RC/1, Coniston Missing Enquiry

1

At the Sycamore Road Apiary, a dozen beehives formed a horseshoe in the clearing of a small copse. A new patch of Himalayan balsam was already at waist height and would soon be in flower. Good for the bees.

It was the first Sunday in May, and the start of the swarming season. The roof of Rick's hive leant against the base and smoke billowed from his smoker. A trick to keep the bees down in the hive. It made his eyes water. Blinking, he prised loose another frame and lifted it up for inspection. There was a steady hum of activity. Over a thousand bees crawled around on each side. Some flew around his white smock and one or two buzzed his veil.

He spotted a queen cup. The shape and size of half a finger, it hung off the bottom of the frame. He lifted the frame higher. The cup was still closed which meant the new queen was still developing. With thumb and forefinger he crushed it.

He destroyed three more before replacing the dummy board and hive roof. There was no doubt about it: the colony wanted to swarm – *would* swarm – which meant he'd have to induce it. A process as simple as nuclear fusion.

As he corked the smoker he saw another beekeeper

approaching. Like Rick, they wore a white smock and veil and with the exception of one detail could have been any club member. Yellow washing up gloves. Rick picked up his gear and walked towards his boss. They met halfway and unzipped their veils.

'Did you get a pass?' said Rick.

'She got out the wrong side,' said Robbo. 'She wants lunch at a pub, but it's not good for my diet. Beer and a roast. Custard.'

'You could skip dessert.'

'How are your new bees?'

'I need to split them,' said Rick. The previous season his colony had lost their queen and been destroyed by laying workers. He stared into the horseshoe of hives. Squadrons of bees taking off and landing. Balsam swaying in the breeze.

'I want to reopen the Coniston missing enquiry. Arrest Khetan.'

'You do, do you?'

The reply was inflected as a question, but Rick knew it was an answer. And not the one he was looking for.

He pictured the long suspension bridge where he'd last seen Khetan. He saw the snowy mountains, the flapping prayer-flags. Heard the thunder of the river. Watched Khetan run.

'You found Calix Coniston.'

'I lost Khetan.'

'You had other priorities.'

'Three people died. There's been muttering and I want to put things right.'

The superintendent pinged off a Marigold and chucked it on the grass. 'Do you know where he is?'

'Nepal.'

'I meant an address.' The second glove followed the first. 'Do you even know he's in Nepal?'

'No.'

'Intel?'

Rick shook his head.

'He'll have changed his name.' Robbo scratched the tops of his hands which were red and puffy.

'Probably.'

'Jesus, Rick, have you got anything?'

Rick had known his boss would take some persuading and he harnessed the strategy lesson from his SIO course. Body recovery, searches, arrests – everything needed a strategy. McTavish, the bald Scottish instructor, had finished by saying they could use it at home. Want wifie to wear a catsuit and smear honey on Saturday? Then Friday, take her out for dinner and invite her maw for Hogmanay.

Rick never forgot strategy. Three points for Robbo: head, heart, and conscience.

'It's your fault.' Point three.

'*My* fault?'

'You said not to flag him.' Rick removed his leather gauntlets. Their biosecurity wasn't as good, but they were less itchy.

'Brigadier Coniston was a brave man and I owe him.' Point two, heart – Robbo was no robot. During the hostage negotiation the soldier had volunteered to be exchanged for his son. 'The brigadier's death was my fault.'

'We've been over this, Rick, several times. You've been debriefed by three senior officers. You've read the review document. Accept the criticisms, learn the learning points and move on.'

Robbo picked up his rubber gloves. 'In any case, it's not a priority.'

'Not a priority – conspiracy to kidnap and manslaughter times three? And that's just by us.'

'No.' Robbo flapped his gloves hard against his leg, trying to turn them the right way around.

'You know he's the FBI's Most Wanted in Southern Asia?'

'It's still no.'

'They think he could be the next Bin Laden.'

'Well, they can worry about that. You've got a lot else on your desk.'

Only one prong of Rick's strategy remained – head – the weakest. He'd been thinking about how to find and arrest Khetan for a year, but still had no big idea. No USP. The sticking point was the lack of an extradition treaty because even if he located Khetan he'd be unable to bring him to the UK.

'Anyway, you've not mentioned an arrest plan.'

'I've a few ideas.'

Robbo held a glove up to his mouth. 'Details?' He blew into a finger. It popped out with a crack, leaving him red in the face.

'Entice Khetan to the UK and arrest him on British soil.'

'Details.'

'Still being fine-tuned.' Khetan would be suspicious of everything and everybody, so whatever Rick came up with had to be clever. Subtle, restrained, unremarkable. Adjectives were as far as he'd got.

'There's another problem which you're avoiding. Do our courts even have jurisdiction?'

Rick wanted to punch the air: not only was Robbo wavering, but the answer was positive. 'They do.' He paused for effect. McTavish would be proud of him. 'Khetan's a dual national – he was given British citizenship when working in London.'

Robbo blew out the final two fingers on his glove. It induced a coughing fit and he bent over.

'Are you okay?' Rick picked up the second Marigold and popped the fingers, one after the other. Like a kid with a cap-gun.

Robbo stood up. 'Bloody show off.'

'Diet's only half of it. Exercise—'

'Dual citizenship still needs the CPS to be willing to prosecute – the deaths were all in Nepal.'

'I've pushed it around with one of their senior lawyers and she says they will.'

'In writing?'

'No.' Which wasn't surprising as Louise was a friend and they'd been in the pub.

Robbo puckered his lips and was silent.

'Fuck, Robbo. If I was a violent no-neck like Harris or Khan, you'd say yes. You know you would.'

'Maybe, but—' The superintendent paused, looked round the apiary. 'How's your dad?'

Rick shook his head. Stepped a few paces away, stepped back. 'This has nothing to do with him.'

'You are on the SMT's watch list – you're still seeing Emma. They – we – don't want you to blow.'

'She's about to sign me off: I've only got one more session.'

Rick held his boss's stare.

The superintendent picked up his washing up gloves. 'If that's true—' He eased the gloves back onto his fingers. 'Okay, Rick, here's the deal: firstly, *if* you get CPS authority to prosecute in writing, and secondly, *if* you come up with a convincing arrest plan to lure Khetan to the UK, then, and only then, will I sanction reopening the file. Agreed?'

Robbo had finished as he'd started: an answer masquerading as a question. But it was enough. Rick nodded. He'd have to manage the fallout later, but inside he was doing the waggle dance.

*

On his way home, Rick stopped off at Three Views to see Dad. Reception was unstaffed and he walked towards the main recreation room. Singing leaked through the double doors. Taking a deep breath, he walked in.

Around the piano in the corner, alongside the row of French doors, a group of white- and grey-haired residents were belting out 'Jerusalem'. Dad, tall and thin, was obvious. He wore his old Arran jumper, and pale slacks which Rick hadn't seen before. He was singing and smiling.

Michael, one of the assistants, nodded at Rick and walked over.

'Did you look it up?'

Rick shook his head. He hoped someone like Michael would be around to care for him. He was young, kind, and at least looked interested in what was going on.

'Your mum's not coming as much. Once a week, sometimes not at all.'

Rick frowned. He thought she'd been coming every other day. 'What about Becky?'

'Your sister? Every Saturday afternoon, like clockwork.'

The hymn finished.

'Go on,' said Michael, his eyes ushering Rick forward.

Rick walked towards the piano, tapped his dad on the shoulder.

'Dad.'

His dad turned to look at him, his face frowning. 'Hello. Are you new here?'

The piano restarted. Rick recognised the tune from school.

'*I danced in the morning ...*' Two or three people started clapping. Dad, too. Rick had never seen him clap. He retreated back to Michael, with each step seeing Dad – on the touchline, winning the fathers' race, fishing for crabs.

'Do you want a cup of tea?'

Rick shook his head.

He watched his dad singing and clapping. Then looked away and stared out of the glass doors. One day *he* would forget everything. Darkness, for ever.

2

After a month in Strangeways, Calix Coniston changed cells. Flanked by guards, he stood on the metal catwalk, holding his cardboard crate. The three men waited, Calix staring at the crate. There were air-holes in the sides, and in a former life it had held apples for a supermarket.

The cell door jerked into life and rattled from right to left.

Third time lucky?

The first had been a drink-driver who'd killed an old man on a pedestrian crossing. A prison epiphany meant Kaiden was constantly praying and quoting the Bible. To be woken every day to Psalm 118, verse 24, '*This is the day the Lord has made, let us rejoice*', had driven Calix nuts. Two weeks of that and then for a reason never explained, Calix had been moved to a different cell. Havel was a Slovakian lorry driver who'd been stopped at Dover with thirty-eight kilos of heroin hidden behind a false compartment. Didn't speak a word of English. Hummed to himself at night and always on the bog.

Or worse?

Calix said a silent prayer, his stomach heaving. He never prayed, and he blamed Kaiden.

The door juddered to a halt and he walked in. The cell smelt of cigarettes and pot noodle.

As the door rattled shut a man stared down from the top bunk. He was mid-twenties, ginger-haired and freckly. The tattoo of a lion's head dominated his bare torso. Thick red headphones were angled back on his head. He held a comic. Calix nodded a greeting, then glanced around. A plastic table and two chairs. On the table sat a small TV with the sound down low. Above it was a shelf, and the bog was in the corner. There wasn't a mirror because it could be smashed and the shards used to wound, or kill.

Three square metres. Every one identical, like bird boxes.

Calix slid his cardboard crate onto the scratched and graffitied table. Inside was a spare set of clothes. Three books, his toothbrush, and last week's paper. Resting on the clothes were clingfilmed sandwiches and a banana – changing cells meant he'd missed lunch. His gratitude was pathetic.

The man on the top bunk put down his comic and swung his legs over the side. He was all muscles and tattoos. He pushed his headphones off. 'Darren. From Oldham – Oldham Edge, the skinter side.' He lit a roll-up, and the smell of fresh tobacco flooded the room. He stretched out a hand, the cigarette pinched as if it was a detonator.

Calix took it and nodded his thanks. He inhaled and passed it back.

'Have a seat.' Darren flipped his legs back onto the bunk and picked up his comic.

Calix looked at the two plastic chairs. The back was missing on one, and the arms flopped down on the other. 'Which one?'

'Which one?' Darren chuckled into his roll-up and shook his head. 'Either fucking one.'

Calix sat down alongside the TV and peeled the banana. Next to him, images flickered and voices merged. A drip fell from a corner of the ceiling, onto a wet patch on the floor. The cave in Nepal. Held hostage with Barney and Spencer, feeling cold. Scared. Having to take charge, act for the three of them.

He finished the banana and pushed the skin onto the table. He wondered if he should say something, but Darren was looking at his comic. On the cover a black-hooded figure waved a chainsaw.

After eating the sandwiches Calix still felt hungry. He walked over to the bunks and slipped off his shoes. The black elasticated plimsolls were the same as the ones he'd worn at primary school. He was twenty-four years old, and he'd got nowhere. He clambered across the stained mattress and lay down.

Above Calix's ceiling of graffiti and old chewing gum and less than an arm's length away, Darren muttered to himself as he tried to read his comic. Calix had taught Havel a few words of English, and could help Darren, too. He closed his eyes.

Darren jumped down onto the floor, wobbling the bunks. 'What you in for?' He paused. 'Oi, fuck-face.'

Calix opened his eyes. 'You heard of Special K?'

'For fuck! Makes you want to piss and see shit that's not there.'

Calix snickered gently. 'No, not ketamine. Hant Khetan – he's wanted by the FBI.'

'Course I heard of him.'

'I worked with him,' said Calix. '*For* him,' he corrected himself.

Darren whistled. 'You some sort of caped crusader?'

Calix scratched his neck and looked away. He'd been duped by Khetan. But he didn't say that. He wished he hadn't said anything.

Darren shuffled across to the table and rummaged in the crate. Calix stood up. He was six foot two. Taller. Darren placed a finger on his chest and pushed.

Calix sat back down on the bunk and watched Darren empty the crate onto the floor. Two photos flew up, floated down and skidded away. Darren picked them up and studied them. The first was of Calix's old man in uniform, and the second his parents on an anniversary, smiling. Before.

'Was them it?'

Calix nodded and took back the pictures. He gathered his things. He put everything back in the crate, checked the photo of Megan was still there, and toe-poked the crate under his bunk. Darren leant back against the wall. A guard walked past and the metal floors reverberated. 'How long you looking at, Capeman?'

'Brief says two to nine.'

Darren grunted, eyes on the TV.

Calix found a drink carton amongst his things. He poked in the straw and lay back on the bunk. He read some of the graffiti. Prisoner BN 89511 would dress up as the governor's wife. He felt sorry for prisoner GH 53976. He drank some of the juice. Two years would be okay: time spent on remand and early release meant he'd not have long to do. Three would be bearable, four hard, and anything longer, obscene. Eight or nine would mean ticking 30–35 in the exit questionnaire. He couldn't stay behind bars that long.

He put the empty carton down on the floor and fingered the photos out of the crate. The one of his parents was torn. Asking the guards for tape was as pointless as asking for a bicycle or a hedgehog. Or a bicycle for a hedgehog. He brushed away hairs, checked the sticky on the back and pressed them to the wall.

Resting his head on the lumpy pillow, he stared at his old man staring back. His pristine white gloves, his sparkling buttons and braid. His old man had wanted him to be a soldier, like father like son. He turned to Megan – she was sitting at her desk, the two of them had been talking late into the night. She looked sad, as if she also was disappointed in him.

Calix rolled over, picked at his fingernails. Every second he remained aware what Darren was doing. Maybe he should have offered him his lunch.

On the wing a prisoner started singing. '*There was ten German bombers in the air, there was ten German bombers in the air.*' More prisoners joined in, coining the pipes in accompaniment. '*And the RAF shot one down. The RAF from England shot one down. Shot one down.*'

It could have been much, much worse: bruises and boredom, but nothing broken and no trips to the infirmary. Calix remained on the fence about his third cellmate. Darren was moody and violent, but could be amusing, and stuck up for Calix outside the cell.

Two things alleviated the monotony. The first was Prison Skool. Subjects included chivs, laundry, disguise, anti-forensic. Two months after being incarcerated, he'd found out he shared a cell with one of the teachers.

Darren taught muling.

There were two basic methods: packing, hiding things by swallowing; and stuffing, hiding things in the rectum. 'Every fuck in this place should be a proficient stuffer,' Darren had told him. 'But packing is more of a special taste. Lit'ra-fucking-ally, ha-ha. Big rewards, but big fucking risk.'

An experienced packer could swallow a kilo in weight in a hundred small packets. Packing was for the longer term and used for drug smuggling on international flights. Stuffing was for a day or two, used to overcome prison and dibble security, and with the added advantage of being employable at short notice. 'Very fucking short notice, Capeman – if you practise.' According to Darren, the urge to defecate came at 100ml, but even a novice stuffer could store twice that. With practice, an experienced stuffer could store objects as large as mobile phones.

There was a downside: the prison infirmary invariably held a packer or a stuffer who'd been greedy or miscalculated. So Darren had made him practise. A wad of tissue double-wrapped in condoms packed in the morning, and a pound coin, similarly wrapped, stuffed in the afternoon. Packing required a knack and confidence which he'd soon mastered. Stuffing had been as unpleasant as he'd anticipated. Hands covered with shit and a feeling of violation.

The second thing was visitors. His mum came once a fortnight. The first time she'd cried a lot and said little, but gradually she'd hardened to being searched and the smell of disinfectant. He asked about his parrot Bird Bird, and she told him about Joe, his increasingly frail grandad. Calix didn't like her visiting, but he didn't like her leaving.

Occasionally, he phoned her. There were public phones on the wing, but they were, as Darren said, like Ron-fucking-seal. In addition, numbers had to be approved, there was always a queue and credit was limited. Darren didn't bother with wing phones. So neither did Calix.

He had a more surprising visitor, too: The Big Red, his former employer. At the time Calix hadn't been able to fathom why. TBR had asked about trial dates and his plea. Later, Calix realised TBR had been assessing whether Calix was going to give him up to the dibble in return for a lighter sentence. The tactic had backfired. Before the visit, Calix had not contemplated anything, but afterwards he'd worked it. TBR knew people and like Darren, he also knew about things. How to buy things, find things out, get things done. On the outside, and on the inside.

He was living a new life, as if he was a salamander emerging from the water onto the land. A new life with new rules and a new pecking order.

*

But, in May, after being locked up for almost a year – a mistake and a delay in the timing of his trial – Calix had received a new visitor.

3

Rick still had no plan to arrest Khetan.

Holding a basketball and pondering, he sat in a wheelchair on the mid-court line. He turned to the day's cases: a three-handed student on student rape, a false call of abduction, and a suspicious house fire – one dead man with special needs. He sniffed the air, then his watch strap. Smoke and post-mortem.

The sports hall was deserted. He bounced the ball, which made a satisfying thwack. He played most weeks and when he was there he quite enjoyed it. But it was one more thing on top of everything else. No one loved a man who couldn't cope.

The door crunched open.

Maggie wheeled in, and threw her bag down at the side of the court. Rick rolled over and pecked her on the cheek. 'You okay?'

'Work shit.'

'Now?'

'Later.' She squeezed his hand. 'What did Robbo say?'

'Ditto.'

'You smell of dead people.' She moved away, laughing.

Rick set off right, his left-handed dribbling still being weak. Maggie came after him like Boadicea. Two bounces with the ball in his lap. He spun his wheels. And again. Another bounce, but too far, and he found himself in the corner. He dribbled along the baseline, but he was clumsy and Maggie was quick. She knocked the ball out of court.

Maggie's turn to attack. She flipped the ball behind her from one hand to the other. Again. A third time. She was toying with him, and he edged forwards. She set off to his right with the ball in her lap. She bounced the ball and changed direction, across his front.

Tracking her, he feinted a lunge. She smiled, but kept going. She entered the three-point zone and scooped up the ball. Paused, steadied, the ball raised between her hands. But instead of shooting, she bounced and moved further left. Rick went with her, but wasn't quick enough to even raise his arms.

The ball was in the air.

Bang. Back board and clean through.

After an hour, he'd made up his mind. In the morning he'd charge all three students. Which meant he could concentrate on the Khetan case.

Rick waited for Maggie in the bar. He ordered two bottles of beer and carried them to a table from where he could see Maggie entering. People sat in small groups, a quick drink after squash or badminton.

He sipped his beer. Entrapment was the crux issue. Trying to think of something that would make Khetan return to Britain. Trying to think like him, to understand him. He'd tasked Maggie – without Robbo's knowledge – to research Khetan, and they'd come up with some good ideas. A friend or girlfriend in Britain? Who was in debt, or a drug addict. An ill friend or relative? Someone who needed Khetan's help, and possible only by him travelling to the UK. Good ideas, but only questions.

Still no sign of her. He checked his phone for messages.

Hunter: *House 2 house negative*
Becky: *Call me*
Maggie: *Drying my hair 2 mins beer please X*

He sat back and waited. They had been together a year, a surprise to everyone. Himself, his family, friends. Colleagues had been agog. Wheelchair wheelchair, cue flashing lights and sirens. Sex was one of the most frequently debated issues at South Manchester. Were they? Weren't they?

He stared into the future. One potential problem was sharing a workplace, but they'd dealt with that. They had a Chinese wall, not at home where they often discussed work, but at the police station. Home life was sacrosanct, not even to be hinted at. She was an analyst in the intelligence unit and he was three grades higher, but it didn't seem to bother her.

There were practical issues: holidays needed creativity and planning, and having her to stay at his house was tricky with the bathroom and bedroom upstairs. One thing still worried him. She hadn't told him how she'd lost her legs. He knew she had stump disease and couldn't wear prosthetics because they hurt too much, but the rest of it he didn't know. He wasn't moving in together until he did.

Maggie came into the bar, and attracted attention as she moved towards him. Her hair was shiny and she'd put on make-up. She caught him staring, and smiled. He smiled back. *Of course they were having sex.*

'Siobhan?'

'She went sick again, but at lunchtime I saw her coming out of a nail bar. I took your advice, stopped the car, wound down the window and told her it had to stop.'

'And?'

'She said that I was a bitch. That I had it all. That I was only saying it because I'm going out with you. And because I'm in a wheelchair.'

Rick stroked Maggie's hand. 'Do you want me—'

She shook her head. 'It'd only make things worse.' She drank some of her beer. 'So come on, what did Robbo say?'

'He agreed on two conditions: one, I clear it with the CPS, and two, I come up with a convincing arrest plan.'

'That's great.' She clinked bottles.

'It is, except I haven't got an arrest plan.'

'What did you expect – a plane ticket to Nepal?'

Rick rolled the bottle across his forehead.

'Maggie! How're you?'

They turned to see a woman Rick recognised from Maggie's team.

The two women started chatting and Rick zoned out. Two people had inside knowledge on Khetan, intelligence which couldn't be gleaned from police databases or from open-source forums. And, even if all the correct channels and protocol were followed, not even from the FBI. One of them worked at a twenty-four-hour rental near Heathrow, the other was in Strangeways.

'How's the big case, Rick?' said Jenny. 'The next Osama Bin Laden?'

'Oh, you know.'

There were kissed goodbyes, Rick included, and Jenny wheeled away.

'Maggie!'

'What?'

'You know what.'

'It's a turn of phrase. Everyone's looking for the next Bin Laden.'

'Yeah, but I really am.' He sipped his beer. 'I had a thought, though, while you were talking to Jenny. I'm going to debrief Barney Williams again.'

'When?'

'Soon as.' He glanced at his watch. 'Maggie, I've got to go – Emma.' He pushed his beer across the table. 'Love you.'

'Rick.'

He turned.

'Siobhan.'

'Don't worry, tomorrow I won't know who she is.'

'I thought,' said Emma, 'we'd try something different to access the mother and triplets incident. I want you to try telling it backwards.'

On the stiff sofa Rick said nothing. His earlier optimism supplanted.

He looked around the room. There was a desk, and a few books, but no posters or anything to distract him. He'd tried before. On a shelf, the spider plant was multiplying like Mickey's brooms.

He stood up, and walked over to the window.

Cold Manchester rain lashed the glass. It pattered, as if the window was in pain. Droplets streamed downwards, slowed, and stopped. They coalesced, and set off again.

If Rick left for Heathrow soon, he could be back by the early shift. Otherwise, Robbo would start moaning, and might even renege on their deal.

For a moment the rain eased and he could hear Emma's clock ticking.

'Rick, if you don't say anything, we won't get anywhere.'

His theory, if he arrested Khetan, the flashbacks, daydreams, visions and nightmares would stop.

The pounding on the panes resumed. Rick stared out through the cascades of water. And into the misty evening of office blocks and streets of grey. Wet and besmirched, the light already fading. Two men were unloading a lorry, boxes on the tail-lift. A woman in high heels struggled to light a cigarette. Red and white vehicle lights: organised, red one way, white the other. The images were fuzzy, and rain-distorted. Like a dream.

He turned away.

Walked to Emma's desk and ripped off a sticky note.

Sorry.

'Maybe bring Maggie next time,' shouted Emma through the doorway. 'As we discussed.'

The words echoed along the corridor.

4

Rick drove south, heading for London. Cars flipped past in the opposite direction, lights momentarily breaching the dark. Single drivers mainly, staring straight ahead. Alone with their fears, and their aspirations.

Pop music washed from some vehicles, but like Rick, most drivers preferred a silent wallow in what had gone on, and why, and what could have been different. The swaying bridge in the snowy foothills of Everest, the failed negotiation with Khetan. *His* failed negotiation. The needless deaths of Spencer Williams and David Coniston. Khetan's escape.

He drummed on the steering wheel.

Robbo had not said no.

Obtaining the necessary paperwork from Louise would be easy, which left coming up with a convincing arrest plan.

He passed a service station, a nasty spread of yellowing lights and stained concrete in the deep darkness of the British countryside.

Barney Williams was his first hope.

After a pitstop to buy coffee and a sandwich, he reached Easy Cars. Under floodlights as bright as a football stadium's, new vehicles lined up on the forecourt. A cleaning crew were washing a four-wheel drive and a woman was marking up a clipboard. Music played from a hidden speaker.

Rick parked, and headed for the office.

The rental company was new, the office shiny and tasteful. Prints of European capitals on the walls, two drinks machines, a large fish tank. The room smelt of coffee, and was quiet except for bubbles from the tank.

Rick rang the bell.

Multi-coloured fish lazed.

Barney Williams appeared from a back room. 'Children love the fish, and they bring their parents back.' He stopped. 'Oh, it's you.'

Rick nodded. Williams had put back the weight he'd lost in Nepal and had shaved off his beard. It made him look younger, and coupled with his shaky voice, he still appeared not to have recovered from the kidnap. Rick shared the same demon, but had others too.

'I'd like to ask you a few questions.'

'Do I need a lawyer?'

'You're not in trouble.' Rick walked closer to the tank. A zebra-coloured fish with a yellow tail drifted across. 'I want to arrest Khetan.'

'We hoped you'd have done it by now.'

'Me too.' Rick held up a pot of fish food. 'May I?'

Williams nodded.

Rick sprinkled the flakes across the surface. There was a flurry of movement and fish darted across the tank. There was jousting and clashing of fins.

'Have you driven all the way from Manchester just to see me?'

Rick nodded. 'How's the course at uni?'

'Alright.'

'How're you?'

'How do you think?'

'I can imagine. But at least we got you back across the bridge in one piece. Got you home.'

Williams looked down and toe-tapped the counter.

The woman with the clipboard entered from the forecourt. There was a blast of reggae, then the door pulled shut, and silence. She looked Rick up and down, clicked her tongue, and went into the back.

'I didn't kidnap you, Barney, or your brother. And I didn't prevent Spencer getting the medical attention he needed. I want to see Khetan punished for what he did, and you and your family to get justice.'

Williams scoffed and kicked again at the counter.

'Closure, then. But I need your help.' Rick set down the fish food and walked back to the counter. Williams looked across. 'You spent a lot of time with Khetan. I wondered what you know about him. Habits, addictions, names of his associates. Medical issues.'

'He'd taken me hostage. I was hardly concerned with his welfare and what he was doing.'

'Weren't you trying to escape? Coniston was, wasn't he?'

'Calix is a fruitcake, you know that.'

'Have you been to Strangeways to see him?'

'Course I haven't.'

'Why not?'

'Is that not obvious? He conspired with Khetan – he's partly responsible for Spencer, for all of it.'

Rick looked across at the tank. Fish swimming slowly, back and forth, back and forth, quiet bubbles rising up. He felt Williams follow his stare. 'Anything might help.' He let the silence build, and expand, and intensify. Allowing the pregnant pause taught on every police interviewing course to do its work. Behind the counter, Williams rubbed the back of his neck.

'Khetan smoked cigarettes.'

'How many?'

'A packet a day.'

'Brand?'

Williams shook his head.

'Drugs?'

'I don't know. Maybe.'

'Ketamine?' It was the obvious question.

Williams shrugged. 'He drank beer, I know that. Different brands.' Williams closed his eyes – he was trying. 'I was scared, petrified.'

'I know you were. Anyone would have been.'

The woman reappeared again from the back, tutted at Rick, and returned outside, slamming the door behind her.

'He cried out in his sleep,' said Williams.

'Interesting,' said Rick. His response, the same as a social media smiley. 'What did he say?'

'Nothing intelligible.'

'How often?'

'Most nights.'

Even Khetan had demons. No one didn't. It wasn't much, but it was something, and justified driving down.

Rick laid a card on the table. 'Call me if you think of anything else, however insignificant.' He walked to the door.

'DCI Castle?'

Rick turned.

'Get that bastard.'

The hairs rose on Rick's neck. He pushed through the door and crashed it shut behind him. He was going to, or receive a telegram from the queen for trying.

5

Calix filed into the visits hall with the other cons and sat down at a table. Some of the men spoke in low voices, one obese man to himself, but most were silent. One con sniffed his armpits and cleaned his teeth with a finger. Another con sat sobbing. Guards stood like gnomes, twirling keys and whispering about last night's football. Calix glanced up at the nearest roving camera, down at the table microphone. On the table leg were dried lumps of chewing gum and scored graffiti: *dibble are cunts, screws are cunts, my dads a cunt.*

His old man wasn't. His old man was the bravest, most selfless person he knew.

Castle, the dibble detective who'd led the search and hostage negotiation in Nepal, was the second.

A buzzer sounded. 'Attention!' The voice came from hidden speakers. 'Attention, staff and prisoners in the visits hall. Due to an incident in reception, there will be a twenty-minute delay to all visits.'

The room groaned.

Calix didn't join in with the banging on the tables. He leant back against the wall and inspected his nails. They were short, apart from the left thumbnail which he left long on purpose.

He looked around, but couldn't see any signs of muling. Darren had told him it often happened during visiting. The obese man was still mumbling, and at the next table sat a prison kingpin, his fetcher the seat behind.

From nowhere, a spider abseiled down in front of Calix. It landed on the table, darted off one way, then turned and ran back. At the edge of the table, he blocked it with his hand. The spider backtracked. He toyed with it for a minute or so, fencing off its escape routes and watching it roll back on itself. Each time, the spider set off again. It was trapped, but never gave up.

Neither would he.

Calix placed his thumb on the spider's cephalothorax and pushed down. The pressure of his thumb was slight, but it restricted any movement. All eight of the spider's legs flailed. He pushed harder. Until the spider was dead. He shuffled it onto a palm. The spider was dark brown, hairy and had long legs. It was a house spider, the most common type. He'd never seen a purse-web, but was always hopeful.

He used his long thumbnail to sever the eight legs, then laid them out in order. Left side, right side. Next, he severed the large abdomen away from the cephalothorax. At the end of the abdomen were spinnerets, tiny protruding organs. He counted four. Children could guess their function, but adults often couldn't. Finally, he worked on the cephalothorax. It had eight eyes, which was normal. He severed off the palps – feelers which males used for mating. Then the chelicerae which looked like pincers but were hollow.

A buzzer sounded. 'Visiting will commence in two minutes.'

Calix arranged all the parts of the spider on the table so it looked like a diagram in a manual.

The heavy door rolled open. The door to the outside. To women and children, sunshine, beaches, ice-cream. Bird Bird.

To his tray of scalpels and tweezers and his work bench. To sitting on the bog in peace. To private property, personal space, limits on surveillance. To going where he wanted, when he wanted; *doing* what he wanted. The only private activity in prison was daydreaming.

Noncons streamed in, and immediately the hall was alive, noisy, and even more unpredictable. Like a pub at chucking-out time.

In front of Calix stood Barney Williams. He was as tall as any of the guards, and he'd shaved off his sun-bleached beard. Calix had been surprised that Barney was allowed to visit, or even wanted to, but he'd agreed to it – Calix was responsible, indirectly, for Spencer dying in the cave while Castle had been negotiating.

Barney sat down. His cheeks had filled out again and he'd put back the kilos he'd lost in Nepal. 'I wanted to see for myself. You. Here.'

Calix could tell him about Darren's moods, the noise at night, his fear of the showers. But he wasn't going to. He picked up one of the palps, twiddled it. 'Can you name any spiders?'

'Eh?'

'Do you know the names of any spiders?'

'Tarantula. Redback.'

'This one's a house spider.' Calix put the palp down and surveyed the dismembered arachnid.

'I've been back to Nepal,' said Barney. 'The cairn was still there on Spencer's grave, untouched. The cross too.' He described the visit with his parents. Back to the damp cave and his brother's grave that Calix helped dig. With the help of the Nepalese authorities, they had exhumed the body and repatriated it to the UK.

A loud noise at a nearby table made the two of them look sideways.

The obese man had fallen off his chair, and crawled under a table. The guards didn't even stop talking.

'I will never forget what you did, Calix.' Barney's hair was short, shaved at the sides and back. He looked younger but sounded older.

'Do you know the difference between a spider and an insect?'

'Will you shut up about spiders.' Barney swept the parts of the spider onto the floor. The abdomen, the cephalothorax, the chelicerae, the legs, and the palps. Only one leg remained, and he brushed that away too.

'Castle came to see me.'

Calix looked up.

Sat up.

'He wants to arrest Khetan, and wanted to know anything and everything I knew about him.'

'And did you tell him?'

'I couldn't think of much. Told him Khetan smoked a lot, and sometimes cried out in the night. But that I was in a daze out there, too scared to take it all in.'

'And why are you telling me?'

'I want you to help him.'

'Help Castle?'

'Tell him about Khetan, tell him anything he wants to know.'

The buzzer sounded for the end of visiting time.

Barney stood up.

'I thought I was the enemy,' said Calix.

'You both are: you and Khetan. But you owe me, Calix. Me and Spencer.'

Calix shuffled up in the queue. Ahead of him cons were being searched. The obese man had gone first, bundled away somewhere. Calix scrutinised the faces, still trying to identify a muler. Nervousness, fidgeting, sweating, even repeated swallowing. According to Darren, packages sometimes lodged in the throat.

He pictured Barney emerging into the pale sunshine, staring at the dirty sky, breathing deeply.

In his hand, he sorted the rescued spider appendages. He twiddled a chelicera between thumb and finger. It contained the gland used to inject venom into the spider's prey. The queue moved up. He sandwiched the chelicera between two fingers and dropped the rest to the floor. The lino was stained and worn from the feet of thousands of pent-up men.

He held his arms out to the sides and waited to be patted down.

Felt the chelicera.

Daydreamed about hurting Khetan.

6

Interview room three smelt of damp trainers. There wasn't a window and the single bulb was weak. A fly buzzed around the light.

'Getting searched still gets me,' said Hunter. He took off his jacket, rolled up a shirtsleeve and scratched his elbow. 'We're the police, for fuck's sake.' Rick's new sergeant had already made his point to the guards in the gatehouse. He was fifty-two, stocky, and wearing a tie which he must have been given as a present. A transferee from the flying squad after a stink that had made the news.

'Your man ain't coming.'

Hunter was wrong about being searched. And, Rick was in no doubt, wrong about Coniston. It wasn't an auspicious start.

'Family okay with the move north?'

Hunter scratched his arm. 'I'm divorced – twice.' He stared at Rick. 'And before you ask, I've got two kids, and one of them's separated.'

Rick tracked the fly, then looked away, the light's after-image staying with him. He wondered if his bees were swarming at that very moment.

Hunter took out a tube of cream and spread some on his

elbow. 'Bloody incontinents – could have been explosive gel.'

Mistake or joke, Rick wasn't sure. Hunter's face gave no clue. 'I heard you paint, Gary?'

Hunter scowled.

The door opened, and a guard ushered in Calix Coniston. He was clean-shaven, and paler than after his month in Nepal. He wore jeans, a light blue t-shirt and prison pumps. Hunter rolled down his sleeve and put on his jacket. He shuffled his chair and Coniston sat down, the three men at compass points.

'Usual rules,' said the guard. 'Nothing to be given to the prisoner, and, Coniston, you can leave at any time. I'll be outside. Enjoy your little tea party.'

Hunter glared at the guard, and Rick sensed another argument. But the guard left and a key rattled in the lock.

'Coniston, this is Detective Sergeant Hunter.' Rick glanced from one man to the other.

'Did you bring any cigarettes?'

'You deaf?' said Hunter.

'We've got something better,' said Rick.

'What?'

'Years of your flyblown life,' said Hunter.

'Gary.' Rick looked across at his new colleague but Hunter avoided his gaze.

'I'm listening,' said Coniston.

'We might be able to reduce your sentence,' said Rick. 'At least get you moved to a lower cat.'

'Why?'

'Because he's Mother Teresa.' Hunter scratched an elbow through his sleeve.

'We want you to tell us about Khetan.' Rick paused. 'It could be something obvious – a child or a girlfriend we don't know about. A drug habit. Names of associates. But it's likely to be something we don't even know we don't know.'

Coniston scoffed. 'You think you can succeed where the FBI have failed?'

'With your help, maybe. You know Khetan better than them. You *camped* in Nepal: can't be much you don't know.'

'We all got an Achilles,' said Hunter. 'Coke or slots, or a fondness for ladyboys.' Rick wondered if his new sergeant had said more than he'd meant to.

'I get it,' said Coniston. 'And in return you'd slash my sentence?'

'No guarantee, but I'd write to the judge. You'd also be helping to prosecute the man responsible for the deaths of Vicky Brant, Spencer Williams and—'

'My old man.'

Rick nodded. It was a big deal for him. It was a huge deal for Coniston. 'Your father, the brigadier.' He waited a few seconds, Coniston's eyes becoming glassy. 'You get out of here sooner and Khetan goes down.'

Rick could hear the fly, but couldn't see it.

Coniston stared into space.

Hunter jiggled a leg.

'We've heard that Khetan calls out in the night.'

'You've spoken to Barney.'

'Is Khetan addicted to ketamine?'

Coniston smiled. He eased his chair backwards and stood up. As quick as a cobra, he shot out an arm and flicked the air. The fly hit a wall and fell to the floor. He bent down, picked the dead insect up by a wing and dropped it on the table. Then rapped on the viewing-hatch.

The door lock clicked across.

'So?' said Rick.

'I'll think about it.'

*

Outside the prison, Rick and Hunter sat in their unmarked car, Rick updating his notes and feeling buoyed by the interview. Coniston was always contrary. A woman walked past, pushing a double buggy with a family bag of crisps shoved into the hood. She stopped pushing and took a great handful.

Catching Rick staring, she stuck up a middle finger and mouthed, Fuck off, copper.

The police radio jabbered: two shoplifters detained at Boots, van requested. Rick threw his notebook in the back and put the key in the ignition.

'Coniston was playing you, *sir*,' said Hunter. 'Enjoying himself.'

The police radio cut across. A man's voice, loud. '1-0-7-8, Charlie Mike, I'm in the high street. Security guard requesting my assistance.'

'More units, robbery at Fine Wine—'

Hunter turned the volume up and Rick started the car.

'Russell was our adviser in Nepal on the Coniston enquiry,' shouted Rick. 'Now a friend of mine.'

Opposite Fine Wine, Rick and Hunter waited in the car. Takeaway coffees steamed up the windscreen. Parked in front of them was an ambulance with the rear doors open, and inside, paramedics were treating Russell and the off-licence assistant. The ambulance gurney was still on the road. A blue blanket hung down and sunlight reflected off the wheels.

'Russell's a mountaineer – climbed Everest five times and runs Nepal Adventures. Speaks fluent Nepali. Russell Weatherbeater, you've probably heard of him?'

Hunter pursed his lips like a guppy fish.

Rick didn't believe him. 'Russell liked what he saw in Nepal and joined the specials when he came back. Job's lucky to have him – built like a number eight and great with people.' Through the windscreen Russell was laughing with the paramedics.

Rick opened the door. 'You coming?' Hunter moved his head from side to side. Rick got out and closed the door.

Russell walked towards him, his shirt sleeve flapping over bandaging. 'Rick! Sorry, *boss.*'

'You okay?'

The big man shrugged. 'Rick, there's something I need to discuss with you.'

'Not now.' Rick nodded at the car.

'Who is it?'

'New DS from the Met. Moodier than a custody sergeant.'

They got in the car, Russell shuffling across the back seat and Rick pulling his seat forwards a notch. 'Gary, Russell. Russell, Gary. The mountaineer thrust a hand between the front seats.

Hunter glanced into the rearview but didn't move.

A rear window zipped down.

They set off. Rick took a short cut through a housing estate. Crop circles of brick with alphabetical road names. 'This is the Wallington, Gary. Paramedics won't enter without us as backup. Patrols always double-crewed.' They passed a blackened and boarded-up pub. An old man wearing carpet slippers waited while his dog had a shit on the pavement.

They drove up a hill, past a recycling plant. Police operations on the estate formed up in the plant's car park.

'You been climbing, Gary?' said Russell.

Rick changed down a gear, the car's small engine protesting at the gradient.

'Gary?'

'Oh, *yeah.*'

'Never too old to start.'

'Like coppering?' Hunter looked out of his window. 'Job's a young man's game: fights, nights, and foot-chases.'

They drove the rest of the way in silence. Hunter scratched

the tops of his hands. Rick continued to ponder the interview. Would Coniston agree to help? Could Rick improve on his proposal to write to the judge? At least if Coniston refused, Khetan's ketamine addiction gave possibilities.

They passed the new Memorial Gardens, its front hedge already full of cans and chip wrappers, the bridge where Benny-the-tramp slept, and the town hall, standing tall and proud with its clock and date of construction – 1835, the decade of the first Peelers. For the moment it was him, Hunter and Russell, but soon there would be others. His time, gone in a flash.

At South Manchester, Rick parked in the DCI bay and switched off the engine. 'Russell, you get on with your arrest notes. Gary, debrief in my office.'

The two of them headed up.

More silence.

'Close the door, Gary.'

Rick sat down. 'I don't know how it worked in your previous unit, but in my team when we're facing out, you keep your thoughts to yourself. And you mask your body language. Then at the debrief, you get a chance to say what you think. Got it?'

'Yes, boss.'

'In the car, you said Coniston was playing me. Which is fine. Let him play, all that matters is the end result.' Rick paused. 'Would you re-interview him?'

'Nah, I'd give him up.'

'Really. What other ideas have you had then for luring Khetan to the UK?'

Hunter twitched his nose.

'You did read the interview briefing I gave you?'

'Yes, boss.' He scratched the back of his neck.

'Don't hold back, just because you don't have an audience.'

'Not much, to be fair.'

'Okay, this is what I've got.' A two-point McTavish.

'Coniston is Tactic A: we'll give him a day or two, and go back. I'll up the ante and tell him if he helps us, I'll not only write to his trial judge and get him moved to a different prison, but give him a pseudonym too. He's probably worried about recriminations for being a grass. If he refuses to play ball, then Tactic B is to explore Khetan's ketamine addiction. Depending on his stage of dependency, maybe a lifetime supply or specialist treatment would lure him to Britain.'

Hunter nodded.

'And just to be clear, that stuff before the interview about your family and your art, that was me playing you.' Rick needed his new sergeant to work for him, and would do or say whatever it took. Same with Coniston.

Hunter nodded a second time.

The door opened and Robbo stood on the threshold eating a banana.

Rick stood, tensed. Playing another game.

'At ease,' said the superintendent. 'How'd it go with Coniston?'

'Nearly. Re-interview tomorrow.'

Robbo nodded, chewing. 'And how're you settling in, Gary?'

'Fine, sir.'

'Is that right, Rick?'

'Yes, sir. A1.'

Rick sat on the bench in the apiary. He wore gumboots, but no smock or veil. The seat faced into the horseshoe and was far enough away for him not to be pestered. He often stopped there on the way home, even for ten minutes. An injection of wellbeing.

A few bees flitted about, most done for the day. There was no sign of swarming, which was a relief as he didn't have the energy to deal. It wasn't late, but it felt like a long day. Maybe he should speak to Siobhan. He should definitely phone Mum and ask her about visiting Dad.

Trees swaying in the breeze sounded like the sea. Hidden birds called. A young rabbit scurried along the perimeter. The birdsong was all around him: whistles, tweets, trills. If their sounds were matter, the air would be full.

He closed his eyes, and the day came back. Hunter winding everyone up. Coniston killing the fly. *I'll think about it.*

Rick would nail Coniston in the re-interview.

He had to.

The day was replaced by another. He saw the three blood-soaked cots in the nursery: Martha, Mark, Marissa, an IVF miracle. Nameplates, tiny pillows, and a turning zoo mobile, all dripping with blood. *His* fault: *his* decision.

The Khetan case could be his redemption, both professional and personal. His hand gripped the rough wood of the armrest and squeezed and squeezed.

7

Something smacked Calix in the face, waking him up. He groped around. The cell felt cold and small, and smelt of human waste. On the wing, someone was already shouting, '*Ten German bombers.*' He pulled out an earplug and opened an eye. Finding Darren's trainer, he threw it on the floor.

From the top bunk his cellmate's inverted head appeared. Hedgehog hair. 'I'm a morning person.'

Calix faked a laugh.

'You got another dibble visit?'

'Yeah.'

'Same pair of Sherlocks?'

'Yeah.'

'You talking?' Darren's good humour vanished. He balled his fist and punched his cupped hand. 'Because if you are.' He punched again.

'I'm not, I swear on my old man's gravestone.'

The scheduled return after only twenty-four hours of Castle and his deputy looked sus, but there was nothing Calix could do. It was sus.

It was also good news, and required careful consideration.

Castle was intelligent, mannered, wary. Calix could push him, but not so far he withdrew his offer.

Mid-morning, the cell door was ajar and Darren was out. Calix was alone and he'd trapped a mouse. It was not only a good omen, but dealing with it needed a similar approach to the second interview.

He held it up by its tail. It tried to right itself, twirling one way, then the other. Not a mouse, a short-tailed vole. They had similar greyish-brown coats, but smaller ears and eyes, rounder heads and far shorter tails than house mice.

He lowered the vole into a beaker of water where it adopted a curious form of doggy-paddle. Using his hand as a lid, he poured in more water between his fingers, closing the gap until the beaker was full and touched his fingers. He could feel the vole struggling, pushing against his skin.

He waited.

How could he make the interview look less sus? He couldn't, except to say he'd said nothing, even if Darren held his head down the bog. Next question, how could he make Castle agree? Reverse psychology. Demand more for his cooperation, his own cell for starters.

The vole had stopped struggling.

After checking the door, he dried the vole on Darren's blanket and laid it out on the table. From a flap in the underside of a chair he extracted a razor blade which had cost three packs of cigarettes. He'd still have to manage without a clamp, and with bog paper rather than cotton wool and wires. Normally, he preferred larger animals – squirrels and rabbits – and birds. Once, he'd even worked on a badger, but never again. It stank, before, during and afterwards, and filling it felt like stuffing a sofa.

He made the first cut with the blade, lengthways from the

vole's neck to its stubby tail. The cut was skin deep, or there'd be intestines and fluids everywhere. He pushed his index finger underneath the skin and eased it away from the belly. Once the carcass was almost free of the skin he worked on the four limbs. On a hind leg, he peeled back the skin to the ankle and cut through the bone. With increasing pressure, he wiggled the blade from side to side, keeping the cut as neat as he could. He repeated this three times. Skinning an animal was like removing someone's coat, but with their hands and feet attached. He remembered working on his neighbours' cat, Riley. Run over, he'd said.

After the legs, the tail. A long shiny sock that needed loosening, but not cutting. It popped and came free. Finally, the head, which was fiddly and always took the most time. Eyes, nose and ears, he left intact.

He pulled the skin the right way, and stuffed it with cotton wool.

Stood it up.

Dead, but alive.

Like him.

At lunchtime the wing was locked down for a spot search. Food was passed through the hatch in paper bags. Darren lay on the top bunk watching celebrities cooking on the TV. Calix sat on a chair, chewing a sarnie.

'I got a question, Capeman. If dibble is looking for yer, say you've burglarised or done the Post O, how can you avoid being spotted?'

Calix shrugged. On the metal corridor, a search dog called Prince was padding up and down. It would be their cell soon.

'Two rules, Capeman. Distract and Blend. Distract means giving dibble a reason why it's not you. Wear a blue hat and chuck it when you're round the corner. Or, wear two different coloured t-shirts and chuck the top one.' Darren jumped down. 'What the fuck? I can do cheese on toast.' He switched TV channels.

It was the royals, a bald one and a pretty one wearing a flower. They were opening something and smiling and shaking hands. Every day for them must feel the same, Calix thought, like being in prison. If he hooked Castle, maybe he'd be out of it soon.

Darren hurled his crusts at the TV and switched back to the cooking.

'You're Mr Chatty.'

'On the edge of my seat for Rule 2.'

'*Careful* – or you'll get a slap. Rule 2, Blending In. If you're doing pockets in the Arndale, carry some shopping bags. If you're nicking on Blackpool beach, wear shorts.'

Darren lit a roll-up, sucked on it and passed it down. Calix inhaled. Distract and Blend were both common sense, and the only difficulty Calix could foresee was having to do them in a panic. He passed the rollie back.

'Now for my tips,' said Darren. 'Top of the pops is a reflective jacket. With one of them you can get away with murder. Lit'ra-fucking-ally.'

The door clanged open. Guards entered with their salivating dog. They pulled and poked and Prince ate Darren's crusts and the vole.

Calix looked through the small glass panel into the interview room.

The London man oozed dibble. He was heavy, wore an old suit with a loud tie, and his eyes never left you. Castle was a different species, younger, smarter, with a voice that wasn't dibble. Spook, Calix had once thought. Fast-track?

The two of them weren't talking. He pushed open the door.

'Usual rules,' said the guard over Calix's shoulder. The smell of garlic followed him in.

The door closed. Calix scraped a chair back, sat down and waited. In front of Castle was his notebook. It was open and dated, and his pen was at the ready. The pen wasn't cheap. A ruler poked out of the top of the book. Victims of crime would lap it up.

'Khetan's nightmares,' said Castle. 'Has he got K cramps?'

'Come again,' said London dibble.

'Ketamine cramps. Abdominal pain typical of long-term users. Coniston?'

Calix wanted to feed them a titbit, and early. He nodded.

'And what does he shout out in his sleep?'

'It's mostly in Nepali.'

'Mostly?'

Calix said nothing. It was a slip, a small one, but still a slip. London dibble scowled. 'Listen—'

'Gary,' said Castle, cutting him off. 'Coniston, we're not coming back again.'

'I want three things in return.'

'Boss ain't a frigging genie.'

Darren would like that. A dibble with a sense of humour – as rare as a screw who could make a decision on his own.

'What things?' said Castle.

'The letter to the judge you promised. Second, my own cell.'

Castle wrote on his notepad. Neat handwriting, degree-educated without a doubt. Hunter scraped a stain on his tie. 'Third?' said Castle.

'I don't know the information you're after.' Frankness, Calix hoped, would give credibility. 'But I know someone who does. He lives in Nepal – in Saklis, Khetan's village. To find out what you want, you'll have to take me there to meet him.'

Hunter guffawed. 'You're 'aving an 'at and scarf.'

Castle laid down his pen. He tapped the ruler down through his notebook, and back up again.

'Let me get this straight,' said Hunter, loosening his tie. 'You want us to take you, a serving Her Majesty's prisoner looking at five years plus, to Nepal. To meet a man who *might* know something. What do you take us for – specials?' He stood up.

'Sit down, Gary,' said Castle.

Hunter sat and yanked up his cuff. The shirt caught on his arm, straining the button, and he scratched the skin as if he was scrubbing the floor.

'That's unlikely, Coniston, probably impossible. What you've got would have to be good. Very good. A guarantee.' Castle paused. 'We'll need some details.'

Calix took a deep breath. 'You remember the Nepalese boy with the yellow rucksack? Ferried messages between you and Khetan.'

Castle looked a touch desperate.

Like Calix.

'His name's Ram Subba. We became sort of friends – he taught me some Nepali, and I gave him Barney's watch. Ram is Khetan's nephew, but more like a son. Ram's father went missing in the Maoist uprising – presumed dead – and since then Khetan has looked out for the boy. Ram'll know.'

'We could find the boy, boss, speak to him through an interpreter. We don't need Coniston.'

'You could try,' said Calix. 'But even if you find him, he won't tell you what you want to know. He'll tell me – he trusts me.'

Castle sat motionless, and stared.

Calix felt butterflies in his stomach. The dibble had to go for it. If they did, it would make his mission – he deliberately used the word his old man would have used – a reality rather than a prisoner's daydream.

'Ram will know where his uncle is. Guaranteed.'

Castle closed his notebook. 'You can shut up now, Coniston. It's my turn to think.'

8

Rick paced around Robbo's office. Opposite the desk, an internal door led to the annexe. It was a privilege of rank and the source of gossip.

He noticed a photo frame caught in the maelstrom of wires behind the computer. It showed Robbo's wife Janice and their two children eating ice-creams on a beach. He pushed out the stand and set it clear of the wires.

The superintendent walked in, his PA close behind. Robbo nodded at Rick, but kept talking. 'Letter to the boy's parents, disciplinary for the PC.' He closed the annexe door and stood behind his desk. 'Ask the community inspector to draft a press release, then come and see me.'

Elaine wrote shorthand on a pad. She was petite, quiet, of mixed race. She smiled faintly at Robbo. She was a keen baker. 'In the bottom drawer, still warm.' She walked out, closing the door with a click.

'Thought you were on a diet,' said Rick, tutting.

He took a deep breath. There was never going to be a good time. 'I went back to Strangeways, and re-interviewed Coniston.'

Robbo folded down into his chair, the springs creaking and his body taking a moment to settle. 'And?'

'Coniston knows someone who's in touch with Khetan. My plan is to go back to Nepal, locate the informant and find out what he knows. Small team: me, Kate, and Russell Weatherbeater, the mountaineer who came with me last time – he's now a special. Maggie running the incident room here. A quick visit, week or ten days max. In and out, you won't even know I've gone.'

'That's because, Rick, you're not going.'

The desk phone buzzed. Robbo pressed a button and leant forward to the microphone. 'Lainey?'

'Sorry, Mike, I forgot to ask, do you want coffee?'

Robbo shook his head. 'No, sweet— No. Thank you.' The button on the phone snapped back.

Sweetie? Sweetheart?

Robbo cleared his throat. 'Four hundred reasons, but I'll start with four. First, you've not mentioned the CPS. Second, there's no way you can take the coroner's officer – last time the coroner summoned me to the courthouse. I'm also not sure about Weatherbeater. You know he's under investigation and they're thinking of suspending him? Third, Nepal. It's a mess after the earthquakes and it'll take longer to get around, probably prove impossible. Four, budget. We're cutting our frontline services, so foreign trips are like growing asparagus up north.'

Rick opened a folder. 'I spent the morning with the CPS.' He handed Robbo a memo.

Crown Prosecution Service
Sunlight House
Manchester M60 3PS

Cold Dawn

Date   28 May   Ref. SLN3170/15

DCI Castle
Case: Hant KHETAN, DOB 30.09.1982
Charging Decision
(1) Conspiracy to Kidnap Spencer Williams and Barnabas
    Williams, contrary to Common Law
(2) Manslaughter of Vicky Brant, Homicide Act 1957
(3) Manslaughter of Spencer Williams, Homicide Act 1957
(4) Manslaughter of David Coniston, Homicide Act 1957

Rationale
The key point for a charge of manslaughter is that the malicious
intent from the commission of a crime can be considered to apply
to the consequences of the crime. Hence, although Khetan did not
intend to kill the three victims and cannot be charged with
murder, he can, due to the doctrine of transferred malice, be
charged with their manslaughters because they died as a result of
the kidnap. Put simply, if they had not been kidnapped, they
would not have died.

Jurisdiction
Which country has jurisdiction depends on three factors: (i)
where the offence happened, (ii) the nationality of the suspect
and (iii) the nationality of the victim. The significant point for
manslaughter, like murder, is that an offence by a British subject
can be tried and punished in England and Wales wherever in the
world it took place and whatever the nationality of the victim.
Therefore, Khetan, who has both Nepalese and British
nationality, can be prosecuted in England.

CPS Charging Test
(i) Is there sufficient evidence to charge?

Count 1: witness testimony, phone records, CCTV, exhibits inc.
    banker's drafts, fraudulent Newcell
      documentation, emails   YES / ~~NO~~
Counts 2, 3 & 4: witness testimony   YES / ~~NO~~

(ii) Is it in the public interest to charge?
Counts 1, 2, 3 & 4:   *(a) punishment*   YES / ~~NO~~
                 (b) deterrence   YES / ~~NO~~
                 (c) incapacitation   YES / ~~NO~~
                 (d) rehabilitation   ~~YES~~ / NO

Good luck, Rick, in getting hold of him!

Louise

Louise Nottingham
Senior Counsel

Robbo put the memo down and pushed it back towards Rick. 'Okay, you've twisted the arm of the CPS. Still—'

'Nepal is desperate for people to visit – they've suffered a double whammy of natural disaster and plummeting tourism. The current disarray might even be an advantage because my visit will avoid the usual official scrutiny.'

'*Will?*'

'Would.' Rick tried a smile.

Robbo missed it – he was looking at his feet. Rick heard a drawer being opened. His boss was thinking about something else – the treat from Lainey?

'In respect of cost, I've found an HQ budget specifically for arresting GMP's Most Wanted. Foreign trips aren't excluded. So, it wouldn't cost the division a penny. And, it's Khetan – the FBI want him. You'd get Brownie points for the next chief super's board.'

Robbo was expressionless.

'Finally, staffing.' Rick had anticipated objections in respect of the CPS and the budget and had prepared counter-arguments, but he hadn't expected a problem with who he might take. 'Russell told me it's a personal matter, nothing to do with the Job. So he shouldn't be suspended. And I don't have to take the coroner's officer. Kate can stay. I'll take Hunter.' Even as the name left his mouth he regretted it, despite it making sense. 'He's only just arrived on the division so he's no case-load and has no close family.'

'What about your cases?' said Robbo.

'We've got two DCIs – Jack can cover. It'll be a quick trip and I'll take it as annual if I have to.'

'You're beginning to sound, Rick, like Captain Ahab.' Robbo frowned and glanced down at the CPS note.

'Khetan was responsible for three deaths – on my watch.'

Robbo looked up. 'Do you really feel up to a foreign trip?'

'I'm fine.'

'I phoned Emma. You told me it was the last session. And you walked out.'

'I'll go back.'

'I thought the sessions were helpful.'

Rick walked over to the window. In the yard two PCs were standing by a patrol car, arguing across the roof. He turned. 'What's not helpful is you using them as a stick to beat me.'

Robbo picked up a pen and twisted it in his fingers. 'You've put some work into it, I can see that. Leave it with me.'

Rick went over his next line like a rehearsing actor. Outside, the two PCs ducked back inside the car, and raced out of the yard. Blue lights flashing, sirens blaring. Sometimes, he wished he'd never been promoted. 'There's one more thing: I need to take Coniston with me to Nepal, to liaise with the informant.

Produce him from prison for two weeks.'

Robbo stared at him for a few seconds. 'Have you been eating rhubarb leaves?'

'I'm serious. I need a temporary release licence for him.'

'Well, it's not up to me – and there's no way the prison governor would agree.'

'It could be a standard application, no mention of Nepal – extended leave to attend a funeral or something. Coniston's been on remand a year. Human rights and all that. Or you could explain things to the governor. Up to you.'

'You have gone mad. But you're right about one thing – it is up to me. NO.' Robbo pushed the CPS note aside and started to write in his daybook.

The moment had come: nothing would ever be the same. Like pressing the button or pulling the trigger.

'Sir, before you write anything down.'

Robbo stopped writing and looked up. Rick rarely called him sir when it was just the two of them.

'Rick, you're a good DCI: committed and sometimes inspired, and you could go all the way. You had a knock last year, but you're almost over it. Don't spoil things.' He paused again. 'Shut the door on your way out.' He resumed writing.

Rick looked at the photo on the desk. Janice and the children on a beach. He tried to convince himself he was doing it for them. He looked at the annexe door and imagined the two of them, Robbo taking off his tunic, hanging it up. Elaine locking the door. He thought about Khetan in Nepal, plotting anew. He thought about Vicky Brant, and Spencer Williams. He thought about David Coniston: the brigadier, his olive cravat, his standards, his belief in doing the right thing.

'Sir, there've been rumours.'

For the second time, the superintendent stopped writing. There was an audible click as he retracted his pen. His eyes met Rick's.

'It's like that, is it?'

Rick nodded. 'I think Janice should know.'

'How very noble of you.' The superintendent laid down his pen. 'And if I authorise your application for Coniston's release licence, you won't tell her?'

'You'll need to do more than that. You'll also need to persuade Hainsforth, the Strangeways governor, to sign it. I know you know him.'

'Everything I did for you last year – checking your bees when you were away, smoothing the internal enquiry when you returned. Our friendship means nothing?'

'I only want this one thing.'

'What about next time you want something?'

'I won't mention it again.' Rick felt sick. 'I promise.' He could hear the hollowness.

Robbo stood up. 'What makes you think a Rick Castle promise now has one iota of value? Trust is a once-only thing. Like bread – once it's toast, there's no going back.'

Rick knew that. He agreed. He also thought it was a bit hypocritical.

'I don't know why you even bothered with this.' Robbo picked up the CPS note. He scrunched it up and threw it at the confidential waste sack. It hit the side and fell away. The superintendent walked over to the screw of paper, dumped it in the sack, and walked out.

On the beach Janice and the two children were still holding ice-creams.

Rick went to his office and shut the door. He wrote a list of actions. Phone calls to Flights.com, admin, Hunter, Russell, and the airport police, his top five.

He picked up the phone, and dialled.

Waited.

This was what he'd wanted, what he'd engineered, what he'd bulldozed through. His mouth was dry, his stomach moiling.

'Flights.com. Where do you want to go?'

'Nepal.'

Rick hovered in the doorway of his bedroom, cleaning his teeth and watching the TV news. Wearing a white hard hat and a yellow tabard, the prime minister walked around a building site.

The picture changed to a flattened village with a snowy mountainous backdrop. *Nepal, Langtang Village – 50 dead, 150 missing* on the tickertape. Rick killed the buzzing. The earthquake was on the news every day. More deaths, more misery. The screen showed the BBC reporter in Kathmandu. The capital was a mess and millions were affected. Robbo was right – but wrong. Khetan was out there somewhere, laughing at British *bobbees* – at Rick. Criminals who were difficult to arrest deserved prosecution as much as those who ran to the doorbell. Prison was for everyone.

He walked into the bathroom and spat in the sink.

In bed, Rick texted Maggie. *Robbo (finally) agreed, flight's day after tomorrow. Time for a last supper? Rick xx*

Amazing! And yes! Snogs, Mxx

He picked up Hooper's and turned to the index. *Artificial swarming, 138–41.* As he feared, it was more complex than calculus. He swapped books to a beginner's guide. *Move the old hive three feet to one side, find and remove the old queen, and put her into a new hive on the original site. Flying bees will return to the new hive.* He closed the book and threw it onto the floor. His appetite for hobbies had gone.

He turned off the light, his brain restless as a beehive. So much to sort out. He missed the semi-conscious murmuring with Maggie, which calmed him down and allowed him to sleep. Although he couldn't tell her how he'd persuaded Robbo. Not ever.

9

Rick walked up the ramp to Maggie's ground-floor flat. He carried a punnet of peaches and held out a large bunch of flowers as if he'd grown them himself.

He pressed the doorbell. A dog barked in a back garden – a deep vicious noise capable of lowering house prices.

'How long have we got?' said Maggie, opening the door. She wore a sparkly-silver top and her brown bobbed hair was damp and shiny.

'An hour or two. As soon as I get a call from the prison confirming Coniston's release, we'll collect him and drive him to the airport. Keep him in a holding cell there. Flight's at six am.'

She took the bouquet. 'They're lovely. Thank you.'

Rick bent to kiss her. Her breath was warm and her eyes mischievous and he wondered if dinner would be substituted.

'It's all happened so fast,' said Maggie, wheeling backwards. 'The governor of Strangeways has really signed the release licence?'

Rick's bedroom thoughts disappeared. He closed the door, the dog still barking. 'His name's Hainsforth. Robbo said he would.'

'So, he hasn't actually signed?'

'I don't know. I'm waiting for the call.' He pulled out his

phone. No missed calls, no messages. 'Assume I'm going.'

'Are you taking Russell?'

'Yes.'

'Kate? Am I going to be jealous?'

'No, and no.' Rick answered on auto-pilot. 'I said I'd take Hunter instead – no cases and no family.'

'Don't I count?'

The frisson that Rick would normally have felt didn't materialise. 'Not to Robbo.'

'I still can't believe he agreed you could take Coniston out of Strangeways.'

'Well, he did.' Rick did his best to smile.

'Unbelievable,' said Maggie, heading for the kitchen.

Rick followed. 'It's been done before. Prisoners come out for funerals, and this isn't much different. Coniston's going back to visit the place where his father died and to pay his last respects. That place simply happens to be in Nepal.'

The kitchen was wide and uncluttered. A large central space with a sweeping C-shaped marble counter at one end, wheelchair height. No high cabinets, and low cabinets with circular shelves, which could be rotated. The sink was shallow and the bin was on wheels.

Rick sat down at the table and immediately checked his phone. Still nothing. He called the Strangeways gatehouse. Then security. Both were engaged.

Maggie opened the fridge and placed two beers in her lap. She rolled over to him, pulled him nearer by his tie and kissed him again.

He unscrewed the beer caps. 'To arresting Hant Khetan.' They clinked bottles.

'You don't sound that excited.'

'I am.' He paused. 'But it's way down the line. First thing is Hainsforth's signature, and I won't believe that until Coniston's sitting next to me on the plane.'

Rick leant back against the wall, watching Maggie chop up garlic and onions. The aroma wafted around. He swigged his beer. Unlike him, Maggie could talk and cook at the same time. She teased him about it, and in return he was always hoping to catch her out – putting sugar in the stir fry or salt on the *tarte tatin*.

She picked up the wok and gave it a sharp shake. 'You don't think Coniston will abscond?'

'I said I'd write to the judge and ask for a lighter sentence in return for his help. In any case, where would he go?'

She put a wooden spoon to her mouth. 'Ho-ho-hot. Nice, though. Sat phone? Box of tricks?'

He nodded, and glanced at his phone. Still nothing. He tried the prison liaison officer but it went to voicemail.

'Almost ready.' She wheeled over and gave him another kiss. 'Did you catch the breaking news about FIFA?'

Rick shook his head.

'The FBI's announced a major investigation into corruption, and the awarding of the next two World Cups. They've arrested FIFA officials, including a vice president.'

'Not Terry Williams?'

'No. Someone else, I can't remember. Seems that FIFA's rotten from top to bottom. And get this: the next but one World Cup might be re-awarded and *we've* been put on standby.'

'You know what that'll mean?'

'The chief'll moan about his overtime budget?'

'Probably,' said Rick, smiling. 'But I was thinking about the foreign workers in Qatar – all that suffering for nothing. And they're still dying. Play Fair Qatar estimates that if things continue as they are, sixty-two workers will have died for every game.' He picked at the label on his beer. 'FIFA have been useless. At least Khetan's aim was laudable even if his method wasn't.'

Maggie put noodles into a saucepan and added water from the kettle.

'You've not mentioned Siobhan,' said Rick.

'She made me a cup of tea today.'

'But?'

'Ten sugars. At least ten. And she keeps taking my stuff out of the fridge.'

'You want me—'

'No!' She came over to the table. 'Sorry.' He touched her arm, then placed his fingers against her cheek. She put her hand on top of his and squeezed the fingers. 'What about you? How was Emma?'

'Not now, Mags.'

'You look pale.'

'I'm fine. Wondering why the prison haven't called.' He stood up and wandered into the tiny dining room. Her canteen of silver cutlery was open, and the table already laid. Maggie liked to do things properly. So had he, once.

Against one wall there was a low bookcase with family photos along the top. Her parents and their dog. Her brother John at a car rally. Larger frames of family groups with overlapping photos, some of them guillotined to fit. No one he recognised. He didn't know anyone else to recognise. None he could see of Maggie.

Below the photos were rows of books. He squatted down. A mixture of classics and modern novels, some he'd even heard of. After the novels there was non-fiction: travel, sport – mainly basketball – and *Bees at the Bottom of the Garden*, a present from him. Finally, a couple of large hardbacks, an atlas, and several on the army. Which made sense. Before the police she'd been a sapper. The brigadier had told him and although Maggie had confirmed it, she refused to elaborate.

'Have a seat,' Maggie shouted from the kitchen. He liked the idea of reading novels, but there never seemed enough time.

His phone rang.

He snatched it up.

'Rick,' said his mum. She told him about her greenhouse, and a great uncle's gout.

'Mum,' said Rick, closing his eyes, 'I can't speak for long, but why aren't you going to see Dad?'

'I am.'

'Once a week. Sometimes not even that.'

'Who told you?'

'Does it matter?'

Silence. Rick opened his eyes. 'Mum?'

'Not much point in going at all – he doesn't know who I am.'

'Mum!'

'Well?'

Rick stared at the floor. 'There is a point.'

'What?'

'To prevent feelings of guilt for one thing, if not now then in the future. Also, to get the best possible care. I've read reports on care homes, and residents whose families stay involved receive the best care. Then there's God.'

'Come on, Rick, you're an atheist.'

'I am, but you're not. Agnostic, you tell people. Mum, I've got to go, I'm waiting for a phone call. Tomorrow, I'm going back to Nepal.'

'Send me a postcard.'

'Love you. And Dad.'

No missed calls, no messages. He tried the gatehouse and security again. Both were still engaged. He tried the prison helpline. Office hours only.

They ate quickly, Rick constantly checking his phone or watch. Maggie said she'd clear up in the morning so they moved to the lounge where a huge bookcase ran down one wall.

Maggie lit a couple of candles on the mantelpiece.

His phone beeped.

A text from Hunter: *Are we on?*

Don't know. But assume we are, meet you at the gatehouse in 30.
He sent a similar message to Russell and received a confirmatory reply.

'I'm going to have to go, Maggie.'

'Ten minutes?'

'Five.'

They manoeuvred onto the sofa, and Maggie spread a blanket with tassels over them.

'That was delicious. In another life, Mags, you could be a chef.'

'In another life I could be a detective. A CSI, a paramedic, a vet, a tree surgeon. In another life I could cycle to work or walk to the bus. Run if I was late.'

Rick glanced over at the bookcase. Helps me forget, she'd once told him. 'Maggie, would now be a good time?'

'I will tell you.' She lifted a section of tassels, folded them one way, then the other. 'I need to be ready. When you come back from Nepal, I promise.'

The word stabbed at him. A Rick Castle promise? He drifted back to Robbo's office: the annexe, Elaine.

Seconds or minutes passed, he wasn't sure. Rick looked at his watch, then at Maggie. 'Sorry.'

She shook her head and edged up close. He put his arm around her and stroked her hair. The tension dissipated, like early-morning fog.

'Shame I've got to go.'

'Do you remember that time in the Conistons' house when you carried me up to the attic?'

They kissed. Then went out to the hall.

The roses stood in a vase. Rick's overcoat hung on a peg. One of the pockets was ripped where he'd climbed over a barbed-wire fence searching for a missing three-year-old. It was his job to tell the parents when, a week later, they'd found the boy in a storm pipe.

He knelt to hug Maggie.

'He might surprise you.'

'Coniston?'

'Hunter.'

They hugged again, kissed again. 'I'll miss you.'

'Me, too. Good luck, Rick.'

He put on his coat and stepped outside, squeezing the door shut. The dog was still yowling.

10

Rick parked outside the prison, and showed his badge at the gatehouse window.

'DCI Castle, South Manchester. I've been expecting a call about Calix Coniston. Your governor should have signed his release licence.'

The guard stared blankly. His short-sleeved shirt exposed tattooed arms tight as rolling pins. He scanned down a clipboard, scowled, and made a phone call, covering the mouthpiece as he spoke. He put the phone down.

'Five minutes. Get your car into the dock. Escort vehicle waits outside.'

'Hainsforth signed?'

'Must have had a funny turn.'

Rick phoned Hunter. 'We're in business. They'll let your car into the dock, Echo Two waits outside.'

The side door of the gatehouse buzzed open, and he went inside.

The guard pointed Rick to a revolving door. He stepped into the cubicle, and the door swung shut. He held up his arms, and stared at the camera. The opposite door opened and he walked through. Two more guards, clones of the first, appeared from the gatehouse, and escorted him along a corridor towards the van dock.

Rick could smell smoke and hear faint sounds of screaming from the prison's dark interior.

Halfway along, one guard unlocked a barred door. They walked through, and the second guard, chewing liquorice with stained teeth, locked it behind them.

At the end of the corridor, another barred door led to the van dock. The door was unlocked, they trooped through, and it was locked again. They walked down the steps into a cavernous garage, large enough for a twenty-prisoner court van.

There were racks of under-vehicle mirrors and firefighting equipment. A covered inspection pit in the centre, and an empty dog kennel in the corner. There was a prominent red panic button, and a sign in huge red letters on one wall: *ONLY ONE GATE OR DOOR TO BE OPEN AT ANY ONE TIME, by order of C Hainsforth.*

A buzzer sounded and one of the guards raised a thumb at the overlooking glass window.

The front wall of the van dock shuddered and began rolling up, chains either side clinking and clanking. Yellow hazard lights flashed. The huge door stopped, and one of the guards curtsied at the unmarked police car.

The car drove into the van dock, a uniformed constable from South Manchester at the wheel. Hunter sat alongside him, and Russell in the back despite being six inches taller. The huge door unrolled back down until it struck the floor. A spiked device secured it in place.

'Sign here,' said one of the guards.

Rick signed. But he remained nervous. He'd signed for prisoners before, only for a frantic knocking on the control room window, and the prisoner release rescinded.

A second buzzer sounded and a hidden door opened, beeping like a reversing van.

Coniston strolled forward, swinging his handcuffs from side to side as if he was practising pass-the-parcel. Behind him, a guard as big as a bear.

Rick advanced with a pair of handcuffs.

Coniston whistled like a promenader.

The bearlike guard unlocked the prison shackles, and Rick clicked the police cuffs on Coniston's wrists. He ratcheted them tight, and two notches further. The early skirmish was his. A glint of a smile from the guard, and a rare moment of camaraderie between prison and police services.

Coniston didn't murmur. No doubt he was also nervous about the exeat being overturned. Which was both useful to know, and a warning.

Hunter stepped forward to grip Coniston's arm, but Rick moved faster. Applying a wrist lock, he guided their prisoner to the car.

Russell climbed out, wearing mountaineering boots and apparel. One of the guards wolf-whistled. Rick shoved Coniston into the back of the car. Russell climbed back in, and Hunter the far side. The doors slammed.

Rick turned towards the waiting guards. He felt a little heady, and was tempted to exchange wisecracks or talk about football. He climbed into the car, still not believing. His stomach roiled and his throat was dry. But in his repeated nocturnal visualisations of the handover, not one had gone so smoothly.

The buzzer sounded, the hazard lights flashed, and the door rolled up.

No one in the car spoke.

Still, Rick expected a shout, and Coniston's recall.

The door clashed to a halt, and the police car backed out. The door rolled down, and clunked tight.

'To the airport,' said Rick. He sneaked a look behind, the three men sombre as conscripts heading for the front.

The constable reversed, then headed towards the road. Behind them, Echo 2 with two more uniformed officers, and all of their kit.

A black Range Rover with tinted windows shot out of a parking space.

Forcing them to stop.

Rick's stomach turned over.

'Reverse,' said Hunter. 'Quick!'

The uniformed driver slammed the gearstick back.

But Echo 2 blocked their path.

'It's okay!' said Rick. 'It's okay, I recognise the plate.' The driver relaxed, and Rick climbed out.

The driver's window on the Range Rover buzzed down to reveal Robbo's chunky profile. He was in full uniform and listening to classical music. On the passenger seat was an open packet of sweets. He turned down the volume.

'What did you tell Hainsforth?'

'That doesn't concern you,' said his boss. 'What does, is that I've requested a Nepalese liaison officer and a local police escort.'

Rick hurled silent expletives. 'Cancel them. It will only make Ram suspicious, much better if we enter his village unannounced.'

'Handcuffs. Coniston must be kept in handcuffs.'

'Okay, but cancel the liaison and escort.'

The superintendent unwrapped a sweet, and started chewing. Weighing things up, or trying to show he was weighing things up.

'We've got to go.'

'If your wild goose chase yields a golden egg, then you'll be hailed as a wonder cop. But if you lose Coniston, then you'll see out your service in the central property store. No pressure.' The superintendent held out the bag of sweets. 'Eclair?'

Rick shook his head. 'You need the calories.'

The window buzzed up, the music resumed, and the Range Rover reversed back into the parking space. The two-car convoy set off again, and as it entered the traffic, Robbo flashed his headlights.

'Morse code,' said Hunter, looking over his shoulder. '*Don't Fuck Up.*'

11

'Stop here,' said Rick to the taxi driver.

'Yes, *sahib.*'

The minibus crunched across the gravel at the viewpoint. The Kathmandu Grand View and G's Terrace restaurants were garlanded with flowers and flags, and fronted with small rose gardens. A dozen ramshackle huts stood opposite, filled with soft drinks and strings of sweets and salty snacks. The smell of onions wafted thickly from a hut where a woman was making *samosas.* Customers sat on upturned crates or squatted on the ground. People were everywhere, mainly locals but some tourists – strolling around trying to ignore their personal entourage of hawkers and children. The air was grey with exhaust smoke and the ground strewn with diesel pools. A coach stood jacked up, and young boys rolled a tyre with sticks. Greasy mechanics argued by the coach. Next to a line of taxis, a huddle of drivers smoked and bet on two men rolling dice. An emaciated dog ran under the coach and two more dogs gave chase. A mechanic slid out from underneath, swore, and spat out a line of phlegm. At the side of the restaurants, a man urinated behind a wall of clucking chicken crates. Five hundred people, Rick estimated.

The taxi slalomed slowly through the crowd and stopped at the far edge of the parking area. Beneath them, the vast low-rise city sprawled in every direction, and disappeared into a grey-white haze. On the plane Rick had read Maggie's briefing sheet.

Kathmandu is known for its smog, the result of a soaring population (two million and climbing), insufficient traffic checks, and incompetent town-planning. The smog is the least of the population's worries. In April, a huge earthquake killed 9,000 people and injured 30,000. Entire villages were flattened and hundreds of thousands made homeless. The epicentre was only eighty kilometres NW of Kathmandu, and much of its low-quality housing and many of its historic buildings were destroyed.

They were silent as they stared down into the valley. The city was a patchwork of tents and plastic sheeting.

'Their worst natural disaster for eighty years,' said Russell.

'Well, London, it ain't,' said Hunter. He rolled up a sleeve and scratched the underside of his arm.

Rick climbed out and pulled back the sliding door. Russell, Hunter, Coniston, and two Nepalese men climbed out. A crowd of hawkers rushed towards them. The two local men shooed them away as if they were livestock, then headed for the larger of the two restaurants, the Grand View.

Rick stood with Coniston.

Lorries belched fumes, cars hooted and tooted, scooters weaved and cleaved, cyclists rang bells and wheeled impossible loads. Old folk, men, women, youths, children. Everywhere. Hefting; lugging; lifting; loading; unloading. Shuffling; running; pushing. Dallying. Shouting; laughing; spitting. Sitting and staring; squatting and staring. Staring and staring. The chaos, the confusion, the hustle and the bustle, were even more than last time. Kathmandu; the aftermath of an earthquake; June.

'Brings it all back,' said their prisoner, his handcuffed hands in front of him and concealed by a rolled-up jacket. His eyes were watery.

Rick nodded. It was the same for him. The bridge, the brigadier, Hant Khetan. For him, it was relief that it hadn't been worse, as well as anger and frustration. For Coniston, it seemed only a quiet rage. Which, if Rick could harness, could work out well.

'Well, let's do something about it,' said Rick.

Coniston grunted, and together they followed the others.

If anyone was perfect for the operation, it was Russell. An experienced, charismatic mountaineer who spoke Nepali and knew his way around – plus he knew the rudiments of policing. If anyone wasn't perfect, it was Hunter. Rick had spoken to Hunter's DCI on the flying squad, Harry Baker. Hunter had been moved on following the bungled safety-box investigation that had made international headlines. Gary cuts corners, Baker had said, but can be useful.

'What's the story on those two?' said Hunter, nodding at the team's Nepalese hires.

'Lok and Uttam are Sherpas,' said Russell. 'I've known them since they were very young. Their father was one of my best *Sirdars* – head Sherpa. Not much English but I'd trust them with my life.'

Rick checked his watch. The sooner they were at the Jyatha Hotel, had recovered from their jetlag and started up the trail, the sooner he would be able to relax – at least, a little. Maggie said he was incapable of relaxing.

The team gathered in an upstairs room of the restaurant. The tables were part laid up and streamers ran around the walls. Rick looked out of the window. Their driver was sitting cross-legged on the roof of the minibus. The mechanics were still arguing. A bus pulled up, horn blaring and trailing smoke. Hawkers scrimmaged at the door.

A waiter entered with a tray of soft drinks and a plate of *momos*.

'Menu, *sahib?*'

Rick shook his head and the man went out again.

He poured himself a drink from the water cooler and faced the room, his heart thumping.

He should have sent one of the Foxtrot units to the domestic. Martha, Mark and Marissa would still be alive.

He could cope. He *was* coping. And if he wasn't, no way was he showing a weakness. He drank the water imagining it was vodka, and dumped the paper cup in the bin.

'Okay. You don't know each other very well now, but you will do in ten days' time. I see us – the six of us – as a team.'

'The Dirty Half-Dozen,' said Hunter.

'We may have different motivations, but we've got one goal. And yes, Gary, that includes Coniston.'

Their prisoner held up his handcuffed hands and shrugged.

'Jobs,' said Rick. 'Lok and Uttam are to watch Coniston twenty-four-seven. One on, one off.'

Russell translated.

'Yes, *sahib.*' Two big smiles.

'Russell, prisoner security, Hunter, searches, and Coniston, your job is to elicit information from Ram so we can entice Khetan back to the UK.' Rick's job was Coniston's welfare. Like a racehorse trainer or an athletics coach, he had to ensure his charge was fit, and motivated for the task. The operation in Nepal, and probably his career, depended on it, and he'd spent much of the flight pondering how to achieve it. He could allow Coniston some of the luxuries he'd been missing in prison. And he could befriend him, even share something personal. His key message was, they wanted the same thing.

'Hunter,' said Rick. 'Search him, then take his cuffs off. Rucksack, too.'

Coniston stood up, and Hunter patted him down and removed the plastic cuffs. Coniston sat on a chair and removed his socks and trainers. He unpeeled his t-shirt and undid his trousers. He piled them all on the cement floor, next to his rucksack and amongst a few forgotten rose petals. He dropped his boxer shorts to the floor.

'Okay,' said Hunter.

Coniston pulled on his shorts and Hunter searched the clothing. Piece by piece, throwing them at Coniston as he finished.

Their prisoner sat on a chair. Hunter unbuckled the rucksack and emptied it out. As he searched he made a second heap. Walking boots, sleeping bag, duvet jacket. Wash kit, book, binoculars, head torch. Walking clothes, underwear. From the top pocket he took out a letter, a pocket Nepali–English dictionary, and a plastic container.

Hunter turned to Rick. 'No phone.'

'I told his mum not to pack one. Not much point you taking one, either. Reception is patchy away from Kathmandu. There are masts in Lukla, but not beyond. I'm carrying a sat phone for checking in – and for emergencies. It's all on the kit list.'

Rick picked up Coniston's plastic container. Flapjack. Everyone's mother loved them. He put it down, sat on a table and waited while Hunter went through the clothing. 'The letter, Coniston, is from your mum. She also gave me two hundred dollars for snacks and anything else you might need.'

Their prisoner nodded. In front of him, Hunter was feeling along the collar of a short-sleeved shirt. He paused, frowned, and ripped out the stitching. 'Boss?' He held up a tiny wrap of cling film. 'White pills.'

'Sleeping pills,' said Coniston. 'We're not allowed them inside. Take one if you don't believe me.'

Hunter put them in his pocket and turned to Rick. 'Binoculars?'

'They're a present for Ram,' said Coniston.

'Not a bad idea. He can keep them.'

'Razor?'

'No, he'll have to ask for it.'

Hunter opened the plastic container, picked up a lump of flapjack and took a bite.

'That'll do,' said Rick.

'Just doing my job,' said Hunter, throwing the container onto the pile of gear. Coniston dressed, then squatted down, put the letter in his wallet and repacked his rucksack.

'Leave the cuffs off, Gary.'

'The fat man said to keep them on.'

'Well, he's not here and it's operationally impractical and self-defeating. We've got to hike miles along the trails, and enter Ram's village in as low-key a way as possible.'

'Who'll catch him if he runs off?' said Hunter.

'Not you,' said Russell from the doorway.

'If you're not careful, Special Constable Weatherbeater,' said Hunter, 'I'll find you a shoplifter.'

'You mean tea-house-lifter?'

Rick forced a smile. Banter would make things go better or at least make it feel that way. 'Lok and Uttam – they've spent their lives running up and down mountains. Anyway, Coniston's not thinking about escaping.' Rick looked at their prisoner. 'Too much to lose. As long as you help us, we'll put in a good word to the judge.'

Rick picked up a *momo* and walked to the window. All four wheels were back on the ground and the coach was hooting its imminent departure. Clouds of smoke billowed from the exhaust and passengers mingled outside. Two boys play-fought with sticks. In his fingers the pastry was greasy and warm. He took a bite. His lips tingled, his eyes watered, and his mouth throbbed with burning.

Coniston winked at him.

Rick stopped chewing. He went to the door and out into the corridor. Ignored the shouts of his colleagues.

A woman sat at the end.

He dumped a few coins into her bowl and hurried into the bathroom. He spat in a sink and stared at the remains of the *momo*. Gripping the enamel, he worked it through. The *momos* had been brought into the room. Coniston didn't eat one, and went nowhere near the plate.

Slapping the sink, Rick looked in the mirror. He felt fine and he was fine. Next time, if there was a next time, he'd grin and deal with the consequences.

12

Calix walked alongside the Jyatha Hotel's golf course, listening to the cicadas. It was flanked by a strip of scrubby grass, a track and a high fence. The heads of half a dozen children protruded above it, staring at the four wealthy white men clubbing small balls towards a red flag. Behind the children, stretching into the distance, stood the rectangular blocks of Kathmandu. Traffic growled, and smog and fumes rolled over the fence. The hotel, with its golf course, swimming pool and spa complex, was a fantasy land in a world of hardship.

If only Darren could see him now: staying with the dibble in a swanky hotel in Nepal. A week ago he'd been stuck in a cell at Strangeways, and two weeks ago he thought he might be stuck there for a decade. With Darren from the skinter side of Oldham, teacher of muling and Distract and Blend. It had been Darren's distraction tips that had led Calix to sewing sleeping pills into his t-shirt collar.

He glanced behind. Lok and Uttam trailed twenty metres back, and Hunter the same distance again. The dibbleman stopped to light a cigarette.

Calix's head ached from the jetlag. He felt lethargic, and his legs soggy. But he walked on, wanting to meet the locals.

There was a hole in the fence near a fruit tree, and three or four children sat underneath. They fell silent as Calix approached. The fruit was sparse and looked like apples.

'*Namaste*,' said Calix. He put his hands together, trying to remember scraps of language from last time.

The children tittered. They wore vests and shorts, and were barefoot, and dirty.

'*Namaste*,' they all said in a rush.

Calix looked over his shoulder. Lok and Uttam squatted down, and waited. Hunter was doing up a shoelace. Calix looked at the hole in the fence. He could crawl through and be away. Lose himself in the city and get it done that way.

But he felt crap. And his mission might be harder – talking to Ram could actually be useful. The boy might know where Khetan was hiding.

He pocketed a hank of string on the ground, then plucked a fruit from the tree. It was green-brown and the size of a small apple. The skin was rough as sandpaper. '*Ramro?*' said Calix, putting it to his lips. Good?

The children laughed, and imitated his poor accent: '*Ramro, ramro!*'

He took a bite. It tasted dull.

'Apple?'

The children laughed as if he'd made a joke. '*Naspati, naspati!*'

'*Naspati*,' repeated Calix.

He thought of Megan lying on the Australian tarmac, bleeding out. The van driver speeding away. She'd have been a great mother. He hoped his sister was watching him with the Nepalese street children.

Behind him, a shout. He turned to see Hunter gesticulating at Lok and Uttam. They passed the message on to Calix with jerks of the head, waves of the hand.

He raised a thumb.

In front of him, the children all raised a thumb. They giggled and jiggled. Raised thumbs on both hands.

'*Namaste*,' said Calix. He put his hands together to say goodbye. And to say good luck. He hoped their gods would look after them.

On the walk back, Castle was waiting at the hotel's terrace bar and indicated Calix should sit with him. But not Hunter, who slouched off muttering.

A line of monkeys squatted nearby. They took it in turns to groom each other, chewing whatever they found. Occasionally they bared their teeth and shrieked.

A waiter appeared.

'Like a beer?' said Castle.

Calix knew he was also being groomed, but he nodded and when two cold bottles of Everest arrived, he took a swig and waited.

Lok and Uttam sat nearby.

On the far side of the green was the high fence, and behind it a huge concrete block of flats. In the fence, a couple of boards had been forced aside to create a squeeze-through and two small boys sat on the ground, throwing things at each other. Calix wondered what chance the boys had of working for the hotel. One in a million?

'Cigarette?' said Castle, offering a packet.

Calix took one and tapped it on the table. He wondered, if he asked nicely, whether the senior dibble would read him a bedtime story. He swigged his beer.

'What do you want?'

'You know what I want.' Castle poured half his beer into a glass. 'I want the same as you – information from Ram so we can arrest Khetan.'

Calix breathed out two arrows of smoke.

'What do you believe in?'

Nothing, Calix almost said. But Castle was talking to him as if he was human, not a piece of prison trash. It made sense to at least be civil, to make Castle think he was playing ball. 'Two things, I suppose. Self-reliance, which I get from my old man; and never giving up, which I get from Megan.' Calix picked at the label on the beer bottle. 'You? Wait, let me guess. Other people?'

'Friends, you mean?' said Castle. 'I've never had many friends, that's something I think we might have in common.' He stood up, afraid perhaps he'd said too much. 'Wait here.'

Leaving the cigarettes on the table, Castle walked into the bar, stopping to talk to the Sherpas.

Calix imagined few dibble had many friends.

He finished Castle's bottle of beer and pushed it back across the table. To prove Darren's distraction theory once more, he tipped the cigarettes out of the pack and into a heap, piling up the ones that rolled away.

Lok and Uttam hovered in the doorway, but there was no sign of Castle so he pulled out his wallet and the letter from home.

Dear Calix,

I'm writing this in a hurry as DCI Castle said you'd be flying out in the next few days. He explained you might be able to help him arrest the man responsible for all this madness. That really would be a brightening in a really dark time for me. And for you too. I hope you're OK, I often think about you. I'll see you on a visit when you get back. (DCI Castle said he'd let me know as soon as you've landed.)

Hope everything's in your rucksack that you need. I found your Nepali dictionary, and I packed your dad's binoculars. He won't need them now of course. Look after them.

There's also a box of flapjack. A girl, a woman I suppose, dropped it off. Strange looking, all dressed up to the 9s, at 10.30 in the morning. Said she was 'Red's girl'. I didn't know you had a friend called 'Red'. Maybe you can give some to the police, or just to DCI Castle if there are a lot of them. What a nice man!

Sorry if I'm waffling.

Hope it all goes OK.

Say a prayer for Dad when you visit the bridge. DCI Castle said there would definitely be time to visit the bridge.

Lots of love
Mum x

PS Thanks for going, Calix. Really, I should have visited. But you know how scared I am of flying – so silly really.

Say a prayer for his old man? He was going to do a lot more than that.

Castle sat down.

'KerPlunk?' said Calix, stuffing away the letter and nodding at the pile of cigarettes. He tipped back on his chair.

'Funny,' said Castle, nodding at the cigarettes. 'They're for you, anyway.' He refilled the packet but didn't mention the missing beer. Another distraction success.

The senior dibble lunged forward and grabbed a chair leg. 'Well, I can be funny too.' He yanked it upwards.

Calix tumbled to the tiled floor. Slowly, he picked himself up. He understood: carrot and stick. Basics.

He stared out into the weakening light. The monkeys and the children had disappeared and the cicadas were quieter. He could hear faint chatter from the hotel restaurant and smell the arresting spices. Timmur, crushed cumin, chillies, ginger. On the opposite side of the fairway a groundsman was mending the hole in the fence. Lights were flickering on in the block of flats and washing fluttered in the tiny balconies.

He was feeling better. Up for it.

13

From Kathmandu Rick and his team flew to Lukla, a large village in the mountains and the trailhead for Everest expeditions. They met with one of Russell's support teams for Nepal Adventures – a cook, porters and equipment – and started walking. Following a rocky trail they climbed steadily, and after three hours reached a tea house.

The building lay in ruins. A heap of wooden beams, glass, and corrugated iron. Water dripped from a hose and a child's flip-flop poked out of the rubble. A wheelbarrow rested against it, holed and missing its wheel.

'I can't believe this place has gone, too,' said Russell. 'Been stopping here for years.'

The support team kept going, but Rick's group sat on the stone porter's bench and rested. Another group of trekkers sat nearby. Two men and a woman wearing matching t-shirts. They were fundraising for a Nepalese charity.

Rick drank from his water bottle and watched the team's equipment disappearing up the trail, which worked back and forth up to a ridge line.

The sky was eggshell blue with streaks of sparkling white. A huge valley fell away to the right. Rocky scrub all around. Behind the ridge were snow slopes and in the distance were mountains. Waves of hills in every direction, as if they were rolling off a massive production plant. Rick could smell woodsmoke and honeysuckle. He could hear unfamiliar birds and a child crying.

'Where's Coniston?'

'Gone to find the *chirpi*,' said Russell. 'It's okay, Lok and Uttam are with him.'

Rick remained seated. He needed to show their prisoner he trusted him, even if he didn't. They'd sat together on the Lukla flight, and Rick had asked about his taxidermy. Coniston answered patiently and didn't draw attention. The two of them seemed to have an understanding: get the job done with the minimum of fuss. He pulled out Maggie's briefing sheet.

Three weeks after the earthquake in April there was a major aftershock. Its epicentre was halfway between Kathmandu and Everest and severely affected all the villages on the trekking route. 200 people died and 2,000 were injured. Saklis lies to the SE of Everest, only 20 kilometres from the worst of it.

A group of porters walked past carrying huge loads in wicker baskets. They wore baggy jumpers, long shorts and small wellington boots. Legs like stockings filled with stones. One held a radio blaring out local music.

'So, there are no roads here at all,' said Hunter. 'No cars and no lorries.'

'Porters carry everything,' said Russell. 'Food, building materials, gas. Literally the kitchen sink. Typical load is fifty k-g; some take double loads.'

Hunter scratched around the top of his boot, and turned to Rick. 'I've got a blister coming on. Not sure I'll get to wherever we're going.'

'Saklis, then Mosom Kharka. All on the briefing sheet.'

Coniston reappeared, followed by the Sherpas. All three were smoking.

He sprawled on the ground, propping his head on his daysack.

Two Nepalese people walked up, heading back towards Lukla, the man carrying a young girl on his back. They were silent. The girl's eyes were closed, her face pale and her head lolling to one side. A shawl was wrapped tight around the woman's head and she looked at the ground. They stopped walking.

'*Meder'sun, sahib?*'

Rick looked at Russell.

The mountaineer shook his head.

The local man edged up to Hunter.

'Sorry, cock.'

The man put his hands together in silent prayer and looked from one white man to another. The woman shuffled onwards. The man dropped his hands, and too tired or dejected to plead further, walked after her. Slowly, they turned the corner.

'You can't help everyone,' said Russell.

'Everyone's not here,' said Coniston. He lit another cigarette, and turned on his side. Rick also felt guilty. They had more in common than he'd thought.

'It's better they get proper medical treatment,' said Russell. 'And also not to reinforce their view that foreigners have all the answers.'

Rick threw a stone into the rocks.

The tinny noise of the sat phone sounded. He found the handset in his daysack, and answered.

'Any problems?' said Robbo.

'We've only just left Lukla.'

'So, no problems?'

'No.'

'I want regular updates. Every two days, at least. You got that?'

Rick pictured his boss standing at his desk, Lainey in front of him. The PA taking a note, and Robbo waving his beefy arms as if he was a commander in Afghanistan.

'Rick?'

'Every two days.' He ended the call and pushed the phone back into his bag. 'Operational needs permitting.'

'Robbo?' said Russell.

Rick nodded, and threw another stone. 'You seen Jacob's band again?'

'No.'

'You thought they were good, Russell.'

'They are.'

'So?'

'He's my son. It's complicated.'

Below them in the valley a large bird of prey hovered hundreds of metres from the ground. It dived, but at the last moment pulled away. The bird flew further down the valley, then rose again. Quickly it was a great distance away.

The three trekkers in matching t-shirts started unloading their rucksacks and laying everything on the ground. The woman walked around the back of the ruined building in the direction of the *chirpi*.

Rick unfolded the map – *Shorong / Hinku, 1:50 000* – and shuffled up next to Hunter. 'Hold that side.' He pointed out Lukla, Saklis, and Mosom Kharka. Russell peered over his shoulder and Coniston walked over. 'MK,' said Rick, 'is an abandoned village where we'll set up camp, and Saklis is where Khetan was brought up and where Ram lives. MK marks a three-way junction in the main trekking trail. It's also close to the suspension bridge where Calix's father died.'

Rick paused.

A moment of respect.

His eyes met Coniston's. Their prisoner gave a small nod of agreement, maybe also of gratitude.

Pointing as he spoke, Rick continued. 'North leads to Mount Mera, west back up the steep hill to Saklis and south, after at least a week, leads to Jiri, another trailhead but one that can be accessed by road. There's about twenty kilometres between Lukla, where we started, and MK. Saklis is a few kilometres before MK. Russell?'

'Two great river valleys run north–south, roughly parallel. The Dudh Kosi, here, on the left, next to Lukla, and the Hinku, here, on the right, close to Mosom Kharka. The two rivers carry the freezing meltwaters from the glaciers, which form at the foot of the mountains – some of the world's highest: Everest, Lhotse, Nuptse.'

'I'm breathing funny,' said Hunter.

'Too much smoking,' said Coniston, plonking down on his daysack.

'It's the altitude,' said Russell. 'We're now at three thousand metres. Only two-thirds of the oxygen of sea-level. Saklis is even higher, has even less oxygen.'

'Except, Russ, I'm not training for the Olympics.'

'It's only twenty k, Gary.' Rick handed him the map and pulled out a copy of a sketch he'd made the previous year. When they'd travelled by jeep to Jiri and walked some of the trail – to Ghandar, where he'd interviewed the other trekkers on Coniston's expedition – before backtracking to Kathmandu and flying to Lukla.

More porters walked by, heading up. They carried buckets, plastic sheeting, crates of bottles. Sticking up from the basket of the last man, and protruding above his head, was a shower-head.

'Look at these people – they were born for it. Half man, half yak.' Hunter rubbed his calves.

'Hey, that's my phone!'

Rick looked up.

The female trekker was standing over Coniston. In his hand was a mobile phone.

Her two friends walked over.

'Hey,' she said again.

Rick scrambled to his feet, Russell already ahead of him.

One of the men in the matching t-shirts snatched back the phone.

'What's going on?' said Rick. 'Coniston?'

'I found it in the *chirpi*.' He passed it over.

'And, are they my cigarettes?' The woman grabbed the crumpled packet resting on Coniston's jacket.

'He's got issues,' said Rick, hauling Coniston to his feet.

Leaving Russell to smooth things over, he strong-armed Coniston away. He walked him twenty metres up the trail and shoved him to the ground. Coniston didn't protest.

'I'm disappointed, Calix.' He hoped using his first name would foster a greater respect. 'I cut you a bit of slack, but you've abused it.'

'Sorry, I couldn't resist.'

'Don't let it happen again.'

Eventually, they set off. At the front, Rick set a furious pace.

Two hours later, they stopped again. The path traversed around a gully threaded by a stream, and after balancing across a log they came to a sign nailed to a post. *Sunrise Restrant, Tourist Welcom.* A line of prayer-flags, bleached from the sun and still attached to the post, draped along the ground. Three heaps of rubble – roughly made bricks, thick bamboo poles, and sheets of metal – were all that remained of the buildings. The place was deserted. Behind the ruins were shallow cliffs of rock, and below, stretching as far as they could see, rocky scrub. There were no trees and the plants were knee high and prickly.

They sat by a water tap and took it in turns to fill their water bottles.

'I knew the family,' said Russell. 'Always used to stop here with clients and have a bowl of noodle soup.' From his rucksack he took out paper bags and handed them out. 'Important to keep eating and drinking, even if you don't feel like it.'

Coniston took his bottle and snack and walked to the furthest heap of rubble.

'Make sure you keep an eye on him this time, Russell.'

'Follow him into the *chirpi*?'

'If you have to.'

Coniston improvised a seat and sat down. Lok and Uttam hovered, like shadows.

Rick surveilled with his peripheral vision. He ate a wrap and glanced at the stony soil. On the ground there were plants in miniature: tiny intricate leaves, and a shock of bright flowers.

The smell of sweaty feet cut across.

Hunter unpeeled his socks and hung them off the top of his pack. He scratched the tops of his feet and inspected the heels. Each had a fat weepy blister. He poked them with a finger. 'I haven't done this much walking since I was in uniform.'

More locals walked past. A thin man, with slick hair in a centre parting, carrying a red suitcase. Two young men in combats with rolled berets under their epaulettes. A woman carrying three kid goats in a wicker basket, the head strap straining. She didn't look up, but plodded on.

'In Saklis,' said Rick, keeping his voice low, 'we need to get the politics right. The village is pro-Khetan; he was their *Sunto Keta*, their golden boy. The first person from the village to go to university, and despite his international reputation, he's still a hero of the villages for his efforts to bring FIFA to account in Qatar.'

Rick glanced over at their prisoner. 'So, we'll keep Coniston out of Saklis. I don't want to risk a confrontation.' Following the theft of the mobile phone, his trust in their prisoner had weakened.

'Makes sense,' said Russell.

'Gary, you'll wait nearby with Coniston and the Sherpas, and I'll enter with Russell to find the boy. Then we'll all trek down to MK and camp there.'

'T-b-h,' said Hunter, poking at his blisters. 'Not sure I'll even make Saklis.'

At 3am Rick woke up. For a moment he wondered where he was. His backside ached and he was cold. He stretched out an arm from the sleeping bag and touched the roof of the tent, knocking off ice crystals. They sprinkled onto his face, and started to melt. He brushed them off, feeling the day's stubble. He needed a piss, having drunk a lot of water to combat the altitude sickness. One of Russell's suggestions.

He fought his way out of the tent, laced his boots and stood shivering a few metres away. The black sky was studded with brilliant stars and he could see his breath as he stared upwards.

At the bright, three-quarter moon.

He waved at Lok who was sitting on a chair outside Coniston's tent. The Sherpa was wrapped in his sleeping bag, but extricated a hand and raised a thumb. During the trek from Lukla, he'd told Rick he wanted to join the Nepalese police force. Become a detective like *Sahib* Castle.

Rick walked further away.

He wondered how Dad was doing; where Maggie was, and, if she was at home, that the doors and windows were locked. The Foxtrot units, screaming through the streets of Manchester, but to the wrong incidents.

He stopped to urinate.

The damaged moon was climbing.

They were on the trail. They'd started. 'Khetan,' Rick whispered. 'I'm coming for you.'

14

The climb to the top of the ridge was steep: all zig-zags and rocky steps. Calix was sweating, the drips splashing onto the stones of the path. Lok and Uttam were on the zag behind him, and the others way back.

He stubbed his toe and swore. The Sherpas practised their English. 'Fu–ukkk.' It reminded him of Darren.

He wouldn't have minded hiking for a month. His outlook no longer framed by bars or wire, his ears no longer filled with swearing and daytime TV, his range no longer that of a household pet, cage to feeding trough. Darren not present in every waking minute, not appearing in his dreams. Instead, he was breathing mountain air, his muscles were tired and there was sun on his face. Nepalese people to interact with.

And he had a mission. He could walk for ever.

At the top of the ridge line Weatherbeater sent the porters on ahead, but called a halt for the main party. A small cairn and prayer-flag tat marked the summit. The Sherpas rested on the stone bench.

'Saklis is over there,' said Weatherbeater, pointing.

Calix followed the direction of the mountaineer's finger. Rocky scrub eventually gave way to rhododendron forest. The view was enormous, like looking out to sea. His eyes settled on another distant ridge line and followed it upwards. Rocky scrub. Rocks. Scree. Then snow slopes, glistening in the sunshine. The snow steepened. The ridge met another ridge, and together they led to the summit.

He dug out a bog roll and held it up. Weatherbeater nodded. Calix pushed his way through the rocky scrub, still feeling uncomfortable. Maybe it was all the sitting on the plane. Screened by a boulder he pulled down his trousers and shorts. He squatted. He inserted a finger, moved the package around, and hoped it sat better. He stood and pulled up his clothes. Rubbed his fingers in the dirt, wiped them in the vegetation. Used some sanitiser. Returning to the others, it already felt better.

He sat down again, and ate a piece of the flapjack from TBR. One without nuts or raisins, same as the piece Hunter had eaten at the Kathmandu viewpoint. Calix had been lucky.

He lit one of the cigarettes Castle had given him, and exhaling, snickered to himself at the senior dibble's epithet of disappointment in him. He took another drag and reflected again: Castle was a brave and decent man.

Four local men appeared from the direction of Saklis, half-running, half-walking. Their baskets were empty, and they didn't stop at the summit but headed straight down, scree-running through the zig-zags.

Hunter was still on the first, Castle waiting for him.

Flicking away the butt of the cigarette, Calix noticed a discarded metal skewer on the ground. He glanced around, bent down, retied his shoelace, and secreted the skewer up his sleeve. He scanned for other stuff.

A beetle was investigating a flapjack crumb. He pulled out a matchbox and emptied the matches into a pocket – except for the last match, which he used to make air-holes in the lid. Trapping the beetle with his boots, he scooped it up into the box. As a boy he'd kept half a dozen beetles in an old ice-cream container with a bed of sand and a few sticks to climb over. He'd fed them dead wasps and flies and left water in a teaspoon. After a while he'd forgotten about them, and when he remembered, weeks later, he found five empty shells and one dead beetle.

His Nepalese beetle – Beetle Beetle – walked round and round its new cage. Round and round.

Finally, they arrived. Castle first, and a few minutes later, Hunter, moving stiffly and sounding like a wheezy dog. The Sherpas rose from the bench and squatted nearby. Hunter dumped his small rucksack on the ground, and sat heavily, head in hands.

'Are you okay, Gary?' said Castle.

Hunter raised his head from his hands, and sighed. Calix expected a wisecrack, but it didn't come.

Castle put down his water bottle. He was still standing, damp with sweat but clearly a fit man. 'Russell, can you search Coniston.'

It took Calix by surprise. He cursed himself: earlier, he'd been too impatient to try the trekker's phone, and now he was lulled by Castle's friendly approach.

The mountaineer walked over. 'Okay.'

Calix needed to play for time – a child would be able to find the skewer. Cons wanting to delay a search fought, or injured themselves; he had a third option: he could run. He glanced down the steep slope, the tiers of zig-zags. All three revealed guilt.

'I'll search him,' said Hunter. 'I'm not dead, yet.'

'Don't you trust me?' said the mountaineer.

'Not really.'

Calix realised he had another option not available to cons: he could talk his way out of it. Or through it. But how?

Hunter heaved himself up.

'What are you looking for?' said Calix. He needed more time to think. What would his old man do? Fight, probably.

'Spot check,' said Castle. 'Think of it as a compliment.' The sky had darkened and he put away his sunglasses.

'It's true,' said Calix. 'I could have stashed anything since the search in that restaurant. Fashioned myself a bamboo club, or nicked a *kukri* from a porter.'

'You could have done. It's a test of your trustworthiness.' Castle turned to his colleagues. 'I don't mind who does it. You two decide.'

Weatherbeater shrugged, and put on a jacket. 'Whoever searches him needs to get a move on. The weather's changing.'

Slate-grey clouds were welling up in the valley.

'Why don't you both do it?' said Calix. 'One of you can search my daypack, the other, me.' His voice had an edge to it. If he couldn't dissuade Castle, there would be consequences: a greater scrutiny going forward, and Calix's mission endangered. In addition to the humiliation of stripping for a second time.

'I told you, I'm doing it,' said Hunter. He lumbered forward.

There was a rumble of thunder in the valley.

'Tell you what,' said Calix. 'I'll hide something, see if either of you can find it. Castle can decide what, and ensure fair play.'

'Mother of God!' Hunter picked up Calix's daypack and unzipped the main section.

A spatter of rain struck them.

'We should keep going to Saklis,' said Weatherbeater. 'This might come to nothing, but we're exposed up here.'

Hunter stopped rummaging, and the three men looked at Castle. Calix's heart thumped. Maybe he could fool Hunter when he removed his base layer. Hide the skewer under some vegetation. But he wasn't Derren Brown, and Hunter was a dunderhead but not a fool.

'We'll keep going,' said Castle. 'Do a spot check another time.'

Hunter threw down Calix's pack, the water bottle, jacket and flapjack spilling out. The dibbleman walked away, scowling and scratching his ear.

Calix squatted down and picked up the flapjacks. He brushed them free of dirt and set them back in the box, the five with nuts, the one with nuts and raisins, the majority plain. He pressed down the lid, and stuffed the box along with his things back in his pack.

His heart still pulsed against his ribcage. The metal skewer cold against his forearm. He hoped his old man would be proud of him.

15

At the edge of a large clearing just outside Saklis, two posters had been attached to a tree. One in English and one in Nepali.

They showed a headshot of Khetan wearing a black beanie and the caption, *FBI Ten Most Wanted South Asia: Hant Khetan aliases Special K, The One, Rama H Khetan.* Under the photo was a list of his crimes. Murder of US Nationals outside the United States. Conspiracy to murder US Nationals outside the United States. Manslaughter of UK Nationals outside United Kingdom. Kidnapping of UK Nationals. A footnote carried a warning: *Caution: Considered Armed and Dangerous.*

Across both posters Khetan's face had been daubed with a single word of graffiti.

NAYAKA.

'Means hero,' said Russell.

Rick took a photo, then walked across the clearing towards the buildings. He sat on a porter's bench and watched Coniston and Hunter stop to look at the posters. The two Sherpas didn't even glance, and when they'd walked past, Coniston tore them down and put them in his pocket. His reaction confirmed Rick's reluctance to allow their prisoner to enter Saklis, even if it would slow the search for Ram.

The team sat on the bench alongside Rick or sprawled on the ground. They were silent, alone with their thoughts on the posters and the long hike from Lukla. On dinner. Coniston reflecting on his lucky escape from being searched.

Above them, a desert of blue sky and a well of yellow sun.

The largest of the three buildings was the original school, a long, narrow single-storey with doors that opened towards the central playing area. Five blue doors, five classrooms. The doors were still in place, but the walls had caved in and the roof had collapsed. In front of it a temporary school had been built from chunky bamboo poles, blue plastic sheeting and corrugated iron. The third building was a *chorten,* now a heap of blocks and stones, some showing the lurid paintwork.

Three men with hammers and chisels were taking down the old building, stone by stone. Another man stacked them up. There were piles of timber, and corrugated iron. Two men removed nails from the timber. Everything would be reused.

A stone landed nearby and rolled closer.

Rick looked towards the builders. They didn't seem to have noticed, or were pretending it hadn't.

A local man walked up. He was young, early thirties, with bandaged glasses and a small beard, wearing jeans and sandals. He wandered around the ruined school, picking things out of the rubble.

The man wandered closer. His sandals revealed Morton's toes, cracked and sore-looking. He caught Rick staring.

'*Namaste!*'

'*Namaste.*' Rick put his hands together.

'I hear you talk. Who look for?'

'A boy called Ram Subba,' said Rick. 'About fifteen years old.'

'I teach here,' said the man, and like a soldier, stood to attention. 'Two-hundred-child school. Two, three boys name Ram. Perhaps he leave school. Perhaps never go school.' He waved an arm. 'Earthquake make much damage. Many people leave Saklis to stay family whole Nepal. Perhaps Ram not here. Very sorry. Why look?'

'He'd better be,' said Hunter. 'After all this effort.'

Rick pointed at Coniston. 'Calix was involved in a trekking accident last year. Ram was very kind to him, and he wants to thank him.'

The teacher nodded. 'I very sorry. Lots of sad in Nepal last three years. My brothers all dead.' From a battered wallet he extricated a photo. It showed five small boys doing pull-ups on a makeshift bar. 'Me,' he said, pointing at one of the boys. 'We want be Ghurkhas, but not enough strong. Now just me.'

'In the earthquake?' asked Russell.

'Two earthquake. And two Qatar. Building football ... *chortens.*' He searched for the word.

'Stadiums,' said Rick, but he was hardly listening. *Perhaps Ram not here.* He pulled out his own wallet. 'I'd like to make a donation to the new school.' He still felt guilty about turning away the request for medicine.

'I no ask.'

Rick handed the teacher a fifty-dollar note.

'Thank you, thank you. Buy lot new books.' He pressed his hands together. 'Name Prakash.'

'Give him my money, too,' said Coniston.

'How much?'

'All of it.'

There was silence as Rick glanced at his colleagues. Russell raised his eyebrows, Hunter pulled a face. Rick looked back at Coniston. 'Are you sure?'

Their prisoner nodded.

Rick handed over the money.

Prakash looked at the wad of notes. 'You very very good man.' He put his hands together, then walked away.

'Puts the Qatar situation into perspective, doesn't it?' said Hunter. 'Compared to the earthquake.'

'No, I don't think it does,' said Russell.

'I didn't think *you* would.'

'The earthquake's a natural event whereas the deaths in Qatar are the work of man. The situation there is avoidable.'

The team fell quiet, Coniston closing his eyes. Rick would have paid another fifty dollars to know what he was thinking. Did it mean he had a heart, and felt compassion for strangers, not just his family? Or was that what he wanted Rick to think, to distract him from what he was really up to? Escape? But, as Rick had told Robbo, where would he go?

Another stone landed nearby.

Carelessness, or a warning?

'Boss?' said Hunter.

'Workplace hazard,' said Rick. 'We'll move further away.' He wasn't so sure, but he didn't want to spook Hunter before he and Russell left to search Saklis.

Rick remembered the village from last time, the hundreds of houses set on the hillside connected by a maze of steep cobbled paths. Many buildings lay in ruins or were in the process of being rebuilt. Scaffolding and plastic sheeting were everywhere. The sounds of stone chisels and saws echoed.

The atmosphere felt subdued. Many people would have died.

Half a dozen children tagged along behind the two of them. Chickens roamed freely along with goats and cows. They passed elderly women squatting in a backyard. Strings of corn cobs hung from eaves. Wicker baskets stacked with kindling leant against a wall. Washing hung at a water tap. Faces appeared at windows, and disappeared again. Smoke rose from chimneys, and a young cockerel crowed erratically.

He hoped Hunter and the Sherpas would be okay with

Coniston. That they remained at the edge of the clearing, and didn't interact with the builders.

Russell stopped at the small *chorten*, as per Rick's instructions. They removed their sunglasses, sunhats and shoes.

The mountaineer put a finger to his lips. Then pulled open the door and ducked inside. Rick followed.

The interior was dark and smelt of incense. Candles provided a gloomy, eerie light. The windows were shuttered, the wooden floor shiny with polish. A large altar dominated the room, leaving only a small space by the door and down the sides. The altar was a bright multi-layered display of icons and godheads, candles, jewelled ornaments, gold plates. Along the front were offering bowls, some containing coins and dried foodstuffs. Grains of rice, flower petals and, incongruously, *fusili* twirls lay amongst the ornaments.

A bald Nepalese man in blood-red robes appeared from one side. He held his hands in greeting. He smiled and indicated they should sit.

Russell and Rick sat cross-legged.

The priest produced a tatty leather book from under his robes, and passed it to Russell. The mountaineer opened it, and Rick read a few of the entries of tourist names and their donations. The priest closed his eyes and nodded back and forth. He chanted softly.

Rick took an offering bowl from the altar and placed a hundred dollars inside. He laid it in front of the priest. He took another bowl and placed a folded piece of paper with the question – translated by Russell – he wanted answered. Where could they find Ram Subba? He positioned it next to the first bowl.

Russell nodded.

Rick bowed his head, put his hands together, and went back outside into the sunshine. Meeting an informant under a railway arch in Salford would never be the same again.

Ten minutes later, Russell emerged. 'We have the Lama's blessing to enter the village and he hopes we find who we're looking for. He suggests we speak to the village council.'

'Really!'

They trekked on and up through the village. The cobbles were muddy and uneven, and a filthy gutter ran down one side. They passed an old man sharpening a *kukri*. He gaped at them with a toothless mouth.

The council building was one of the largest. The shutters were open and trays of plants decorated the ledges. The walls were painted bright purple, the decking swept. The tables and chairs new.

A plump middle-aged man wearing a *topi*, the traditional woven hat, appeared at the front door. He wore beige robes and new black sandals. He put his hands together. He looked tired, his face deeply lined.

Rick smiled, put his hands together.

'This won't be quick,' whispered Russell.

They sat at a table.

Russell did all the talking. Explained how they'd been to see the Lama, they were looking for Ram Subba, and Russell would be hiring porters and cook crews for his autumn expeditions.

A tray of drinks and snacks was brought by a young boy. He was barefoot and didn't smile.

The drink was locally brewed *raksi*. The snacks were goat meat, which Russell whispered were reserved for distinguished guests.

Two young women came out of the house. The headman's daughters looked like they were wearing their mother's clothes. They danced slowly with much tittering and confusion.

Rick nodded along, doing his best to avoid the *raksi*.

'Why you want find Ram Subba?'

Russell repeated what they'd told the teacher.

'Are we getting anywhere?' whispered Rick.

Russell drank more *raksi* and ate more goat snacks. Talked at length. Rick picked at his fingernails, glanced at his watch. Wished he knew more Nepali.

Lok appeared at the edge of the decking.

Rick beckoned him forward, knowing it could only mean a problem. The Sherpa passed him a note. '*You need to get back here, boss. Coniston's had a standoff with the builders. A couple more stones were thrown.*'

Rick stood up. 'We need to go, Russell. Is Ram here, or not?'

'Easy, Rick,' said the mountaineer, winking. 'Ram Subba does still live here. He works in the fields, but sometimes takes a herd of goats to pastures lower down. To Mosom Kharka. He might be away a couple of nights. Sometimes a week. If he's in the fields he'll be back by the evening.'

By his side, Rick clenched his fist. The boy was close.

'You wait here, Russell. I'll swap with Hunter, and take Coniston and the Sherpas down to Mosom Kharka. If Ram is here, bring him down tomorrow.'

'Aye, aye, boss.'

Rick shook the headman's hand. Smiled. Then handed Russell an envelope with money. It wasn't enough for what the village had suffered, but it was something.

16

The descent from Saklis to Mosom Kharka was steep as a staircase, and over two kilometres long. From halfway down it alternated between rocky steps and tight zig-zags.

If the boy didn't turn up in Saklis, what then? Hope he turned up near MK, scour the local villages, or look for a different informant? Seeing the posters, rereading the havoc Khetan had wreaked, had tightened Rick's resolve to lock up a very dangerous man. On top of his promise to get justice for the brigadier.

He caught Coniston, and grabbed his sleeve.

'Calix.'

'What?' Coniston stopped, and turned. The two Sherpas waited, patient as statues.

Rick hoped using his first name again would foster teamwork. 'What was all that back there with the builders?'

'It was nothing.'

'That's not what Hunter said.'

'He was panicking. They were annoyed I'd taken the posters down, that's all.' Coniston scowled. 'Khetan's no hero.'

'Any ideas where Ram might be, if he's not sleeping at Saklis?'

Coniston shook his head.

Rick gripped harder. 'We want the same thing.'

'You keep saying that.'

Coniston shook his arm free, and kept walking. Quickly, too quickly, as if he did know something.

Rick replayed the incident with the mobile phone, and the two-hundred-dollar donation. He wondered if they were distractions, and he'd missed something. Maybe they were delaying tactics, and someone was following them. A replacement spot search was overdue.

Looking back up the trail, he couldn't see far. The path jinked between rocky bluffs and short ramps.

He hurried after the others.

At the edge of a cliff, he edged forward to a bamboo ladder strapped to the rock. He looked down to see Coniston with Lok and Uttam, and past them to the valley floor, a long way below. The river a faint blue line, trees and vegetation green smudges alongside.

Rick stepped back and closed his eyes. He hated ladders, almost as much as bridges. But he had no choice. He turned, gripped the wooden rails and climbed down, his sweaty hands sliding down the wood. At the bottom he stopped, held the ladder. Counted to ten. Then set off again, shuffling round the corner and not looking down.

Ahead, the path widened, and the others were waiting. Coniston was teaching a wrestling move to the Sherpas. Leaving Hunter and Russell in Saklis meant Rick was exposed if there was a problem, but with limited time, he'd had no option.

They continued down, the path descending through a series of tree roots protruding above the earth, like the claws of a giant bird. The roots shone in the shafts of sunlight that made it through the thick rhododendron flanking the trail. They were stripped of bark and kicked smooth by thousands of pairs of feet. It was a reasonable possibility that famous mountaineers had trodden the very same path: Hillary, Mallory, Weather-beater. He walked on, his list exhausted.

He thought of Maggie, back home in the incident room. The path from Saklis to MK was now impossible for her, but hadn't always been. Statistically, a traffic accident was the most probable but didn't explain her reluctance to tell him. If it had been a car accident, there must have been a complication – she'd had a drink or been at fault. Killed someone, even.

An incident in the army was the most likely, and he'd looked up the role of sappers. They were engineers with a variety of functions, including bridge-building, road and airfield construction, and laying or clearing minefields. It could have been a training accident, or possibly, the result of an actual deployment. He didn't even know whether she'd seen active service. There were no mementoes in her flat, and she never talked about it.

Whatever the answer, it wasn't straightforward. At least now she'd promised she would tell him.

He came to a second and much longer ladder. Again, the others were waiting at its foot. Coniston looked up, raised a hand in mock greeting. Rick stepped back from the edge. The ladder was in two sections, a short diagonal over a giant boulder and a chimney, and then a ten-metre vertical. He drank from his water bottle. No choice. He turned and backed down the near-horizontal ladder, over the boulder and the chimney. Moved slowly, looking down, Coniston's leering face staring up. He reached the vertical ladder. Wondered if they should be roped up. He took another step down, his hands wet with sweat. He wiped them on his trousers and inspected a bolt. It looked okay. Nepali voices below. Another step. Another. Halfway.

He took his foot off the rung and lowered it. The ladder juddered forcibly. His hand came off the downward rail, and he swung away from the ladder like an opening door. His left hand and foot on the ladder, his right hand and foot in space.

He glanced down. Three faces staring up. Beneath them, the river, streaks of dark blue and black.

'Sorry,' shouted Coniston.

Rick grabbed at the ladder with his right hand. He hauled himself back round, replanted his right foot. Stared straight ahead at the rock behind the ladder. He let his heart-rate settle, then continued down. One hand at a time, one foot at a time, slowly, slowly. All the time wondering what Coniston meant and whether he'd strangle him when he reached the bottom. If he reached the bottom.

He reached the short exit ramp, and finally stepped onto solid ground. His legs wobbly, like a landlubber stepping off a boat.

There was a small rocky outcrop, hidden from the top, which pushed through the rhododendron and formed a viewpoint. The rock was scratched with graffiti and cigarette butts spotted the floor.

Rick slumped down next to the Sherpas. On their far side, Coniston sat on his pack taking it all in.

The view was incredible. Part of a suspension bridge, almost a hundred metres long. The bridge where Khetan had released Coniston, where the brigadier had jumped into the freezing river and where Khetan had disappeared into the hills beyond. Downstream was the clearing of Mosom Kharka, mostly hidden, but two blobs of orange revealed their campsite.

'I tripped,' said Coniston, 'and grabbed the ladder for balance.'

'Really?' Rick glared across.

'Really.'

'And that trekker's phone?'

'I was going to give it back.'

Rick jumped to his feet. 'Stand up.'

'Eh?'

'Stand up.'

'Here?'

Rick resisted the temptation to look over the edge. He hauled Coniston up, spun him round. 'Hands on the rock.' He patted him down, checked his pockets. A matchbox with a beetle. Sweets he'd been allocated, and some string and wire, which he must have collected. Rick confiscated the wire, and shoved Coniston back to the floor.

'Careful.'

'Just remember who I am, who you are.' He glanced at Lok and Uttam who looked shocked, and approving. They were on his team, even if he was paying them.

He grabbed Coniston's daysack and emptied it out on the ground. Jacket, gloves, hat. Nepali pocket dictionary. The box of flapjack. No knives, or mobile phones.

'Just remember.'

Coniston looked defiant.

Smug.

Rick examined the daysack a second time. There was a padded waist belt. He pressed along it, and felt something hard and long. He found a slit and pulled out a skewer.

'What's this?'

'I found it.'

'So why hide it?'

'I didn't. It's rusty, didn't want it spoiling my things.'

Rick hurled it over the edge.

For a second, the skewer hung in the air, glinting in the sunshine. Then it plummeted out of sight.

'Last warning. Then you're back in handcuffs.' Rick leant

back against a rock and flapped his sticky shirt. He drank some water. A light breeze blew up from below and cooled him down.

The skewer was rusty, so was it a beachcombing, or a weapon? And the wobbling of the ladder, was it an accident, or had Coniston tried to kill him? Or only test him? Usually he would make a case – witnesses, CCTV, interview – and dwell for weeks.

Snap judgement: guilty, or no?

The purple-blue river pounded along below. Over the millennia, smashing great rocks to pea shingle.

17

Rick stood at the table outside the dining tent at Mosom Kharka. In front of him were a cold coffee and a newspaper he'd picked up at Lukla airport. The remains of breakfast and Russell's first aid kit at the far end of the table.

He looked up the hill towards Saklis, but there was no sign of his colleagues. He turned a page of the paper, looked up again.

Still no one.

The blue sky was cloudless. An aeroplane streaked across, leaving a dissipating vapour trail. It had been a cold night and the ground was crisp, but the orange sun was naked and the day warming up.

Mosom Kharka covered a large flat area of land. A tributary of the Hinku River ran along one side and low rectangles of stone revealed the sites of the old houses. Camp had been set up in the middle. Sleeping arrangements still reflected the old world order. Rick and Coniston, and when they arrived, Russell and Hunter, each had their own tent. Lok and Uttam shared, the cook and the cook boy slept in the kitchen tent, and when they were staying, the eight porters used the dining tent.

Rick flicked more pages of the newspaper.

The international section carried two articles on Nepal.

The first concerned the arrest of a BBC TV crew in Qatar despite being on an official visit. They'd been inspecting the accommodation of migrant workers building stadiums for the World Cup.

He surveyed the steep slope. A train of porters was heading up. Small but solid men who wouldn't look out of place in a Samoan front row. But no one was coming down.

'*Roti, sahib?*'

In front of him, the cook boy held a steaming plate. Rick nodded. The boy pushed it onto the table and scurried away.

Coniston emerged from his tent. Lok, who was on sentry duty, shuffled his chair out of the way.

'Morning,' said Rick. He would try again.

Coniston nodded, yawned. He fitted his feet into his boots, and slopped over. He poured hot water from a flask.

'There's a shepherd's hut near the bridge.' Their prisoner grabbed a couple of *rotis* and spread them with jam. He looked up. 'I think Ram sometimes stayed there.'

'What? Why didn't you say last night, or when we arrived at Saklis? Or at the hotel in Kathmandu, or even on the plane?' Coniston's inputs were like social media posts: untimely, random, distracting, often deliberately false or misleading.

Coniston shrugged. 'Remembered in the night, you know how you do.' He pocketed some coffee sachets, and blister packs from the first aid kit.

Rick kept his eye on the jammy knife, which Coniston had lined up on the edge of the table. He did know. But didn't believe him.

'Knife.'

Coniston picked it up.

Rick shook his head.

Coniston slipped his hand over the sticky cutting edge and passed it over, handle first. Eyes glinting, he sauntered back to his tent.

Rick set the knife down. Unzipped his jacket. Mulled the new information.

He scanned the trail from Saklis but the only movement was the line of porters. If Russell and Hunter didn't appear soon, he would check out the shepherd's hut. Maybe Coniston was trying to help.

He checked the sat phone. There was a forwarded email from Michael at Three Views on the therapeutic effects of singing.

Abstract: Over the last decade, there has been significant research into the physiological, neurological, and emotional benefits of singing. Regular singing can have cognitive effects.

Rick read some of the detail. There was hope for Dad. There was hope for everyone. He looked up at the slope.

Still nothing.

Where were they?

Draining his coffee, he glanced at Lok sitting outside Coniston's tent. The Sherpa was alert and uncomplaining. Rick rummaged in his bag and walked over. He handed Lok a small police notebook with the GMP crest on the front. Lok gave him a thumbs-up. No surprise Sherpas were such a trusted part of the British army. David had told him that.

The synthetic trill of the sat phone broke the silence. Rick walked back. Fifty-fifty, Maggie or Robbo. He pressed a button.

'I thought we agreed updates every two days. Come on, Rick, I'm out on a limb here.' The superintendent sounded crabby, as if he'd eaten too many of Lainey's homemade cakes.

'This isn't nine to five.'

'Have you reached Mosom Kharka?'

'We have.'

'Located the boy?'

'Yes.'

'Started the debrief?'

'Early days.'

'Any issues?'

Rick thought of Coniston stealing the trekker's phone, Coniston wobbling the ladder on the cliff face, Coniston hiding the skewer. No sight of the informant. 'No, no issues.'

'And if I said, I don't believe you?'

I'd say, hop on a plane.

'Let me know the moment you learn anything useful. And, Rick, you had better hope the boy does say something useful.'

Rick threw the phone onto the table, and glanced at the second newspaper article about Nepal. A familiar name caught his eye. It described efforts by the Nepalese authorities to encourage trekkers to return. Visitor numbers had dropped ninety per cent since the earthquake, and travel advice was negative. Even so, trekking companies were still organising trips.

According to Russell Weatherbeater, five times Everest summiteer and owner of Nepal Adventures: 'It's business as usual. All our Nepal trips are going ahead.'

The piece finished with a warning. If trekkers didn't return in significant numbers, then more people would be forced to work in Qatar. And more lives would be lost.

He looked up.

Four figures were descending, one a long way ahead, one a long way behind. Rick recognised Hunter's red jacket on the backmarker. The leader was careering down, taking every short cut, slipping occasionally. He had to be a local, and Rick dared to hope.

'Coniston, I think it's them.'

A tent zip ripped, and Coniston climbed out.

'That's him, that's Ram.'

The two men stared at each other, and for a second or two, shared the good news. In another life, Rick entertained, they could have been colleagues. The police was well known for having misfits and oddballs in its ranks.

The moment over, their prisoner laced his boots and walked a little way out of camp. Lok on his heels.

Ram was streaking ahead. At the foot of the slope, he didn't slow, but bounded towards MK. Ten minutes later, he met Coniston. They embraced.

Rick felt cheered as if the boy was hugging him.

Finally, they were in business.

Rick introduced himself and held his hands in the prayer position. Then he gave orders.

He sent Ram to the cook for a plate of *dal baht.* He told Coniston the interview would take place sitting on the stones of the ruined village of MK, and told him to wait there with the two Sherpas.

When they'd gone, he debriefed Hunter and Russell, then described how he'd swung out on the ladder, and Coniston's admission. The question mark over intent. He briefed them about the skewer. He told them to stash their kit, and Russell to bring the boy over when he'd eaten. Hunter to search Coniston's tent.

Rick walked over to Coniston. In front of him, marmots ran around the flat scrub. The far side of the valley, streams coursed down the hillsides, and in the distance, snowy mountains teased. He could hear marmot whistles, the crash of stonefall and avalanche.

Their prisoner was throwing pebbles into the tributary. Lok and Uttam squatted nearby and backed away when Rick arrived.

'Rules for the interview,' said Rick.

'Shoot.' Coniston tossed a pebble from one hand to the other.

Rick sat down on a foundation stone. He wanted to ask Coniston to put the pebble down but it seemed petty. He found another question.

'There's something I want to ask you. Something I wanted to

ask your father, but never got round to. Why did your parents call you Calix?'

Coniston lobbed the stone into the water. 'My old man was on some army course in the US – at Westpoint. One of the American generals was called Calix – General Calix Lee Cooper.'

Rick nodded. 'Calix, we need to have an *entente cordiale.*'

Coniston looked across.

'It's a military phrase your father might like. We're here for him, doing this for him. And I want to make this interview work, make the boy talk and hopefully tell us something useful. So, you and I need to clear the air. Why did you wobble the ladder on the descent from Saklis?'

'Why did you over-tighten the cuffs in the van dock at Strangeways? Why did you tip me off the chair in the bar at the hotel in Kathmandu? For the same reason: one-upmanship, nothing more I assume. I didn't mean you any harm.'

'Not an accident, then?'

'You wanted to clear the air.'

'Let's start anew. We both want the same thing, and we need to work together.' He didn't believe it, not completely, but he had no choice.

Coniston picked at a muddy fingernail. 'Okay.'

'Interview protocol: I ask the questions, Russell translates, Ram answers. You cheer the boy on. Clear?'

'I'll need some time to warm him up a bit first. Two hours should do it.'

'You can have an hour.'

'Ninety minutes.'

'One hour.'

Coniston gurned.

Rick looked away, at Lok and Uttam squatting in the scruffy grass nearby. In the distance, a frozen waterfall was melting in the sun. The ice was cracking and creaking, and echoes reverberating down the valley. A bird of prey took off and swept down the cliffs, searching for a kill.

18

Calix sat facing Ram, each of them on a lump of stone. He stared at the boy through his sunglasses. He had short black hair, short enough to stand up, and light brown skin. The boy looked happy enough being the focus of attention, but he must have been wondering why. Or maybe he wasn't.

There was work to be done – the dibble's work.

Calix beckoned the boy, and together they walked over to the tributary, to a place where it curved and the water fanned out and split into two streams. Downstream, it rejoined into one. The water rushed over the protruding stones, muttering to itself.

Lok came with them. He was the smaller of the two Sherpas, and like his brother and Ram, glided over the land like a gazelle. He squatted down on the bank, and watched.

Calix moved a boulder, blocking part of the smaller stream's flow. The water piled up to it. He placed more rocks to form a barrier, and waved at Ram to help him. The boy added a boulder, and together they worked, building and damming.

They succeeded in stopping the water.

The pool was two metres wide and half a metre deep. Two trickles made their way through the barrier, the river less talkative. Calix glanced at Lok who was still as a rock.

The camp stood a football-pitch distance away. Outside the dining tent Castle was looking in their direction. The senior dibble's backdrop was the steep trail towards Saklis. A path of switchbacks, zig-zags, and ladders, one in need of repair. Distract and Conquer, a refinement of Darren's lesson.

Calix looked back at the dam. It was deep enough to drown someone. He'd read somewhere, you could drown in a puddle. He glanced at the lifeless Lok, at young Ram.

More work to be done.

He rummaged in his jacket for a chocolate bar, and offered half to Ram. They munched in silence, staring at the dam, at the half-metre deep pool of water. Ram had to have questions about the dibble, and about Calix. Maybe, he didn't.

'*Prahari*,' said Calix pointing at Castle and the MK camp. Police. '*Sodhnu.*' Ask. He pointed at Ram. '*Prasnaharu.*' Questions. 'Okay?'

The boy nodded. 'Okay.'

'But,' said Calix raising a finger and waggling it. '*Prasnaharu* about *mama* Khetan, *na javaphaharu.*' No answers about uncle Khetan. He'd looked up the Nepali words while he ate jam *rotis* in his tent. '*Bujhe?*' Understand?

'*Prasnaharu mama* Khetan, *na javaphaharu.*'

'*Ramro!*'

Calix took out the matchbox containing Beetle Beetle. He wished he'd taught the insect a trick: jumping through a burning hoop, eating a whole raisin. They cleared space between their feet and let the beetle run around. Calix scratched around in the scrub and uncovered a few ants. He squashed a few and laid them as offerings. Ram walked away and came back with a dead spider. Not one Calix recognised, and on a different day he'd have taken it apart.

The show continued. Life required food and water. He spat onto a finger and let it drip down onto the ground. Beetle Beetle investigated it with its pincers. He glanced at the motionless Lok.

It was time.

Calix took off his boots, unzipped and removed his trouser bottoms, and waded into the pool. He gasped: the water reached the top of his shorts, and was icy cold. He waved at Lok to come closer.

The Sherpa rose and slid down the bank to the water's edge. Calix waded towards him, put out a hand, as if he'd stubbed his toe and needed to steady himself. Lok took his hand.

Calix tugged the Sherpa's arm, lost his footing and fell back. Lok, unbalanced, unsuspecting, plunged forward into the freezing water.

They were both fully immersed. The water was cold and shocking. Calix rolled on top of the Sherpa, kept him under. He wondered if Lok could even swim. His plan was not to kill him. But to scare him enough so he – and ideally his brother, too – would flee the expedition. Reduce Calix's supervision and make his mission easier.

The margin of error was small.

He went up for air, took a half-mouthful, glimpsed the azure sky. He went down again. Underneath him, the Sherpa was struggling, fighting, panicking. Every child should be taught to swim. Calix pushed down on Lok's head, his shoulders, his torso.

Strong hands grabbed his shoulders, yanked him up and out of the water. Castle's face backdropped against the blue blue sky. Calix waded out of the water, coughing and spluttering. Behind him, Weatherbeater hauled out the Sherpa. Shoved him onto the far bank where Castle helped pull him out.

Lok lay on the bank, his feet still in the water. His eyes were closed and water streamed from his face and clothes.

Calix stood up, mud oozing up between his toes.

'Is he breathing?' shouted Weatherbeater.

Castle knelt down and tilted the Sherpa's head back. He moved closer to listen for breathing. He shook his head. He pinched the Sherpa's nose and bent lower. He gave two breaths, then began chest compressions. Weatherbeater climbed out of the water and knelt down next to him. Castle gave two more breaths and the mountaineer took over the chest compressions. Ram stood opposite them, looking worried as a trailside icon.

Calix waded out of the water. Castle was dibble, Weatherbeater was a mountaineer. Both would be trained.

Castle gave another breath.

Calix glanced at the camp. The cook and the cook boy were walking over. Behind them, the prayer-flags were trilling.

Weatherbeater started compressions.

The cook sent the cook boy back to camp. Towards the Sherpas' tent. Towards the sleeping Uttam. The prayer-flags were spinning round and round, and somersaulting.

Lok coughed, and spewed up a jet of water. He sat up, coughing and spluttering. Gasping. Breathing. Breathing and breathing and breathing. He hoiked and spat.

The two heroes sat back on their haunches.

'Fuck,' said Weatherbeater.

'Okay, Lok?' asked Castle.

The Sherpa closed his eyes and see-sawed his head. Water spilled from his ears. He blew snot from his nostrils. He opened his eyes and grabbed Castle's arm. '*Ramro.*' He didn't sound *ramro*, he sounded *naramro*, but that was Sherpas for you.

Castle waded back across the river and climbed out next to Calix. 'What was all that about?'

'Just mucking about.' On the opposite bank, Ram was whispering to Lok in Nepali.

Castle punched Calix in the stomach.

He doubled over, and collapsed to the ground. He lay diagonally across the riverbank, gasping. He was an idiot for even attempting a near-drowning. He needed to bide his time, he had a plan – he'd made preparations – and should have stuck to it. His old man would have called it an ND – a negligent discharge.

'Good on you, Rick,' said Weatherbeater.

Minutes passed. Five, ten, Calix wasn't sure. The cook appeared, and went again. Calix's breathing settled, his stomach felt sore. Such an idiot.

Castle kicked his foot. 'Mucking about?'

'I don't think he can swim.'

Castle booted Calix's other foot. 'You're meant to be socialising with the boy, preparing him.'

'We built the dam, and we're getting on well.' It was a chance to backtrack, rebuild. Calix glanced at Ram who was showing Beetle Beetle to the Sherpa. 'The boy's ready. All I need is a change of clothing, then we can start the interview.'

'Is that right?' said Castle. He took out a set of plasticuffs and fixed them over Calix's wrists. Ratcheted them tight.

Twisting and turning his hands, Calix watched Weatherbeater escort Lok back to MK. Above them, the mocking blue sky.

19

In front of Rick, and behind the boy, the steep hillside led up to Saklis. The rocky hills became snow slopes. Snow slopes led to the summits. Pyramidal peaks covered in an icy sheen. Majestic, sheer, impossible.

Police station niceties were for the UK. Solicitors, tapes, jugs of water. This was interviewing in the freshest of air, with the best of backdrops, and the least of regulations.

The most at stake.

Rick glanced at Coniston, and nodded at Weatherbeater. They sat on the huge foundation stones in a rough circle, two metres across, Rick opposite the boy. Coniston remained in handcuffs, and Uttam squatted a short distance behind him, ever alert to Rick's instructions.

'So, Ram, what's your favourite football team?' He smiled.

Russell translated.

'Manchester United,' said Ram.

Rick patted himself on the chest. '*Ramro*. Me, too.'

The boy grinned.

'Who's your favourite United player?'

Russell translated.

'Messi,' said the boy.

Even Rick knew Messi didn't play for United. He raised a thumb, slapped his chest. Grinned.

The boy raised a thumb, grinned back.

Mirroring was a good start. Despite the handcuffs, Coniston was passing stones from one hand to the other.

'How old are you, Ram?'

Russell translated.

Ram answered.

'He's fifteen, born in February 2000.'

Rick nodded, smiled. 'Can you tell me about your family?'

Russell translated.

The boy nodded, smiled, and spoke for over a minute.

'Good news,' said Russell. 'Ram wants to improve his English, and he's keen to talk to us.'

'Great,' said Rick. He raised another thumb at the boy, and in his peripheral vision caught a scowl from Coniston. Still smarting over the handcuffs?

'Ram's been through a lot,' said Russell. 'Him and his family. His father was taken by Maoists, his grandfather was killed in the Falklands and he lost his brother and several cousins in the recent earthquake.'

'I'm very sorry to hear about his terrible losses,' said Rick. 'Ask him more about his family, his mother and father and so on.'

Russell translated, and again the boy spoke at length.

'Ram's full name is Ram Subba. His mother, Neera Subba, is Khetan's sister and his father, who was captured by the Maoists, was Rajesh Subba. Hant Khetan is his mother's brother, and their father is Manu Khetan.'

'Who was killed in the Falklands in 1982,' said Rick. Accidentally, by David Coniston, Rick thought – the revenge for which was the reason Hant Khetan had kidnapped Barney and Spencer Williams the previous year. He took out his notebook and drew Ram's family tree. They were getting somewhere. He glanced at

Coniston who was passing stones the other way. Giving the impression he was bored, but Rick wasn't taken in. Coniston was paying close attention, as if he was supervising. Biding his time, but for what?

The boy started talking again.

'Okay,' said Russell. 'The boy's filling in the gaps. On his father's side, his grandmother is dead, but his grandfather is still alive. His name is Hari Subba. The two grandfathers were good friends and joined in the same intake of Ghurkhas. However, Hari Subba was posted to a different battalion and wasn't sent to the Falklands. He went on to have three children, the youngest of which was Rajesh Subba, Ram's father.'

'How does Ram know all this?' said Rick. 'Most people haven't a clue about their family history.'

'The extended family's very important here.'

Rick added more details to Ram's family tree. Circles for women, boxes for men. 'Good stuff, Russell. Let's focus now on Hant Khetan.'

Russell translated.

Coniston stilled his stones.

The boy spoke.

'Ram is Hant Khetan's nephew, and because his father went missing during the Maoist uprising when he was very young – and not been since – Hant more or less adopted him. Not officially, but he did pay for him to go to school.'

'Which means they're close,' said Rick, leaning forward. 'So, Ram, Hant Khetan is your uncle?'

Russell translated.

The boy looked at Coniston.

'Ram?' said Rick. 'Ask him again, Russell.'

The mountaineer repeated the question.

Again the boy looked at Coniston, looking uneasy.

Coniston nodded at the boy.

RAM'S FAMILY TREE

DCI Rick Castle

June 2015.

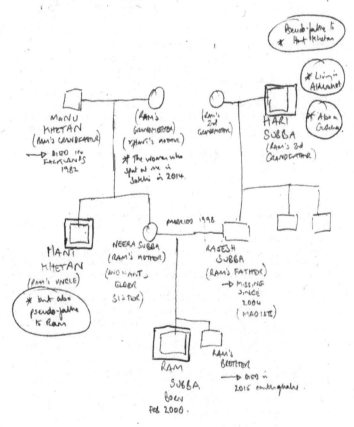

MANU KHETAN
(RAM'S GRANDFATHER)
→ DIED IN FALKLANDS 1982

(RAM'S GRANDMOTHER)
(KHETAN'S MOTHER)
The woman who shot at me is Jakhi in 2014.

(RAM'S 2nd GRANDMOTHER)

HARI SUBBA
(RAM'S 2nd GRANDFATHER)

Pseudo-father to * Hari Khetan

* Living in Allahabat

* Also a Grandma.

MARRIED 1998

HANI KHETAN
(RAM'S UNCLE)
* but also pseudo-father to Ram

NEERA SUBBA
(RAM'S MOTHER)
(AND HANT'S ELDER SISTER)

RAJESH SUBBA
(RAM'S FATHER)
→ MISSING SINCE 2004
(MAOIST)

RAM SUBBA BORN FEB 2000.

RAM'S BROTHER
→ DIED in 2015 earthquake.

'*Chaa.*'

Even Rick knew the Nepali for yes. 'And which football team is your uncle's favourite? United?'

Russell translated.

The boy grinned. '*Chaa.*'

Leading question, slapped wrist. Rick asked another. 'Tell me about your uncle Khetan.'

Russell translated.

The boy glanced at Coniston who remained blank, and refused to meet Rick's glance.

Russell tried again, and slowly the boy responded.

'I asked if Hant had hobbies, but Ram didn't really understand the question. Bit of a Western concept maybe. Says he's quite a serious man.'

'Where does Hant live?'

Coniston whispered in Nepali.

The boy shrugged.

'What did you tell him?' asked Rick.

'That it was important,' said Coniston, holding Rick's gaze.

'Did he, Russell?'

'I didn't catch it.'

'Ask him again.'

Rick observed the boy as Russell asked the question a second time. The boy's eyes flicked to Coniston and back to Weatherbeater. Then he spoke.

'Says he doesn't know.'

Rick didn't believe him. 'Ask him if they write to each other.'

Russell translated.

The boy shook his head.

'Does Hant send the boy money?'

Coniston whispered in Nepali.

'Russell?' said Rick.

'Sorry, too quiet.'

'Coniston, no talking in Nepali, if you want to say something, say it in English, and Russell will translate.' Rick wished he'd thrown their prisoner's Nepali dictionary into the void with the skewer.

Coniston tossed his pebble from hand to hand, glancing around the circle.

'When did Ram last see Hant?' said Rick.

Russell translated.

The boy looked at Coniston, then at Weatherbeater, but not at Rick. He seemed confused and torn. As if he was about to fib.

Finally, the boy spoke.

'He's not sure,' said Russell. 'During the winter.'

'Where?'

Coniston whispered in Nepali.

Rick stood up. 'Shut up, Coniston. I'm warning you, any more and you're back to the camp.'

'I'm encouraging him!' Coniston's pebbles chinked from hand to hand. 'He's probably been sworn to secrecy by Khetan.'

'Well, unswear him.'

'I'm trying, but I don't know enough Nepali.'

Rick sat down, knowing, despite himself, it was a good point. 'Russell, can you persuade Ram on Coniston's behalf?'

Russell spoke to the boy, who thought for a long time before speaking again.

'He can't remember.'

Rick drew a row of increasingly unhappy emojis on his notebook. 'Okay. Does Hant own a car? Or a motorbike?'

Russell translated.

The boy shook his head.

'How does he get around?'

Russell translated, and the boy answered.

'He walks, like everyone else.'

'Does he stay with friends?'

Russell translated.

The boy answered.

'Maybe.'

'Does he know any names?'

Russell translated.

Ram shook his head.

'Does he have a girlfriend? Or a boyfriend? Any children?'

Russell translated, and explained at some length, the boy colouring.

'*Chaina*!'

'No boyfriend. Doesn't know about children or girlfriends. Not around Saklis or MK.'

'Is he suffering from any illnesses or diseases?'

Russell translated.

Ram looked frightened. '*Chaina*.'

Rick toned it down. 'Does Hant drink beer?' He smiled, beat his chest, and pretended to hiccup.

Russell translated.

The boy smiled weakly, and nodded.

'What about cigarettes?' Rick puffed from an imaginary cigarette.

The boy nodded, pretended to cough.

Rick drew a smiley face on his pad. The interview was back on, despite Coniston. 'Ask him which brand, and about drugs, and spell it out. Heroin, cocaine, ketamine of course, and whatever the Nepali equivalents are.'

Coniston's pebbles clinked louder.

'Careful, Coniston, remember our *entente cordiale*.'

Russell translated the unusual words slowly.

The boy also thought for a moment. Then answered.

'Khetan smokes Surya. And he eats mushrooms! Funny ones, what we call magic at home. They all do. Ram used to get hit with a stick if he was discovered.'

At South Manchester, Rick would have filled out half a dozen reports following such an admission. 'Nothing about ketamine, or harder stuff?'

'No.'

Which didn't necessarily mean Khetan wasn't using hard drugs, only the boy didn't know or wasn't telling the truth. 'Let's go back to Khetan's whereabouts. Ask him again where he is.'

Russell translated.

The boy answered.

'Says he doesn't know.'

'You sound as if you don't believe him. Let's push him a bit.'

'This isn't Manchester,' said Coniston. 'Ram's not a criminal, he's not even an adult.'

'Whose side are you on?'

'I'm just saying. He's only a boy, and he's doing his best.'

Is he? thought Rick. 'Keep going, Russell. Ask him, does he think Hant's living in a different country?'

Coniston threw a stone over Ram's head.

'I warned you!' said Rick, standing up.

'It's the handcuffs, they're putting him off.'

'Rubbish! It's you.' Rick shouted towards their camp. 'Hunter!' He beckoned his colleague over, and told Russell to keep chatting to the boy, to keep him sweet.

Hunter lumbered over, marmots whistling and scurrying away. Rick had been so absorbed he'd forgotten where they were. A mountain nirvana. Gurus lived in remote caves for years at a time, meditating and praying.

'Yes, boss?' His new sergeant sounded breathless even on the flat.

'I want you to take Coniston back to camp with you.' Rick hauled their prisoner to his feet. 'He's worse than a solicitor.' He nodded at Uttam to go with them.

Rick watched them leave. Why had Coniston deliberately tried to scupper the interview? It didn't make sense. They wanted the same thing. Unless, Coniston had his own agenda, wanted to bypass the criminal justice system, and seek out his own form of retribution for his father's life.

He sat down again.

Ram was talking to Russell, but also watching Coniston. He fidgeted with his boots and looked bewildered.

'Tell the boy, not much longer, Russell.'

'He's confirmed over and over, he doesn't know where his uncle's living. No one does in Saklis, it's a bit of a mystery, and a source of speculation.'

Maybe the boy didn't know. 'Okay,' said Rick. 'Let's go back to the family tree, and see if there is someone else who might know where Hant is hiding. I know where they all are now, except Ram's grandfather on his father's side. Does he live in Saklis?'

Russell translated.

The boy smiled, pleased the questions had shifted, or he liked his second grandfather. Or both. Or neither. Non-verbal communication was often more helpful than spoken replies, but could equally be misleading. The key was to build a web of cohesive answers.

'Blimey! He lives in Aldershot.'

'In Hampshire?'

'Yeah! Not been there for that long. A couple of years, three maybe.'

'Makes sense,' said Rick. 'There was a government ruling a few years back following Joanna Lumley's campaign.' He raised a thumb at the boy. 'Tell him, well done. It's not an address for Khetan but it is something.'

'Meaning?'

'Maybe we can concoct a reason involving Subba to lure Khetan to the UK.'

The boy started speaking again.

Rick flicked to the back of his notebook and the briefing material.

In the late 1990s the Ghurkhas relocated from Hong Kong to Aldershot. Ghurkhas who retired after that were allowed to settle in the UK, but not the ones before. Lumley led a campaign, and the government caved in 2008. The PM declared that all ex-Ghurkhas could settle in the UK, regardless of when they'd left the army.

The timing fitted. Rick drew another emoji, this time a very smiley face, then updated his diagram of Ram's family tree.

'There's a bit more,' said Russell. 'When Khetan started looking out for Ram, the boy was told that Hari Subba had done a similar thing for him, as he also had lost his father.'

Rick looked at his diagram. 'That's even better for us.'

'Is it?'

'It strengthens the relationship of Khetan with Hari Subba, Ram's grandfather living in Aldershot.'

'You've lost me.'

'Have you got a sister?'

'No.'

'Brother?'

'Yes.'

'Is he married?'

'Yes.'

'Think of your sister-in-law.'

'Okay.'

'Now think of your sister-in-law's father. I bet you don't even know his name.'

'True.'

'Compare that to Hant Khetan's situation. Not only does he know the name of his brother-in-law's father – Hari Subba – but Hari Subba was his surrogate father and played a significant role in his life. Has done and *still does*. So—'

'I get it,' interrupted Russell. 'So, if anything happens to Hari Subba then it will affect Khetan significantly. He might want to do something about it.'

'Exactly.'

'Like what?'

Opposite Rick, the boy was yawning.

'I don't know, but Ram's had enough for today. He has though definitely earned another plate of *dal baht*. We'll try again tomorrow.'

20

Rick walked back to the Mosom Kharka camp with Russell. The boy was ahead of them, bounding from rock to rock, trying to stay above the scrub. Woodsmoke billowed from the cook fire and the brightly coloured prayer-flags raced and rattled.

'Are you okay, Rick, after that thing with the ladder?'

'Coniston's constantly poking us, seeing how we'll react. Question is, why? For kicks, or distraction tactics hiding some master plan?'

'We're in the middle of nowhere.'

'I know, but we all need to be careful. I'm going for a leg-stretch, hour or so. You and Hunter okay with him?'

The mountaineer nodded. 'Why did you bring him?'

'Coniston?'

'Hunter.'

'I didn't have much choice. But he was a good 'tec: came from the flying squad.'

'Exactly. When did they walk anywhere? But it's not only that. He's so obstructive, and I'm fed up with it. And he calls me Russ.'

'I'll speak to him.'

They walked on, Rick replaying the interview, the interruptions and obfuscations by Coniston. It appeared that their prisoner had told Ram to stay quiet about Khetan. Which suggested Ram knew where their target was hiding, and so, now, did Coniston. Or maybe their prisoner didn't: maybe Khetan had sworn the boy to secrecy.

'Keep him in cuffs, Russell.'

'Hunter?'

Rick's mood lifted.

A kilometre north of MK, he reached a clearing at the bottom of a dark cliff. Under an overhang at the top were half a dozen bright yellow patches the size of dustbin lids, and across their surface were thick black semi-circles, like giant smiles.

He raised his binoculars, realising he'd stumbled upon half a dozen colonies of the Himalayan cliff honeybee, the world's largest. The smiles were bees, the yellow half-lids honeycomb. Each colony could contain sixty kilos of honey.

He let the binoculars drop, and sat down on a log seat surrounded by noodle wrappers and burnt tin cans.

What if the family tree was all they gleaned on the entire trip? Even if Ram knew something about Khetan, he seemed unlikely to tell them. They could beat the boy, or employ thumbscrews or waterboarding. Succumb to the red mist of interviewers and their controllers. In the Nepalese foothills, he was both.

He pulled out the remnants of the trail mix, and his notebook. It fell open at his most recent entry – Ram's family tree – but upside down.

Like his thinking.

The investigation was not about Ram, but about Hant Khetan. He reread Maggie's briefing sheet.

Born 1982 in Saklis, Nepal. Studied at Kathmandu University, then worked in the Nepalese telecoms industry for ten years. Worked overseas, mostly in London.

Khetan believes in Dharma (respect), and the importance of family and country. He is suspected of planning terrorist activity on behalf of his countrymen around the world.

Rick ate a handful of trail mix. Where was Special K? What was he doing? He wasn't going to be content tilling fields and growing subsistence crops in a remote corner of Nepal. He'd be searching for another FIFA target, or something else to believe in, and fight for. A cause which accorded with *Dharma*.

The sat phone rang.

He didn't answer. Maggie would follow up with a text, and if she didn't, the caller would be Robbo.

The grating noise resumed. No messages, which meant it was his boss. Rick killed the call. Robbo could fret and dwell.

Like he was.

He sent Maggie a message to research Hari Subba, and when it had gone, sent another one. To take her pepper spray whenever she went out, and to set her house alarm at night. Coniston was making him jumpy.

Three local men arrived at the foot of the cliff. One was hunched over and carrying a large roll of rope ladder on his back. He looked like a giant snail. The other two carried wicker baskets. All three set their loads down and stared up at the bees. The older man, his skin wrinkled like bark, turned to Rick and gave a toothless grin. The man with the rope ladder picked it up, and returned the way they'd come. The other two men emptied their baskets. Smaller baskets and plastic containers were placed on the ground in a semi-circle.

Everyone needed an absorbing project. Whether it was keeping bees or collecting butterflies, building a patio or organising a motorcycle rally. Everyone needed something. Juvenile to junkie, surgeon to psychopath.

Could he foist a new project onto Khetan?

He stared up at the bees. Behind them, the black rocks of the cliff glistened with moisture. A rivulet of water ran down and puddled on the ground. He wondered about his own bees, and whether they'd swarmed.

There was a shout from the top of the cliff, and a second later, the rope ladder unfolded in violent jerks down the cliff face.

How could one of Khetan's relatives living in Aldershot lure him to the UK? Previously, Khetan had been motivated by *Dharma*, the Nepalese concept of honour, and by familial revenge.

Rick smelt burning.

The two men at the foot of the cliff crouched around a thin line of rising smoke. A single rope was thrown down the cliff and came to rest alongside the rope ladder. The old man attached a shallow basket of smoking leaves and gave the rope a yank. The basket rose until it was three-quarters of the way up the cliff, near the circular bee colonies. Smoke billowed everywhere. Bees lifted off in their thousands. The air was full of smoke and angry bees.

Rick stuffed his gear into his bag and retreated to the edge of the clearing.

The man at the foot of the cliff covered himself in a blanket. The old man pulled on a mosquito veil and started to climb the ladder. He carried a long pole, sharpened at one end. Smoke and clumps of bees drifted around him. When he reached the level of the honeycomb more ropes fell down the cliff. Using the sharpened pole he made two holes in the lower half of a yellow disc, then pushed a rope through each. He used the pole to saw through the comb, which fell away and was caught by the ropes. The old man guided it into the basket.

Familial revenge. He could recreate that. Revenge for something that had happened to Hari Subba, Ram's grandfather and Khetan's surrogate father. An ex-Ghurkha who had recently taken up residential rights in the UK. An old soldier, a man who

132

would have discipline and standards, reasonable education, good English, relative wealth for a Nepalese man, but relative poverty now that he was in the UK.

What about a Nepalese issue? Justice or fair play for his countrymen was something that Khetan felt passionate about. Passionate enough to kidnap and kill.

The old man climbed down the rope and the basket was lowered alongside him. As soon as his feet touched the ground he scooped a chunk of honey into his mouth and licked his fingers greedily.

How could he link the two things that motivated Khetan? He needed to make Hari Subba the centre of them. The target for anti-Ghurkha harassment? The target for protests by far-right thugs against the change in the law?

Racial harassment could work. Racially harass Hari Subba. It would get Khetan's blood up. It might even make him fly back to the UK.

If Ram couldn't – wouldn't – provide any more info, it might do.

Might convince Robbo.

Might even work.

At the edge of the clearing, Rick turned for a last look at the cliff. The ropes still dangled, but the smoke had dissipated and the bees were calmer. The two younger men were picking dead bees out of the basket.

He set off back towards MK, soon breaking into a run. He would like to have tasted the honey but he had a bad feeling he'd been away from camp too long.

At Mosom Kharka, the cook was chopping chillies and singing to himself. Ram was rolling dice with the cook boy. Hunter and Russell were playing darts, and eating popcorn. Lok sat outside Coniston's tent.

'Where is he?'

'Relax,' said Hunter. 'He's in his tent, still handcuffed. Uttam's having a kip.'

Russell fetched a giant flask of tea and a packet of the local butter biscuits. The wrappers littered the trails. Rick sat down. Russell opened the biscuits and poured tea into insulated mugs which wouldn't fall over.

'Any ideas using Hari Subba?' said Rick. He ate a biscuit.

Hunter dumped sugar in his tea.

'What about a competition?' said Russell. 'Like the one you told me about, Gary.'

'You tell him, Russ.'

'Okay,' said the mountaineer, shaking his head. 'Basically, we tell Khetan he's won a competition, but the prize has to be collected from the UK – in person. Gary told me he ran one when he was at Clapham. You wrote eighty letters, Gary?'

Hunter tapped the table like a spoilt child.

'To fine defaulters, telling them they'd won a TV which they could collect from the town hall. Twenty-three arrests, Gary?'

Tap-tap.

'It's got symmetry,' said Rick.

'Come again?' said Hunter.

'It's in the file. Last year, Khetan used a competition to lure the Williams twins to Nepal. But, I can't see him falling for it. From what we know about him, he's not interested in anything material.'

'You got anything better?'

'Maybe.' Rick explained his idea of racist harassment of Hari.

'You mean like pushing dog shit through his letterbox. Daubing *Go Home* in Nepali across his front door?'

'Racist abuse would provide Khetan two reasons – his love of kith and kin – to risk travelling to the UK. Love, honour, duty, patriotism, whatever you want to call it.'

'Won't there be a problem with us harassing Hari Subba?' said Russell.

Hunter snickered. 'Specials!'

'We have to make Khetan *think* that Hari Subba has been the subject of racial harassment. How we do that is where I'm at.'

Hunter raised a hand. 'Isn't there another problem? How's Khetan going to know about this harassment? We don't know where he is, and even if we did we can't simply send him an email.'

'My turn,' said Russell, pouring out the last of the tea. 'Even if Khetan does get to know about the harassment, he's not going to fly over to the UK. He'll phone Hari up, and Hari'll tell him he's okay.'

'But at the moment,' said Rick, 'we've got nothing better. Three problems, so now we need three solutions. Or, Coniston convinces Ram to tell us more about Khetan. I'm going to give him – them – another chance tomorrow.'

He stood up, and walked to the edge of the camp to urinate. For Coniston to persuade Ram, he needed to persuade Coniston.

He would sweeten their deal. Offer Coniston a cash bonus, or a night in a Kathmandu massage parlour. He would empty the expedition's sundries account.

Ignore, bend, or circumvent every regulation in the book.

He'd then brief Coniston to give Ram the binoculars, to offer him money, a place at an English school, *anything*, so even if the boy had been sworn to silence by Khetan, then maybe he'd relent. Which meant he'd have to remove Coniston's handcuffs, remove every impediment to success, however risky. He'd post both Sherpas on watch. The situation couldn't get any worse: if Ram told Coniston and then Russell, great, and if he didn't, then no one, not Coniston or his mother, not Robbo, not Rick's own demons, could say he hadn't tried everything.

Couldn't say he'd made the wrong *decision*.

He stared out.

The ice-encrusted mountains were bathed in a pink ethereal light. The steep ridges gleamed, the jagged peaks poked the heavens. In the distance, the marmots were shrieking.

21

Everyone was observing everyone else.

Calix was watching Ram paddling in the pool and making minor improvements to the headwall. Sitting on a high rock on the opposite bank, and now armed with whistles and sticks, the two Sherpas were noting every move of both of them. And at the MK camp, where the three dibble sat around the mess table, Castle stood occasionally, and looked over with his binoculars. Our last chance, he'd said.

Castle was right – and wrong.

'*Ramro!*' said Calix.

The boy added another rock, and smeared a handful of muddy grit to cement it in place. The pool was deepening.

It was possible to drown in a puddle.

Calix checked on Beetle Beetle, then inventoried his pockets. A few coins, some string. The neckerchief used as a mask on dusty trails. His balaclava. The tent peg he'd substituted for the skewer.

He checked through his daysack. His old man's binoculars. His jacket, dictionary, and the box of flapjack. His KFS – in old man speak. Plastic to save weight, and permissible under Castle's new regime. The small cooking pot he'd borrowed from the cook. The other items he'd collected: a plastic bottle, a small flask, some cold charcoal from the fire, and three sachets of coffee. Lastly, the pouch of useful things which his mum had taken from his old man's kit bag. Castle had confiscated the 5mm cord and the spare bootlaces, but the rest of the items were still there: sachets of salt and sugar; iodine; needle and thread; a candle; fishing hooks; tent patch; waterproof matches. His old man had often talked about the pouch – how he lectured junior soldiers on self-reliance and small things making a difference. Calix hadn't been a junior soldier but his old man had never seemed to notice.

After repacking the bag, he lay back and closed his eyes. Marshalled his thoughts for the boy, for Castle. For Khetan.

He started with the premise that Ram knew where Khetan was hiding. Which meant it was only a matter of coaxing and terrorising. Calix knew from pushing cannabis to students and dopeheads that finding the right balance was an art, and satisfying as the money. Too much cajoling and debts never got paid, too much oppression, and debtors returned with a weapon or an army.

Ram plonked down next to him, and Calix opened his eyes. The boy threw a stone in the water. 'You no like Sherpa?'

Calix heaved himself up. 'Just playing.' The boy frowned. Calix didn't know the word and he hoped Ram would understand from his tone. Children understood more from actions, not words, so it wasn't surprising he was confused.

'*Kina daai?*' Ram balled his fist and punched his hand.

'Why did Castle punch me?' said Calix. 'He was also playing.' He pushed Ram's shoulder and pretended to laugh, hoping it would be enough to convince the boy.

At the camp, the junior dibble were playing darts but Castle stood looking through his binoculars.

Calix threw a stone into the water. The rings worked their way outwards, slower and smaller.

'*Mama Hant kaha chha?*' Where's your uncle Hant?

Ram shook his head.

Calix threw another stone.

He extricated the binoculars from his bag. The last person to have used them would have been his old man. Queen, country, family. Castle had thought they were a good idea and he hoped the senior dibble was right. He handed them to the boy.

'*Mero buwaa.*' My old man's.

Ram held them as if they were made of china. He'd also lost his father so maybe he understood.

The boy looked around, his face lighting up. Calix showed him how to focus. The boy scanned around again. He focused on the mountains, and on the dibble camp. Castle had disappeared inside his tent. On the high rock, Lok and Uttam watched and whispered.

Speaking excitedly in Nepali, the boy wandered off, observing all around.

Calix took out the small pot. He broke the charcoal into small pieces and dropped them into the pot. He ground them with the stick and added some water. He mashed it all together and added more water to form a paste. He added the coffee granules and hot water, and stirred again. The paste became a thick liquid.

The boy was still spotting things. A shrieking marmot, a bird. An aeroplane. More marmots.

Calix rolled up a trouser leg, revealing a very white shin with curly blond hairs. Using the flat of his hand, he smeared it with the gooey liquid. He rubbed it in, twisting some of the hairs so they received a good coating. His leg turned dark, but so did the hairs. Brown-black rather than coal-black, but it would do.

Ram wandered back with the binoculars. He walked up to Calix and looked at him through the glasses. He let them slip and stared at Calix's discoloured leg as if he'd chopped off his foot.

Calix poured the gooey liquid into a bottle and stashed it in his bag.

Next, he looked around for a piece of wood. He found a branch, snapped it to length and hollowed out the middle with a pointed stone. It was the rough shape of a boat, but it needed stabilisers, otherwise it would roll. He used the tent peg to force holes at either end, and pushed two thin sticks through the holes so they protruded on both sides. He fashioned four floats from offcuts of wood, like those on a trimaran. With the tent peg he bored holes, then forced them onto the ends of the sticks. He had a boat with stabilisers.

Ram walked over, letting the binoculars dangle round his neck.

'Okay?'

The boy nodded as if it was his birthday.

Calix started on the sail. He ripped his neckerchief in half, then half again. He made a wooden square of thin sticks. He joined them at the corners by making crude joints – a hole in one stick and the second stick whittled with the stone to a point and forced through until it was wedged. It looked rough, but it worked. Four of them. Like his old man, he was good with his hands.

With the needle and thread from his old man's pouch he sewed one of the neckerchief quarters onto the wooden square. He fixed a mast into the centre of the boat, and lashed the sail to the mast with string.

Then he handed the boat to Ram, and the boy pushed the boat out into the dam. There wasn't much wind, but it floated well. They watched it turn a lazy circle.

On the water, there were broken reflections of the

sky and the mountains and the two of them.

Loud voices broke the quietness. At the MK camp the junior dibble were arguing about the darts. Their bright jackets, the mountaineer's grubby yellow and Hunter's shiny red, moved back and forth, and their voices carried on the air. Uttam and Lok perched on their rock like two birds.

Calix threw a stone at the boat, deliberately missing. He threw another. Again, the stone missed but water splashed onto the boat deck. He gathered more stones, handed one to Ram.

The boy threw a stone. Calix threw, hitting the boat. Ram hit the boat. The deck shipped water. They threw together, they kept throwing. The boat capsized. Ram found larger rocks, threw larger rocks. One holed the deck. Another smashed the mast. The sail sank. The boat capsized and floated away.

They'd built the dam, they'd sunk a boat. They were almost a team.

Almost.

Calix cleared a patch of ground with his boot and the two of them squatted down. Using a stone, Calix drew an X in the middle of the cleared area. 'Mosom Kharka.' He scratched two stick men. 'Calix and Ram.'

The boy nodded, and grinned.

Calix drew an arrow to the west. Another X and the word *Saklis*. Another arrow, another X and *Lukla*. He drew a bridge and a wavy line for the River Hinku. He marked another arrow to the north. He scratched triangles and pointed at the mountains. Ram nodded. To the south Calix drew an arrow and wrote *Jiri*.

'*Kati din laagchha Jiri?*' How many days to Jiri?

Ram held his chin while he thought. An adult gesture and Calix's turn to grin.

'*Ek haptaa,*' said Ram.

One week – the first of two answers he needed from the boy.

'*Mama Hant kaha chha?*' Where's your uncle Hant?

Ram avoided eye contact.

'Binoculars,' said Calix. He held out his hand and pointed to the dangling glasses.

The boy clutched them to his chest.

'*Mama Hant?*'

The boy looked torn.

Calix reached over and unhooked the binoculars from Ram's neck. He set them down in the top of his bag, and looked over at the camp. Castle was poring over a map.

There were some things he wished Megan could see him doing and saying, and others he was glad she couldn't. 'Can you swim, Ram?' He mimed breast-stroke, then front crawl, and pointed to the water.

The boy shook his head, and rose to his feet. Calix glanced at the camp, then stepped towards the boy. Ram backed away but Calix grabbed his arm. He smiled, smiled for the Sherpas, smiled at Ram.

'Lummle.'

'*Lummle kaha chha?*' Where's Lummle?

Ram put two fingers together to indicate small. 'Tibet.'

Calix nodded. A village called Lummle, close to Tibet. He handed Ram back the binoculars, and feeling giddy, raised an ignominious thumb.

He wanted to punch the air, wanted to whoop, and shout huzza, like his old man at a regimental dinner. Carrot and stick never failed.

The boy still looked apprehensive.

Calix waggled his thumb.

Ram finally raised his digit, and smiled weakly. Then turned and wandered off to MK, the binoculars swinging around his neck.

The wind picked up, and Calix stared at the ripples on the

dammed river. Deep enough to sink a boat. Deep enough to drown in. He donned his jacket and balaclava, and followed the boy. Suddenly, he felt freezing cold.

22

'Ram wants to go home,' said Russell.

'Why!'

'Says he has to get back, boss, his family will be worried.'

'We'll pay him to stay. A stupid amount.'

Russell conducted a second tense conversation with Ram, the boy staying at a distance, as if he thought someone was going to do him some harm. His trouser legs were wet and the binoculars hung like a millstone around his neck. He refused a plate of *dal*, refused to come closer, refused eye contact.

Coniston sat down by the cook fire and unlaced his boots. Smoke swirled round and about. The Sherpas squatted nearby, silent and uncertain.

'Sorry,' said Russell, 'he's adamant.'

Rick wheeled round. 'Coniston. Why's the boy going?'

Their prisoner tipped out his boot, and shrugged. 'Said he had to go. I gave him the binoculars, tried everything.'

'Did he say anything about Khetan?'

'I asked him again, of course.' He rummaged inside his boot and pulled out a stone. 'Nothing.' He tossed the stone aside.

Ram turned to go.

'Russell, tell the boy to wait, and ask the Sherpas what went on.'

The mountaineer spoke to the boy as he was walking away. He started following him. 'He's going, boss, nothing I can do.'

'Pay him anyway. A hundred dollars, and thank him. The British government are grateful, I'm grateful.'

Rick waited, eyeing Coniston remove his second boot and empty it of unseen detritus. Next to him lay his daysack, the Nepali dictionary sticking out of a side pocket.

Russell walked back toward the Sherpas.

Behind him, the boy was now running towards the foot of the hillside, and the steep path back to Saklis. Running like a startled marmot. Back home, back to his family, back to his fields and goats. And away from Coniston. The risk of letting Coniston have a second go had backfired. But then, it was a risk. Robbo would never understand, and Rick would never tell him.

Nepali voices, to and fro.

'Lok says Coniston grabbed the boy.'

'I told you I tried everything.' Their prisoner tucked the laces into his boots, slipped his socked feet inside and picked up the daysack. 'Oh, when I did grab Ram, he said he thought his uncle might be in Europe.' He set off towards his tent.

Rick intercepted him. Europe had a whiff about it, a whiff of make-believe, a whiff of Coniston, a whiff of smugness.

'Hands.'

Coniston scowled and spat like a lifer.

Rick fixed a pair of plasticuffs in place and ratcheted them tight. He whipped the dictionary out of the side pocket and dumped it in the cook fire. 'Cuffs until we get back to Strangeways.'

They all went to visit the suspension bridge, all six of them. Reneging on a promise to Mrs Coniston, and in memoriam,

David Coniston, would have been petty, and Rick was spitting, but not petty. Later they'd pack up, and in the morning trek back to Lukla. Fly back to Kathmandu, then Manchester, return Coniston to Strangeways.

The bridge swayed in the wind. Seventy metres of wire and wood. Tattered prayer-flags fluttered along the sides – red for fire, green for water, blue for sky, white for air and yellow for earth. Buddhists believed that when the flags moved, they carried messages of wisdom and peace.

'Stay here with him,' said Rick.

Taking a deep breath, he climbed the short ladder onto the bridge and walked partway across. He didn't let go of the rail, tried not to think about falling. Below him the water heaved and roared. Submerged rocks as big as cars lined the edges. A chunk of dirty ice surged along.

Rick stared across the bridge – at the events of last year. The brigadier arriving at MK, and offering to hand himself to Khetan in exchange for his son. The soldier climbing onto the rail, and jumping.

Rick had ousted Coniston from prison and travelled to Nepal to put things right. He had to keep going, to fight his demons, to obtain justice for David. For Spencer Williams, Vicky Brant. For tens, maybe hundreds of others.

He tottered back on the swaying boards, and climbed down. At the foot of the ladder, he sat on a porter's bench and tried the incident room on the sat phone.

Porters from a major expedition began filing across the bridge, returning from a high mountain. Twenty-five or thirty of them, carrying overloaded baskets. Eyes down, headstraps straining, foreheads glistening. The HGVs of the foothills.

'It's me, Mags.'

'God, it's early.'

'Have you found anything on Hari Subba?'

'How are you, too!'

'Sorry. The boy's done a bunk, no second interview. Subba's all we've got.'

'Well okay, then. I've looked a few things up, and I've got some ideas.'

Rick took out his notebook. 'Go on.'

'Hari Subba lives in a council flat. So, we could find an identical one – one that's empty – and daub it with racist graffiti. Maybe smash a few windows. We'd take photos and make good the damage. No one would be offended, and neither Hari Subba nor Khetan any the wiser.'

Rick nodded with the phone. 'It might work.'

He pondered. 'Sorry,' he said after a while. 'Is it Siobhan?'

'I don't want to talk about it. I just need cheering up.'

He was the one seeing Emma, the one who saw shapes in the umbra of the night. Maggie cheered *him* up.

'I could do with a kiss,' she said into the silence.

'You mean phone sex?' Rick grabbed the words from nowhere.

'Sat-phone sex,' said Maggie, surprise in her voice.

'Is that different?'

'Very,' she said, laughing. 'I'm officially cheered. What can I hear?'

'I'm sitting near the suspension bridge.'

'*The* bridge?'

'It's an incredible place.' He paused. 'Hill after hill, as far as I can see. The sky is deep blue and it's warm during the day. At night the river freezes at the edges and ice forms inside my tent. But the sky is usually clear, and there are thousands of stars. Out here, Mags, it feels different. It feels primeval.'

'Sounds cold.'

'I'd like to bring you here.' But not if the operation failed.

Maggie was silent for a few seconds.

147

'Anything else on using Subba?'

'A bit more. I looked up the election results for Aldershot. Independence UK increased their share of the vote from five to eighteen per cent. A local paper ran a story alleging the Independence UK candidate tweeted that Nepalese people were parasites.'

'So racial harassment of a Nepalese man wouldn't be unexpected?'

'Harassment's already happening. Locals have dubbed Aldershot 'Ghurkha Town'. It's estimated ten thousand Nepalese people are living there. Although they're seen as honest friendly people, there have been problems. Graffiti, verbal abuse, and a couple of drunken fights. I could concoct a fake newspaper article, and use the photos of the damaged flat. Then, send it out to Saklis.' She paused. 'I know it's a bit tenuous.'

'We'll make it work. We have to.'

'Another problem was why Hari Subba hasn't told his family about the harassment. Ex-soldiers are all the same. They've spent their lives coping with adversity, and now they're proud old men who don't want to be helped.'

It sounded like someone else he knew, but he didn't comment. Maybe bringing Maggie to Nepal was a terrible idea.

'Even if Hari *was* being harassed it'd be unlikely he'd tell his family, yet alone ask for their help. He'd probably deny it, even if they asked *him*.'

'I hope you're right.' He heard voices and looked over his shoulder. Coniston was arguing with Hunter. 'He's playing up again, Mags.'

'Robbo wants a word.'

'Tell him, no battery. Love you.' Rick put the phone down and rejoined his colleagues. Left-field ideas were all he had.

'Coniston wants to go onto the bridge alone,' said Hunter.

Rick waited for the tail of the climbing expedition to cross the bridge. Dozens of porters, then five climbers carrying daysacks, and ice axes as badges of honour. Finally, a backmarker holding aloft the Nepalese flag.

'Okay,' said Rick. It was a risk, but so was everything after they'd left Strangeways.

Coniston stood up. He climbed the ladder onto the bridge and walked halfway across. Uttam and Lok climbed the ladder and leant against the stanchion. Fifty metres below, the freezing water crashed along.

Hunter sat on the bench and took off a boot and sock. Nursed a large saggy blister. 'I'm not going to say I told you.' Hunter looked up at Rick. 'But we could've done this without him.'

'He got the family tree.'

'Hari in Aldershot! Anyway, Russ could have got that.'

'Russell?'

The mountaineer see-sawed his head. 'Maybe. Some of it. Not all of it. My view, Coniston has earned his plane ticket but only just.'

'Maybe you're both right.' Rick glanced along the bridge at Coniston, leaning over the rail and communing with his father.

Above them, there was another perfect blue sky and a red sun bright as a billiard ball. In the distance, the boom of rockfall.

23

The red sun beat down.

Calix descended the ladder from the bridge, his ears ringing from the river. At the bottom, he gripped the side rails, leant forward and rested his chin on a rung. He closed his eyes. He'd wanted to come. But the bridge wasn't how he remembered it. It was longer, higher above the water, more precarious. The water was louder, frothier. Hungrier. His old man had done it for him.

'Take your time.'

Despite everything, Castle was a decent person. No surprise he'd got on with his old man.

Calix opened his eyes. Behind the ladder a faint path led under the bridge and down the steep bank towards the water. He sat down on a rung. Castle was watching him from a porter's seat. In the wall underneath a stone was missing and a plastic bottle stuck out. Someone had shoved their litter there, as if they were in Manchester. In Failston.

Castle nodded at him. Almost avuncular in his concern.

Calix ran his hands over the side rails of the ladder. They were smooth from thousands of hands pulling and sliding. The finest sandpaper couldn't do a better job. His old man's hands had contributed. His old man had been here, had hauled his body onto the bridge platform.

He looked at the ground. Scraps of silver foil and fruit pips lay between the stones. People had sat on a rung of the ladder before.

'Did he sit here?'

'David?'

'Mmm.'

Castle paused. 'He did.'

Calix nodded, wondering for a second if Castle was just saying that.

A butterfly landed on a stone slab. Then another. The two butterflies rested, their wings spread out, soaking up the sun. Black with red and yellow streaks, like lightning forks at night.

'You know what they're doing?'

Castle shook his head.

'They're taking up minerals and salts which they can't get from flowers. They need places where water is very shallow or has evaporated. It's called puddling.'

'I didn't know that. Bees do the same.'

'How do you know bees?'

'I keep them.'

'You?'

Castle nodded.

The two butterflies took off and flew away. They flew together, circling, landing and taking off again. They merged into the bushes.

Castle took a deep breath, and seeming to forget the events of the morning, told Calix about his bees, about artificial swarming and laying workers. Despite himself, Calix listened and was interested.

He glanced around for the two butterflies, but couldn't spot them. He stood up. The bridge was swaying and he stared across it. He was looking for a ghost. He felt him, but couldn't see him. Halfway across the bridge, a young boy with a stick was driving a small herd of goats towards them. He was tapping the handrail with the stick, and singing. Above the bleating of the goats, above the booming of the river, rose snatches of the boy's lament.

'Before we walk back,' said Castle, 'and I'm sorry to do this now – here – but I need more detail on what Ram said to you this morning. Europe's a big place.'

Calix was still listening to the goat herder's singing, still thinking about his old man sitting on the ladder. 'London, maybe.'

'Maybe Khetan's in London? Or, maybe Ram said, London?'

His old man climbing the ladder. And not coming back down.

'Calix?'

'I'm not sure. Either.'

'What do you mean? You're just making this up.' The thinking man's copper sounded riled. His eyes were bloodshot, his cheeks sunken. 'Something went on this morning. What was it? Did Ram tell you when he'd last seen his uncle? And where? Was it recently?'

'Maybe I pushed him too hard.'

'So what did you find out? And why aren't you telling me?'

Behind Castle, two large trees had grown up close to each other. A branch from each had met and fused together. It looked as if they were shaking hands. But, they were trees, and Castle was dibble. 'Maybe London, I told you.'

Castle shoved him backwards toward the bench.

His legs buckled and he sat. In the cell when Darren had pushed him down, he'd stayed down. But Castle was constrained by rules. Calix took his time, stood up again slowly. 'I wouldn't do that again.'

Castle stepped back, raised his hands at waist height. It looked well practised. It looked defensive.

'Boss?' shouted Weatherbeater and Hunter together.

Lok and Uttam loped over.

'*Sahib?*'

'It's okay,' said Castle. He waved a hand as if he was slowing a car.

The two Sherpas backed off and waited. The junior dibble stayed their distance, but Weatherbeater removed an ice axe from his pack.

'We want the same thing, Coniston.'

'Do we.' Calix glanced at the swaying bridge. Justice for his old man was completely different to revenge.

Castle ushered Weatherbeater closer.

The mountaineer halved the gap, his ice axe at port arms. Old-man language, even now. The ice tool glinted in the sun. It could save life, but equally take it.

Calix held out his manacled hands. 'I can't walk back to Lukla like this.'

'Are you offering a trade?'

'Take them off, and I'll tell you what Ram really told me.'

'Okay.'

'Khetan's near the border with Tibet.'

'I need the name of a place.' Castle gestured for the ice axe. Weatherbeater threw it and Castle caught it, as if they'd been rehearsing.

The senior dibble swung back, and forward, decapitating a section of scrub. It looked improvised. It looked offensive.

'A village near the border, that's all I know.'

Castle swung again, leaving another line of ripped plants.

'Don't do anything stupid,' shouted Hunter.

Castle stepped closer.

'Lummle,' said Calix. 'The village is called Lummle. That's it, that's all I know.' He held out his handcuffs.

'They can come off at Strangeways.'

'You said.'

Castle threw the ice axe back to Weatherbeater, stared up at the pink-tinged sky, and puckered his eyebrows. 'I said, maybe, or maybe I said.'

24

Pockets of warmth trapped in his sleeping bag, two pairs of socks, black dogs wandering around his purple dreams. The last cold dawn at Mosom Kharka. In a few hours, they'd be heading back to Saklis.

Rick forced himself out of the tent. He still felt as if he was drunk. Like a wearied and bloody knight, the night after a battle, enemy flag secured, king's daughter rescued. It was possible Coniston was lying, or Ram, or the boy was mistaken, but Rick didn't think so.

Already he could smell woodsmoke. An urn rested on the cook fire, and the cook was making tea. Uttam sat on a chair outside Coniston's tent, rocking back and forth. The sky was cloudy but spines of the mountains were yellow-edged. Haloed.

'*Namaste!*' whispered Rick.

'*Namaste.*'

The cook brought tea. It was sweet, milky, and hot, and according to Weatherbeater good for combatting altitude headaches. Rick cupped his mug, the steam making his nose run. He could have eaten a full English fry up.

He tested the sat phone but it was inoperable. They were miracles of technology but too much cloud cover rendered them useless. His moment of elation on the phone to Robbo would have to wait still longer.

Behind him, the Sherpas' tent zip ripped, and Lok emerged. The replacement guard slipped on his boots and plodded over. His eyes red-rimmed and crusty. Wide smile. His brother handed him his mug and Lok spoke. The two men chuckled quietly.

'Coniston?' said Rick.

'*Ramro*,' replied Uttam, raising a thumb.

Rick finished his tea and pointed up the valley towards the bridge. The Sherpas nodded, and leaving his mug with the cook, Rick walked out of camp.

One final walk. He slipped on his gloves, and pulled his balaclava down. His breath marked the air. Smoke rose from distant shacks. A rock dislodged on a far crag and crashed to the ground hundreds of metres below. Echoes dissipated.

He stopped at a clearing with a wall and a set of prayer-wheels. He remembered them from last time. Buddhists believed turning them sent out prayers, like the flags.

He walked around the wall, spinning the intricately carved wheels. He wasn't a believer – in anything – but he still assigned prayers. Dad. Mags. That the information from Coniston was genuine, timely, and could be actioned.

The clouds were shifting and the sun emerging, but the sat phone still wasn't connecting. He slumped down by the prayer-wheels, and opened his notebook. The third problem stared up at him.

How would Khetan get to know about the racist harassment of Hari Subba?

If Lummle proved correct, they no longer needed a backup plan. But if it didn't, then informing one of Khetan's relatives in Saklis seemed the only viable option. Russell was staying in Nepal, switching back to his day job of mountaineer, and could hand-deliver a letter. A written message could be relayed to Khetan verbatim so that nothing could be misconstrued or forgotten.

Three problems – three solutions.

The sat phone sounded from inside his bag. He delved inside and pulled it out. The cloud had broken and the phone was transmitting again.

'Must be the middle of the night, Mags?'

'I hoped you'd think it was her.'

'Hello, sir.'

'Battery okay?'

'How's the diet?'

'Bit late for that, Rick.'

'I was thinking you could cycle to work.' Rick stroked a prayer-wheel which clacked around.

'You know what I've been thinking,' said Robbo. 'That it's due to stress. As soon as Coniston's back in Strangeways and you're back here investigating South Manchester crime, then my weight will drop back to normal. You'll see.'

Rick refrained from telling Robbo he'd been overweight beforehand, and instead enjoyed the anticipation before telling his news.

His boss cleared his throat. Rick pictured him in paisley pyjamas sitting on the edge of the bed, his night guard in a glass. 'What has Coniston extracted from the boy?'

'Quite a lot.'

'Such as?'

'Ram's grandfather lives in Aldershot, and we could use him to lure Khetan to the UK.'

'You could?'

'We've also got a location for Khetan.'

'Where?'

'A village called Lummle near the Tibetan border.' Rick spelt it. 'I've checked. It exists.'

For a short while, Rick had thought about not telling Robbo, but he'd got over that. So he might not have the satisfaction of arresting Khetan on UK soil, but if the Americans found him instead, he would have the knowledge he'd helped remove a resourceful killer from the world stage. And if they didn't find him, he had Hari Subba as a backup plan.

'How good is the intel?'

'D4.'

Rick waited.

'Remind me.'

'Unreliable source and uncorroborated information. But Coniston thinks it's true, which is something.'

'Well, I suppose congratulations are in order. I'll pass it on, and let you know. Battery still okay?'

'It is.'

'I met with Hainsforth at the weekend.' Rick turned more prayer-wheels. 'Turns out the governor of Strangeways is also a mason.' His boss paused. 'Elaine came up in conversation. And he was very understanding. Empathetic, if you get my drift. Anyway, we had a nice little chat and we've written it all up so we're covered. When I say *we* I mean the governor and me. Not you, Rick. You're not covered. So best you bring Coniston back, and soon. And then keep your head down.'

Rick shoved the sat phone back in his bag, and leant back against the wall. The sun warmed his face and he felt his eyes closing. The days were so different to the nights. He wasn't sleeping well, unused to the discomfort of a thin inflatable mattress and the cold. Minus four degrees celsius inside his tent.

He never snoozed during the day. Never. Two minutes and he'd jog back to MK and help take down the tents.

He'd lost some leverage with his boss, but so what. He had a location for Khetan and a workable backup plan.

He'd done it.

*

He's doing night duty, visiting the central control room. It's rare he goes there, but he was passing and thought he'd fly the flag. He's the senior detective on duty. The room seems dark. He chats to the duty inspector, Ellis Shears. Ellis sits at three large screens on a raised platform. Rick stands behind him, looking over his shoulder. In front of them are two semi-circles of smaller screens and a dozen dispatchers. Ellis offers Rick a coffee and he accepts.

A 999 call comes in:

> 2333   I768   'steaming' robbery on a 64 bus, 5 or 6 susps,
> knives and hand-gun seen, 2 indep witns

Patrols are sent to an RV and Ellis deploys an armed unit. Rick stays silent, listening to the radio chatter and watching the screens. Units call up at the RV. Foxtrot 2, the armed unit, is four minutes away.

Another 999 call arrives:

> 2334   I770   DV, screams heard, informant a neighbour –
> 3 v young children, triplets, heard stuff
> breaking, does NOT want to be spoken to

A dispatcher taps away on a computer. She's wearing a blue *hijab* and has thick glasses. 'FI marker,' says the woman. 'No other reports, no prior police attendance.' She types it up. 'Armed unit, boss?' Before Ellis can answer, a third 999 call within a minute flashes up:

> 2334   I771   White van LOS fail to stop for DT23, PC
> 376 seen wires around driver's coat, IC3,
> male, 20

'Boss?' says a second dispatcher. He's eating a sandwich. He's also in civvy clothes, and has an earring and a ponytail.

'Control, Foxtrot Three, where do you want us?' In the background, sirens break through the night.

'Control, Foxtrot Two, divert?' More sirens can be heard.

The soft chatter in the control room stops and someone turns the lights up. The young guy puts his sandwich into a plastic box with a blue lid.

'Rick?' says Ellis. 'You're the DCI. I've only got two armed units. Both three up. Foxtrot Three's in Wigan. Twenty minutes, at least, from all three jobs.'

Rick thinks about the relative gravity, real and potential. At the robbery there are no reports of injuries, but a firearm has been seen. The address of the domestic has had no previous calls, but is always a potential murder. The van with wires is very likely to be a false alarm, but is potentially a disaster.

Ellis waits, the room waits. Rick can feel them waiting. Domestics are always volatile and can escalate in seconds. A bomb can kill and maim hundreds. The firearm could be an imitation. He picks up the mic. The police get a bad press for not taking domestics seriously enough, and they are a force priority. He opens his mouth and closes it again. The witnesses at the robbery are independent, but aren't police. No one would ever forget 9/11 or 7/7. Most domestics are verbal.

'Foxtrot Two, divert to the van. Foxtrot Three, you go to the robbery RV. First one free can roll on to the domestic.'

Ellis nods his head and the armed units confirm the commands. Bursts of sirens again fill the room. 'Unless there's another one,' says Ellis.

Rick nods. 'I'll head to the robbery RV.'

'Make you that coffee next time,' says Ellis. 'Thanks for coming.'

All the details, every time. The plastic box with the blue lid, the bursts of sirens, like a radio being tuned, the female dispatcher in the *hijab*.

Did they hate him? Did Ellis hate him? The DV victims' family hated him – they'd written to tell him. They'd told the papers, front page of the *Manchester Evening News. DCI Castle gets it wrong: mother and triplets murdered.* The paper was right and the family were right: he'd made the wrong decision.

25

Calix couldn't sleep. Moonlight lit his tent, and frost sparkled on the inside of the roof. He touched it, brushing off a sheaf of shavings. They sprinkled down like glitter, and melted on his sleeping bag. It was cold inside the tent, but colder outside and he hoped it wouldn't snow. The white stuff would scupper things.

Outside the tent flaps Uttam was singing softly. Sometimes his guard muttered to himself, sometimes he sang, but mostly the Sherpa was silent. He took his job seriously and would earn enough money in the ten days to keep his young family for six months. He would be cold, though, sitting there all night, despite two duvet jackets, a hot water bottle between his legs, and a flask of tea.

Calix stared at the ceiling. It was ironic – he needed a sleeping pill.

His feet were freezing. Not literally, ha ha. But they were very cold, almost numb. Really, it was a good sign. A cold night meant a cold dawn and the reduced likelihood of snow.

He maneouvred the scissors he'd taken from the dibble's first aid kit: up from the foot of his sleeping bag, to his handcuffed hands, and out into the open. They were a serrated pair, and strong enough to cut cloth, maybe even flesh. He turned them backwards and practised cutting the plastic cuffs. It was fiddly and he kept dropping them, but when the time came, it would be possible.

He pushed the scissors back down his bag, and prised open the box of flapjack from TBR. With his hands shackled, everything was awkward and time-consuming. He took out the piece with nuts and raisins and snapped it in half to expose the foil wrap. He unfolded it, removed the blisters of pills and slotted them into his shirt pocket. He fitted the flapjack pieces back in the box and pushed it into the top of his rucksack.

Nestled back inside his warm sleeping bag. He was ready.

So what if he'd told Castle about Lummle. The dibble weren't going to do anything about it, and it took international agencies months, if not years, to implement action on the ground. Calix only needed a few days.

Soft Nepali voices and the smell of woodsmoke drifted into the tent. Which meant it was five thirty. The cook and the cook boy would be starting to heat hot water for early morning tea. Father and eldest son who, when they weren't on a trek, lived in a one-room shack in Kathmandu. Along with the *didi* and four other children.

Kit check – again. *Fail to prepare, prepare to fail*, was one of his old man's phrases. If he wrote them all down, he could write a book.

Top pocket of his rucksack: flapjack, sunhat, sunglasses, sun cream. He put everything back, unzipped a side pocket. Dye paraphernalia.

He stopped, stilled.

Another zip. A tent zip all the way up.

Movement. Someone was climbing out of their tent. It sounded close, but not next door. The next but one: Castle's tent.

Calix checked about him. It should be okay if the dibble

leader looked in. But he was a detective, and not a stupid one. The discarded foil lay at the head of the tent. He balled it and stashed it in a tent pocket. Nothing else. He held his breath and waited.

Castle tied up his boots. He didn't do what everyone else did, slip their boots on and shuffle out for a piss. The tent was zipped back down. Definitely Castle.

'*Namaste!*'

'*Namaste, sahib,*' replied Uttam.

More soft voices. The cook brought them tea.

Calix sat up and slowly, slowly, drew down the tent zip four inches. Did the same for the fly sheet. Now he could see.

Uttam was standing with Castle, both drinking the early morning tea. They wore balaclavas and held their mugs with both hands. Their breath marked the air. Behind them was a line of stiff prayer-flags, frozen overnight.

The next-door tent zip pulled. And his new guard Lok appeared, heavy with sleep. Changeover time. Uttam handed Lok his mug and the brothers shared a quiet joke. It was impossible to dislike them.

'Coniston?' said Castle.

'*Ramro.*' Uttam raised a thumb.

The dibble leader drained his tea, and pointed north, towards the bridge and the mountains. The Sherpas nodded, and Castle strode away from the camp.

Across the valley there was the crash of stonefall.

Castle leaving camp was unexpected, possibly a stroke of luck. If he stayed away for the morning, it would make Calix's job easier, but if the dibble leader returned unexpectedly, it would sink *HMS Mission* before it set sail.

Uttam took off his boots, and disappeared into the next tent. Lok pulled up the plastic chair and sat outside Coniston's door.

Sunlight hit the prayer-flags.

Weatherbeater appeared. He threw down a sack of clanking climbing equipment outside the dining tent, and washed in the bowl of hot water left by the cook boy. Then walked back along the row of tents to rouse Hunter. The evening before, the two junior dibble had boasted about their plan to climb the frozen waterfall in the nearby hanging valley: safer to climb first thing when the ice was still frozen. Which made sense, but meant Hunter had to crawl out of his warm sleeping bag.

The mountaineer returned to the dining table. The cook brought over a plate of steaming *momos* and a box of jams and spreads. Ten minutes later, Hunter shuffled up, and demanded coffee.

The cook boy brought over a flask. He was about the same age as Ram, and the two boys had become friendly. Calix hoped Ram was enjoying the binoculars and would forget everything else. He regretted seizing his arm, but he'd had no choice.

'Real climbers do it at midnight,' said Weatherbeater, scoffing his third *momo*.

Hunter ate nothing and only sipped at the coffee.

Finally, after checking on Lok and the cook, the pair of dibble left for the icefall. It was 7.30, but seemed later. The prayer-flags were starting to drip.

Calix climbed out of his tent, still dressed because of the cuffs from the day before. He said, '*Namaste,*' to Lok.

Breakfast. Lok sat with him, as usual. The cook and cook boy busied. First, popcorn, then porridge with raisins, and finally, a huge plate of *momos*. There were three types of jam, honey, and peanut butter. Calix ate three and when Lok wasn't looking, stashed five honey-spread *momos* in his jacket.

The prayer-flags were fluttering.

Lok was warier now.

Calix took out a pack of cards and showed them to his guard. Big smile; Lok couldn't stop himself. The Sherpa would have smiled if Calix had suggested peeling potatoes. They played a few rounds of Crazy Eights. From the hanging valley, there was the occasional shout and clatter of falling ice.

Calix suggested a different game, hoping Lok wouldn't get suspicious at the over-friendliness. But his guard grinned like he was in on it. They began contract whist, Calix keeping the scores.

Lok won the first few rounds – of course he did – and seemed to relax.

Calix did anything but. He poured them both more tea, trying to remain nonchalant. Four cards each, three cards each, two cards. Lok winning by miles. Calix dealt one card each, set the pack of unused cards near the table's edge.

Then—

He jogged the table, knocking the cards onto the floor, and hoped it was obvious he couldn't easily pick them up.

Lok bent to retrieve them, and while he was under the table, Calix popped pills from the blister and added them to the Sherpa's mug. He heaped in sugar and stirred. Lok raised his head and returned the cards to the table.

Calix handed him the mug, and drank deeply from his own. Thirsty work, cards.

Lok took a sip and set it down.

More cards, then.

They played on. One card each, two cards each, three cards. Lok still winning. Calix clinked tea mugs, made a performance of draining his mug. Lok sipped like a lady. Calix wondered if it had a strange taste. At least there was no sign of Castle, but time was passing. The dibble leader had to return soon. Likewise Hunter and Weatherbeater. It was their last day at MK and the porters would be about to arrive. Maybe it wasn't meant to be.

His old man would have had no truck with that mindset.

Stay positive.

Final round, seven cards each. Lok held up three fingers, and Calix wrote down three tricks. And five for himself.

The cook came over, wanting his flask and the mugs back. Calix waited, hoped. If Lok didn't drink it, maybe he could knock the Sherpa out with an ice axe.

The Sherpa drained his tea and handed the mug back to the cook. Three cheers, Calix wanted to shout.

The cook returned to his packing. The multi-coloured prayer-flags fluttered, prayers billowing across the camp. Calix's entreaties too.

Lok yawned and slumped down on a chair. He yawned again, rested his head on the table. Calix continued talking and laughing for the two of them. He propped Lok up and manoeuvred the chair so the Sherpa faced away from the cook.

Calix glanced around. The cook was packing up his tent, and his son dismantling the fire. There was no sign of Castle or his team. Shouts still echoed from the hanging valley.

He snuck over to his tent, slipped inside and zipped it behind him. He pulled out the scissors, knelt into position, fiddled his fingers and thumb into the loops. He dropped the scissors. Tried again. Dropped them again. Too hasty. Slower. He set the scissors up once more, pointing them toward his chest, poised to cut the plastic shackle. He opened them, closed them. Tweaked the angle of the blades so the plastic was in the cutting sweet spot.

He clamped down again.

And he was free.

He used the scissors to slit open the back of the tent, and pushed his rucksack under the fly sheet. He crawled out, pulled the fly back down.

Shouldering his sack he ran along behind the tents. The Sherpas', Castle's, Weatherbeater's, and finally Hunter's, a pair of crusty socks tied to a guy-rope.

Ducking down, he veered diagonally into a shallow gully, and along it to the foot of the moraine which bordered the old village of MK. He skidded down behind a cluster of rocks, and checked back.

The cook and cook boy were packing the cooking equipment into a line of wicker baskets left by the porters. They were oblivious. And there was no sign of the dibble or the Sherpas.

He crawled up the two-metre high moraine, at any moment expecting a shout. Discovery. The end. But a shout didn't come, and he crested the top, and slid down the other side. At the bottom he turned towards the main trail, and picked his way across the rock-strewn ground. All the time scanning the crest of the moraine for movement.

He reached the main path. He'd done it. Cold all night, he was now on fire. He glanced back one final time, then turned, and after a hop, skip, and jump, ran helter-skelter. Like a pacesetter, the yellow globe was already streaking ahead.

26

Rick felt his arm being jostled. He opened his eyes.

Uttam stood in front of him. '*Chito, sahib.*' Sweat dripped down the Sherpa's face, and he was out of breath.

Rick sat up and brushed away a few ants. His trousers were damp from the ground, and his neck felt stiff.

'*Mosom Kharka, chito.*' The Sherpa jogged on the spot.

Rick hauled himself up. The Sherpa was already walking away and he looked over his shoulder to see if Rick was following. Rick stuffed his jacket into his bag, glancing one last time at the prayer-wheels.

Uttam walked faster, started jogging.

Rick ran after him.

At Mosom Kharka, the tents were still erect. The prayer-flags fluttered in the breeze. The cook was washing pots and the porters sat in a whispery huddle.

Uttam headed straight to the dining tent. The flaps had been tied open and Lok squatted outside. He was smoking and bouncing up and down on his calves. Next to him were helmets, ice axes, and a coil of rope. Uttam squatted down with Lok. He took his brother's cigarette and used it to point inside the tent.

Rick pushed through the tent flaps. The interior was gloomy.

The table had been cleared and a map spread out. Russell and Hunter were hunched over it.

'What's going on?'

The two men turned around. Russell looked serious. The mountaineer sat down – he was too tall to stand inside the tent. Hunter chicken-winged his arm, worked his hand under the collar of his jacket and scratched the top of his back. 'Coniston's done one.'

Rick waited for the grins, the feinted punch to the ribs. He looked from one man to the other, but their faces remained steadfast. Stubbly, sunburnt. In the case of Hunter, blotchy with patches of dried blood on one cheek.

His stomach dropped.

He'd railroaded Coniston to Nepal, and squeezed him and the boy for information to take down Khetan.

Losing their prisoner would not only wipe away that success. It would call into question his professionalism.

'Are you sure? He's probably messing around.'

'Listen, boss,' said his sergeant, 'I was conducting missing enquiries when you were drinking milk through a straw. Sure I'm sure.' He wore a climbing harness which revealed the middle-aged curve of his stomach. His hair was crimped from wearing a helmet, his cheek cut and bruised.

Underrated, Coniston's father had called him when Rick first met the brigadier. They'd discussed his missing son in a room full of military regalia and medals.

He stepped toward the map, shunting the under-table heater out of the way. It turned over, clattering to silence. He bent to right it. 'For God's sake, one of you, open the back of the tent. It stinks in here.'

Russell unzipped each side. He tied up the flaps, his climbing metalwork clinking as he moved. From his climbing harness dangled half a dozen ice screws.

'Where was Lok?'

'Asleep in a chair,' said Russell. 'He's still groggy, and doesn't know what happened.'

'Coniston must have drugged him. You didn't give him the pills back, Gary?'

'Course not.'

'And Uttam was also asleep?'

Russell nodded. 'He'd done the night shift. The cook and the cook boy were packing up, and the porters hadn't arrived.'

'What about you two?'

The two men looked at each other like schoolboys.

'Russell was teaching me to ice-climb on that frozen waterfall. No one's to blame.'

'And your cheek?'

'A lump of ice.'

'Maybe,' said Russell, his ice-screws clanking, 'he's hiked up to Saklis to apologise to Ram.'

'Unlikely. He could have done it today, walking back to Lukla. *He's* not stupid.' Rick took a deep breath. Time was speeding by. Recriminations could come later, when the wheel was back on. More important were the decisions he made now.

Deathcop DCI Castle gets it wrong: mother and triplets murdered.

He was going to get this one right.

'I think Coniston knows exactly what he's doing and where he's going. Kathmandu, then Lummle, close to the Tibetan border. He's going to deal with Khetan himself. At least, he thinks he is.'

Russell nodded.

'Gary, you search Coniston's tent. See what he's taken, and what he hasn't. Double-check he's taken his walking boots. Russell, send Uttam and two of the porters five hundred metres from here, one on each of the main paths, Mera, Saklis and Jiri. Tell them to ask everyone they see, and to wait there. Handcuffs will slow Coniston down, but he won't be wearing them for long.'

Rick walked out of the tent, but ducked his head back in. 'And both of you, take all that crap off.'

Rick went to his tent, rummaged amongst the kit bags and hauled out the metal briefcase. Walking back, he worked out the timings. He'd left MK at six am, Russell and Hunter an hour later. They'd returned at ten to find Lok asleep and Coniston missing. The cook told them he'd seen Coniston at about nine. It was now eleven, which meant Coniston had a head start of one to two hours. Assuming the worst, the briefcase was unlikely to give a result.

Outside the dining tent, the heap of mountaineering gear had grown. Harnesses and ice screws lay on top. Lok was alone, still leaning back against the side of the tent. Rick caught his eye, but the Sherpa looked away.

Inside, Russell was checking through the first aid kit.

'The scissors are missing.'

Rick scowled. Coniston would have cut off the plasticuffs, and so could move as fast as them, possibly faster.

Russell cleared away the red bag, and Rick pushed the briefcase onto the table. He clicked open the latches and pushed up the lid. The case was lined with grey foam with shaped blocks cut out. One piece was missing. The second piece looked like an old-fashioned car radio. Rick lifted it out onto the table. He closed the case and set it down on the ground.

Hunter entered, holding up bits of plastic. 'Coniston's free.'

'He'd planned it,' said Rick, pulling out an aerial. He turned a knob. The red power light came on, but the screen stayed blank and the device remained silent.

'What is it?' said Russell.

'It's a tracking device,' said Hunter. 'I'm guessing the boss has lumped up Coniston's boots.'

Rick nodded.

'Why didn't you tell us? We might have got him.'

'I didn't want you to relax your guard.' He switched the tracking device off, counted to five, and switched it back on again. The red light returned, but nothing else. He turned the volume all the way. Still nothing. He knew it had been unlikely – Coniston had too much of a head start.

'Anything in his tent, Gary?'

'Sleeping bag's still there, but most of his kit's gone. Clothes, duvet jacket, walking boots. He left his gaiters and crampons.'

Hunter picked up the tracking device. 'Shall I?'

Rick nodded, and Hunter walked out of the tent, holding it in front of him like a water diviner.

'What's the range on that thing?'

'About two hundred and fifty metres. It starts beeping and yellow dashes appear on the screen. The closer you get the louder the beeps and the closer the dashes.' Rick bent over the map. They had to give chase, but in which direction?

There were four options. West would take Coniston back to Saklis, then to Lukla and its airport. There was a lot of ascent, and it usually took three days. Easier was to head south, to Jiri and the roadhead. It was mainly downhill, but took trekkers ten days. North led to Mera Base Camp, then Mount Mera. East to Khetan's hideout the previous year.

'Thoughts, Russell?'

'North, no. There's a five-thousand-metre pass which leads to the next valley, but it requires ice axes and crampons which Coniston's not taken. East, no. A cul-de-sac unless you're Messner or Bonnington. So he must be heading to Jiri or Lukla.'

Rick nodded. He checked his watch again. Eleven forty-five. Jiri or Lukla? Coniston was unlikely to head uphill, then again he might want them to think like that. Lukla was a quarter of the distance to Jiri. Lok was now sleeping like a custody-suite drunk, so there were four of them. Uttam and Russell were fit. Hunter wasn't, and Rick was somewhere in between. Uttam and Russell spoke Nepali. There was only one tracker.

Hunter arrived back. He shook his head. 'I walked the perimeter – not a tinkle.'

'What would you do, Gary?' said Rick. He didn't want a consensus, but he did want ideas.

'I think Russell should head for Saklis, and you should head for Jiri with the tracker. Coniston's not going to start uphill and he'd also have the uncertainty of getting on a plane. I'll stay here at MK and coordinate things.'

'Russell?'

'I agree, more or less. I'll go to Saklis, and all the way to Lukla if I have to. You take Uttam and head for Jiri.'

The fireball sun was directly overhead as Rick's team left Mosom Kharka. In front of them reared line after line of hills, like waves on a beach. Red-tinged clouds gathered in the south. Rain looked unlikely but would help, rain always helped. In Manchester, rain was a more effective deterrent than prison.

He led, half-walking, half-jogging, and Hunter and a porter followed. Rick hoped they'd all be back at MK with Coniston before dark, but they might not be, and extra clothes, food and emergency kit would be useful. Hunter had moaned about coming, and was still moaning, but falsely, Rick thought. All police liked to be in the action.

To his right, Russell and Uttam laboured up the hill towards Saklis. They'd reached the first of the zig-zags. They carried small packs, and Russell held the tracking device. In Rick's opinion, Jiri was by far the most likely direction, but Russell and Uttam were his insurance. He'd figured the two of them would move at twice the speed of Coniston, and be able to confirm after an hour or two whether he'd gone that way. If they didn't find him, they'd backtrack to MK, and follow Rick.

Rick's team passed a cairn marking the way. He picked up a stone and tossed it on top, hoping it would be a good omen. He'd have built a *gompa* if he thought it would bring Coniston back. He glanced over his shoulder.

Mosom Kharka was already out of sight. Jagged mountains sat along the horizon, silent, ancient, and judging.

27

Bands of silvery cloud stretched across the lagoon-blue sky.

Imploring the weather to hold, Calix crossed a side stream on stepping stones. The flats of the stones were clear of algae, worn smooth by the thousands of people who'd used them b2re, and his footing was sure. But he still had to be careful: a twist or a sprain would scupper everything. As would slipping off the path, and careering down the mountainside.

Hundreds of metres below, curls of the main river glinted.

On the far side of the stream the path curved up to a long rise with steep rocks at the top. His watch showed midday. Already.

He started running.

His rucksack knocked up and down on his back and his boots felt heavy. He stopped to cinch his pack tighter, then ran on. Ten minutes of running, ten minutes of fast walking. He would jog-walk for as long as he could.

His aim was not to stop until he reached Jiri, but it left him with a dilemma. Too slow and the Sherpas would catch him. Too fast and he'd have to rest up, and they'd overtake. An option was to hide somewhere for a week. But that brought a different set of problems – shelter, food, language – and it seemed easier to get to Jiri and disappear in Kathmandu. Commence the mission proper.

The intervals of walking lengthened. And all uphill.

After two hours he reached the rocks and a porter's bench. One of the rocks protruded like a gangplank. Cigarette butts littered the floor and behind it a line of bedraggled prayer-flags hung from posts. He was soaked in sweat, breathing hard. The straps of the pack were rubbing, and his feet were sore. But he was determined not to stop, determined not to slow down.

He glanced back.

No sign of them. No shouts of alarm, no cries of *stop*.

Skirting the rocks, he plunged down the other side of the ridge. Could hear his old man and Megan urging him on. Knew he'd hardly started.

Slowing to a walk, Calix checked back over his shoulder, then down the path in front of him. All clear. He turned off the path and climbed some easy rocks to a wide ledge. He traversed around and checked he was out of sight of the trail. Every minute was vital, but there was one thing he had to do. He'd been lucky so far, only meeting one trekking party – a large group of Japanese, and all yammering away so he'd been able to dart off the path and hide. But he was bound to meet others. A single trekker was unusual. A single trekker stuck out like dibble in a night club.

He shucked off his rucksack and knelt down. Shoved the sharp stones aside. From the pack he found the plastic bottle. He took out his shaving mirror, and balanced it on a stone. At the bottom of the bottle sat the black residue. He tipped a little into his hand and massaged it into his hair. It smelt like an espresso. He could have done with one. He poured more of the black gunk on his fingers and rubbed it back and forth across his hair. Streaks ran down his forehead. He wiped them away with a sleeve and looked in the mirror.

Brown-black was the new blond. It was one of Darren's principles of disguise: *distract means giving the dibble a reason why it's not you.* Dyeing his hair was better than wearing a hat. Castle would be asking people if they'd seen a white male trekker with blond hair. A trekker with a hat could be him, but a trekker with black hair couldn't be.

He wiped his hands on his trousers, packed everything away, gobbled half the broken flapjack. Time was moving on. His hair was still wet but he'd have to risk someone noticing. It would soon dry. Before shouldering the rucksack, he covered it in a yellow waterproof cover. He then worked his way back down to the trail. The rocks were dry and his fingers gripped the ledges and protrusions with confidence. He swallowed the last of the broken flapjack and jumped the final few feet back onto the trail.

Checked his watch: the pit-stop had taken thirteen minutes.

And jogged on.

The path contoured across a vast scrubby hillside. Streams crossed the path, and over the centuries had cut deep into the hill. The path worked its way around each stream, staying level and curving back into the hillside before crossing the stream and curving forward again. Calix couldn't see into the next cutback or into the previous one.

Ram thought it took most trekkers heading away from the mountains a week to reach Jiri. Calix hoped to do it in two days, but to do that he'd have to walk through the night.

He turned a corner.

Three men. His stomach heaved. Local men, with wicker baskets. The baskets were loaded, crates and boxes protruding from the top. Porters! Smoking and uninterested in him. Not an ambush. And they weren't waiting for him. The men were resting, sitting back on their t-shaped rounded sticks.

Calix slowed to a walk. '*Namaste.*'

'*Namaste,*' said the first man.

He walked past them. They sat absolutely still, like Sri Lankan stilt fishermen or the silver-painted buskers in Piccadilly Gardens. The three porters were part of the landscape. They were the landscape.

The porters laughed softly. The colour of his hair?

He hurried on.

At the next corner, he glanced back. The dibble weren't following. But the hoary runnels running across the sky were wider, longer.

He broke into a run. Mosom Kharka to Jiri was a long way, like walking from Manchester to Liverpool, and who'd want to do that? He had considered heading to Lukla, instead of Jiri. The airport was maybe only two days' walk, one day if he walked all night. In addition, Castle had probably assumed he would head downhill to Jiri. But, tempting as the much shorter distance was, he had no ID, and bribes at the airport would be risky.

Felt blisters forming.

Kept running.

He came to an abrupt halt. In front of him, the trail ended. A landslip had removed the vegetation together with the path, leaving a steep brown scar the size of a football pitch. Small birds hopped across looking for worms. He looked closer. There was a faint narrow path. He wondered how the porters – and the Japanese – had managed to cross.

The scar dropped over an edge, and disappeared. Glistening tree canopies and rocks, and far below, the boom of the river. He would fall, bounce, smash to pieces. Remembering another hostage, Vicky Brant, who'd slipped and died the previous year, he checked his pack straps, his laces.

Leaning into the bank, he set off. His right hand grabbed at the freshly exposed rocks. They were loose, offered no security.

He kept going, reached an island of untouched ground in the middle of the scar. Glanced behind, glad he didn't have to return that way. In front of him, it looked even steeper, the way even more indistinct. A thin rope trailed the ground, muddy from the fresh earth. It was attached to a metal stake. The stake on the island wobbled. He pulled the rope tight. It held but didn't inspire confidence.

He started off, placing his feet and sliding his right hand across the rope. He wiped his greasy hands, kept going.

He fell.

Clutching at the rope, and folding his body into the ground.

He kept falling, the rope stretching, his stomach dropping. The rope tightened. He slammed into the earthy slope. Birds flew up in alarm and dirt skittered down. He swung from side to side, praying the rope and stakes would hold.

He stopped swinging. The three metres he'd fallen had felt like thirty metres. He spat out soil, wiped his face. The cold earth smelt sweet.

Below him, fresh air. Small trees, tiny rocks. The crash and bang of the river.

Time was passing. He stood on a protruding rock, un-weighted the rope, and inspected the burns on his palms.

Time was passing. He found a solid tree root, and hauled upwards. Moved his feet to a wedged branch. Stones fell away taking a slew of dirt. The landslip unstable as a sand dune. He found more holds, and climbed back up onto the vague path across the scar.

Returning the way he'd come would be quicker and safer. But he kept going forwards, shuffling like an old person, using the rope as backup rather than an aid.

He made the far side. He wiped his muddy hands on his trousers, drank some water and looked back. There was no one behind him, at least no one he could see. But Castle would be following: the senior dibble would never give up.

Calix jogged unsteadily onwards. Turned a corner, mounted a short incline, and looked ahead.

Swathes of pink-headed rhododendron, the national flower of Nepal, carpeted the slopes below. Rhododendron meant he'd made some progress.

28

Woodsmoke in the air.

A single homestead stood in a clearing at the front of the hillside. Beside a sputtering hose a woman laid a pair of trousers out on stone slabs, and scrubbed with a block of soap. Behind her, clothes hung on a line. A toddler ran about, naked except for a grubby t-shirt. A dog dozed in the open doorway. Leant against a stack of wood was a chalkboard with a menu for hot drinks and noodle soups. Egg, two eggs, garlic, onion. A young girl emerged from the doorway, carrying a stool. She set it down near the woman, and sat. Resting her chin on a hand, she watched the woman washing the trousers.

As Rick walked past, he couldn't help staring. The girl's face was serious. She was watching her future.

'*Namaste*,' said the woman. A gold ring hung from her nose, and her ears jangled with hooped earrings which glinted in the sunlight. Beads of perspiration dripped down her face.

He loitered on the far side of the clearing, and drank some water while he waited for Hunter. They'd neither seen Coniston, nor spoken to anyone who had. He'd like to have speeded up, but Hunter was slow. They'd walked for two hours, and a large group of Japanese trekkers were the only tourists they'd encountered. Though the Japanese were friendly, they said they hadn't seen anyone. There were plenty of local people on the trail, but his Nepali stretched only to ordering a beer. In hindsight, maybe he should have brought Uttam and left Hunter behind.

After five minutes, there was still no sign of Hunter, and Rick wandered on further. He could hear a river, and after rounding a corner, he found it. Two trekkers rested on the far side, sitting on their rucksacks. Above them the trail curved up to a long rise with sheer rocks at the top.

Rick crossed the river on the stepping stones, smoothed to a fine sheen by the traffic. The water was clear, and he could see smaller stones on the river bed. The man and the woman were eating from a bag of trail mix. On the man's t-shirt was a Bolton Wanderers FC badge.

'I've come all this way,' said Rick, slipping into witness patter, 'only to meet someone else from Manchester.'

'No,' said the man. 'We're from Bolton.'

The woman laughed and offered Rick the trail mix. Her hiking clothes were new, and her face was made up. She wore pink lipstick. 'Natalie. And Tim.'

The man chin-jerked. Tattoos covered his arms like sleeves. Hands like mallets.

'Rick,' he said, refusing the peanuts and raisins. 'You heading for Mera?'

'Yup,' said Tim. 'You done it?'

Rick shook his head. 'Actually, we've had a bit of an argument.' He looked back across the river, and saw Hunter and their porter approaching. 'My friend Gary had a row with his son who's walked off – down this way. Wondered if you'd seen him? White, tall, blond hair.'

'We did pass someone,' said Natalie. 'Quite a while back. Two hours, maybe.'

'I've got a picture,' said Rick. He pulled out the sat phone, flicked through for the mugshot of Coniston, and held it up.

'The guy we saw had dark hair,' said Natalie.

'Are you sure?'

'Pretty sure.' She stepped back.

Rick grabbed her arm. 'Have another look.'

'Easy,' said Tim. He moved alongside his girlfriend.

'It's important,' said Rick.

Natalie nodded. 'It's alright, Tim.' She looked again at the photo of Coniston and shook her head. 'Not him. I'm certain.'

Rick released her arm.

'You?'

'Nope.' He stood with his big hands on his hips. 'You shouldn't go grabbing people.'

'What's occurring?' said Hunter, walking up. He threw down his daypack and sat heavily. His face was wet with sweat and red as a tomato. His trousers were ripped on one knee. He took off his sunhat and wiped his face. 'Bolton! Would you Adam and Eve it.'

Scowling, Tim shouldered his pack, and after a final chin-jerk at Rick, followed Natalie across the stepping stones.

'What was all that about?'

'Nothing.'

Rick watched the two backpackers walk off up the trail. 'They said they passed someone, but he had dark hair.'

'You think they're mistaken?'

'Witnesses get things wrong more often than not. The trekker they saw was white, the same age, the same build. And he was alone. Seems very likely.' Rick bent to tighten his boots, then stood up.

'Come on, let's catch him and find out.' He walked off.

'I need a bit more recovery time.'

Rick backed up. 'We have to keep going. And faster.' He

hauled Hunter to his feet, picked up his daysack and thrust it to his chest.

'I should have stayed at MK.'

The porter hefted his basket, and throwing stones from one hand to the other, walked ahead.

'Come on!' Rick pushed Hunter forward, running his feet. Hunter leant backwards. 'Come on,' growled Rick, 'come on!'

Two Hindu priests in brilliant orange robes arrived at the river crossing.

Hunter stood upright.

Rick fell silent.

The men's faces were painted orange with a red stripe down the nose. Both had long beards, one white, one coloured orange. One priest wore sandals, but his colleague went barefoot. They had orange symbols on their bare arms. They both raised a hand in greeting, nodded their heads in quiet respect.

Rick put his hands together, nodded back.

Hunter stood, and slowly put his hands together. The first time Rick had seen it.

The two priests crossed the river and glided forward, their robes masking their leg movements. They looked like they could walk for ever.

In silence, Rick and Hunter picked up their bags and sloped off, their porter following. Externally, Rick was calmer, but internally he was roiling.

29

Calix clattered down the switchbacks. They were steep and loose, and he slipped and slid. The incline eased and the path followed a stream. The hill was long, and he couldn't see the valley floor because of the rhododendron. He kept jogging. His hips were sore, but it was easier to jog downhill than up. Going up, he'd started to walk.

The air was noisy with bird chatter. And busy with insects which occasionally landed on his clothes. He brushed them away rather than swatting. *When in the land of Buddha.* Trailside shrines every couple of kilometres, and already he'd run out of coins.

He reached small fields of crops where a drainage channel had collapsed and the path had disappeared. Footsteps led off in every direction. He searched for several minutes, panic quickly rising, but found it again. He passed the rubble of a row of abandoned shacks – earthquake damage from earlier in the year.

At the foot of the hill he came to a small village. Outside the first house, stapled to a post, was another of the *Wanted* posters. There was no mention of a reward, but at least it hadn't been graffitied with *nayaka*. Khetan wasn't a hero: his old man was the hero. He let it be, and walked over to the water tap where an old man was smoking a homemade pipe.

The man muttered. Where was he going or coming from? The weather? The state of the trail? The price of beer and bread? The things his grandad Joe had talked about. Calix filled his water bottle, nodded at the old man and hurried on. He crossed a bridge made from tree trunks lashed together, and on the far side looked back up the hillside. He couldn't see anyone on the sections of path that were visible. No dibble, no Sherpas, no locals. No one.

He ran on.

The path snaked between more houses. A scabby dog followed him out of the village. He came to another small shrine next to a tree. It was made of brick with a gable roof and inside was a statue of the Hindu elephant god. The god had four arms, a rotund belly, and a trunk curling down and to the left, like a saxophone. It was reaching for a sweet in one of the hands. Around the god's neck was a necklace of marigolds and on his forehead was a red spot. A brass bell hung from the ceiling and three brass dishes lay in front of him. Coins and sweets and open wraps of paper with brightly-coloured powders had been left.

On the ground was a small light-blue egg, the size of a coin. Calix picked it up. It was cold, but he looked around just in case. There was no sign of a nest or an anxious parent. He placed it on a brass dish.

But the egg didn't seem enough. He looked along the path, then back at the village.

No one.

He knelt down, shucked off his pack, and pulled out the box of flapjack. He counted them: fifteen plain, five with nuts. Selecting a piece with nuts, he snapped it to reveal the foil wrap. Unfolding the foil, he was relieved to find the banknotes were unharmed.

A hundred dollars in twenties. He laid one across a brass dish, and slipped the others into his wallet between the letter from his mother and the photo of Megan. Unable to resist, he pulled out the photo.

His sister was sitting at her desk, looking serious. Pensive. He'd been sitting on the end of her bed, and they'd been talking about the future, about where they saw themselves in ten years' time. Next year. Megan would have been twenty-six, Calix twenty-five. She'd said she might be married. When he said he didn't think so, she'd thrown a book at him. He thought she might be a foreign news correspondent, and appearing on TV each evening. For him, his future, they'd both been stuck.

He kissed the photo, and making sure it wasn't creased, slotted it back into his wallet. He shouldered his pack, and ran on. He'd lost some time.

The trail curved around and headed up again, steeply. His calves were stiff from the long downhill, and he was breathing hard.

They'd both been right about him.

It was nearly four. He'd been going for six hours, but it felt longer. Six hours was a slow time for a marathon and he felt like the people who fell over the line about then. But he'd hardly started and knew he would have to walk through the night. If he didn't make it to Jiri all the planning and physical effort would be for nothing. At Jiri he'd catch a taxi to Kathmandu, find a dingy hotel and check in under a false name. He'd rest up for a couple of days and then head out again. To find Khetan near the Nepalese border with Tibet. Lummle. Thank you, Ram.

'*Aaeee.*' A shout from the opposite hillside.

Calix dived to the ground, and crawled off the trail into the scrubby undergrowth. He wished he hadn't. If it was the dibble, he'd confirmed it was him. If it wasn't, he looked like a madman.

He peered through the fronds and grasses of the scrub. Heart pounding like a village *madal*. He looked back across the river, across the roofs and smoking chimneys of the village, to the opposite hillside.

'*Aaeee*.' The shout came again.

He ducked his head and squirmed lower in the scrub. His nerves jangling as if an entire Nepalese folk band had been locked in his cell.

He counted to twenty, and slowly raised his head so he could see. Just.

A farmer was ploughing a field. The man was driving a pair of oxen and struck out with a whip.

Calix hunkered down. He counted to fifty, and wishing he had a periscope, raised his head once more. The farmer was still ploughing – the only person moving within shouting distance.

'*Aaeee*.' The farmer, urging his oxen.

Calix stood up, brushed himself down and adjusted his pack. He scanned the opposite hillside again, but there was no one apart from the farmer. At least, no one he could see.

He ran on.

Next time, he wouldn't react – just keep going. He felt sick. He was being hunted. He was the quarry. The fox.

He'd never stuffed and mounted one, although he'd thought about it. Birds, cats, squirrels, two dogs and a badger. Never a fox. He'd studied them, in preparation. He always did. Online, in books, and on the ground. Once, he'd even spent a day with a group of sabs – a splinter group of the Derbyshire Sabs with a base in Bolsover. He'd watched them lay false trails, break windscreen wipers, and argue with scarlet-clad horse riders. Afterwards, he'd hung around in their pub.

Sabs talked about foxes as other people talked about their

children. Fox-cubs started on solids at four weeks, found food independently at four months and left the lair at six. When a pack of hounds caught a fox, they ripped it apart. Foxhunters claimed it was quick. It was: death in seconds. But sabs were less concerned with the moment of death than the hunt that preceded it.

Being chased. Hunted down.

He felt like a fox. The possibility at any moment of being spotted. The frequent looking back to see if the hunters were in sight. Ears straining for the sounds of a pursuit.

Foxes didn't always get caught, even without the help of the sabs. Fleeing foxes waded through streams to put hounds off the scent. They went to ground. They ran into another fox's territory. It was a survival of the fittest.

He needed to be as wily as a fox. He'd dyed his hair and changed the colour of his rucksack. But he needed to do something else. He was still a single white male trekker heading towards Jiri. He needed a better disguise or to disappear altogether. Become invisible. Changing the body's refractive index to resemble air was impossible, but remembering it gave him an idea.

Halfway up the hillside, Calix came to another isolated tea house. There was no glass in the windows and heavy wooden shutters had been propped open with fence posts. An old woman wearing a bobble-hat sat on the doorstep, stroking a cat. The woman looked a hundred, but she was probably only fifty. Calix winked at her, and she cackled.

At the side of the tea house were some benches and a table. Two trekkers sat huddled over steaming bowls. Their rucksacks sat alongside them. One man was bald, the second wore small round glasses. Behind them, a juniper tree grew up the wall of the house. Blue berries clung to dark green, drooping foliage.

The squat trunk was twisted and looked as old as time.

Calix had found what he was looking for. Buddha. The Hindu gods. They'd accepted his offerings.

30

'You must be joking,' said Hunter, halting like a horse refusing a jump. He flopped down beside a rock and took out his cigarettes.

Rick examined the landslide with binoculars. Sticks shoved into the ground marked a vague way across. At halfway there was a safe haven of untouched hillside and then a steeper section protected by a rope. Below the landslide, the ground fell over a hidden edge to the valley floor, a long way below. A slip would be fatal.

Hunter was patting his pockets. 'I've lost my lighter.'

'Have one of these,' said Rick, opening a packet of the local biscuits.

Hunter shook his head.

Rick ate a biscuit. A small bird landed in front of them and hopped about. Hunter took out a notebook and began to sketch the landslide. It was almost as if he didn't want to catch Coniston.

'I think we should—'

'Wait for Russ,' said Hunter without looking up.

'See if there's an easier way.'

Rick clambered up the side of the scar, but he couldn't see one. The slope reached a band of steep rock. He climbed back down.

He stared across and down at the lush forests of rhododendron. Bright pink flowers like rosettes. Millions of them. They had a beguiling beauty: their tentacles snaked through the scrub, took root, and advanced, to the exclusion of other plants. Nothing stopped them.

Nothing was going to stop him.

If Coniston had been the trekker seen by the couple from Bolton, then he must have crossed the landslide.

He stood up, and inched across the scar. Rocks and dirt fell away. He took another small step, dislodging a rock the size of his pack. He fell to his knees, grabbed an exposed root. It pulled out further, but held. He turned round and, heart thumping, shuffled back.

Coniston might have headed for Lukla. Which meant Russell and Uttam should have overtaken him, and taken him back into custody. Or found him and had a fight, injuries on both sides. Or not found him.

Then again, Jiri seemed the better option, and made more likely by the sighting of a solo trekker.

He climbed onto a boulder, and looked again for a route across. Halfway, there was a section of blue rope. If he could reach that.

After a deep breath, he again inched out onto the scar.

'They're coming,' shouted Hunter.

Rick edged back, both relieved and disappointed. If Coniston had managed to cross, then he could. He bent over with his hands on his knees. 'Do me a favour, Gary, and don't call Weatherbeater Russ. He doesn't like it.'

Hunter gave him a two-fingered mock salute.

Uttam arrived first, a smear of perspiration across his forehead. 'Coniston?' shouted Rick.

The Sherpa shook his head.

Lok appeared, and Russell carrying the tracker. 'No sign of

him.' The mountaineer took off his sunhat, drank some water. The Sherpas squatted down and surveyed the scar.

'We walked all the way to Saklis to be absolutely sure. And we went at it, there's no way he could have kept ahead of us. We criss-crossed the village with the tracker, then hacked back. We asked everyone we saw on the trail both directions. No one had seen him. Either he'd stopped somewhere and hidden, or he didn't go that way. Sorry.'

Rick booted a rock onto the scar. It created a mini avalanche which cascaded down and disappeared over the edge. Dust rose.

'At MK we collected Lok and came after you.'

'So it *was* Coniston who the Bolton couple saw. Pack up, Gary. Russell, you set up a rope to get us across.'

Rick shouldered his rucksack, and checked his watch. Eight hours had passed.

Russell set up a safe system and roped them all across. Half an hour later, they'd crossed the landslide and were on the move again. Uttam led the way followed by Rick, and Russell brought up the rear.

Rick walked alone in a bubble of concentration. Coniston could have slipped on the landslide and be lying somewhere dead or injured. Either that, or somehow he'd crossed the landslide by himself. He was foolish or desperate enough.

Four weary trekkers walked past, Rick stopping the last, a woman with an Australian flag stitched to her rucksack. She had bright blue eyes. He showed the photo of Coniston, the fifth time that day, but her answer was the same.

She called back as she followed her friends up the path. 'You should visit Perth, you won't regret it.'

Rick hurried on, thinking he probably would.

There weren't so many tourists on the trail despite June being a popular month for trekking. No doubt the earthquakes were to blame. After the information from the Bolton couple, the reports of the single trekker had dried up.

They reached the rhododendron forest. The walking was cooler, the path ridged with greasy tree roots. And there was no view, no chance of spotting Coniston.

Russell caught him up.

'Do you think he slipped on the landslide and fell off?'

'No,' said Rick. 'Not Coniston.'

'So he's ahead of us.' Russell put a hand on Rick's shoulder. 'We'll get him, don't worry.'

Rick was worried. The solo trekker might not have been Coniston. It was also possible their prisoner had hidden somewhere between MK and Saklis, and watched Russell and Uttam sail by – twice – then continued at leisure. But he would have needed to hide more than 250 metres from the path – and he didn't know to do so. It seemed unlikely. But that didn't mean it hadn't happened.

The two of them walked in silence for a few minutes, Rick's head whirring with ifs and maybes.

He needed a break. 'Tell me what Jacob's done.'

'Not just him,' said Russell. He paused.

'Go on.'

'They're called The Sparks: Jacob – he plays bass, then drummer Barry and this girl Velvet who sings.'

'Velvet?'

'Yeah, Velvet.'

Rick guessed what was coming.

'Anyway, the band had a barbecue to raise some money at a pub near Buxton. In the field next door there was an orchard and a shed at the end where they stored the apples. The shed had a wonderful rich, sweet aroma, like overdone baked apple. And me and Velvet, well, you get the picture.'

'You're divorced.'

'I can't stop thinking about her, even now. She's nineteen.'

'Jesus.' Rick paused. 'I thought you were seeing Kate?'

'There's that, too.'

Finally, they emerged from the rhododendron, and walked into a small village, past a wooden post with a Khetan *Wanted* poster. They filled their bottles at the water tap. Chickens wandered around and a dog loped up, yawned, and lay down. Russell spoke to a group of children but they hadn't seen anyone. They kept going, leaving the village via a bridge made from tree trunks.

Rick wondered if his intel on Lummle had been disseminated. Corroborated. Actioned. Khetan apprehended, even. And Coniston foiled. It was a comforting thought, but unlikely. He hoped Robbo had at least forwarded the intel.

An hour later, they reached a small *gompa*. It had earth walls and a metal dome. Blue irises, white sclera, red eyebrows. Lines of prayer-flags were strung from the top of the dome to metal posts at the four corners. The sun was setting, and the light caught the dome, streaking it yellow and green. Above the *gompa*, the hills were disappearing in shadow. The sky had turned light blue and the white clouds were edged with pink.

The flow of trekkers had stopped. Most were resting their tired legs and ordering pizza and apple pie at the trailside lodges. No one hiked after dark unless they were lost or they were escaping, or they were looking for those who were lost or were escaping.

'We've got to keep going,' said Rick, 'so we maximise the last of the daylight.'

'I need a break,' said Hunter, slipping off his daysack. He sat on a boulder and leant back against the *gompa*.

'Two minutes,' said Rick. He set the countdown on his watch and observed the seconds ticking down. Trekking in the dark would be slower. On the other hand, the problems would be the same for Coniston, possibly worse. He might use a torch. Sound carried further at night so they might hear him. They also had the tracker.

His watch beeped.

'Right, onward!' He grabbed Hunter's daysack, threw it on top of his own pack, and strode off.

The soft glow of lights appeared through the gloom. Dogs started barking. Rick rounded a bend in the trail and saw that the lights were clustered. Dark roofs of houses stood out below him. A small village, a hundred metres away, not one he'd been expecting. He hoped they weren't lost and he swore silently at Russell. The mountaineer had boasted he knew the trail better than his back garden.

Rick walked closer. There were only four or five houses. Not a village. He checked the map with his head torch. A village wasn't shown. After another few paces he saw the dark shapes of Lok and Uttam and the porter. They sat on a stone bench alongside their packs so for a second he thought there were six people. The men were quiet and looked like statues. He wondered how long they'd been waiting.

Behind him, there was no sign of Hunter, or Russell who was backmarking. He took off his fleece hat, and ran his fingers through his hair. It was sticky and needed a wash. They weren't fast enough. He'd spent the previous hour flogging the speed-distance-time triangle, but however he did it the answer was the same: they weren't going to catch Coniston. He was probably running some of the route, and even if he was only running the downhill sections, it would make him significantly faster. Which meant if Coniston had left an hour ahead of them, he'd now be two to three hours clear. Worst-case scenario, Coniston would be three to four hours away. They also had to assume that he would keep going all night.

He yanked out knots of hair.

If you keep doing the same thing, you will keep getting the same result. A tip from some course he'd been on. The rank and file saw things very differently: they hated change, and thought the Job was in a constant state of flux. In the canteen they complained that after being away for a few days they returned to yet another new computer system or shift pattern or re-drawn police boundaries. Their view was *if it ain't broke, don't fix it.*

He looked again at the map. It laughed at their progress. The next village was Penja, still several hours away. And about thirty kilometres from Mosom Kharka, a quarter of the distance to Jiri. He turned off the torch.

On the bench, the porter lit a cigarette. The match flared, lighting up the man's face. Eyes intent on the cigarette. The flare disappeared and a red spot replaced it. The spot was passed along the bench to the Sherpas.

Just before eight Hunter and Russell arrived. Hunter sat down heavily, and Russell handed around yet more of the local biscuits.

'Tracker?' said Rick.

Russell shook his head.

'Asleep,' said Hunter, 'as I'd like to be.' He leant back, and closed his eyes.

'I've been doing a few sums,' said Rick. 'We're going to have to walk all night. And speed up.' He explained his arithmetic.

'We don't even know he's come this way,' said Hunter.

'He didn't go to Saklis,' said Rick. He sounded surer than he was.

'Maybe he went north. Maybe he went to Khetan's old hideout in the cave. Or maybe he's stopped along the route and we've somehow missed him.'

'The tracker would have started beeping,' said Rick.

'So maybe he's hunkered down for the night more than two

hundred and fifty metres from the path. Maybe he found the lump in his boot. Maybe he threw his boots away and is walking in trainers.'

Rick turned. 'Russell?'

'Uttam and I pushed it hard to Saklis, and then again trying to catch you. I'm fine to keep going, but not more than that.'

Rick's eyes were becoming used to the dark. The cloud was clearing and he could see the moon for the first time. The night might be clear which would help. But it would also help Coniston. What they really needed was a roadblock outside Jiri. He couldn't ask the local police – the whole operation was under the radar – but Uttam or Lok might know someone there.

'We should keep going.' He shouldered his bag, still thinking. A friend of Uttam or Lok, or better still, Uttam or Lok. To get them there instantly he'd need a teletransporter, or at least immediate access to a helicopter. Neither of which he had. But his chain of thought sparked another idea.

'Russell, how're the Sherpas doing?'

There was a brief exchange in Nepali, and the two men grinned at Rick as if they knew what he was thinking.

'Right, listen both of you. I'm going to send Lok and the tracker on ahead. He's got the freshest legs. He'll move twice as fast as us.'

'Five more minutes,' said Hunter. Behind him, Russell was giving instructions to Lok.

'No,' said Rick. He heaved Hunter to his feet. 'We can't have a row every time we stop.'

'Why not,' said Hunter, pushing Rick away.

Rick was so tired. He pushed Hunter back.

His sergeant hadn't expected it. He staggered, regained his balance, and lunged forward. Rick swayed back but wasn't quick enough. Hunter struck Rick's chest with a flat palm. A jab, no follow through.

But it took Rick by surprise. He turned away, winded. Seeing red. He prepared a haymaker of a punch.

Then thought twice, and sprayed Hunter's face with his water bottle.

'No debate, we keep going.' He nodded at the Sherpas and the porter who loaded up, and scurried off.

The three of them followed in silence. Threading their way between the dark houses. Moving like burglars.

The front door of one house stood ajar, tools propped up outside. The hatch was down on the coop, the chickens stuttering in their half-sleep. In front of the next house a chain had been attached to a metal post. It lay on the ground in hanks and led to a dog kennel in deep darkness.

They left the houses behind. A crescent moon with two sharp points was slowly rising and stars filled the sky. Already well ahead of them, Lok looked like a ghost.

31

In the village of Penja, Calix stood with two men on the terrace outside the Namaste Guesthouse. Plastic furniture was stacked at one side, and tubs of yellow flowers stood at the edges. The *didi* must have seen their head torches, and was waiting for them in the doorway. She was small and plump, and wore a bulging apron. Bottles of beer were lined up on the windowsills either side of her. Inside, a baby was wailing.

Lars was a bald Swede and Noud a tall thin Dutchman. Lars was a chef, and always hungry. Noud worked in telesales and day-traded in his time off. Lars read tarot cards, and Noud had been to forty-seven countries. They'd met in a hashish bar in Amsterdam and were spending six months travelling around Asia.

'Good price,' said the *didi* for the third time.

'We stop here,' said Lars. 'I ready eat horse.' He looked at his watch and tapped it. 'After eight – we never walk long time.'

Noud shrugged at Calix. 'Sorry, Joe.'

'I need to keep going,' said Calix. 'Got that flight to catch.'

'One card,' said Lars. He took the tarot pack from his breast pocket, shuffled like a croupier, and fanned them out. 'Just one card.'

Calix felt it would annoy the Nepalese gods, but he was too

tired to resist. He pulled out a card, and turned it over. It showed two people meeting under a silver moon. The title in gold lettering: *L'étranger*.

'If we visit *Oo K*, we come find you,' said Lars, taking back the card. 'Check you okay.' He turned, the *didi* stepped aside and he walked past her into the light.

'Nice meet you,' said Noud. 'Good luck start café.' He winked and followed Lars. The guesthouse door banged shut, and Calix walked away, wishing he hadn't drawn a card.

He was on his own again. He followed the stone steps through the village. Lights shone from some of the windows, but most were dark. At the edge of the houses, animals rustled in wooden enclosures. He peered over a fence. Red-eyed buffalo lay on a bed of straw, their jaws silently moving.

Switching off his head torch, he walked into the darkness. The moon was up and he could see enough to stay on the path. A torch might attract Castle. He looked again at the silvery moon. Tarot omens were never good, that was their thrill.

He came to a wood. The trees were bent and leaning. Little understorey, branches encased in ivy and lichens.

It was cold and getting colder, but for a while he hardly noticed. He was on a high. Talking to Noud and Lars, concocting a different past and future had distracted him from the walking. His name was Joe, he had a flight to catch, he was setting up a roadkill café at the foot of Snake Pass. But more important than distraction or titillation was his invisibility. One man had morphed into three men. Confuse the dibble: give them three spades and tell them to take their pick. An old joke, but Lars and Noud hadn't heard it.

A fallen tree blocked the path. He switched on his head torch. The trunk was at waist height and there was no easy way past. He was too tired to climb over, so he dropped to his knees and crawled under, his pack scraping the bark and pieces falling down his neck.

He set off again. Wind soughed in the trees. The wood swallowed the light from the torch. The path climbed for a while. The trees were thicker-trunked, the understorey denser. He could see even less. He stumbled on a root. According to Lars's tarot cards, he was in danger – which he knew. And he'd meet a stranger, which he could have guessed. Khetan? But he wasn't a stranger.

Midnight. He emerged from the wood and switched off the torch. The moon was brighter, and his shadow was back. He descended a long diagonal into a valley, worked his way up the far side. He was tired, his feet sore and his legs stiff. Twinges of cramp in the hamstrings. Running, even downhill, was no longer an option. He reminded himself why he was doing it. For his old man. For Vicky who'd slipped and fallen. For asthmatic Spencer Williams who'd died in the cold.

Megan wouldn't stop.

He kept going.

An hour later he climbed a small rise, and as he neared the top he smelt woodsmoke. He ducked down into the scrub and crawled forward to the edge. The ground was cold and damp.

At the foot of the slope a circle of dry stone wall provided protection for a herd of goats. About a hundred. At the entrance two boys sat side by side, backs against the wall. They were asleep, or they looked as if they were. At their feet were the remains of a fire, and a dog which also appeared to be asleep. The trail led past them. All his hard work with Lars and Noud would be for nothing if he woke the boys. They would be sure to remember a single white man walking by in the middle of the night.

He could try to steal past or he could detour. Behind the enclosure were open fields with low walls or hedges. Young crops and no cover.

Before he could move the dog stood up, stretched, and trotted up the slope towards him. Calix held his breath. A bark would be fatal – Lars would point to the cards.

The dog didn't bark. It lumbered all the way up, stiff with sleep.

Calix held out his hand. He was good with animals. He felt the dog's mouth and stroked its ears. The dog lay down. He wished he still had some of the sleeping tablets he'd used for Lok.

He kept stroking, keeping the dog calm and sleepy. It was a working dog, similar in size and appearance to a Border Collie.

'It's okay, boy, it's okay.' Whispers. He glanced down at the boys, kept stroking. The dog whined softly.

He crawled further back into the scrub until he was out of sight of the boys and it was safe to kneel. The dog followed. He gave it a piece of dry *roti*. The dog ate it and licked his hand. It lay down, yawned.

'Sorry about this, soldier.' A phrase his old man had used, and the first time he'd ever said it. There was a first time for everything. He pulled the spoon from his pack's top pocket. He stroked the dog's ears and used the spoon to massage the cartilage. He felt for the small cavity under one ear, and pressed the spoon in hard. The dog groaned, and went out.

But, it wasn't enough. The dog might wake and raise the alarm. Convincing Castle to take him to Nepal, extracting the information from the boy, the physical effort of his escape, would all be for nothing.

He untied his boot and whipped out the lace. Gently, he tied the dog's mouth shut. The dog murmured but didn't wake.

Again Calix considered a long detour. It would take precious minutes, and working his way around off-path would be noisy.

He glanced at the dog. Maybe he could risk slinking past the boys on the path. But even if they didn't see him, they might wake and shout or whistle when they realised their dog was missing.

He had one more choice. Not one he wanted to do, or liked doing, but the only one he had.

He unpacked his rucksack and removed the plastic lining bag. He stroked the dog for a few more seconds, admiring its toned legs, its feathered tail. Gently, he slid the dog's head inside the bag, gently he pulled it tight. Very tight.

He was thankful the lining bag was coloured so he couldn't see the dog's face. The bag sucked inwards as the dog breathed. Tried to breathe. The dog started, tried to stand. Calix gripped hard. The dog half-stood, scrabbled, ran its feet round. Calix pressed his body down on the dog. The animal sank to the ground.

Pathetic slobbery gasps came from the bag.

The dog stilled.

Calix held on until he was sure. He released his cinch hold and laid the dog's head on the ground. He removed his lace, retied his boot. He stuffed the liner at the bottom of his bag and repacked his kit. He pulled the dead dog behind some rocks so it was hidden from the path.

Then he returned to the top of the rise. The boys were still asleep. Behind them, some of the goats were shifting around their pen. The animals were quiet but not silent. It would help.

He crept down the path, planning to skirt around the top of the enclosure. The cleared ground on both sides was trodden and nibbled down. He went slowly, placing his feet.

One of the boys called out in his sleep.

Calix froze.

Crouched.

Some of the goats jostled in their pen. He was close enough to smell them.

The boy stood up.

Calix flattened to the ground.

The boy walked a few metres towards him, whistled and called out for the dog. The second boy woke, and called out to the first boy. Who turned around.

Calix seized his chance, and crawled up to a rock the size of an upturned bath.

The two boys spoke again, and laughed. The first boy glanced back at the rock where Calix was hiding. He spat, and began to urinate. Whistled. Shouted. More goats stood and walked around their enclosure.

The second boy whispered crossly. The first boy scowled and pulled up his trousers. He stared at Calix's rock, then turned and walked back to the other boy. The two of them talked for a few minutes.

The goats settled.

The boys went back to sleep. Not knowing.

Calix felt like he'd been hit by lightning. He was wet with sweat, as if he'd pissed himself. He stood, detoured around the far side of the enclosure. Halfway round, he peered through a gap in the wall at the goats. Pairs of red eyes glinted in the gloom.

Stepping back onto the trail, he glanced back at the sleeping goat herders. He was sorry about their dog.

Then he went on.

After another hour Calix came to a cluster of houses. He was too tired to detour and he followed the trail which weaved between them. The rush of adrenalin at the goat pen had reversed. Now he felt like he'd been awake for a week. His legs were leaden, his body ached, even his head felt heavy.

Dogs started to bark.

He speeded up, dreading the sound of human voices. The path was rough and shadowed, and he slipped and stumbled.

Soon after the last house he walked past half a dozen low stone walls in oval shapes, the size of tents. Windbreaks built by trekkers who camped rather than staying in tea houses. But not that night: the plots were empty.

He walked up a small rise towards a signpost marking the skyline. He stopped beside it. The signs were of the type placed in big cities and tourist spots. *New York 12,000 km, Sydney 9,500 km, London 7,000 km.* Nepalese destinations too. *Kathmandu 260 km, Chitwan 150 km, Pokhara 500 km.* At the bottom was the place he was interested in. *Jiri 80 km.* He wasn't sure whether to be disappointed or pleased.

He looked back the way he'd come: he couldn't see the houses. His pace had slowed, but he still reckoned on two hours over the dibble. If he dozed for an hour, he'd be able to move faster. Dawn would be closer.

He retraced his steps to the windbreaks. He chose the flattest. He put on his duvet jacket and lay down, using his rucksack as a pillow. His legs throbbed, and his calves felt tight as wire. A bat swished past and a dog barked near the houses. He set the alarm on his watch. His fingers were dry and cracked and the long left thumbnail was broken and jagged. It didn't matter: nothing mattered except reaching Jiri. The ground was cold and damp and he cinched his hood tight. He lay down. Khetan had cried in the night. Everyone was equal there.

Above him, the silver moon taunted. He thought back to the *L'étranger* card. Did two strangers count as one?

He curled his knees up towards his chest and closed his eyes. An hour, no more.

32

Cobalt blue was the first colour to appear on the eastern horizon. The pale moon had disappeared and the land remained dark. The patch of blue turned white, then soft yellow. It widened into a streak, and became golden. A rim of brilliant yellow appeared. The streak multiplied, sending orange daggers across the dull horizon. Wispy clouds formed, tinged with pink and coral. But not the sun. The sun didn't show.

Ten past five. The day had arrived and Rick could see again. Colours. Distances and altitudes. Buildings and people. Body language. Nuances.

'Any sign of him?' said Hunter. He was sitting on a rock, head on his lap, the light of his head torch still boring down into the ground. Uttam was now carrying his daypack.

Rick let the binoculars drop. He shook his head.

'*Camdai*,' said Russell. Soon.

'Can you stop saying that,' muttered Hunter. 'And speak in English.'

Rick said nothing, but he too felt irritable. They'd walked all night. Nine long hours since he'd sent Lok and the tracker on ahead. It had been a good idea, but not a perfect one. If – and it was a big if – Lok detected Coniston with the tracker, it would only confirm their fugitive was ahead. He would not be able to stop or detain him. And then he'd have to wait for them to catch up.

But it would confirm they were on the right trail. And that would be something.

They kept walking. Rick felt like a zombie. At home he worked ten-hour night shifts on a rota. Sometimes he worked for eighteen hours, and very occasionally twenty-four. But he didn't walk all night. His shoulders ached, his back ached, and his legs ached. His feet were swollen and sore.

An hour later, they stopped for some breakfast in the shade. The sun had burnt away the haze. They drank luke-warm tea from a flask and ate honey-filled *rotis*. Rick could have eaten fifty. Hunter lay on the ground, his head on Russell's pack.

'Five minutes,' said the mountaineer, 'otherwise we'll be too stiff to move.' He did some stretching exercises against a rock. The sat phone rang.

Rick stabbed at it with a sticky finger.

Robbo's voice.

Rick felt a spike of adrenalin. 'Has Lummle firmed up for Khetan?'

'I've passed it on, and we've had an official thank you back. They'll let us know.'

Rick doubted it. Success would be heralded on the news, anything else would be filed away.

'Maggie says we haven't heard from you for a couple of days.'

'We're in Nepal.'

'I don't need reminding. How's Coniston?'

'Fine, we're trekking back.'

'Daily calls from now on. Understood?'

'Understood.' Rick paused. 'Less fatty foods, you'll sleep better.'

The line went dead.

Hunter opened his eyes. 'We're fucked.'

Ahead was another shadowed ridgeline. Above, a helmet of blue sky and a daffodil sun. Rick handed Uttam his binoculars and pointed at the ridge.

He waited with Russell next to a knee-high statue of Buddha. It was painted gold and reflected the sun. Condensation dripped off its bald head. Beads of water trickled down its rotund belly, caught in the button and fell to the ground.

'There are over a hundred different Buddha postures,' said Russell. 'They're called *rupas*, and all mean something different. This is the Serenity Buddha. His arms are in his lap and his legs are in the double lotus. His eyes are closed and he's meditating, hoping for enlightenment.'

'He's a long way from the nearest house.'

'It's a gift to people who walk past.'

Uttam returned from the ridge at the same time as Hunter and the porter arrived. Hunter immediately flopped down.

Uttam shook his head.

'*Camdai*,' said Hunter.

They walked on. Rick didn't trust his legs not to seize up. Walking seemed so simple: move one foot, then the other, and don't stop. But his legs felt like blocks of stone. It was odd how something so ingrained, so easy, should change and fall apart.

He tried to distract himself with positive thoughts.

Maggie. She's good news, Mum frequently told him. Their one-year anniversary of going out was coming up and he should buy her a present.

What?

Something that showed he'd made some effort, in the

thinking if not in the making. A thing? Jewellery was boring, and she already owned a lot of books. A piece of modern art, something that he could explain in an amusing way? A gadget for her modern kitchen? Maybe, not a thing – a gesture: he'd suggest they move in together. They already spent most nights in one place.

Already, Russell was twenty metres ahead. Rick broke into a trot, but gave up, and settled back to a fast walk. As long as he could see the mountaineer.

Move in – what was he thinking? For a moment, he'd forgotten her promise. He was not moving in until she told him about her legs.

Two men in combats walked past. Berets tucked under their epaulettes and filthy boots. Then a man carrying four kid goats in his basket. He was humming to himself.

Rick put his hands together.

At the next bend in the path, Russell was waiting for him. Rick unlaced his boot and removed a stone. Looked back the way they'd come. Relaced his boot. Looked at his watch. Had a piss.

Hunter arrived and sat heavily on a rock. 'Ten minutes.'

'Five,' said Rick, his stomach churning. He turned to Russell. 'Any jobs going at Nepal Adventures – ops manager?'

Hunter scoffed. 'I wouldn't employ him, big man, he'll be nosing around your employment records, your finances, your health and safety. Couldn't stop himself, he was born a beak.'

'I think that's a compliment, Rick. Anyway, it won't come to that, we'll find him, I know we will.' The mountaineer's intonation told the opposite story.

Climbing a small rise, Rick heard voices.

Coniston and Lok?

Allowing himself to hope, he managed a painful jog to the

top. He climbed onto a rock and looked down and across a cleared hillside. Near a herd of goats two teenage boys were arguing. No sign of Lok, let alone Coniston.

The boys were digging a hole.

Rick stepped off the rock, and followed Uttam and their porter down the slope. There was a stone enclosure but the goats were roaming free. The porter trotted ahead and rested his basket on top of the wall.

The boys stopped digging. They were dressed identically. Gilets of animal hide with fur on the outside, Umbro tracksuit trousers. Near the boys, a dog lay on the ground. The animal looked dead.

Rick sent Uttam to the next ridgeline, and wishing he had more Nepali, waited at the stockade for the others. The porter rolled a cigarette. Rick stared at the dog. Young, no obvious injuries. Arguing owners.

Russell and Hunter finally appeared, the sergeant slumping down by the wall. He pulled out a crumpled pack of cigarettes, and cursing his lost lighter, lit one from the porter's cigarette. The mountaineer drank deeply from his bottle.

'When you've asked them all the usual, Russell, ask them about the dog.'

Russell asked – the boys hadn't seen Coniston but thought they might have seen Lok. The dog was only three years old, and fine the day before. They thought it had eaten a poisonous mushroom and were blaming each other.

'I'm not so sure,' said Rick. He stared at the dead animal. Legs stiff and splayed unnaturally. He would never forget Coniston's attic room with the stuffed birds and rodents.

'*Sahib, sahib.*' Shouts from the ridge. Uttam was jumping up and down on a rock waving the binoculars and pointing toward Kathmandu.

Coniston?

Rick shouldered his sack and forced his legs forward. The ground was rough but flattish until the pull up to the ridge. He willed Uttam to start back towards him. He willed the news to be good – Lok *and* Coniston. Coniston uninjured, apologetic. He tripped, stumbled, and fell, his daysack hitting the back of his head on the way down.

Uttam ran up. 'Okay, *sahib*?'

Rick sat on a rock and rubbed his head. He nodded. 'Lok?'

Uttam ran on the spot holding up all his fingers.

Ten minutes later his team was reunited. Even Hunter had sloughed across from the goat enclosure.

'So?' said Rick.

'It's complicated,' said Russell. He spoke again in Nepali to Lok who kept pointing at the tracker. Uttam intervened. Finally, there was agreement. 'Okay. About thirty minutes walk from here, there's a small village and just after that, the tracker started beeping. Lok turned it off then on again every fifteen minutes to save the battery, as you'd instructed. After an hour, the tracker stopped beeping.'

'Dead battery?'

'No, that's what I was checking. The red light's still showing.'

'About what time?'

'Between four and five. It was starting to get light.'

'Did he see him?' said Hunter. He pushed up his sunglasses revealing bloody eyes and crusted eyebrows.

'No. I checked that too.'

'Come on!' said Rick, charging off. 'Coniston might be just ahead of us.'

As he strode he poured water on his head and down the back of his neck. He was determined to keep going although his legs were screaming.

On the other side of the valley, sparkling streams coursed

downwards. The land was too steep for farming, and covered in stubby trees and impenetrable vegetation. A bird of prey rode the thermals above.

Rick checked his watch every few minutes, and after forty, the team reached the small village of Penja. Hunter not too far behind.

At the water tap, a woman was filling a large metal urn. Russell asked questions but she said she hadn't seen anyone. She placed the urn on her head and walked off, one arm splayed out at the side to keep her balance.

At the side of the nearest house, a crowd of boys knelt round a small fire, roasting corn cobs in the embers. They were taking turns with the end of a cigarette hidden under a broken cup. They grinned like conspirators at the white men and didn't move from the fire. Russell bent down. Asked. Stood up, shook his head.

Under the next house was an animal pen. The gate was open and the ground inside was churned up and lumpy with manure. Outside, an old woman milked a buffalo with a golden hoop through its nose. She sat on a stool and squirted the milk into a plastic bucket. The animal chewed stoically.

Rick and his team trooped past.

On the far side of the village was a small river. A rope had been tied to a tree and children were swinging across. They beckoned excitedly.

'They want you to have a go,' said Russell.

'Next year,' said Hunter.

Lok pointed to the tracker. '*Sahib, beep, beep.*'

Rick took the device out of the case and switched it on. Silence. As he expected, if it hadn't malfunctioned, then Coniston was no longer in range.

Hunter sat on a tree stump and took off a boot. 'Not got much left.'

'We're close, Gary,' said Rick. 'We know we're close.' He gave instructions. Russell and the two Sherpas to knock on doors and show the photo of Coniston. Rick would criss-cross with the tracker. Hunter to rest. As soon as they were sure, they'd need to continue.

After thirty minutes, the four of them converged on Hunter. He'd moved from the tree stump and was leaning against a signpost. His boots lay beside him and his eyes were closed. The signpost was for tourists. *New York 12,000 km, Sydney 9,500 km.* It probably featured in the photos of at least half the trekkers who walked past. *London 7,000 km.* Rick felt that he'd walked that far.

'There are some stone shelters not far from here,' said Russell. 'Trekkers sometimes camp there.'

'He hasn't got a tent,' said Hunter, opening his eyes.

Rick sent Russell and the Sherpas to find the stone shelters, but he wasn't hopeful. If Coniston had been in Penja, he had left again. On top of that, their searching had cost another hour. If Coniston had been there at four and gone an hour later, they were at least two hours behind him and possibly as much as five.

Hunter stood up and hobbled a few metres in his socks.

If, if, if. It was all still speculative. The kids shouted and laughed by the river. A dog splashed through the water, and a rooster took up crowing. Normal life kept going, regardless. Missing person or multiple homicide or motorway pile-up, it made no difference: normal life kept on flowing and eventually subsumed the crisis.

Hunter hobbled back and slumped down. 'I found this.' He held up a dark green cigarette lighter. 'It's mine – Coniston must have pinched it, and dropped it here.'

'One last effort then.'

'I can't.' Hunter nodded at his feet. 'Blisters the size of squash balls.'

Rick looked along the trail, curving down towards a winking river. He glanced at Russell who shrugged, and again at Hunter, picking at his feet, and he looked up at the plum-blue sky with its golfball sun, and summoned up his every last joule of energy.

33

Calix came to another rhododendron forest. The path dove in: a well-walked line through the mulch. Among the trees the world was darker, and the view disappeared in front of him and behind him. The limbs of the stubby trees were sinewy. They winded and twisted, more like tentacles than branches. The large purple flowers were dying, their petals turning brown and falling off in soggy clumps. Forests were scary places for children.

He was no longer a child.

He pushed on, standing on the tree roots to gain purchase on the muddy sections. It kept his mind from feeling tired and away from dwelling on what was happening behind him. The dibble's Sherpas were born in the mountains and used to walking five miles to school and ten miles for supplies. Legs like athletes, cardiovascular systems like Tour de France riders. If the surface area of his alveoli was the size of a tennis court, then theirs had to be the size of football pitches. Their *destiny* was to pursue him, to run him down.

He slashed at a branch with a stick, releasing a flurry of withered petals.

He'd been annoyed with himself ever since he'd woken at four and realised he'd overslept. At least he hadn't had to get dressed. Already, it was ten. He'd been going for twenty-four hours, which was longer than his last girlfriend. She'd told him she was into animals, but she wasn't into animals like him.

He took another drink from the water bottle, but couldn't face any more flapjack. His eyes were prickly and his tongue felt swollen. His boots were heavy and uncomfortable, as if he was wearing someone else's, and his legs were cramping. In Strangeways there'd been a gym, and he wished he'd used it. He had a young man's fitness, but could he outwalk the dibble? He could at least match Castle, but what if they split up? There was no way he'd outpace Weatherbeater, a professional mountaineer, yet alone one of the Sherpas. He could only hope they stayed in a group.

He pushed his hand up behind his back to relieve the pressure of his rucksack. Althought it was light, it chafed against his skin. His t-shirt stuck to the weeping sore. He pulled it off the wound and wished he hadn't.

A con from Barcelona had told him a Spanish judge could sentence a prisoner to six weeks of walking on the Compostela Way. At the time he'd thought it a soft touch, but now he knew.

He looked behind him: Castle was back there somewhere.

Then hustled on.

Khetan was in Lummle.

He stopped for a piss next to a stack of branches that had been trimmed and piled up between stakes. He was so tired he leant against the stack, knocking off a curl of bark. A scuttling woodlouse reminded him of Beetle Beetle. He pulled away more of the bark, and yellow grubs and woodlice fell to the ground like spilt rice.

He extricated the matchbox from the side pocket on his pack. Then picked up some of the wriggling grubs, pushed the box open and dropped them in. Beetle Beetle raced about. He added a few drips of water. They reminded him of Mr Small and the drop of lemonade. The crumb and the pea. His old man had read him that book when he was small. When his world was small. When Megan was small.

Calix set off again. Maybe after he'd been to Lummle, he'd travel to Australia. Find the van driver who was responsible for Megan. He would. It was a decision. Couldn't be too hard, the accident was in all the papers and the driver – Rod Stokes – prosecuted for dangerous driving.

The rhododendron thinned and finally petered out. He reached Jubing, which he hoped was halfway to Jiri.

On the far side of the village, he walked through small fields. Some lay fallow and were dotted with mounds of manure which had been deposited by hand. The path weaved around and he retraced his steps several times. Three women were weeding. They squatted in a line, working the soil with hand forks and throwing weeds into a bucket. All talking at once. A young girl played on the ground in front of them and put everything she could reach into the bucket. A baby in a papoose slept on one woman's back.

The yellow sun overhead, hot and relentless.

In the corner of the next field under a single gnarled tree, a man sharpened a plough. A young boy was watching. The man handed the boy the file, and the boy had a go. His father guided his hands.

'Jiri?'

The man looked up, smiled and pointed at a diagonal across the field. The boy copied his father, then hopped around laughing. He was no older than five.

Calix marched on.

*

He came to a section that had been washed away by a flooding river, and he jumped down into the gully that had been carved out. As he landed, his pack bit into the sore at the base of his back. He swore loudly. Using the new, rough steps he climbed out. In the adjacent field another farmer watched him, a mattock in his hand. He stared at Calix with a wry grin.

Calix took off his rucksack, and took out the box of flapjack from The Big Red. He placed two pieces without nuts on the plastic lid. Then waved the farmer closer.

The farmer walked over. He looked older than Calix, but was probably a similar age. He grinned, revealing perfect teeth. On his head was a *topi*. He wore a shirt with a collar which would not have been out of place in a city, and a v-necked brown cardigan.

'*Namaste.*'

'*Namaste.*'

'*Bhok?*' asked Calix. Hungry?

The man nodded and Calix passed him the lid with the flapjacks. The farmer took one. Broke off a piece and ate it.

'*Ramro?*' said Calix.

'*Ramro.*' The farmer grinned, his perfect teeth now stuck with flapjack. He ate the rest of the flapjack and helped himself to a second.

Calix pointed to his pack, and lifted his shirt to expose the sore on his back. '*Naramro.*'

'*Naramro,*' said the farmer.

Calix pointed again at the farmer, then at his rucksack. He took out one of the twenty-dollar notes and held it in front of him.

'*Kaha chha?*' Where?

Good question. Farmer Barleymow wasn't such a pushover.

'Jiri.'

'*Kahile?*' When?

220

Calix waved another twenty. '*Aba.*' Now.

The man took hold of Calix's rucksack, picked up the wicker basket lying next to the path, and pushed the pack inside. He picked up his mattock, inverted it and slotted it down beside the rucksack.

'Joe,' said Calix, patting his chest.

'Gopi,' said the farmer.

They set off, Gopi leading and carrying Calix's rucksack. Wearing stumpy wellies, the farmer lolloped along humming. The pressure on his sore gone, Calix also felt his spirits rise. Jiri seemed closer.

Above them, the taunting seaside sky.

34

Rick walked through small fields. A farmer was ploughing, encouraging an ox with a stick. The man was talking to the ox, or to himself. Three women sat under a tree in the corner of the field. Between them was a bowl of rice, and they ate it with their fingers, chatting as if they were knocking off early and they were going out. Maybe they were. A young boy and a young girl squatted nearby, their arms around each other, looking at a scruffy book. Rick stared and looked away. He looked back, nodded at the women and smiled. He looked away. He was unsure – did he seem interested or voyeuristic? Friendly or judging?

The path jinked around, but the Sherpas knew where to go – even when the path was new, or diverted. Like a detective's sixth sense in his world. He'd read that to increase the length of your life, you had to do new things, go to new places. The trip to Nepal would count for decades.

He hurried to catch Russell. He owed him for his positive mindset in the hunt for Coniston.

'You still haven't told me about Jacob.'

'He's in a bit of bother with you lot.'

'You're a special now – *our* lot.'

'That's part of it.'

Russell fell silent, and Rick didn't want to push him. They might have all day, and all day the next day.

They walked on.

Quicker now, having left Hunter at the tourist signpost. He was stubborn as an old woman at the front desk.

Rick wasn't sure whether to believe his new sergeant, or even to totally trust him. He thought it more likely he'd lent the lighter to Coniston, or the lighter had dropped out of his pocket when he was having a piss. Maybe Hunter didn't even know and he was guessing – or hoping. At the landslide, too, Hunter had wanted to give up chasing Coniston. Too easily? Lazy self-interest, or something more sinister? A bribe for his retirement?

Rick was so tired he was losing himself to conspiracy theories. Or so tired, only the truth was left.

He stamped on, the muscles in his legs feeling like rods.

They came to a wood. The trees were taller and thinner than in the rhododendron forest. They were covered with lichen and mosses, many crooked and warped. Lots had fallen. The branches were draped in a secondary growth of creepers and vines which made the forest look like a fairyland. Rick was a good guy, searching for the bad guy. Around every twist in the path, he hoped he might see him: Coniston sitting on a stump or a giant red toadstool. Bouncing Khetan's severed head up and down on his knee.

The path climbed up. There were steps made from fallen logs, all decaying with age and use. He counted seventeen, out loud. The path turned back downhill. Downhill felt like flat ground, flat ground like uphill and uphill felt like mountain climbing. He could feel every contour, as if he was on a bicycle with only one gear.

A stream crossed the path. Rick stopped and bent down. He

cupped his hands in the cold water and splashed his face. The water so clear.

He soaked his sunhat and stood up slowly, as if he was following a list of complex instructions. He turned to face the sun, clutching the dripping hat. He closed his eyes, enjoying the contrast in temperature. He sensed the water droplets vaporising, one by one. His eyelids cemented down. Where were his sunglasses? His sunhat? He sensed he was swaying. Horses slept standing up. Or was it cows?

'Rick.'

'Rick!'

Russell's voice.

Rick squinted into the sunlight. 'You seen my sunglasses?'

'On that rock.'

'You must be used to being this knackered.'

'Yes and no. Lack of sleep and legs screaming, yes. But this is a chase. The quicker we go, the quicker it will end. A summit stays still.'

Rick put his sunglasses on. Robbo had wanted him to leave the Khetan file alone. Leave it to sit with the hundreds of other unresolved files in the archive – to be forgotten, to gather dust and be subject to strict weeding criteria. Six years, twenty-five years and a hundred years. The Khetan file with its conspiracy to kidnap and three manslaughters would make it through the first thinning, but at twenty-five years would be pulled out, reviewed one last time and shredded. Even if he was an FBI target.

'Onwards,' said Rick.

He picked up his pack and leapt over the water. The stream never stopped, and neither would he.

They reached an isolated smallholding. In the front yard a boy sat on a chair while a woman cut his hair. She snipped away: short all over. She waved the scissors at Rick and nodded at the chair. He shook his head, and forced a smile. Behind her, the house lay in ruins. Chickens ran around the fallen walls, and two younger children played in the dirt. At the side of the house there was a makeshift shelter with a roof of plastic sheeting. The sound of sawing came from behind the ruined house.

If she could remain positive, then so could he. At home he'd call up a helicopter, or ask for a tracker dog. Here, they just had to keep going, only quicker. Without Hunter, Rick was now the slowest. But he had to be fitter than Coniston. So, where was he? They were on the main route to Jiri, but there were more circuitous ones. The dead dog and Hunter's cigarette lighter suggested they were on his tail. But the first could be a coincidence, and the second an oversight, or a fib, or even a deal between Hunter and Coniston. Maybe Coniston had thrown away his boots. Or found the tracker and smashed it.

Rick sucked on a fruit pastille and followed Russell down the trail. The boy with short hair ran past and fell over. He started crying. Tufts of hair on the shoulders of his t-shirt. Rick propped the boy up and gave him the rest of the packet.

Some time tomorrow, they'd be at Jiri – with or without Coniston. The end of the line. Shower, a proper meal, sleep.

Start over.

Find their escaped prisoner.

Directly or indirectly, take out Khetan.

35

A waxing moon lit up the deserted field. Small cabbage-like plants sat in neat rows, their leaves silvery in the moonlight. *L'étranger* card again.

Stones and rocks lined the edge of the field, and a scarecrow was standing guard. A bucket for a head, branches for limbs, and brushwood for a body. There was no spare clothing. The path tracked along the field and turned around a small stone barn at the corner. The corrugated roof glinted. Underneath its eaves were stacks of firewood. A waymarker had been screwed to the wall.

Bhandar – 6 hours

Jiri – 12 hours

Jiri and the roadhead. He was going to do it. Castle wasn't going to catch him. He shouted at Gopi to stop.

The farmer walked back up the path, and set down his basket and mattock. Calix grabbed his calloused hands and danced back and forth. He let go of him and punched the air. He whooped like a warring brave and ran around hollering and letting off arrows. He danced the can-can, he played the saxophone, he booted a football into the back of the net and into the next universe. Gopi started chanting and waggling his hips from side to side. He bent his arms at the elbows and with thumbs extended, moved his arms up and down in time with his hips. Calix copied him and together they chanted, and danced up and down, and round and round. The farmer whirled his mattock around. He was drooling, unaffected, deranged.

Finally, Calix slowed, and pointed at the barn. The sore on his back no longer bothered him, but his anus was sore and chafing.

'*Paanch* minutes.' He tapped his watch, and held up a gloved hand, fingers spread.

The farmer stopped his crazy dance and threw down his mattock. He lit up a cigarette, the flare clawing at the dark.

The barn was the size of a domestic garage back home, but twice as high. One small window in the second storey. Calix peered through the doorway. It was stacked with hay and logs. He climbed over the gate and went inside. A pair of bats flew over his head and into the night. Hoes and different-sized spades hung on nails. He turned on his head torch. Mice scuttled away. On a shelf, a packet of biscuits in a jar. Plastic buckets in a corner.

Calix pulled out some of the hay and spread it on the ground. He looked over his shoulder at the doorway, but couldn't see Gopi. He turned back to face the heap of hay and removed his gloves. He dropped his trousers and pants and squatted down. The package had made him sore, and he blamed the unusual diet. He felt for the plastic, gripped and eased it out.

The double-wrapped package dropped onto the hay. It smelt, but the vial looked fine. He removed the plastic wrapping and with a handful of hay pushed it deep into the stack. He left it there, wiped the vial on the bottom of his trousers and opened the lid. Push and squeeze. He tapped the contents onto the palm of his hand.

Two white pills with crescent-shaped dimples. Crescents, or smiles? The manufacturer's sick joke.

Calix poured the pills back into the vial. He wondered whether he should have handled them with gloves – even touching skin might be enough. He wiped his hands on the straw and on his sleeves. He zipped the vial into a trouser pocket and lay back against the hay.

A handgun would have been preferable, but he'd not been sure whether he could source one in Kathmandu under pressure of time. So he'd acquired cyanide pills along with the sleeping tablets at Strangeways. Cyanide had been Darren's idea, and research had shown it to be viable. It was no longer used in the UK for homicides because it could be detected in a post-mortem. Only for suicides. He doubted whether Nepal investigated many deaths.

Cyanide had seemed ideal. A small dose would be sufficient. Death occurred within a few hours. And it could be bought on the internet. A prison was a truly free market. If the price was right, then almost anything could be obtained. Size was the main limitation. Darren had boasted, *prison is better than Amazon* – no problems with the law and no VAT.

Through mates of Darren's Calix had bought a pack of five pills. He'd covered costs and a kickback to his cellmate by pushing on three.

Calix pulled out a strand of hay and put it in his mouth. It was the second night without sleep and he was exhausted. He took a puff of the imaginary cigarette, and closed his eyes.

He finds Khetan in the small village of Lummle on the Nepal–Tibet border. Just as Ram had said. Calix follows Khetan for a few days, learning his morning habits and routes. He buys local clothes and wears a hat and doesn't shave. He doesn't rush, only following a small section of the route each time. Khetan leaves his flophouse at sunrise, takes a shit, washes at a water tap and goes for breakfast in a café. The Lummle Lodge. Tea and *momos* at a street table. Calix sits at the next table, waiting. A beggar appears outside the Lodge, his sleeve on fire. Calix has paid him – one of the twenty-dollar bills from the flapjack. Khetan watches, is distracted, and Calix strikes.

Drops a cyanide pill in Khetan's tea. Simple. Biblical. An eye for an eye and all that.

'Bhandar?' said Gopi.

It was nearly a shout, as if the farmer had said it more than once. Calix opened his eyes. He felt a soggy piece of hay draped down his chin and he wiped it away. Gopi was leaning on the gate, looking into the barn.

Calix nodded. *'Dui mineta.'* Two minutes.

The farmer nodded back and Calix looked past him into the night. A solitary tree was caught in the moonlight, like a burglar in a security beam.

He closed his eyes again. He was so tired. Bats squeaked and shuffled in the rafters, and mice moved around in the hay. Outside, Gopi was tapping his mattock. One more minute and he'd stand up.

36

At the end of the valley Rick spotted the first stone bridge since they'd left Mosom Kharka. Two or three valleys after that would be Jiri and the trailhead. Roads and vehicles. Buses, taxis, jeeps and cars. Hotels with beds and showers and baths.

Sleep and more sleep.

The moon was fatter than on the first night, and the stars were brighter. In the ethereal glow, the trail led down the side of a hillside towards a patchwork of fields. Streams cut across the path, heading for the large river in the valley below. The soft noise of the water's progress rose as they reached each stream, then fell as they walked away. The night was more rhythmical than the day.

The first sign of the sun would arrive soon. Rick kept moving his feet robotically in front of each other. A small rat-like animal skittered away from the path, its red eyes staining the darkness.

An alarm beeped.

Rick glanced at his wrist. He angled it at the moon. Ten past three. He'd been awake for almost fifty hours. He turned and waited for Russell to catch up. 'Is that your watch?'

'I didn't hear anything.'

They walked on. He'd been thinking about the moon cycle.

It lasted a month so it waned for fifteen nights, then waxed for fifteen nights. Tonight it was six per cent fatter than last night ... 6.66 per cent recurring ...

The beeping came again.

'Listen,' said Rick.

'That's no watch,' said Russell.

Ahead, Uttam waited on the edge of the patchwork of fields. The bridge was somewhere on the far side and no longer visible.

Uttam was beeping. The Sherpa held the tracker in front of him as if it was a newborn. The tracker was beeping. Adrenalin charged up inside Rick. 'Keep going, Uttam.'

Russell translated, and Uttam glanced over his shoulder. He whispered to Lok, and they walked on.

Rick followed close behind, and their porter brought up the rear. It had to be Coniston.

The path made its way through the fields. Rick stared ahead, but couldn't see any movement. The tracker had a range of 250 metres. They still had to catch him. 'Faster.'

It didn't need translating.

Uttam and Lok speeded up. They all speeded up. Could Coniston hear them? Five people moving at night were not quiet.

They came to a stream and a small homestead. A dog barked and ran at them. It was caught by a chain and its bark strangulated. A baby started crying. They crossed the stream on an old door with the handle still attached. The path climbed a few metres, and continued through another set of fields. Rick walked as fast as he could. He could hear his breathing. He stumbled, but caught himself. He kept going.

They came to another small stream and another homestead. Shirts and trousers hung on a washing line. Outside the door were a heap of shoes and a child's doll missing its legs. A face appeared at an upstairs window. The next second it was gone.

Uttam crossed the stream and waited with the tracker. *Beep, beep, beep.* The reports were louder and closer together. Which meant they were gaining, but too quickly. Something was wrong. Rick glanced at Russell who was behind him. 'It's too quick.'

The path followed along the side of a planted-up field. Rows of small plants. For animals or people? Both?

Rick caught up with the two Sherpas.

Beep-beep, beep-beep. The tracker was at fever pitch. He was at fever pitch, his heart thudding, and the hairs on the back of his neck erect. They were very close: the last fifty metres. But it was too early to count the chicken. They hadn't caught him. They hadn't even found him.

They reached the corner of a field and a two-storey barn with a corrugated roof which shone in the moonlight. As if God, or Buddha, was on their side.

Beeeeeeeeeeeep. The tracker report turned continuous, as if someone was flat-lining. The barn gate was on the floor and Rick trampled over it.

He switched on his head torch.

A haystack filled the back half of the barn. Lying face down in front of it was Coniston. A mouse scurried away. Next to Coniston was his rucksack, the top flap open and his belongings scattered on the ground. A glove, a second glove, a matchbox and the container of flapjack. Both empty. The pockets on his trousers were pulled inside out.

A second beam of light surveyed the scene. 'Is he dead?' said Russell.

Rick felt around Coniston's head. He'd blackened his hair. On the top of the head was a bloody matted mess and a lump. Rick's hands were smeared red and black. He sniffed them – coffee. The sachets he'd taken.

Someone had hit Coniston hard. He couldn't hear breathing,

but the tracker was still crowing. 'Turn that thing off.'

Silence.

With Russell's help, Rick rolled Coniston onto his back. He pressed two fingers against his neck. The pulse was faint and he nodded. 'He's alive.'

Rick had been there before. A body in the dark. Suspects? Motive? Witnesses? Weapons? He looked around, the beam of his torch picking out farmers' tools and a stack of firewood.

'Coniston.' Rick pinched an arm. There was no response. He held his head up and poured water down his face.

Coniston's eyes flickered open. He frowned. 'C-c-a-s-stle?'

'What happened?'

Coniston's eyes closed. They moved him back, so he leant against the hay. His head lolled. Rick slapped him on the cheek. 'Coniston, what happened?'

'Goppeeee, where'ssss Goppeeee?'

Rick stared out through the doorway of the barn at the first sparkle of daylight. A single tree stood in the middle of a field. It had stood for ever, but one day it would be gone. Like everything and everybody.

37

Four days later Rick lay in bed, unable to sleep. 4.05am gleamed the clock radio. Mid-morning in Nepal. He stroked Maggie's hair. She lay asleep beside him, breathing deeply.

In – and – out.

In – and – out.

Comforting, like the ebb and flow of the sea.

Jetlag wasn't the only thing responsible for his insomnia. Also to blame was Maggie's ridiculously comfortable bed with its duck-feather duvet, fresh sheets, two standard pillows and a reading pillow. Three pillows *each*. The reading pillows were somewhere on the floor. Since he'd got back, they'd not done much reading.

His brain whirred as he continued to stroke Maggie's hair. Coniston was back in Strangeways. Would be lying there now, in some dirty cell, listening to the coughing and moaning of tens of prisoners. No reading pillows for him.

Few people, not the Nepalese authorities, not the prison governor, not Robbo, were any the wiser. Only five other people knew. Three he could trust, and of the other two, Coniston had already made a move. Driving back from Jiri to Kathmandu, their prisoner had threatened to tell the Nepalese police. Rick had countered with the letter to the judge – which he still had to write, and soon, because Coniston's trial was only weeks away. As a stalling manoeuvre, it had worked, but would evaporate after the trial.

After delivering Coniston back to prison, he'd driven straight to the police station to report to Robbo. An abridged version.

'No problems?' said Robbo when he finished. A jam stain sat halfway down his white shirt. It was a typical Robbo question: more of a statement.

Rick shook his head. His only thought during the report, and his first question afterwards, was Khetan. 'What's the update on Lummle?'

'I haven't heard anything.'

Rick pulled a face. 'It's D4 intel, I bet they've done nothing.'

'Well, you've done your bit, so you can now get back to what you're supposed to be doing. Suspicious deaths and murders at South Manchester.'

'I will.'

'But?'

'No point in me taking Coniston to Nepal if I'm not going to use the intel we gained. Lummle might not come good, so it makes sense to write the letter to Khetan and concoct the fake newspaper article, and get Russell to deliver them. Only take a day. Then I'm sus deaths and murders.'

Robbo walked over to the window. He'd worn a faint path in the lino.

'Did I mention,' said Rick, 'I bought you some duty free. Chocolates of the world and a kukri-shaped bottle of Nepalese rum.' Rick dumped a lumpy plastic bag on Robbo's desk.

Robbo turned. 'Take Monday off, write the damned letter, then forget about Khetan.'

*

Maggie stirred again.

'You could stroke my head for ever.'

He ran his fingers through her hair, pushing out a couple of the tangles.

'What happened out there?' she murmured. 'You've hardly said anything.'

'I *have*. Flying to Lukla, walking to Saklis, finding Ram. The Lummle intel.' He paused. 'I want to hear how you are, Mags.'

'I've been at work mainly. Robbo's been odd. Avoiding me and very sarcastic whenever your name came up. Or highly critical. Did you two fall out?'

'We had a difference in opinion, that's all.'

Maggie looked at him, wanting more.

He changed the subject. 'How's the thing with Siobhan?'

'Last week she broke one of my spokes.'

'How do you know it was her?'

'Oh, aren't you Mr Detective, Mr Detective.'

Rick tickled Maggie's stomach until she started to shriek. She threw off the duvet and pushed him out. He went to the bathroom. So civilised not to have to find his head torch, unzip the tent, work his boots on and stumble around in the dark.

When he returned the duvet was back in place, and he eased back into bed. Maggie nestled alongside him. 'When're you going to move in?'

'Soon.'

She stroked his arm. He couldn't face asking the question that stood in the way. Not in bed. It could wait until the morning.

'Tell me a story, Mr Detective.'

'Once upon a time,' said Rick.

Maggie smiled. 'I've heard that one.'

'Three detectives took a bad man to a place with mountains.'

Maggie closed her eyes. 'I'm still listening.'

'The bad man was going to lead them to a boy who knew about an even badder man. One of the baddest men in the whole wide world. When they arrived, there'd been a terrible earthquake. Almost every building had been damaged and all the people were hurting. They met a teacher called Prakash. He'd already lost two brothers building football stadiums in Qatar – *temples*, he called them – and two more in the earthquake. Now, there's only him left. Yet still he managed a smile. The detective in charge and the bad man gave Prakash some money. The detective wondered if there was some good even in bad men. After trekking for many years, the detectives finally met the boy. His name was Ram. The bad man spoke to Ram, and the boy told the detectives what they wanted to know . . .

'Maggie,' murmured Rick, but she'd fallen asleep.

He finished the story without her: the bad man escaped but the detectives chased him. Up and down steep mountain passes, through many streams, across rocky terrain. They became very tired and very cross. Their feet wept with sores. But they found the bad man, and a few weeks later, they found the very bad man.

The detectives send the very bad man to prison for the rest of his life.

And the senior detective and his beautiful girlfriend live happily ever after. He kissed Maggie on the forehead and closed his eyes. He'd never tell her the full version.

In the kitchen Rick served out a generous helping of cereal and added milk from the fridge. He poured a large glassful of orange juice. Fridges: such a good invention. At the table, he sat down and ate a few mouthfuls. After trying the tongue twister on the back of the cereal packet, he pulled over the newspaper cuttings which Maggie had saved.

Nepalese deaths in Qatar reach 500.
FIFA President Blatter re-elected for a fifth term.
Blatter resigns following outcry over re-election.
Blatter to go, but to stay on until the spring.

Frontrunners to replace him were a Jordanian prince and Michel Platini, the UEFA president. Also one of the FIFA vice presidents, but no mention of which one. Possibly Terry Williams, father of twins Barney and Spencer kidnapped by Khetan.

Rick poured another glass of orange juice, fired up his laptop and worked up the letter he'd been thinking about half the night.

Maggie came in, wearing her dressing gown.

She kissed him, then filled a coffee pot and set it on the stove. Her kitchen was so clean and so full of gadgets and foodstuffs. Herbs, condiments, a veg rack. That fridge again.

'What do you want to do today?'

'I've got a few work things to tidy up.'

Maggie scrunched up her face. 'It's a Sunday.'

'Compromise? You help me this morning and we'll go out this afternoon.'

'O-*kay*.' She poured coffee into mugs and put the mugs on the table.

'First of all, can you read that.'

Dear family of Hari Subba,

I regret to inform you that Hari is the victim of a campaign of racial harassment. His flat has been daubed with graffiti and several windows have been smashed and excrement pushed through his letterbox.

We are doing all we can to help, and have already installed a panic alarm and stepped up local uniform patrols.

Hari is of course an ex-Ghurkha, and a proud and strong man. He has been very reluctant to accept our help, and has also refused any help from his friends and the local ex-servicemen support group. He may not even have told you about his problems.

We think the only answer is a visit from a close relative. That person or persons will be able to liaise better with us, and also with other ex-Ghurkhas.

Then, hopefully together, we can sort this problem out.

Please don't hesitate to call the number at the top of this letter if I can help.

Yours sincerely
PC 432 Richard Knight

'Why won't Hari's family simply ask his Nepalese neighbours to go round and see him? There're always strong links in migrant communities like the one in Aldershot. You need to add a line.' She paused. 'How about *Hari is refusing to engage with the local Nepalese community*.'

'Yes, like it.' Rick made a note.

'Do you think anyone will phone?'

'No. The obvious person in that family to sort it out is Khetan, and he won't. I've tried to imagine someone writing to me about Dad. If they said he was getting harassed, I'd go to him like a shot.'

Rick ticked his list. 'Have you booked a photographer?'

Flag Khetan, and link alias name
(Himal Limbu)	(Rick)	✓
Aldershot flat	(Maggie)	✓

'She's meeting you and Hunter in Aldershot at midday tomorrow, at an identical flat to Hari's. Can we go out now?'

'One more thing, Mags.' He took her hand and uncurled the fingers. 'About us.' Three prominent lines ran across the palm. Three children? 'Before I went away, you said you'd tell me.'

Maggie withdrew her hand. 'I did.'

'How about now?'

'I need to tell you something else first.'

Rick's heart started to thud. He closed the laptop.

'There was someone else, Rick. Someone before you.' He had a feeling he knew what was coming. 'Not just boyfriends.' She looked away. 'I used to be married. I was married back then. Married when I had legs.'

Her splatter of words was unusual. He waited for her to look at him. When she did, her eyes were watery.

'I thought you might have been.' He put his arm around her and moved closer. 'It's okay.'

'It's not okay, I should have told you.' She rested her head and wept quietly, her tears falling onto his shirt. 'How did you know?'

He smoothed her hair. 'The photos of your family cut in strange places, no photos of you. Rarely talking about special occasions in your past, not introducing me to your wider family. The canteen of silver cutlery in the dining room.'

'Why didn't you say?'

'I wanted you to tell me.'

Maggie took a deep breath. 'I was in the army. You know that. And that's where I met Ian, my husband. My ex-husband.'

'Okay.'

'We were in the same intake at Sandhurst – he was another officer cadet but heading to a different unit. After passing out we got married and bought a small house in Aldershot. Which is why I knew about the Ghurkhas there – and why it was easy for me to find a flat identical to Hari Subba's. We had our army careers, we had a house, and we had each other. Life looked good. And then I lost my legs.'

She looked away, then back at at Rick.

'Ironically, it was Ian who struggled to cope. When he came to see me in hospital he hardly touched me. A peck on the cheek and a brief squeeze of a hand. His visits became sporadic. I found out during rehab he'd been given compassionate leave. Which was then extended. Six months later, Ian left the army – and me.'

'*In sickness and in health.*'

'I don't blame him.'

'He was a soldier, you were a soldier. He must have thought about it.'

'Nobody thinks about it. Nobody thinks it'll happen to them. To somebody else, yes, but not to them.'

'Who do you blame?'

'Not him.'

Rick blamed him. Hated him. How could he have left her when she needed him? 'I'm sorry, Mags.' He held her hands.

'No, I'm sorry, I should have told you a long time ago.'

Mid-morning, Rick opened Maggie's front door.

Warm sunlight struck his face. A car drove past in the road. She hadn't been married long, and she was divorced now.

The rest of Sunday beckoned: brunch, a stroll in the country, and supper in a pub with the woman he loved. And maybe she'd tell him the rest.

38

Beads of sweat rolled along Robbo's forehead. The superintendent flicked his arm down, lengthening the telescopic baton with a click.

Rick held his ground, eyeing the weighted tip at the end of the baton, like someone staring at a swarm of bees. The tip delivered the punch. It looked like a small ice-hockey puck, and a strike held for a full second maximised the pain by spreading it through the leg.

He stepped forward. 'Come on then.'

Robbo struck him. A leg strike, then two to Rick's torso. His body shuddered each time and he dropped to the floor.

'Hands out to the sides, palms up.'

He did as he was told. The floor was cold against his cheek, and it vibrated as Robbo crashed the end of the baton into it. His boss holstered the baton, and pulled out his quick-cuffs.

PCs stopped to watch.

Robbo shoved a knee in Rick's back making him gasp, then grabbed his left hand and snapped a cuff over his wrist. His left arm was swung round and pushed into his lower back. Robbo weighed a tonne.

'Right hand.'

Rick swung his right arm back to mirror his left. The second cuff clicked shut and tightened. Then over-tightened, reminding him of restraining Coniston. He bit his cheek and lay there waiting.

'Okay, everyone,' shouted the officer safety trainer, 'that's it for your refresher. See you all next year.'

Condensation from the showers fogged the mirrors. Rick wiped one with a towel and set out his shaving kit. In the mirror, blurry images of colleagues changed for their next shift. The air smelt of sweat and deodorant, and carried a confusion of accents. He lathered his face and wiped the mirror again. His body ached, bruises already showing on his leg. Being paired up with Robbo wasn't unusual; they'd been the two senior ranks. But the ferocity of the strikes and the vicious handcuffing had surprised him. Both his wrists were bruised.

He swiped the razor and rinsed it in the basin. Perhaps he should have expected it, along with an impossible case-load, the worst management duties and being undermined in meetings. Their easy friendship in and out of work had simply ceased. Now they never talked unless they had to, even avoiding each other at the apiary. Moving stations seemed the only answer.

Next to the basin his phone rang. 'Rick Castle.'

'DCI Castle, South Manchester CID?'

'Yes.'

'Border force at Heathrow.'

Rick stared at the half-shaved face in the mirror. He looked gaunt. He hadn't put back the weight he'd lost in Nepal and he'd been back three months.

'Did you flag Himal Limbu, date of birth 31.05.1982? Himal Limbu, aka Hant Khetan, 30.09.1982?'

'Yes.'

'Well, he's here.'

244

Rick half-smiled at himself. 'I'll get a van organised.'

'I'm afraid, sir, that won't be necessary. When I say *here* I don't mean in a cell, I only mean in the country. There's been a cock-up.'

Rick put the phone down, gripped the basin and stared down into the water. Scum floated on the surface.

'Van for who?' At the other end of the mirrors, Robbo straightened his tie and epaulettes.

'Khetan.' Rick's sharp tone made the nearest two men stop talking and glance over. 'But they've not arrested him.'

'I thought you'd flagged him?' The tone matched Rick's and the silence of the nearest men spread.

'Big queue at passports – new guy made a mistake.'

'Case'll be the death of me,' said Robbo, banging out through the door. Conversations resumed.

In the fogged mirror, Rick scrawled *YES!*

Rick sat down at his office desk and ate a banana. The graffiti on Hari Subba's Aldershot flat had to become a reality, and quickly, before Khetan arrived. No guarantee Khetan would go there, but it was at least possible. Convincing Robbo that Rick also had to go there – with a team – would be totally impossible.

He stood up and looked out of the window. A tow truck waited to unload a public order van with a broken windscreen and dented bodywork. No one could argue the division didn't need every officer to combat the late summer spike in street crime. *But*, the centre didn't care about that. They'd be more interested in a high-profile arrest, something to fight their battles in the next funding round. He picked up the phone.

'Deputy Chief Constable Grayson, please. Tell him it's DCI Rick Castle, South Manchester CID.'

'Hold a minute.'

Rick stretched the phone cord to the window. A second public order van drove into the yard. PCs stepped out, hardly saying a word, and slumped down in the shade of the wall. A canteen assistant arrived with a crate of soft drinks and sandwiches.

'Grayson.'

'Sir, you won't remember me, but I was attached to your unit once. A murder you ran in Wigan, summer 2008.'

'Yes, DCI Castle.'

'To cut straight to it, I've got a chance to arrest Hant Khetan, FBI's Most—'

'I know who he is. How?'

As Rick explained, he watched the PCs outside gather round their sergeant for a briefing. They kept drinking, like runners after a race. A garage hand pulled down the security grille on their van and screwed it in place.

Rick put the phone down. The serial had a group hug and climbed back in the van. It drove out of the yard. Behind him someone cleared their throat.

Hunter stood in the doorway with Maggie. 'We've heard the news,' said the sergeant. He scratched the back of his ear. 'I'd eat my hat if I had one. But I ain't.'

In the yard the hydraulics on the tow truck screamed. Rick shut the window. Hunter remained cantankerous but at least he'd not mentioned Coniston's escape. Despite that, Rick still wasn't sure he could trust him, and wondered if Hunter was holding the escape back until needed.

'What's first?' said Maggie.

She'd been married once. So what.

'We have to do Hari's flat.'

Hunter rolled his eyes. 'That's what I said months ago.'

'You're serious?' said Maggie.

'Yes and no. We have to create the *impression* that he's been racially abused, and without him knowing it. So we have to get him out of his flat – and keep him out for a few days. Ideas?' Rick pulled up a flip chart and turned to a fresh sheet of paper.

'Just shout 'em out,' said Hunter.

Rick wrote on the chart:

Tell Hari he's won a holiday

Gas leak

'Making a film for TV,' said Maggie.

Rick marked it up, then waited. Marker pen on his fingers. Shouting in the yard.

'Gary?'

Hunter shook his head.

'Leave Hari in situ,' said Maggie, 'and arrest Khetan if and when he turns up.'

Rick added it to the board. 'But he might recce the address first.'

The desk phone rang.

'Did you phone the centre?' said Robbo.

'Why?'

'They've heard about Khetan being in the UK and they're interested. Distract the public from the unrest and the thin blue line.'

'It would.'

'Is that special back in the country?'

'Russell Weatherbeater – he is.'

'Okay, you've got one week. DCI Gibbs can cover but you'll owe him one. But just you and DS Hunter, and Weatherbeater. You'll have to arrange local arrest teams. And, Rick, before you head south, go and see Emma again. I don't want you blowing, not now.' The phone went dead.

'Gary,' said Rick, 'we're going to Aldershot. Maggie, I need you to run the incident room again.'

'Did Robbo clear it?'

'Either way,' said Hunter, 'I'm not going.' He slipped off a shoe and scratched his heel. 'Nothing personal.'

Rick sat in his car in the multistorey closest to Emma's office. He stared at the driving wheel, and kept staring.

He saw himself walking up the garden path in a smart neighbourhood with large houses. There's a PC standing by the front door. The PC says, they're upstairs, sir. Rick bends his head and goes into the hall. The thick curtains are drawn and it's dark. Wooden beams, old house. Flies buzz. He keeps his head low and heads to the staircase. Sunlight through a small window floods a halfway turn. The bloody footprints of paramedics mark the carpet. A wide landing at the top, lots of options. He peers into the first bedroom and the second. They're in the third. Three cots in a row and above them a zoo mobile. Blood spatter on the ceiling and on the mobile.

The children's father had shot himself. But it wasn't enough: it felt like he'd got away.

Rick started his car and drove out of the car park, heading to the apiary. Where he could smell the autumn leaves and watch the bees. Let his circadian rhythms relax and attune.

And afterwards, before he collected Hunter and drove to Aldershot, there would be just enough time to call in on Dad.

At Three Views the two of them sat in the lounge. Cups of cold weak tea and crumbs of cheap biscuits littered the tables. Snippets of conversation reached across from the dozen residents and visitors but nothing made much sense. Always worse before mealtimes, according to Michael.

'You know my son's a policeman?'

Rick held the dice cup stationary and looked across the backgammon board. If he'd thought Dad's question was a moment of lucidity, a sudden break in the clouds of his dementia when everything – past and present – had become clear, then it would almost have been funny. But it wasn't.

'He's a chief superintendent in London. At Paddington.'

Rick nodded, and shook the dice. They'd played backgammon when he was a child, on Sunday nights, *to warm your brain up before school in the morning*. He turned the cup upside down and the dice rolled out. One dot and two dots.

His dad smiled. Rick moved two black counters. Dad collected the dice, and shook again. The dice rattled in the cup. Pot plants filled the nearest windowsill, and below them, covering up the chequered carpet, lay crinkly brown leaves.

Dad threw the dice across the board.

Double six.

Rick would have paid for it. Dad smiled again.

After the game and he'd said goodbye, Rick stopped by the office. Michael sat tapping away at the computer but looked up.

'Who won?'

Rick smiled. Behind Michael, the notice-board bulged with duty rosters, check-lists, and residents' details. 'How is he?'

'Going slowly downhill – you know that. How're you?'

In the Three Views car park Rick picked at his nails. Rain drummed on the roof and dripped down the windscreen. He closed his eyes. Going slowly downhill, the same as Dad.

39

Rick peered through the blind, marching his fingers through the dust. The yellow wallpaper hung in peeling curls and the whole flat smelt musty. But, from the first-floor window he could look down and diagonally across at the front door of Hari Subba's flat, number 43 Stanley Close – and it was only forty metres away.

'It's perfect. How long can we have it?'

'As long as,' replied the Aldershot crime squad DS who stood in the centre of the room, cradling his phone. 'Estate agent's a friendly.'

In his mid-twenties and with shaved hair, Foulds looked the typical hardball crime squad sergeant. Every division in the country had a similar unit, ready at a moment's notice to solve a problem. Rick's request was straightforward: surveillance from an observation point with the aim of arresting a suspect. Khetan's status had gone down well at the briefing, but Rick's name had caused whispering at the back.

'Half an hour before they knock on.'

Foulds nodded. 'I'll stand the van down.'

Rick left him to watch and went to look around. Even before they'd properly set up there was a chance that Khetan might show. Possible he'd been already, even with one of Foulds' team watching from the back of a van since Rick's first phone call.

There were three rooms in addition to the front room. The bedroom was empty except for a phone sitting on a dog-eared *Yellow Pages*. Rick tried it, but the line was dead. He glanced at the pink paisley wallpaper in the bathroom, and went into the kitchen. Four wooden chairs and a small table. He opened the fridge door. The stench from a can of dog food flooded out, and he pushed the door shut.

He opened a window, and heard faint announcements from a railway station tannoy. The open window was a tell-tale and a risk, but they might be there a week, or longer. The small lawn was overgrown and behind it a line of tall fir trees screened the alley. Crows flapped in the treetops. A line of flattened grass led from the gate to the back of the flats. Another tell-tale, but again they'd have to risk it. Using the alley to enter the OP was ideal: plenty of people used it to get from the close to the nearby shops.

Recce over, he slotted together a couple of chairs and walked back to the front room.

'Anything?'

'Nothing.'

'Kitchen window needs whitewashing.'

'I'll sort it.'

Rick picked up the *A to Z* and looked up Hari's address. Stanley Close was an egg-shaped cul-de-sac, number 43 in the top right quadrant, the OP in the top left. Between the OP and Hari's flat there was a second alley connected to the main one. He went over to the window to see if he could see it.

'Where's the second alley between us and Hari's flat?'

'Just to the right of the garden with the bird table,' said Foulds, not turning from the window.

Rick looked around the close. The grey pebbledash flats had been built in blocks containing two storeys of four flats. Number

43 was a mid-terrace with a front garden. 'Hari's is the one with the hydrangeas?'

'Big pink and white jobs?'

'Yes.'

'And forty-three on the door.'

Rick double-checked, but the number wasn't there. Foulds, he thought, would get on well with Russell. Not so well with Hunter. No one did.

An ice-cream van drove in, tune jangling. It parked up. Rick could just see the junction with Wolfs Drive where it had entered. 'It's possible that Khetan might arrive in a car.' He watched an old woman shuffle out to the van.

'Only one vehicular access. It's a close, boss.'

'Thank you, Neil.'

'I've borrowed a stinger from traffic. If they unroll it across the road next to the post box, and then park their car on the opposite pavement, there'll be a barrier all the way across. We've done it before.'

Foulds answered his phone. Rick watched the ice-cream van drive out of the cul-de-sac.

'Not tonight. I can't. I told you, I'm working late.'

Rick checked his watch: 5.30pm. Hunter and Russell should have arrived. But the close was deserted, except for two young boys riding around on BMXs. He was beginning to have a good feeling about the operation. The OP was good, Foulds was efficient, the tactic original: Khetan really might fall for it.

But where were his colleagues?

A pushchair emerged from the right. The young Asian mother, possibly Nepalese, pushed it across the close towards Wolfs Drive. Rick checked the *A to Z*. Wolfs Primary School lay behind him, and the alley behind the OP started in the school entrance.

Foulds put the phone in his pocket and turned to Rick. 'I was thinking: Khetan might turn up at night. We're not supposed to work round the clock, health and safety and all that. But we will, of course.'

'We'll run a listening post at night: eyes and ears in here rather than full arrest teams. When do the kids go back to school?'

'Next week.'

A large minibus pulled up. *Forest Green Day Centre.* Two men in staff t-shirts helped people out. One man in a wheelchair lowered down on the rear lift. Watching made Rick think of Dad, then of Maggie. Still no sign of Hunter, so he sat down and drew a sketch map of the close. He positioned the two arrest cars: Alpha One next to the parade of shops to cover the alleyway, and Alpha Two on Wolfs Drive, to deal with vehicles entering or exiting the close.

'Boss, I don't want to be rude, but the lads are talking. You're the Manchester deathcop, aren't you? Twenty-five deaths in a week, said the paper.'

Rick clicked his pen in and out half a dozen times. 'Don't believe what you read in the papers, Neil, you should know that by now.'

'So it's not true, then?'

'Seventeen.'

'Six is my record.'

Rick went into the kitchen and stood by the sink. He wasn't safe even in Aldershot. He rinsed a glass and filled it.

'Boss.'

'Sir.'

'DCI Castle!'

Rick had no idea how long he'd been standing there, but he wrenched the tap closed and ran into the front room.

Khetan?

His stomach lurched.

'They're here.'

For a second Rick was disappointed. But he joined Foulds at the window, and the two of them peered through the dusty blind like middle-aged executives at a peep-show.

A van with ladders on the roof had parked near Hari's flat. *Smith & Son, Painters & Decorators. No Job Too Small.*

Hunter and Russell climbed out and walked down the path of number 43. Hunter wore white dungarees, heavily paint-stained. He walked with his hands in his pockets and a pencil perched behind his ear. Well-versed, he'd told Rick. Armed robberies were dying out in the capital, so the flying squad were turning proactive and targeting major crime groups. He'd posed as postmen, TV crew and meter readers, anything that involved a reflective jacket and a clipboard. Painter and decorator was an easy one and he even owned a set of overalls.

Russell knocked on the door. Acting as Hunter's translator, he wore a shirt and tie. He knocked again.

The door opened, and a small Nepalese-looking man stood on the threshold. Rick raised his binoculars. The man wore a *topi*, the traditional Nepalese hat, and baggy clothing. *Star Wars* slippers.

The man kept a hand on the door, and a discussion began. Hunter spoke, Russell translated, and the man nodded or shook his head.

Hunter passed over a letter which confirmed the man was Hari. Dated three weeks ago, it purported to be from Rushmoor council and advised Hari that he would have to move out to a local hotel while his flat was repainted.

Hari disappeared into his flat, followed by Hunter and Russell. The door closed.

Foulds went to the bathroom and Rick watched the close. A crow landed on the road and pecked around. He heard more rail announcements and a train braking. The two young boys sat next to their bikes and threw stones at the crow until it flew away. They set up a ramp and took turns to launch themselves over a traffic cone. A straggle of early commuters walked through the close.

Foulds came back. The two of them watched the boys trying to do tricks. Wheelies and hops, on one wheel and sideways. One boy lay down lengthways at the end of the ramp.

Hari's door opened and Hunter stepped outside, pulling the door behind him. He made a phone call.

Rick answered.

'He won't go. Says he'll stay, he won't get in the way and he makes a good cup of *chee-ah,* whatever the fuck that is. Russ says it's tea but I wouldn't like it.'

'I'm sure you can persuade him.'

'He's an old man!'

'Offer him fifty quid of expenses.'

Hunter went back inside the flat, leaving Rick to rue that his moral positioning was now lower than Hunter's.

Khetan to Blame.

For Everything.

The second boy raced down the road towards the ramp but as he reached it the boy lying prone rolled out of the way. The boys shared a cigarette, the smoke clearly visible in the warm still air.

Another line of commuters took the short cut home.

Two male joggers ran out of the alley. One white, one Asian. Rick felt his heart quicken but the runner was too tall to be Khetan.

More commuters. One woman bent to remove a stone from her shoe.

Rick swept dust along the blind.

Finally, Hunter, Russell and Hari emerged from the flat. Hunter carried a small brown holdall and they were smiling and talking.

Hari was out.

Lift off!

Rick sat down at the table and removed a clip of photos, copies of the ones sent to Hari's relations in Saklis showing the graffiti and damage to the flat. Except that it wasn't Hari's flat, but an identical one in some other Aldershot estate. He took measurements with a ruler, and made some notes for Russell and Hunter. Three large stripes and two smaller stripes would do it. The idea to show Khetan the graffiti had been painted over without causing any actual offence. Sitting in the OP and seeing the plan take shape, Rick felt excited as a burglary squad trainee running his first obbo.

He balanced a coin on the edge of the table, flicked it up and caught it. Slapped it on the back of his hand. Heads they got the painting done before Khetan turned up. Tails they didn't.

Foulds answered his mobile and spoke briefly, then flipped the phone shut. 'Hari's on his way to the Travelodge and my men will monitor him there. Your two will start the painting shortly.'

Rick took his hand away.

Tails.

Best of three, or twenty-three, or a hundred and three. However many it took.

40

Calix sat on the end of a bench in the exercise yard. Cons shuffled around the perimeter in twos and threes, and kicked a football. A pair of guards patrolled, and more guards observed from a tower. Cameras swivelled on the high walls.

Beyond them, cranes worked in a nearby building site and into the yard came the splutter of diesel engines, the whining of drills, and the heavy *whump* of jack hammers. Occasionally there was a brief silence, and if Calix listened hard, he could hear the faint sounds of schoolchildren.

The bench was wooden, not slate like the ones in Nepal. Already, they seemed a lifetime ago. He'd been unlucky, very unlucky, to engage a Nepalese thief as a bagman. And Castle had been lucky, very lucky.

The long dull days were back.

Lock up, greyness, sameness. The pervasive smell of boiled cabbage and drains. Walls of dirty brick and razor wire and broken glass. Jangle of keys and doors. Barking of dogs, and shouting of hopeless men.

Megan would never give up. He would never give up on Khetan, on his promise to his old man.

Two men sat down. They nodded at Calix and offered him their cigarette. He shook his head and stood up.

Dark clouds lined up in the distance. Calix listened for the children, but couldn't hear them.

He slipped into the shuffling circuit of men and walked. No one was chasing him. No one was interested in him. He reached the wall of an accommodation wing, eight storeys high. He could walk with his eyes closed, the cons' feet having worn a path like a goat trail.

In the shadow of the wall Calix saw the wing of a bird. He stepped away from the path and bent closer. Small, not moving. He crouched down. The wing of a young bird, maybe only a few weeks old. As it became aware of him the bird fluttered, but moved only a few inches and stayed on the ground. Calix cupped the bird, and clicked gently. 'Easy, girl, easy.'

'What you found?' said the man shambling behind.

'Stone in my shoe.'

'Call these shoes?'

Calix tucked the bird into the pocket he'd added at the bottom of his trousers. Into the small *khalti*, the word reminding him of his first trip to Nepal when he'd had special pockets sewn into his trailpants. He glanced behind him at the waiting man, cleaning his glasses.

'You going or what?'

Calix walked on. Each time putting his right foot down with care, rolling it from the outside. Looked like he was limping. He needed to stop, to check on the baby pigeon, but prisoners and guards and rules were funny things. Impossible to argue with, but possible to circumvent, like rivers—

Or Castle. There was still the letter. If the senior dibble didn't come good on his promise to write to Calix's trial judge, then he would reveal to the press all the sensational detail of what had taken place in Nepal.

Locked back in his cell Calix put a towel on the table. He ripped up a t-shirt and wrapped thin strips around the hot water pipe. Resting his foot on a chair he took the injured bird out from his trouser leg pocket. New cellmate Toose watched him from the top bunk. The pigeon was a young female, only three or four months old. Blue-grey with dark wingbars, and a purple sheen on her neck, like jewellery. He laid her on the towel and folded it around. All the time stroking her head and whispering. 'Easy, girl. Easy.'

Toose jumped off the bunk and loomed over his shoulder. 'So yous gonna look after this one?' He dropped down to the floor and began to do press-ups.

Calix nodded, still stroking and whispering. 'Easy, easy.'

Toose paused, mid press-up. 'How yous decide, help or no?'

'I sort of know,' said Calix, washing his hands. He scrubbed his nails. The only prisoner, Toose said, that owned a nail brush. He filled the kettle and switched it on.

He pulled away the towel and examined the young pigeon. Her eyes flickered open and shut and her heartbeat was faint. He felt her body for an injury but found nothing. He felt her head. He extended a wing and pressed gently with his fingers. All seemed okay. Pulling out the second wing he found the problem. A clear bump and twist in the feathers. Probing gently with his fingers he found a break in the thinner of the two bones. The radius, same as the human forearm.

'So's?' said Toose, standing up and breathing hard.

'Good and bad. A bone in the wing is broken and bent, but it's not pierced the skin. And she's a pigeon: pigeons are Glaswegians of the bird world.'

'Fucking ay.' Toose gripped his bicep. 'Can yous fix her, chief?'

'Maybe, but I need to borrow a needle.'

'Nae problem.'

While Toose rummaged in the floor behind the bog, Calix filled a mug with boiling water. He added sugar and salt, and stirred until they dissolved. He took the pieces of t-shirt from the pipe and used them to strap the injured wing to the pigeon's body and healthy wing. The final strip he tied in a bow. It was far from perfect but good enough. He felt the temperature in the electrolyte solution with a fingertip. Then, holding the young pigeon with one hand, her head between his thumb and forefinger, he squeezed open her beak and pushed Toose's syringe into the back of her mouth. She didn't like it, but she was weak and seemed resigned to her fate.

His cellmate began to sing softly. 'Yous dain good, yous dain good. Nows slee-eeps, nows slee-eeps.' The harsh accent defeated by his intent.

Calix straightened the pigeon's neck so it was easier to aim for the oesophagus and push the syringe down into her crop. Too far might pierce the crop and lead to further problems. He pushed down gently on the plunger.

Toose crooned some more.

Calix sucked up more of the electrolyte, and repeated the process. 'Most birds are at least ten per cent dehydrated, much more if they've been injured.' He gave her to Toose to hold.

In the corner of the room the hot water pipe jinked around a bend in the wall. Calix stuffed clothes behind the right-angle of pipe and spread a towel on top. He took the pigeon from Toose and set her down. Toose knelt by the pigeon like a new dad.

Calix lay down on his bunk.

She probably wouldn't make it but either way he needed a name for her. He wondered how Bird Bird was faring, whether she still called at his attic window, and Beetle Beetle, who'd escaped when he'd been turned over by the Nepalese highwayman masquerading as a farmer.

He settled on Girl.

And hoped Gopi had swallowed one of the cyanide pills. Serve the thief right.

His mum sat down in the visitors' hall. Gloves, no make-up or perfume. She'd learnt, and Calix was sorry she'd had no choice. Behind her, the sound of scraping chairs and a blur of yabbering cons and their relations.

'You look well, you've caught the sun. But you've got a bruise.'

'Playing football in the exercise yard.'

She nodded, not believing. Her eyes were bloodshot and her face pale. 'Did you say a prayer on the bridge?'

Calix gripped the table legs. The one thing she'd asked him to do, the one thing. On top of a failed mission. He looked away. One visitor was already leaving. He looked back at his mum. 'Of course I did.' He wiped the corners of his eyes.

'I miss him.' She braced herself, fiddled out a tissue. 'Didn't think I would.'

The lone con started humming to himself.

'I've got some bad news, Calix, about your grandad.' She waited for him to nod. 'Joe died while you were in Nepal. In his sleep, he didn't suffer.'

Calix winced. Joe, his old man's old man who'd come round every Sunday for lunch. He always took the carving knife out of the drawer and sharpened it with the steel, even if they weren't having a roast. He'd taught Calix how to use it, and the whetstone, and how to sharpen the axes and tools in the shed.

'The date for the funeral's not been decided. Do you think?'

Calix shook his head. 'Sorry.' He closed his eyes. It was only three weeks to his trial but even if Castle wrote to the judge, there was no way he'd be released from custody for his grandad's funeral.

'He left you some money, quite a lot: twenty-five thousand pounds. I've put it in your account for when you come out.'

'Time, ladies, please!'

The visitors shuffled out, his mum the last to go. Wearing her long mac and sturdy brown shoes. And thin as a stick.

Calix kicked back his chair which toppled and clattered to the floor. He picked it up and slammed it under the table. Sorry was cheap.

41

'Standby, standby. Possible approaching from Wolfs Drive into Stanley Close. Asian male, blue baseball hat, grey top, blue jeans. Alpha Two.'

Hunter peered through the dusty blind. 'That's received, Alpha Two. To confirm, possible for suspect one now approaching target. Control.'

'Received, Alpha One.'

Rick jogged to the window, and stared out at the fifth possible sighting. Already it was day three. The man walked towards the OP. A supermarket delivery van drove up. The driver climbed out and a shutter clattered open.

Russell came to the window.

Fifty metres.

Khetan?

Forty metres. The man in the baseball hat was oblivious as a deer approaching stalkers. Behind him, the delivery man hefted crates to a front door only three up from Hari's.

The arrest cars were in place. Each three-up, and crewed by Foulds and his team. Both were proving reliable and competent so when the time came there shouldn't be a problem. There were always problems.

'Possible still approaching target. Thirty metres.'

Rick stared at the small man through binoculars. He was smoking a cigarette. Khetan smoked – Barney and Ram had told them. And the man was about the right height, about the right age, about the right build. But he had his baseball cap pulled down tight.

'Russell?'

'Could be.'

'Hunter?'

'Only seen photos.' His sergeant pressed the transmit button. 'Standby. Male now at gate of target.'

Russell clicked away with the camera. No one answered the delivery driver's knocking. The Asian man turned and stared at Hari's address.

If the man in the baseball hat was Khetan, he couldn't miss Hari's flat. Three straightish fat white stripes made it look like a giant national flag. Opening the gate increased the probability of Khetan but didn't confirm it. And if he walked past, it didn't mean he wasn't Khetan because he could be having a recce.

Rick had established a protocol to confirm either way. Each possible would be followed away from Stanley Close and at a safe distance stopped and his identity confirmed. If he left on foot, then Alpha One or Alpha Two would drop a footie to follow. If he left in a vehicle, then Alpha Two would follow and request a marked unit to pull it over. Following the protocol meant if Khetan was watching Hari's flat, then he wouldn't be spooked.

The man in the baseball hat walked past the gate and around the curve of Stanley Close. He took a drag on the cigarette and flicked it into the road. The driver of the supermarket van reloaded his crates and drove away. Two boys on BMX bikes – the same two boys from three days earlier – rode past the van, one giving the driver the finger.

'Possible is now into alley B,' said Hunter. 'And a loss to control. Alpha One, standby to drop footies.'

'Received, Alpha One.'

Rick listened as the protocol swung into action, his hopes rising for a fifth time. The first two possibles had been delivery drivers, one in a car and one in an unmarked van. A third had entered number 57 and after emerging two hours later had been stopped by Alpha Two on Broadoak Road. The fourth had entered from alley A, sat on a nearby fire hydrant playing with his phone and then wandered away via Wolfs Drive.

'Footies are down, Alpha One.'

'Thoughts?' said Rick.

Hunter shrugged.

'Why walk around the curve of the pavement to the alley?' said Russell. 'Quicker to cut across the road. Everyone else has.'

Hunter pressed his radio. 'Foxtrot One, Foxtrot Two, either of you got eyes yet?'

'Negative, Foxtrot One.'

'Negative, Foxtrot Two.'

A second minute ticked by.

A third minute.

A fourth minute.

'Jesus!'

'Maybe,' said Russell, 'he's making a call or having a piss.'

'Long bloody piss,' said Hunter.

'Sounds painful,' said Russell.

Hunter clapped.

'Russell, check out the back. Use the kitchen – we need to find out what's happening in the alley. Gary, send a footie down the alley.' A front door banged shut. Rick glanced out and saw a woman setting off to walk her dog, a skinny miniature.

'Foxtrot One, control.'

'Foxtrot One.'

'It's a loss in the alley. So we want you to do a walk through. Alley A into alley C, and check alley B as you go past. Exit from Stanley Close into Wolfs Drive. Take a roundabout route back to Alpha One.'

'Received, Foxtrot One.'

Rick took a radio into the kitchen and stood in the doorway. 'Anything?'

'No.' Russell stood hunched by the window, looking out through the hole in the whitewash.

Above the hob the ceiling was shiny-black with grease. Curling brown newspapers stuck out from the top of the cupboards.

'Here's someone. No, wait – it's the Aldershot guy: Foxtrot One.'

Rick relayed the information on the radio. Pencil marks and dates were written on the jamb of the doorway. He bent to look closer. Initials to go with dates: children's heights? Grandchildren's?

'No one in the alley, Foxtrot One.'

'Unless Foxtrot Two missed him,' said Russell, 'he must have entered a garden backing onto the alley.'

'Yeah, but why?' said Rick. 'Why not enter from the front?' If he and Maggie had kids, he would record their heights in his kitchen.

'Up to no good? Nicking or dealing.'

Rick returned to the lounge and made a few notes.

'Control, Foxtrot Two.'

'Go ahead.' Hunter used the radio antenna to scratch his neck.

'I'm back in Alpha One, so is Foxtrot One. We've moved position so we can see the end of alley A but no trace of the possible. Only a woman with a rat of a dog, a white man and two elderly Asians.'

Rick spoke into the radio. 'Anything of interest in the alley?'

'The usual rubbish and dog crap. A few used condoms.'

'Any ideas?'

'Neil's going to phone you, sir.'

Rick pressed the green symbol on his phone.

'Could be a girl working along there,' said Foulds. 'I've spoken to our intel unit and they're checking. If that is where baseball-hat man has gone, then he should reappear pretty soon. Otherwise, it might be a big nothing: some people use the alley to access the houses alongside.'

Rick pressed the red symbol. Might be nothing, but *might* be Khetan. He updated Hunter, then went into the kitchen and told Russell. 'You okay in here for a bit longer?'

The special constable nodded, and kept looking out.

'How's your dad?'

'Okay,' said Rick. 'How's Jacob?'

'You know what happened?'

'Some.'

Russell turned from the window. 'He'd started snooping. Seen too many films, thought he was a PI, Magnum or someone.'

'Keep watching.'

The special turned back to the window. 'He stumbled into it – literally. He saw the father of one of his friends with a woman in a parked car. Jacob told his friend who told his mum. And she paid Jacob thirty quid to find out a bit more. One thing led to another and within a few months he had two more enquiries. He's good with computers and was able to dig online as well as do the legwork.'

'What happened?'

'One fella spotted him and reported him as stalking. It got a bit nasty. They thought I might be involved – through my access to police databases as a special. I was suspended for a month.'

'A mess,' said Rick. 'Any movement in the alley?'

'No.'

'Let me know the second there is.'

Rick picked up Russell's newspaper, and went into the bedroom. He sat down on the floor and leant back against the wall. His dad wasn't okay – every visit he was worse. He seemed happy enough but goldfish happy. Maybe that *was* okay.

His phone buzzed.

'Anything?' said Maggie.

He told her about the man in the blue baseball hat. A possible, but somehow he'd disappeared.

Rick dragged his fingers across the greasy carpet, and settled on a matchstick. He imagined the old man sitting in bed, lighting a cigarette and flicking away the match. Watching it cartwheel through the air. Listless as—

Someone in prison.

'I've had an idea, Maggie. If Khetan doesn't turn up today, I'm going to have another go at Coniston in Strangeways.'

'You can come and see me.'

'If there's time. Can you tell Robbo.'

Rick put the phone down. He struck the match on a leg of the bed, and watched it flare into a hazy orb of white and gold. And die back, and burn down the stick, and, finally, expire.

42

Girl was showing signs of improvement. Her eyes no longer flickered open and shut, and her heartbeat was stronger. The young pigeon could walk about, but often fell over due to the strapped-up wing. Toose had hardly left her side.

It was time.

The lack of an anaesthetic remained a problem. They had ibuprofen and there was an active ingredient in cough mixture to which Toose was addicted. Calix was also unsure how to administer the pseudo-anaesthetic – intravenously or tube-feeding into the crop. He watched Toose scrabble behind the bog for a syringe. Puncture-marked and lean as a hunger-striker, his cellmate passed it over. The answers were staring Calix in the face.

'My gear?'

'She'd only need the tiniest of drops, barely enough to see.'

'Git tae fuck.'

Toose removed the cement pieces for a second time. Calix boiled the kettle and sterilised the syringe. Toose prepared the weakest solution he could. Calix scooped up the young pigeon and felt for the vein on the side of her neck. Using the syringe, he sucked up a tiny drop of the solution on Toose's spoon and injected Girl. He laid her back down. If he'd judged it right, she'd be out for an hour or two. Wrong, and that would be the end of Girl.

Toose turned off the TV and shuffled up a chair. His breath smelt like a blocked sink.

Calix re-boiled the kettle, cleared the table and laid out his equipment. Toothbrush fitted with a razor blade. Scissors. Curved metal tie from a bread bag. Syringe. Sharpened piece of wire. Thread from a button ripped off a shirt. He'd have liked his Anglepoise and his tray of gleaming tools. He sterilised the metalwork. He scrubbed up, and flapped his hands in the air while Toose washed his hands. As rare as a full moon.

Calix picked up Girl, unwound the strapping and laid it aside. He scratched her neck with his long thumbnail, grown back after Nepal. She seemed unconscious, her eyes closed but her chest moving. He snipped off the feathers to expose the patch of skin covering the break in the bone. Red, sore and bumpy.

'Dain okay to smoke?'

Calix glanced over his shoulder. Toose clamped the cigarette in his mouth but put the lighter back in his pocket.

With the toothbrush-blade Calix made cuts down the wing, each side of the fracture. He peeled the flap of skin down, like a door on an Advent calendar. In the thin pale flesh, the two bone ends protruded at sixty degrees. Toose inhaled sharply on his unlit cigarette. Calix straightened the two pieces of bone into a straight line so the broken ends touched. He cut the metal tie of the bread bag so it would wrap around the bones one and a half times. Any longer and it would be too difficult to remove. He hugged it around the bone ends so they couldn't move. He folded the flap back up.

'Belting,' said Toose, sucking on his cigarette.

'Wire.'

Toose passed the makeshift needle and Calix used it to make

holes in the skin. He threaded the cotton in a blanket stitch and tied the ends. He replaced the strapping and laid Girl back in the apple box.

'Fucking ay,' said Toose. He checked the temperature of the hot water pipe, then held up his cigarette.

Calix nodded. He looked out of the window, through the bars and the smudges and the cobwebs. Another wing playing football, another circle of shambling prisoners. In prison most days were as long as years.

But not today.

The wicket clanged open. 'Coniston.'

Calix turned around.

'Dibble are here,' said the face in the hole.

In the interview room Calix sat down, still thinking about leaving Toose with Girl. He'd told him to leave her alone and to let her rest, even if she regained consciousness. But a prisoner like Toose was as predictable as an octopus. The dibble allegation against him proof enough.

Hunter rapped on the table. 'Anyone at ho-ome?'

'How's the head?' said Castle.

Calix felt the slug-shaped weal, and for a moment he returned there. To the barn and the waymarker: *Bhandar – 6 hours, Jiri – 12 hours.* Sitting down in the barn, Gopi pacing up and down outside. Gopi hitting him. He owed the farmer, like he owed Khetan, but as with Khetan he had no chance of doing anything about it.

'We want to talk about my letter to the judge,' said Castle.

For a moment Calix daydreamed of a return visit to Nepal to help them look for Khetan. A second chance to avoid a long prison sentence. Hunter winked at him and scratched the back of his hands.

'You won't be surprised that I haven't written it, but I will, if you help us out.' Looking earnest as a recruit, Castle looked directly at Calix. 'Khetan's here – in the UK.'

Castle continued to stare, but Hunter looked half-asleep. They must be playing with him. He wondered if Girl was conscious and whether the stitches were holding. His gran had taught him blanket stitch, had said she'd taught his old man, too. His old man mended clothes and repaired his gear, part of army self-reliance.

'But we don't know where,' said Castle. 'Khetan must have an associate in the UK. Tell us, and I'll write that letter.'

Maybe they weren't playing. Castle seemed genuine; he always did.

Calix's family was a family of ghosts. Only two things mattered: Girl surviving, and getting Khetan. He took a breath.

'He'll assume you're trying to trace him, and he'll be paranoid about phones and computers. He worked in telecoms.'

'Go on,' said Castle.

Calix said nothing. If Khetan was arrested he'd get sent to prison, probably Belmarsh. Unlikely to be Manchester. But prisons were as connected as motorways, and there might be a way.

'Calix, this is your last chance. We're not coming back.'

Castle had called him Calix only once before, on the suspension bridge in Nepal. When he'd told Castle about puddling and butterflies, and the senior dibble had said he kept bees. Explained the likelihood of his bees swarming while he was away.

Castle kept bees, and said he understood about Khetan. Maybe he'd understand about Girl. 'Last year,' said Calix, 'Khetan had someone in the UK who did things for him: got things, sorted things out. A Mr Fix-it.'

'What things?'

'Anything, I think. Cost though.'

'He *thinks*,' said Hunter, closing his eyes. 'Sounds like Hollywood to me.'

'False documents,' said Calix. 'PNC details. Other stuff.'

'Why didn't you tell us this before?'

'Because you wouldn't have taken me to Nepal.'

Castle's eyes glinted. He knew it was the truth. 'Does this Mr Fix-it have a name?'

'Manoj.'

'Second name?'

'Ager – *Agasti.* He's also from Nepal – started off driving for Khetan but moved on. Now manages a restaurant near Leicester Square, called K2.'

Castle glanced to his left.

Hunter's eyes remained closed. 'I know it.'

The dibble jostled their chairs and stood by the door. Castle turned around. 'One more question: Khetan smokes Surya in Nepal, but what about in the UK?' The door swung open and Hunter stepped out into the corridor.

'Did they swarm?' Calix half-whispered.

Castle nodded. Slowly, his face pained.

'Marlboro,' said Calix.

Castle nodded, and followed his colleague. Their footsteps drummed away, and the door swung shut. The room smelt like a chicken coop.

43

At South Manchester, Hunter detoured to the canteen, but Rick went straight to the incident room to find Maggie. She wasn't there, but two doors along the corridor in the intelligence unit, she was working on a standalone. Two colleagues sat nearby.

Rick touched Maggie's shoulder. Her colleagues exchanged glances but said nothing.

She turned, squeezed his hand. 'Isn't that against the rules?'

Rick replied in kind. 'Anything on Manoj Agasti?'

Maggie nodded. 'Lots. I phoned the intel unit at West End Central and chatted up my opposite number. Turns out they've got a camera near the K2 restaurant. I explained it was urgent and she emailed me the footage straight away.'

'Khetan?'

'Yes. The day after he landed at Heathrow, he visited the K2. He came out again twenty minutes later. Each time he was by himself, and no sign of a vehicle.'

'Was he carrying anything?'

'Not obviously.'

'Has he been back?'

'Rick, that's three days of film. It'll take a while. I've also been researching Agasti. He served a year for supplying fraudulent docs. Part of an attempted murder investigation which never went anywhere – about five years back. Clean, apart from that.'

'Intel?'

'Various reports, several different sources, saying he provides information and puts criminals in touch with other criminals. A sort of criminals' LinkedIn.'

'Well done, Mags. Agasti gives us another lead if Khetan doesn't show at Aldershot. Can you watch the rest of the footage asap?'

Maggie nodded, and glanced round at her colleagues who were passing sticky notes.

'Hunter and me need to get back down to Aldershot. Khetan could strike at any minute, and I want to be there.'

'I was thinking, Rick. Well, I've been thinking since you drove down south.' She nodded behind her. 'Can we go somewhere?'

'Hunter's grabbing a bite, we've got a few minutes.'

Rick pushed open the emergency exit door – *Warning, qualified personnel only* – and stepped out onto the roof of the police station. Until the Khetan case, he'd been an instinctive rule-follower, but rules now seemed to be for other people. Two more broken in ten minutes, and he'd led Maggie astray both times.

She followed him out, the breeze pulling at her hair.

'Never been up here.' She smiled at their complicity.

At the guard rail they looked down at the back yard, five storeys below. The van waited outside the custody cage.

Rick leant back on the bar, his fingers twisting off curls of rusty paint. He looked across the rows of suburban housing with their tiny gardens like beer mats.

'How did it go with Emma?'

'It didn't.'

'You have to talk to her. Otherwise the SMT will deem you unfit for duty.'

'She keeps saying I should take you with me. Anyway, how're you?'

'Okay,' said Maggie.

'You don't sound it. I thought the Siobhan thing had gone away.'

'It has. She's really on the sick now: had a double mastectomy – came from nowhere. I went to see her. She's alright really. Makes you think though, doesn't it?' Maggie stared out at the city. 'It's made me realise, Rick, that I need to tell you what happened to me before any more time passes.'

An aeroplane roared overhead. One of the new Dreamliners, its wheels down, heading for Manchester airport.

'I know you were in the sappers, Maggie. What kind of sapper were you?'

She half-smiled. 'Bomb disposal. I was in the Royal Logistic Corps.' She paused. 'I lost my legs in Afghanistan – in Helmand.' Tears wet her face.

Rick's stomach turned over.

'We defused IEDs, made safe conventional weapons. I just wasn't a very good one.' She laughed between her tears. She dabbed at her eyes with a tissue.

'Why didn't you want to tell me?' He felt cold all over.

'Lots of reasons, but mainly I didn't want you to know I'd been married before. I worried it might stop you getting, you know, serious. Also, I didn't want you to think, like Ian, there was something wrong with me.'

'*Is* there something wrong with you?'

Maggie smiled. 'Thanks. I like hearing it even though I don't believe you. There's also another reason – I wanted you to know only the new me, not someone I once was. You either wanted to be with me or you didn't, but at least there'd be no wishing that time could go backwards or things had turned out differently.'

Rick nodded.

Maggie ran her hands over the arms of her chair. 'Anyway, I can't do anything about it: I haven't got any legs. I don't want to even think about before: county hockey, running, basketball not wheelchair basketball. Police analyst, wheelchair basketball, a ground-floor flat, asking people to reach things in shops: they're the new me. It's not all bad. I like my job.'

Rick took Maggie's hands, and squeezed. He kissed the top of her head.

Together, they stared across the Manchester skyline. Minshull Street Crown Court with its steeple and clock. The Civil Justice Centre known as the filing cabinet. The thirty-storey City Tower. The even taller Beetham Tower, the second tallest building outside London and a hotel where they'd once spent the night together.

His phone rang.

'Take it,' said Maggie.

Helmand. Bomb disposal. IEDs. Maggie. Rick imagined the explosion, the ripping shrapnel, the smoke, the pain, the terror.

The phone kept ringing.

'Rick!'

He let go of Maggie's hands.

'I've just seen Khetan at Hari's,' said Russell.

'You're sure it was him?'

'One hundred per cent. He didn't stay long, but a footie's housed him into an address about a mile away. They're sitting up on him and want to know if they should knock on, or wait for you to get back down there.'

'Tell them we're coming. Tell them to get a warrant, and to prepare arrest and search teams.'

'Okay.'

'Tell them four hours, and if he moves before then, to arrest him.'

Rick pocketed the phone. And tell them not to fuck it up. He phoned Hunter and told him they were leaving in five.

He looked at Maggie, part of him wanting to stay and hold her. The images of Helmand in his head. One moment Maggie had legs. The next she didn't. He would give up his legs for her. She was a better person than he was.

'Go on,' said Maggie. 'Go and get Khetan.'

He kissed her, and ran across to the exit door.

'Next time,' shouted Maggie, 'I'll come with you to see Emma.'

44

Rick stood in front of the officers at the junction of Beech Avenue and Elmhurst Road in north Aldershot. They bristled with kit: body armour, batons, cuffs, torches, and fluorescent *Police* armbands. More plain clothes units and a dog van were parked up in the road which backed onto Elmhurst, and uniforms cordoned the surrounding roads. A mile away, on the other side of the railway station, Russell remained in the Stanley Close OP. A liveried police van and an ambulance waited in the station car park. The sky had turned dark and rain looked likely. Station announcements floated through the muggy air.

Rick phoned Russell. 'We're about to go in.'

'Enjoy your big moment, you've earned it.'

'You're positive it was him?'

'I told you, one hundred per cent.'

Rick slid the phone away, and cleared his throat. 'Okay everyone, this is your chance to make history: arrest South Asia's Most Wanted and get one over on the FBI.'

They lined up: the doorbusting team at the front, then Foulds and two of his crime squad. Then Rick, Hunter, and two more crime squad.

'This is on Russell,' whispered Hunter. He forced a hand down the front of his armour and scratched his chest.

Foulds turned to Rick. 'Okay, sir?'

Rick nodded and Foulds gave a thumbs-up to the door crew. The file moved off like a wounded centipede, around the corner and into Elmhurst Road.

Rick's heart thudded. It always did, no matter how many he'd done. Nailing Khetan would draw a line under so much, and create some breathing space. He would do what Emma kept telling him: take a week off, take it easy, take stock. Maybe he would ask Maggie to go with him.

As they reached the address, a two-up two-down mid-terrace, the rain broke. Cold diagonal pokes in the face. The door crew pushed open the gate and fitted the hydraulic to the door, and Foulds whispered into the radio. In the front yard a wheelie bin lay on its side, rubbish everywhere. Rotting bodies of moles dangled from the side fence, like dystopian wind chimes.

Whoosh.

The door fell in and the door crew stood aside. Foulds entered first, followed by his men. Rick stepped over the threshold, Hunter at his shoulder. Rain streamed down his face and his heart beat even faster. He'd know any minute.

'Clear,' shouted an officer from the first room.

The house smelt of fried onions. Pizza leaflets and takeaway boxes lay in the hallway, scattered and crumpled by the falling door. Rick climbed the stairs, his feet clopping like hooves on the bare wood. Water dripped off his hair and clothes, leaving a trail. He was first, and only slightly reassured by Hunter following behind.

'Clear.' Another room downstairs.

Upstairs, the windows were all shut and the smell of onions persisted. The wallpaper on the landing was torn and marked with graffiti. A dark void loomed above them.

'Loft hatch's open,' shouted Hunter.

Rick went into the front room, dominated by a single bed with a dirty mattress. Drug paraphernalia covered an upturned cardboard box and pornographic magazines protruded from under the bed. He looked underneath. More magazines, dustballs, a garden fork, and silverfish racing about. 'Clear,' he shouted. 'Clear.' He peered out of the front window. A marked car pulled up and officers climbed out. Children on bikes cycled towards them.

He went back into the corridor, glancing up at the loft. Standing on the banister, even a small man could reach the loft hatch, and a powerful man could pull himself up. He found scrape marks on the wall. 'Hunter?'

The detective walked into the hall. He shook his head. 'All clear, bedroom and bathroom.' They looked up at the dark hole and Rick cupped his ear. He could hear movement.

'Quiet,' yelled Hunter down the stairs.

They listened again. Nothing – or someone else was listening.

'Need a ladder, Neil,' shouted Hunter. 'And a torch.'

Rick climbed onto the banister and peered into the darkness. He could just make out the sloping roof. He leant forward and grabbed the sill. A swing and a mighty pull-up with feet scrabbling on the wall would do it. Foulds came up the stairs with a chair and a torch. 'Want me to go up?'

Rick shook his head, and stood on the chair. He reached upwards, and with Foulds and Hunter keeping the chair steady, walked his feet up its back until his elbows were either side of the sill. He took a breath. Hunter and Foulds took hold of his legs and shoved him upwards.

He was up. His heart banging like a door.

Foulds passed up a pencil-torch.

Rick switched it on and looked around. Empty, except for a water tank. Next to the tank, a hole in the wall and a sheet of plywood on the floor. A floor which only consisted of rafters and insulation. In the adjacent loft – the next house – there was a crash. Then another. Tiles were being broken.

'Boss?' shouted Foulds.

'Tell them outside,' Rick shouted back. 'I think he's trying to get out on the roof.' Holding the torch in his mouth he balanced across the beams, walking his hands across the underside of the roof as he moved. He heard a commotion outside, and the muffled sounds of more tiles breaking. He reached the water tank and the hole, and he peered through. A similar hole had been made at the end of the next loft and in the darkness he could see a shaft of light. 'Two houses down,' he shouted. 'Elmhurst side.'

Rick put a foot on the water tank, and climbed through the hole, ripping his trousers on a nail. Outside he heard shouting and screaming. He balanced across the second loft of rafters, using his palms as before. He reached the hole, smaller than the first. Through it he saw a jagged hole in the eaves. The shaft of light revealed suitcases and boxes. Sirens blared in the road.

He couldn't climb through the hole feet first. So, with his arms leading, he wormed through, ripping his shirt and scraping his stomach, and collapsing down onto the rafters of the third loft. In the road the sirens fell silent. A round of applause. Khetan had been arrested?

A shaft of light shone through the jagged hole in the eaves. Rick stood up and worked his way forward. Rips of underlay and busted battens hung down. He bent down to the hole and peered out.

Tiles hung precariously. A small boy holding a large dog pointed up at him. Puddles dotted the road but the rain had stopped. Next to the boy stood an ambulance with its rear doors open. Further up the road stood a group of plain-clothes and uniform officers.

'Have you got him?' A yell. He was losing his voice.

The officers parted and three men walked forward. A plain-clothes officer frog-marching a handcuffed Asian prisoner, Foulds walking alongside. Khetan was limping. Khetan!

'Brilliant,' shouted Rick. Screw his voice. He would take Foulds and his crime squad out to the local curryhouse and buy them as much beer as they could drink. 'Brilliant,' he shouted a second time.

Foulds glanced up at Rick, and yanked back Khetan's head.

It wasn't Khetan.

Similar-looking.

But not him.

Definitely not him.

Rick lashed out at the loose tiles. Five or six pulled away and slid down the roof. Half a second of silence. Then a crash as they hit the path below.

'Foulds!'

'Yes, sir?'

'Get the force surveyor down here. Right away.'

Rick withdrew into the loft and slumped down onto the rafters, hardly caring if he fell through.

In the Stanley Close OP Hunter watched from the window. Rick sat with Russell at the small table, the two men a knight's move apart. He pushed back the half-finished crosswords and Sudokus, the chewed pens, the sachets of sugar and plastic stirrers, the two police radios. Only the log remained, opened at the page of Russell's entries that had promised so much.

1530 Asian male to Hari's door. 5ft 6 ish, slight. Believed ident Khetan. Circulated PR.

1531 Male knocks on Hari's door. No answer. Looks in front window. Knocks again. Waits, then disappears through passage to rear.

1533   Comes back. Knocks on Hari's door again. No answer. Looks through front window.

1534   Walks away.

1536   Turns left into Wolfs Drive. Loss to OP. Alpha 2 drops Foxtrot 3 to follow.

'Sorry,' said Russell. He pulled forward a sachet of sugar and tore it open. Poured it onto the table and used a stirrer to divide it into heaps. He tidied the heaps up, then divided them into new heaps.

The man who Rick had followed into the loft, and who had broken out through the tiles onto the roof, looked like Khetan. The man who had shinned halfway down the drainpipe looked very like Khetan. The man who had fallen onto the water butt and broken his arm was nearly Khetan, very nearly. But he wasn't Khetan. He was Tashi Bhattarai, an illegal immigrant and petty thief awaiting immigration. Before then, an interview by Foulds, but Rick wasn't hopeful.

Nothing for nearlies.

Russell glanced towards the window. 'Anything?' Hunter didn't reply. 'Hopefully it won't have spooked him.'

'You know what I think,' said Hunter. He leant down to scratch his shin. 'He's not even here.'

'Well, you're not the DCI.'

Hunter stopped scratching and stood up. 'Russell, can you do one for a minute.' He flicked his head at the door.

'Boss?'

Rick nodded.

Russell walked out.

'No, I'm not the DCI, and I never will be.' Hunter turned back to the window. 'I should have drunk less, thought about the future more. Worked harder at my marriages. But I was young and foolish, and now, well, I'm bitter and argumentative. I fell out with Baker my old DCI who made me a scapegoat for the safety box investigation. Then again, I probably needed a change.'

'Okay,' said Rick.

'I keep thinking about what you said to me in your office, boss, when I started. To be fair, I sometimes need a bit of that.'

'Some people would have given their right arm to go to Nepal.'

'Others wouldn't.' Hunter scratched his cheek. 'I still want to lock up villains. Just didn't want to be doing it on the other side of the world.'

'I'll bear that in mind if there's a next time.'

'God, I hope not.'

'We can agree on that.'

'You also told me not to hold back. So here's my tuppenny worth: I think we should return to Manchester and work the intel. Put an OP on the K2 restaurant. Task a handful of the Met's informants.'

'Noted.'

Rick went into the kitchen. He poured a glass of water, and drank it staring out through the hole in the whitewash. He felt sure Khetan wouldn't return to Agasti's restaurant. In any case, an OP was probably a non-starter, as facial recognition on the London bus and tube network had drawn a blank. Hari's was the best bet. It was Hari who'd lured Khetan to the UK.

A sketchpad lay by the kettle. On the first page the two boys on BMXs, one in the air having cycled off the ramp, and the other straddling his bike and watching. On the next page, an old woman wearing slippers, walking a small skinny dog. He heard footsteps on the stairs and a key in the door. He put the pad down and stood in the kitchen doorway.

Neil Foulds pushed the door open.

'Did Bhattarai say anything?'

'Seems he befriended Hari in a local café, and wanted to borrow some money from him. When there was no answer at Hari's, he went on the scrounge, and ended up in Elmhurst.'

Rick nodded. The lead cold as rice pudding.

'And there's more bad news, I'm afraid, sir. We've been pulled.'

'When?'

'Now,' he said, picking a fingernail with the key. 'We can send an arrest car if you get a shout but we can't sit here waiting. The super's spoken to our governor.'

For the last shift of the day, Russell stood at the blind, watching Hari's front door. At the table, Hunter turned the pages of a newspaper he'd already read, and Rick paced the flat. No arrest cars, and no night listening post. If Khetan came at night, that would be that, and if he came during the day it would be a dash-and-roughhouse.

'I found your sketchpad in the kitchen, Gary.'

Hunter glanced round.

'They're good,' said Rick quietly – so Russell couldn't hear. 'I mean that.' He paused. 'When I said in my office I was playing you, well, I wasn't. I said it to make you work for me.'

'And?'

'Jury's still out.'

His phone vibrated on the table, *Robbo* flashing up on the screen. Rick put him on speaker.

'One more day, Rick, twenty-four hours. Sunday, get back up here and Monday, I want you and DS Hunter back in the office.'

Hunter stared at his newspaper. At the window, Russell stood still as the curtains.

Rick turned off speaker and grabbed up the phone. 'The centre are—'

'I've spoken to the deputy chief con. Told him about the stunt you pulled to go to Nepal.' Robbo paused. 'Can you hear me?'

'What about—'

'Janice? I've told her about Lainey. And Rick, there's one more thing you should know.'

Rick hung up and threw down the phone. On the inside of his notebook he drew a honeybee. But it looked grotesque, proportions all wrong.

45

Two cons crouched among the kale plants, weeding. Another one hoed along the rows of leeks. Three older cons sat on a bench at the side, sharing a cigarette and arguing about the best way to sharpen secateurs. Two murderers and an arsonist. One for kitchen steel, two for whetstone. A guard leant against the wall, swinging his keys and humming.

As a new con to the prison garden, Calix had been tasked with an easy job: taking down a wigwam of runner beans. Above it the plants' tentacles waved in the wind. Half a dozen beans hung down – tiny or dried out or half-eaten by birds. He untied the string at the top and pulled away the first bamboo pole.

Megan wouldn't believe he was in prison, in Strangeways. With killers and firestarters. With stabbers and biters and cutters and shooters. With psychos and stalkers. With the drugged and bugged. With the screamers, the self-harmers, the freaks and deaks.

The guard undid the zip on his flies and scratched his balls. Calix knelt down on the far side of the bean wigwam. The old men on the bench debated the meaning of organic. He removed Girl from the pocket on the inside of his trouser leg. Her eye stared at an acute angle, and he tried to fold down the eyelid. He kissed the top of her head. Then dug a hole, and laid Girl inside with the envelope from Toose on her breast. Raisins and buttons for the next life.

Toose had wanted to be there but he'd lost all his privileges. He said he should be in a Glasgow lockup. He was probably right. He said he was misunderstood, which was questionable.

Calix pushed the soil back and patted it down.

As he finished, a second guard entered the fenced enclosure, and spoke to his colleague. The guard on garden duty turned around.

'Coniston, you've got a visitor.'

Calix slipped some of the wizened runner beans into his pocket. He walked past the bench on his way to the gate. The two murderers and the arsonist had fallen asleep leaning up against each other, like books fallen over at the end of a shelf.

Calix waited in previsits with the other cons. Twenty of them sat on low wooden benches all facing one way, like at kindergarten. Prison, the great reducer. Calix stared at his feet. He expected his visitor to be Castle wanting more information on Khetan, more details on Agasti. Still no word from his brief about a letter of mitigation, and he feared Castle had got one over him.

On the bench in front of him two cons whispered about Toose. How he'd fed out-of-date sausage rolls to dibble horses during a riot in Glasgow. They were laughing about it. What they didn't mention was Toose unseating a rider and battering him with a piece of rusty-nailed four-by-two. The dibbleman invalided out, would only ever eat through a tube.

A guard blew his whistle, and read out the list for legal and the dibble. Calix's name wasn't called and he was herded along with the others into the visits hall.

He chose a table by a wall and sat down. If it wasn't Castle, it had to be his mum. He fingered the beans in his pocket and placed them on the table. Eighteen shiny purple beans, like opal stones. He moved them into a grid: six by three.

A klaxon sounded, the door opened and noncons streamed in. He scanned them for his mum. She always wore her long mac, even if it was warm. His old man would have worn his olive cravat, creased slacks, buffed brogues. His old man wouldn't have come.

Darren slid onto the chair in front of him.

Calix's heart sank. Darren had been released after the dibble had lost the exhibits, and Calix was in no mood for his former cellmate's gloating.

'This feels fucking weird, Capeman.' Darren looked around at the guards and the cameras, and the table microphones, at the grid of beans, then back at Calix. He had more tattoos on his arms. 'Got myself a girl haven't I. Wendy. A looker, you'd be surprised. Show you a photo but phone's in the locker.' He nodded over his shoulder. 'Got *The Sun* in there too.'

'The newspaper?'

'Well not the big ball of fire you daft fuck. Locker would melt.' He turned to a sign on the wall. 'Con-ver-sat-ions. Conversations – may – be – re-cor-ded. Conversations may be recorded.'

Calix clapped silently. Surprised.

'You opened my eyes, lit'ra-fucking-ally, ha-ha. And I owe you, Capeman.'

Another surprise.

He told Darren about Girl. Darren sat solemn as a Buddha and listened without interrupting. Calix felt his vision blur.

'Why've you come, Darren?'

'I heards Special K's here. Saw it on the news. Shouldn't be approached, all that. Dibble fucked up, but they didn't say that.'

In front of Calix was what his old man had called an

opportunity. When Calix had been in the sixth form at school, his old man had kept saying things like: This is a great opportunity for you to hear Lieutenant-Colonel X; or, Do you want to do a weekend's adventurous training with the regiment's junior soldiers? It's a great opportunity. His old man hadn't really got him, and yet he'd taken the bullet for him on the bridge.

Joe had left him a lot of money.

Had to forget about Girl.

Calix moved twelve of the beans into a single row in the middle of the table. One by one, he pushed them closer.

'For special?'

Calix nodded.

'Fifteen.'

Calix pushed three more across.

Darren swept up the beans, glanced round, and put them in his pocket. The klaxon sounded, haunting as an air raid warning.

The mission was back on.

46

Saturday, the last day in the OP. They started at six, the three of them, like the musketeers only in number. Hunter watched at the window, intermittently scratching his elbows; Russell observed from the kitchen while doing strange finger-stretching exercises; Rick sat at the table reviewing his case notes.

Monday, Khetan had arrived at Heathrow, and later visited Agasti at K2. In response, they'd pulled Hari from his flat and set up the OP. Tuesday, Khetan had again been caught on the K2 CCTV. Sorting false documents and tickets back to Nepal? Wednesday, the first loss in the alley: the man with the blue baseball hat. Khetan carrying out a recce, confirming the address of Hari and seeing for himself what was going on?

Day four, when Rick and Hunter were re-interviewing Coniston, a second loss in the alley. Khetan for the second time, or for the first time, or not him at all? Friday, the failed house search and arrest of Bhattarai. Foulds returning to base and Robbo pulling the plug on the whole shebang.

Zero intel from the Met's informants. One facial recognition camera on the London tube had recorded a forty-three per cent likeness for Khetan – but a South Manchester taxi firm would have scored better.

Rick still felt sure the OP on Hari's flat was their best bet. Hunter's opinion hadn't changed and Russell was on the fence.

His phone vibrated with a message. *Phone Dad its his birthday!!*

Rick tapped out a reply. *I'm working he wont know*

But you will

It was the argument he'd used on Mum. Indisputable, and Becky unassailable.

Today was their last chance to arrest Khetan before the three of them returned to Manchester. When Rick would find out what else Robbo wanted to tell him. A transfer away from South Manchester? Back to uniform? The community safety unit? Or, the fag ends: the firearms register, licensing, property.

Their last chance.

Was the brigadier's killer in Aldershot, and if so what was he waiting for? Rick doodled underneath his notes. A basketball net and a basketball heading towards it, dashes to indicate movement.

Today was Saturday, the weekend. He shaded in squares on the ball. Most people would get up late and go out, to visit friends or watch the football or take the kids to a park. They would go out again in the evening. Get drunk, act the fool. Some would get drunk and fight and damage things. Uniforms would run around picking up the pieces. Saturday nights saw fifty-five per cent of anti-social behaviour.

Including graffiti and racial harassment.

Was Khetan waiting for a Saturday night? The dual Nepalese–British national had lived in the UK for ten years so he was familiar with British culture. If Rick was right, then they had to provoke him.

'Russell, can you come in here a minute?'

Rick found three of the plastic stirrers and broke one in half. How had he forgotten Dad's birthday? Mum would think he was stressed at work, Becky that he couldn't multi-task.

Russell walked in. 'What about watching the alley?'

'I've had an idea, and if I'm right you're not going to see Khetan in the alley. I think he's waiting for something. And one of us is going to provide it.'

'La la land,' said Hunter.

Rick explained his thinking and suggested they draw lots. He held up the three plastic stirrers.

'We should be going back to Manchester and working the intel.'

Rick held the stirrers so all three protruded the same length. He walked over to Hunter at the window and held his hand out.

'I'm not drawing,' said Hunter. He scratched an elbow.

Rick walked back to the table. 'Just me and you, Russell.' He removed a complete stirrer, and held the other two out to Russell.

The mountaineer gripped a stirrer and pulled.

The half.

They made preparations. Russell drove out to a hardware store, Hunter stayed at the window, and Rick phoned Foulds.

He told him to put an arrest car on standby. While he spoke, Hunter stood by the blind, scratching like an ape.

Rick left him to it, and went into the bedroom to call Three Views. This life, the afterlife, and a previous life? This life, and two versions of the afterlife, heaven and hell. Three versions of the afterlife: heaven, purgatory, and hell. At least Dad had been spared all the conjecture.

'Three Views. How can I help?'

'Michael, it's Rick Castle.'

'How are you, sir?'

Michael sounded calm, respectful, and on top of things. The home was lucky and Dad was lucky. In the background Rick could hear music. 'Can I speak to him?'

'He's singing at the moment. Probably best not to

disturb him – he loves the singing and it's good for him.'

Rick took a deep breath. 'Maybe I could join in on the phone.'

'First time for everything.'

Rick sensed Michael carrying the phone along the hall, the singing getting louder. Michael pushed through the swing doors into the piano room.

'*We all live in a yellow submarine*' blasted out.

'Mr Castle,' shouted Michael, 'it's your son. He wants to sing with you.'

'Who?' said Dad on the phone.

'Dad, it's Rick.'

Rick sang. He wished Mum and Becky could see him, but was glad they couldn't hear him. Hunter could, though. He didn't care: it was good for Dad, good for both of them.

The three of them argued about the time. Russell thought five-thirty, Hunter eight-thirty. Rick said it didn't matter because if he was right, Khetan would be watching from midday to midnight. The FBI's South Asian Most Wanted had flown from Nepal and wanted not only to check on his surrogate father but to solve his problem. Hand out a little Nepalese justice. A little *Dharma*.

And if Rick was wrong, well, it was his career on the line.

At seven pm Rick and Hunter watched through the dusty blind as the tall hooded figure opened the gate of number 43. His small rucksack sagged with two halves of a brick and his jacket pocket hid a can of black spray-paint. He wore an earpiece for the radio.

The close was quiet. A cat ran along a wall, jumped down and loped off. At the far end, a man slammed a front door and ran out to a car.

The hooded figure walked up the path.

'Walk slowly,' said Rick into the radio.

The car started, and drove out of the close at the same time that the hooded figure reached the front of Hari's flat.

'Okay, Russ,' said Rick, glancing across at Hunter.

Russell reached into his pocket, and pulled out the can of spray-paint. He pushed off the top and shook the can up and down. They could hear the rattle in the OP.

'Now?' whispered Russell into his mic.

'Now.'

The mountaineer cum special policeman waded into the hydrangeas and began spraying.

Big arm movements.

Capital letters, about a foot high on the front wall of Hari's flat.

F
U
C
K

Russell moved along, shaking the can.

O
F
F

The mountaineer stopped and shook.

B
A
C
K

He moved again.

T
O

A shot rang out, and Russell fell forward, hitting the wall. He slid down and disappeared in the bushes.

Silence, except for the echo of the bullet and the flapping of wings.

47

Rick clattered down the narrow staircase and flung open the front door. He turned right, cut diagonally across the tiny patch of scrubby grass and wrenched open the gate.

'Police, don't shoot!'

Still shouting, he sprinted across the pavement, past the end of the stubby cul-de-sac, across the opposite pavement and into Hari's front garden. For the last few metres he ran with his hands in the air, and despite his booming panic, he felt sure there'd only been a single shot.

Russell lay in the hydrangeas with his boots sticking out, toes pointing up. A good sign.

'Russell?' Rick bent to look closer. He felt sick from the sudden exertion, and a mushrooming sense of guilt.

'You okay? Speak to me, Russell. Are you okay?'

'No.'

Rick was almost sick with relief, and he yanked at the hydrangea plants to clear some space. 'At least you can talk.'

'You know, Rick, they smell pretty good.' Russell's words were slow and slurred. He sat slumped with his back against the wall of the house and with his legs out in front of him. His right shoulder bled from the bullet.

Rick stood up and swivelled around to face the OP. 'Need an ambulance.' He yelled again, his voice still sore from shouting at Foulds in Elmhurst Street.

He took off his shirt and ripped a piece from the front. He folded it into a pad, then bent down and pressed it on the wound. 'Hold that,' he said, clamping Russell's hand down.

The mountaineer nodded and did as he was told. He closed his eyes. He looked pale as paper.

Rick inspected the back of Russell's shoulder. Blood was pouring out, and he hoped it was positive news: the bullet had exited. He ripped off another piece of shirt, folded it, and held it against the back of the wound.

'Hang in there, big man.'

Next door an upstairs window opened and a woman leant out. 'Oh, my God.' Another window opened and a teenage boy with a phone started taking a video.

Rick checked the bloody pads on Russell's shoulder. He put a hand on the mountaineer's hand and pressed from both sides. 'Russell?'

'Mmm?'

'Stay with me.'

'Not going anywhere.' He sounded drunk.

A motorbike accelerated hard on a nearby road. Train announcements carried from the station. Still no sirens. 'Talk to me.' Rick paused. 'I'll call your parents. What about Jacob?'

'Velvet.'

'Do you know her number?'

Russell didn't even pause.

Two cars screeched to a halt. Crime squad officers ran up the path followed by a paramedic. Behind them stood a small group of people, whispering and pointing. Rick recognised the two BMX lads.

Foulds arrived first. 'Is he alright?'

'Breathing,' said Rick. His voice was gravelly. He could hear a cacophony of sirens in the distance.

The paramedic set down his bag and knelt. He worked the ABC, examined the wound. Took out a needle, tapped it, scissored up Russell's sleeve. Stabbed the mountaineer's arm, injected. The crime squad sergeant asked questions.

Rick pointed at the school.

'One shot. Came from the school, a classroom at the front. Shooter will be on his toes, and may not be alone. Heading for a vehicle I should think. Lock it down.'

Foulds issued commands on the radio, and the others headed back down the path.

An hour later Rick sat on the rear bumper of a crime squad car, the boot raised above him. He wore Foulds' jacket, and was trying to write notes. Beside him, a mug of treacly tea. Uniforms and detectives were busy everywhere, cordoning the scenes and marshalling the crowd. Even with the helicopter, there had not been a single sighting of the shooter.

Rick spotted Hunter, walking around the curve of the pavement, and limping. He hobbled up to Rick. Hunter's blue shirt showed sweat patches under the arms and down the chest, and one trouser leg was ripped at the knee. A bloody gash shone out. He'd lost a shoe. The surviving one and the bottom of his trousers were filthy.

'How's Russell?'

'He was shot in the shoulder. But he should be okay.'

Hunter picked up Rick's mug of tea.

'What happened to you?'

'I saw someone.'

Rick felt a tremor of hope. 'So?'

Hunter sat on the kerb and sipped the tea. 'The shot came from the direction of the school so when you came here I went there. I saw him near the back fence. Way over.' He put the tea down, and took off the shoe.

'I didn't hear you put it up.'

'Didn't have my radio.'

Rick said nothing.

He counted to three, braced himself.

'Khetan?'

Hunter stretched up and pulled a bin liner from the car boot. He dropped his shoe inside. 'Maybe.'

'Come on, Gary.' Rick slammed his hand down on the bumper. They both knew what was at stake: an identification was only worth something in court if there wasn't any doubt.

'Don't worry, I'll write it up.' Hunter picked up the mug. 'I should have taken a stirrer. I'm sorry.'

'Talk about that later,' said Rick. He passed Hunter a small report book. 'Sign and date. Do it properly.'

A car stopped at the cordon and Foulds climbed out. He walked over, phone in one hand, radio in the other. 'You've lost your shoe, Gary.' He turned to Rick. 'Dog should be here any minute. I've sent my team to the station and taxi bases, and I've got our intel unit contacting buses and social media. I'm getting a flyer done with Khetan's photo and the whole nick's turning out. We haven't got the staff for a proper lockdown on the roads, but motorway and neighbourhood patrols have been briefed – or they soon will be. One of our DIs will take the scene here. I'll introduce you as soon as they arrive.'

Rick stood up. 'Get your DI to phone me, Neil, I'm going to the hospital.'

Hunter thrust the empty mug at Foulds. 'I'm coming. I want to apologise to the big man.'

Rick shook his head. 'You're more useful here, Gary, work the scene with Neil.' He clicked down the boot. 'If I can, I'll tell him.'

Frimley Park hospital was a familiar spaghetti junction of vast corridors. Rick sat in one as wide as a road. A trolley rushed past, attended by a phalanx of emergency staff.

'Dr Jammu and anaesthetist Milssen to theatre A immediately.'

Rick sat on the floor with his back against the wall. It was as close as he could get to theatre B. Next to him was a set of double doors with rubber skirts and above his head was a sign – *Operation in progress* – illuminated in red. Through the double doors was a second set of double doors with rubber skirts and through them Russell lay on the operating table. Rick had been sitting in the corridor for half an hour, his backside going slowly numb. He hadn't bothered moving because he deserved to suffer.

He stared at his phone, wondering whether to try Russell's parents again. A woman steering a floor cleaning machine approached and he drew up his legs.

His phone rang. Robbo. He pressed the red button.

It rang again. Green button.

'Neil. How—'

'Nothing yet, sir, but thought you'd like an update. Dog's a muppet – hasn't even picked up a trail. And the helicopter's had a mechanical and returned to base. *But*, five hundred flyers with Khetan's photo have been printed and are being distributed. Over a hundred officers and civvies have turned out from the nick. Local radio are running an appeal every fifteen minutes. And we're all over social media asking for info. If we get anything, I'll phone again. Hold on, Gary wants a word.'

The floor cleaner went past again. In its wake a young black nurse with crinkly hair bursting out of her cap and a man in a football shirt herded three crying boys.

'Hunter here. DCI Matt Bailey from the local shop has taken it. Scenes of crime just arrived. The murder team have sent a homicide assessment car and CID have begun house-to-house. Bailey is setting CCTV parameters. Local super wants you to call pronto, will text you his number. How's Russell?'

'In theatre.'

'Did you tell him?'

'Not had a chance.'

Hunter rang off. Rick's stomach rumbled. A text arrived. Then another call. Robbo. Red button.

He stood and walked stiff-legged to the nearest vending machine. Selected coffee and sandwiches, and slotted in coins. As he opened the cellophane Hunter rang again.

'Robbo just contacted me to say you're not answering your phone. I told him I'd spoken to you.'

Rick sat on a plastic seat and bit into a sandwich. The nurse with crinkly hair walked past with two pillows and a clipboard. His phone rang, the screen showing an overseas number. He swallowed the bready lump and answered.

'Sorry, Inspector, been on the beach. I'm Peter Beater, Russell's father. We're on the Algarve.'

Rick started to explain.

'How bad is he?'

'He's alive. Still being operated on. The bullet went into his shoulder, but it came out.'

'Thank you for telling us.'

Rick didn't deserve thanks and almost said so. He wanted to tell them that according to one of the doctors it was a straight-forward operation. But he resisted. A colleague had recently made a mistake with the parents of a young girl who'd died after an asthma attack.

'It's funny,' said Mr Beater, 'we always thought it would be a mountaineering accident, not his role as a special that would end up like this.'

The call ended. The words were all wrong. It wasn't *funny*

and it wasn't an *accident*. But words on the phone were always wrong. He put the mobile on the floor and spun it around. A pair of ward shoes stopped alongside and he looked up to see the nurse with crinkly hair.

'Got a Superintendent Robinson on the phone for you. Do you want to follow me?'

Rick stood up. His backside still ached. He followed the nurse along the corridor to a door marked *Staff Only*. She punched a code on the keypad. Further doors led to small offices and she opened the door of the third. *Dr V. Sagaratharanathum – Registrar*, on the brass plaque. 'In there.' On the desk was a landline, the receiver lying next to the base. 'He's on that phone. Vic's away, so afterwards you can stay in the office. I'll tell the theatre sister. Code for the corridor door is ten-sixty-six.'

'Thank you.'

'Fiona, but they call me Fi.'

When the door had eased shut behind her, Rick picked up the phone receiver and dropped it on the base.

He walked over to the window. Stared out at the expanse of parked cars, glinting in the fading sunlight like a silent robot army. Behind the cars, men in hard hats and fluorescents were felling a copse of trees, and a bulldozer was razing the scrub. Birds wheeled across the dirty white sky.

48

Bats scrabbled behind the loose brick in the window alcove. Just out of reach if he pushed a hand through the bars. A bright day, outside.

Calix lay on his bunk, staring at the photos of his old man and Megan. He took the pen from under his pillow and drew a picture frame alongside. Inside, he wrote *Joe*. Surely, photos of family were a human right. He'd filled in two forms, had both signed by the wing supervisor, both countersigned by the block principal. But Hainsforth had refused.

He wondered if Darren was making any progress on finding Special K. If he did, he would only take the next step if he was paid. Which was a conundrum. The money left by Joe was in his bank account, but his mum would refuse to make payment, even if Calix repaid her and provided a cover story.

He stared at the photos. Behind Megan sat her computer, her gateway to the world. Where she'd researched cycling round Australia. Where she'd paid for her trip. And how.

The internet.

The world wide web had supposedly originated because a Cambridge professor was too lazy to walk to the faculty's coffee machine to check whether there was any coffee. To save the walk, he rigged up a CCTV camera to a computer. Urban myth or not, people on holiday could now water their plants, draw their curtains, check their home security. And everyone, wherever they were, could buy stuff, and transfer money.

Even if they were in prison.

The metallic clinking of a coin on a water pipe started on the wing. More cons joined in. There was shouting from cell to cell. Toose jumped off the top bunk and pushed off his headphones.

'A bizzie gone down.'

Toose switched on the TV and flicked through the stations to a news channel.

Tickertape ran along the foot of the screen: *Police officer shot in Aldershot. Suspect still on the loose.* The picture showed a reporter holding a microphone at the scene. 'At just after three o'clock this afternoon on a quiet residential street in Aldershot a male police officer was shot and injured. The suspect has not yet been arrested, and police are advising the public to stay indoors and not to approach anyone suspicious.'

Toose punched the air. 'Gonna be bangers for scran, bet yers.'

The camera switched from the reporter to a small front garden on a council estate, then panned away. It showed blue and white tape bobbing up and down, dibble cars, uniforms standing around and forensic bods in white overalls. A crowd of onlookers and two men in suits. And a third man without a jacket, and with a rip in his trousers.

Hunter.

Calix couldn't believe it. Hunter. Coincidence?

Couldn't be.

Toose jigged up and down.

The camera returned to the reporter. 'The wounded officer is currently being treated in hospital but his injury is not believed to be life-threatening.'

'Booo.'

His cellmate dropped to the floor and started doing press-ups.

The TV showed an old woman in a rocking chair. 'I'd just sat down to a cup of tea when I heard a bang. Thought it was a firework.' She was followed by one of the men in suits. *DCI Bailey, Aldershot CID* flashed up on the screen. 'We're looking for Hant Khetan known as Special K – he might also be using the name Himal Limbu. He's Asian in appearance, five foot six, mid-thirties.' A photo was shown.

Toose locked out a press-up. 'Special fucking K, man.'

On the TV the reporter reappeared. 'So far no motive has been given for the shooting, although local speculation is that it's drugs- or gang-related, an overspill from London.'

'Not Special, man,' said Toose. 'He's skyrocket.'

Calix wondered whether it was Castle who'd been shot. The visit three days earlier must have been part of it. But he'd not mentioned Aldershot – only Agasti and the K2 restaurant in London.

Nothing made sense.

'We are just hearing,' said the reporter, 'that the police officer shot in Aldershot was a special constable. And that makes it one of the very few occasions in modern times that one of the police volunteers has been shot on duty. His family have been informed.'

Not Castle. Weatherbeater, the mountaineer. Bumps prickled on Calix's neck. In Nepal, Weatherbeater had talked a lot about the death zone and killer storms and high altitude pulmonary oedemas. But he'd always checked Calix had enough water, always talked to Calix as if he wasn't a con.

The news programme moved to golf. Toose turned off the TV, and climbed back up to his bunk. He slipped on his headphones and played music so loud the next cell could hear.

Calix dragged a chair to the window. He stepped up and

opened it as wide as possible. Bat droppings littered the alcove. He pushed his arms through the bars and stared out into the shadowy yard, listening to the pattering of the bats. He ground the droppings with a finger and blew the dust into the yard. One con had told him guano was carcinogenic and was suing the home office.

The yard grew darker.

Darren couldn't work a miracle. Aldershot was a start, but he, they, needed an address or a venue for Khetan. And they needed it before the dibble got their act together. And before Khetan skipped back to Nepal.

The yard grew darker still. A bat edged out from the loose brick and keeled off into the dusk. The night air would soon be full of them, pinpointing their insect prey like snipers.

*

The registrar's office was small but tidy. A skeleton dangled from a hook on the back of the door and cancer diagnostic charts hung on the walls. An umbrella and a squash racket stood in a corner. Above the tiny sink was a mug with a toothbrush.

Rick sat at the desk, laptop open alongside his notebook. Nine pm. He felt exhausted and empty: he'd only eaten half a sandwich since breakfast.

There was a light knock on the door. It was opened by a small man in a theatre gown. His face had a waxy yellow sheen, and heavy stubble, and there were sweat patches under his arms.

'I'm Doctor Fisher. Russell's now out of surgery, but there've been complications. He might lose the use of his shoulder.'

Rick nodded.

Fisher went out and the door closed.

Rick ran a basin of hot water. Russell's blood remained under his fingernails. He doused his face and soaked his fingers. It made no difference. With a pair of scissors from the desk drawer he scraped under the nails until they bled. He dried his hands and threw the paper towels in the bin.

He sat down and read his note of his last call with Foulds. *Two cars stolen in Aldershot within an hour of the shooting.* House-to-house and scene boards were in hand. *Thirteen sightings of Khetan: 1 hoax; 3 genuine but mistaken; 8 extremely vague; 1 being followed up.* Which was normal – unless there was a betrayal by a relation or an associate, information from the public was rarely useful. Very occasionally, however, it was the golden ticket.

Rick phoned Maggie.

'How's Russell?'

Rick relayed the information from Dr Fisher.

'What can I do?'

'Lots. Phone your contact at West End Central. Explain the circs and ask her to speak to her boss about an OP on the K2. Say I've authorised it. Double-check a port alert has been done. He'll head for an airport or the coast, but maybe not for a day or two. Circulate a description countrywide to transport police; yes, escaping by bus or train is unlikely, but Khetan's smart and might think like that. Send taskings to force informant controllers: us, the Met, Thames Valley, Hampshire and surrounding. Anyone in the intel office who's spare, get them to start trawling the internet chatter. Finally, ask DS Ali to put a team together for tomorrow morning, and await further instructions.'

'Something will turn up, Rick.'

'Something has to, Mags.'

The door opened.

Hunter walked in and shook his head. 'Khetan's proper done one.' He shook the skeleton which tinkled, and sat down. 'Russell?'

Rick repeated the doctor's update.

'Have you spoken to him?'

'Still in recovery.'

Hunter held up an arm and scratched it. 'I wish I could turn back the clock, take a stirrer, take my chance.'

'Even if there were three stirrers, Russell still might have pulled the short one. Thirty-three per cent chance is not so different to fifty.'

'That's not my point.' Hunter scratched harder. 'I had *no* chance.'

'We shouldn't even have drawn straws.' Rick wondered if Russell had only agreed because the mountaineer felt guilty for the botched raid following his mistaken identification of Khetan. 'It was my idea to spray racist graffiti and I should have done it.'

Rick inspected his fingers: blood still clung to a nail. 'What would you do if you were Khetan?'

'Run to the station. Then backtrack to a car, zig-zagging along alleys which I'd recced beforehand. Car hired from a backstreet. Driven ten miles to a second car. Driven back to London, and gone to ground. Or possibly to Dover. I'd have my exit route out of the country all arranged, and I'd use false details.'

'My thoughts, too.'

'Bailey wants copies of your files and he also wants a call.' Hunter scratched the underside of his neck. 'So, if you're ready, I'll brief you.'

Rick picked up a pen. He stared at the blood. Russell's. Martha's, Mark's and Marissa's.

'Are you okay, boss?'

'Prop the door open. I can't breathe in here.'

Hunter stood the refuse bin in the doorway, and started on the detail. The first scene, Hari's front garden, had been photographed and searched and closed down. The bullet hadn't been found, but a fingertip search would take place in the morning.

The second scene, Khetan's hideout in the classroom, had also been photographed and searched, and forensic analysis would take place the following day. Rick would get copies of all the photos. Exhibits included train ticket receipts to London, a blue baseball hat (all but confirming the sighting from the OP – a scientist would examine it for hairs), and a bullet casing. Forensic analysis on the casing might provide a link to Khetan which would be important: the two other parts of the connection between Khetan and the shooting, the bullet and the firearm, remained outstanding. The next day further search teams and a police diving team would check dustbins, drain grids, and water bodies within Bailey's search parameters. These included the close and Khetan's possible routes to the railway station. They had no information about a getaway vehicle – car hire firms and the seven vehicles stolen since the shooting were still being followed up. Nothing of significance had come from any witnesses, and house-to-house enquiries had also drawn a blank. The CCTV trawl was still under way, and would take a week, maybe more, to be fully analysed.

Rick stared at his notes, then glanced at the clock. One am. He felt light-headed.

'Last thing. A PC dropped off a confidential memo for you from Robbo.' Hunter pushed an envelope onto the desk. He stood up, pushed a hand down the front of his collar and scratched for a few seconds. 'I'll let myself out.'

The door at the end of the corridor banged shut.

Rick ripped open the envelope and unfolded the memo.

DCI Rick Castle
Attached is a Regulation 15 Notice for gross misconduct: taking Coniston to Nepal.
Superintendent M. Robinson

He stepped forward and punched the skeleton in the head. Rattling and railing, the body of bones swayed back, swayed forward. Rick punched again. The skeleton fell off the hook and collapsed in a heap on the floor. He picked it up. Khetan. The father of Mark, Marissa and Martha. Robbo. An arm lay detached. He picked it up along with the rest of the bones and stuffed them cranium-first into the bin.

Arresting Khetan was his only way out. His only release. The warm orange glow at the end of the valley.

He walked over to the window.

And breathed the cool night air.

49

Two cups of strong black coffee from the vending machine, and two bars of chocolate. A piss. Then Rick got stuck in.

After the sea- and airports, the most likely destination for Khetan was London. He sent a tasking to the night detectives in every borough. He sent a tasking to the police control room on the underground. Another to the super-recognisers in the CCTV room at Scotland Yard.

He read Coniston's missing enquiry file, hoping for something to jump out at him. He finished the first coffee, and ate some chocolate. Looked at the cancer charts: a hundred horrible ways to die. Doctors never gave up – they'd taken the Hippocratic Oath.

He phoned the night detective at Aldershot to see if there was an update. There wasn't. But DCI Bailey was still hard at it.

Rick phoned him, and for half an hour, detailed everything he knew about Khetan. His UK links: Aldershot, and London and Oxford where he'd worked in the telecoms industry. Agasti and the K2 restaurant. Coniston. Hari Subba. Khetan's criminal history, the FBI's interest.

'Makes sense if you email me the appeal sheets,' said Rick.
'Will do.'

Rick drained the second coffee. Then stood up and

walked to the window, and ate the second chocolate bar.

He started on the 137 appeal sheets. He read them all, discounted ninety. He graded the rest, and actioned the top five. Three sightings of Khetan, two in London, and one in Dover; and two addresses of Nepalese nationals and alleged associates, both near Manchester airport. He failed to corroborate any of the information on police databases, but they were the best they had. He emailed the closest police stations, attention of the DI. DS Ali could deal with the ones near the airport.

He opened the window wider.

The car park was almost deserted, yellow beams of light revealing hundreds of numbered bays. A fox stood by a toppled litter bin, the rubbish strewn around. Voices carried from the hospital, and the fox padded into the darkness.

Rick stared at the cancer charts. Doctors didn't surrender, and neither would this detective.

An email at 3.25am brought the first positive result. An informant in the Met had provided an address in East Ham. A telecoms colleague of Khetan's from way back. Previous for employee theft and fraud. Information graded as A2 which was enough for a warrant.

Rick phoned Hunter.

Who answered on the second ring.

'Need you to pull in a favour from your old unit. Get them to do a door first thing.'

Hunter took the details without a murmur. 'Anything on Russell – let me know.'

At 3.45 Rick went for another piss. He walked up and down a flight of stairs ten times, then went back to it.

He read internet chatter for ten minutes hoping to get lucky, but there was nothing. Dreamers, conspiracists, and time-wasters. Drunks, punks, and skunks. Wastrels, wassocks, and wankers. He was getting tired.

He went out for more coffee, but when he came back to the office someone had removed the doorstop. He tried a credit card without success, then busted the lock barging his way back in.

Hoping for inspiration, he again dipped into the Coniston file. He wrote a list for the morning. He texted Bailey but received no reply.

At 4.50am a second positive result: a witness to one of the lost or stolens in Aldershot. The woman's husband had returned home from a night shift to find the police note, woken his non-English-speaking wife, who told him what she'd seen. Theft of a car, and later, Khetan's face on a TV news report. Uniform had attended, and bulletins sent countrywide.

At five, Rick started waking people up.

Tenth ring. 'Wakey, wakey, Sergeant Ali.'

'Boss?'

'Just emailed you some information on possible addresses for Khetan near the airport. Need you to look up an out-of-hours magistrate, swear the warrants, and execute them as soon as possible.'

Ali phoned back five minutes later.

'Not enough here, boss, beak will never sign.'

'Course they will, just fill in the gaps a little.'

'Boss, listen.'

'No, Arjun, you listen. In fact, just do it.' Rick slammed the phone down.

He phoned Maggie. 'Anything?'

'OP's up and running on the K2. Nothing so far. Port alert, transport police, taskings all done. Nothing from social media. You slept at all?'

'No. You?'

'Had an hour in my chair.'

'We'll go somewhere nice.'

'When you retire?'

Rick drank the last mouthful of coffee, and crumpled the cup. Then phoned the stations where he'd sent actions from the appeal sheets, hoping to speak to the early turn DI. Nothing like the personal touch. He spoke to DIs in Dover and Stansted; no problem, their response. If there had been, he was prepared to persuade, shout, exaggerate. Lie.

At 6.15 he went over to the window. Grey light revealed a damp car park, and already there was a queue at the barrier. Alongside the cars, a man picked up litter with a grabber.

Rick headed out to the washroom, passing the broken skeleton in the refuse bin. He would write to Dr V. Sagaratharanathum – Vic – and apologise, and for the broken door lock. Offer a donation to hospital funds. He rinsed his face. Looking ten years older, smelling of yesterday.

On the way back, he met Hunter carrying paper bags of breakfast.

'You look like shit.'

Rick pushed through the broken door. 'East Ham?'

'Negative. Russell?'

Rick shook his head.

They sat either side of the registrar's desk and Hunter unloaded coffee and orange juice and greaseproof wrappers smelling of bacon. Rick summarised the manhunt while Hunter ate a burger, relish oozing down his thumb. His sergeant glanced at the dumped skeleton but didn't comment.

Rick drained a juice. 'OP?'

'Closed,' said Hunter. 'Given the keys back to Neil.' He ate a clasp of chips and wiped ketchup from the table with his finger.

Rick took the lid off the coffee. He would never sleep. 'During the night, I reread the files from last year.'

Hunter wiped his mouth with a serviette. 'Do you want your chips?'

Rick shook his head. 'Did you ever read them?'

'Not every word.'

On the table the phone rang.

Rick snatched it up.

'Russell's awake,' said Fiona. 'You can go and see him.'

Rick replaced the receiver and tapped on the laptop. He swivelled it around. 'Read this – it's the postscript to Coniston's missing person enquiry. Then we'll go and see Russell.'

Hant Khetan appears to have been motivated not by greed or drugs but by faith, and by honour – familial and for his country. He had two aims, the first to force FIFA to effect meaningful change in the working conditions of Nepalese workers in Qatar. The second, revenge for the death of his father in the Falklands War. In the second he was successful, Brigadier Coniston jumping to his death in the face of almost certain torture and / or death at the hands of Khetan.

'What's your point?'

'I think I'm missing something.'

'You need to think about something else for a few minutes. Let's go see the big man.'

An armed officer stood outside Russell's room on Wheatley Ward. Rick and Hunter showed their warrant cards and the woman nodded. 'Thank you, sir. He's already got a visitor. And you need to wear gloves.' She nodded at the dispensers on the wall.

They rubbed their hands with sanitising gel, pulled on disposable gloves, and went in.

The room was surprisingly large. Two machines like Mars exploration rovers were parked along one wall, and opposite them stood a round table with a vase of artificial flowers. A horseshoe of monitors curved around the bed, their tubes attached to Russell's arms and disappearing into the V of his hospital gown. A woman with a dyed blond bob sat at the bedside, holding the hand of his uninjured arm with both of hers.

As they entered, the woman released Russell's hand, and looked up as if she'd pulled out one of the tubes. She wore a black dress and black patent shoes. She had a mole above her lip, and her face was made-up. She was young and turnaround pretty.

Rick and Hunter walked to the end of the bed. Russell's eyes remained shut, his face pale and badly shaved.

'Russell?' said Rick. 'I'm here with Hun— with Gary.'

After a pause, Russell said, 'Hello, Rick. Hello, Gary.' He sounded weak and hesitant, like someone else. 'Have you met Velvet?'

'We're just meeting her now,' said Rick.

Velvet stood, and adjusted the strap of her dress. Rick imagined her in The Sparks. Russell's son Jacob playing bass guitar, Barry on drums, and Velvet singing, and adjusting the strap of her dress. He'd buy the CDs, follow them around the country and hang out in the after-gig bar. He'd leave his wife for her. She leant across to peck Russell's cheek and squeezed his hand. 'I'll come back later.' She walked out, leaving a smell of youth.

Hunter sat on her chair. 'Still warm.'

Russell smiled but didn't open his eyes. 'Did you like her?'

'Yeah, we liked her,' said Hunter.

Rick walked around the other side of the bed and peered at the flashing and beeping monitors. The shoulder was bandaged and the gown had been cut away to make room.

'Did you get him?'

'Not yet,' said Rick.

He watched Russell's face, hoping the mountaineer's eyes would appear. For the mountaineer himself to appear, the man who'd summited Everest five times. A mountain of a man – until Rick had come calling.

'I'm sorry, Russell,' said Hunter.

'Why's that?'

'Not taking a stirrer.'

'You should have done.'

'Yeah.'

'Next time.'

Rick went over to the larger of the two machines. The back half consisted of a cabinet with flexible tubes clipped to the sides and a monitor on top, and the front half a giant C with an upturned bowl for the head like a dryer at a hair salon. All sparkling white and stainless steel. He could see parts of his face, distorted and deformed.

Monstrous.

As if he was standing in a hall of mirrors.

Part of a horror show.

50

The shower block was noisy with banter: the evening football game, Dirty Harry, the new guard on the wing. Two cons were singing an army chant. Calix pictured all sorts getting done – CCTV in the shower block was against prison regs.

He hung his towel over a cubicle wall and pulled his t-shirt over his head. Keeping his running shorts and flip-flops on, he stepped into the shower and let the wooden three-quarter door swing shut behind him. He slid the bolt. Then angled the showerhead so it pointed to a wall and pressed the knob for water. He stood in the dry by the opposite wall. From inside his shorts he took out the phone and marker pen and placed them on the soap rack. Day to day, Toose kept the phone under a tile by their bog. It might get picked up in a sweep, but the phone didn't matter so much. The SIM card was the important thing.

He took off his shorts and squatted down. Closer to the scratched graffiti, the residue of filth on the tray, the pubes stuck to the chipped tiles.

He inserted a finger.

Delved, hooked, pulled the small shitty bag out slowly.

And let it drop. He stared at it for a few seconds. Stuffing now as routine as cleaning his teeth. He smacked the water knob again, and soaped and rinsed his hands. Cleaned the bag. Dried his hands and removed the SIM. He slotted it home and waited for the phone to power up.

To-and-fro volleys of abuse replaced the singing.

Calix's stomach churned. Prison regs were the least of his worries: the phone call and online transaction would take time. The red light on the phone blinked. He tapped through for the number, pressed dial. Hit the knob for water.

'Coniston, how long you gonna be?' The door shook.

'Only just started,' shouted Calix, pulling on his shorts. He hit the water knob and checked the door bolt.

'Yeah?' said a voice on the phone.

'You seen the news, Darren?' Calix whispered. 'Special K shot a dibble in Aldershot.'

'Relax, Capeman, I'm on it. But my man needs the real beans now. His brother Ant works in a petrol station, he's the white fucking baa-baa of the family. He's got an account.'

'Sort code?'

Calix wrote the number on his arm. Fail to prepare, prepare to fail. His old man was with him.

'Account number.'

Calix wrote the eight digits under the sort code.

'Need an address,' said Darren.

'I'm still working on it, I'll call again.'

There was hammering on the door. 'What you doing in there, Coniston?'

'Washing my hair.'

The wheezy cackle hopefully meant he'd won some time. He clicked through to internet banking and entered his user ID.

Password.

BirdBird!

The bank's website didn't like it.

A pockmarked face appeared under the door. Albino eyes, long greasy hair, leering grin.

Calix ripped down his shorts and started masturbating, and grunting.

The face disappeared. There was a stream of imaginative swearing, and more wheezing. Then: 'I'm going to count to twenty.'

!BirdBird!

Success.

Two more questions. His old man's middle name. His favourite country.

They shared both answers, he was sure.

Jack. Nepal.

He was in. He hit the shower knob.

'Ten, eleven . . .'

He copied the bank details from his arm.

'Fifteen, sixteen . . .'

Calix transferred fifteen k.

'Seventeen . . . beating the bishop or not . . .'

He unclipped the back of the phone and pushed out the SIM. He took a new plastic wrap from his t-shirt pocket and covered the SIM. He pulled down his shorts, squatted and reinserted the wrap. It didn't hurt, but nagged like a splinter and always took a while to forget. He yanked up his shorts and hid the handset in the gusset.

'Nineteen . . .' The door juddered, the bolt rattling in its catch.

Calix hit the shower knob one last time and thrust his head under the spray. He pulled on his t-shirt and grabbed his towel.

'Fucking twenty!'

Calix retracted the bolt, pushed through the swing door, and walked out with his hair dripping and his flip-flops slapping the damp hard floor.

51

They headed north, back up the motorway.

'Do you think we'll get him?'

'We have to,' said Rick.

Hunter drove faster. From time to time he flexed his fingers against the steering wheel or itched his neck.

Rick stared out of the window. A landfill site appeared in the mist. A great sea of rubbish, thin chimneys poking out like periscopes. Two caterpillar vehicles worked up and down, triangular claws embedded in the tracks helping to keep them upright. Their car ploughed through the smell of decomposing rubbish. Next, a field with cows huddled around a feeder, and then a housing development, Lego-like in its simple repetitive geometry.

Stoke 34 miles, Manchester 87 miles.

They'd all be waiting for him: Robbo and the chief super, the discipline board, Dad, Emma. Enough for a firing squad.

At least he had Maggie – she was on his side.

Aldershot was no better. Khetan wouldn't go back there, not unless he was taken in a prison van. And Russell was in Aldershot – Russell, Russell's parents, and Velvet. The mountaineer cum special constable had been moved to the ICU, his wound having become infected. For Rick to be the lightning rod for the only thing the two bedside factions agreed on wasn't attractive, but staying nearby was the right thing to do. What he wanted to do, what Maggie would want him to do.

Ali phoned.

'All done. Two were vacant; nine asleep in the third. Seized phones. Nothing stood out. Magistrate v unhappy. You owe me, sir.'

Fuck you.

They drove alongside a vast warehouse with numbered bays and steel shutters. Dozens of trucks lined up outside, like piglets with their mother.

'Velvet's a piece,' said Hunter.

The miles ticked down.

They overtook a convoy of military vehicles. Soldiers smoked and peered out from the backs of the lorries. Then Land Rovers with jerry cans strapped to the roofs and spare wheels held down by netting on the bonnets. Long antennae reached into the air. In the first vehicle a driver with a rolled-up beret in his epaulette glanced across at him.

The phone rang.

Rick grabbed it up. 'Got something, Matt?'

Hunter glanced across.

'We've not found the weapon or the bullet. But, we have recovered hairs from the balaclava. And, the DNA profiles match both those on the bullet casing and on the soft-drink cans found in the temporary classroom.'

'Anything else?'

'No.'

'Well, it's a start.' If Khetan had shot Russell, there was sufficient forensic evidence to connect him with the classroom and with the bullet casing. Even with a No Comment interview, there ought to be enough to convince a judge. Convincing a jury was very different: a jury was no better than two rows of coin-tossers.

But first they had to find him.

'How's the journey?'

'The journey, Matt?' Rick thumped the phone back into its cradle.

Then picked it up again and checked for messages. Negative from the DIs at Dover and Stansted. No movement at the K2.

'Do you think he's still in the country?'

'Not a bloody chance.'

Rick tended to agree: if he'd been Khetan he'd have sorted out an exit strategy – another false ID, passport, plane ticket – as soon as he'd arrived in London. But, until it was confirmed, there was a chance.

There was still a chance.

Hunter slowed, flashed his lights, and accelerated again. Glared across at the driver of a Mini.

They sped on.

The DI from Hounslow phoned.

'We've found your LOS from Aldershot – dumped in an industrial estate. CCTV trawl underway.'

Rick balled his fist. 'At last, we've got something.'

'Keep going,' said the Hounslow DI.

Rick told Hunter. If it was Khetan, he was heading for the airport. Or the underground, or the train network. Or wanting the police to think like that.

And a very big if.

Rick relaxed his grip, and Hunter drummed his fingers on the steering wheel. He sang a ditty about a girl called Velvet. Then leant across and switched on the radio.

The weather. A cold front about to sweep across the UK

from the west, temperatures below average.

After the weather, the news. The worsening European migrant crisis was the lead story: bodies had been washed up on Greek beaches amongst holidaymakers. The next item was the Aldershot shooting. 'The search for Hant Khetan, the Nepalese gunman known as Special K who is believed to have shot Special Constable and five-time Everest summiteer Russell Weatherbeater, continues. Although the police are following up what they say are promising lines of enquiry, they also admit that Khetan may have left the country.'

The newsreader paused.

'We are just hearing unconfirmed reports that Weatherbeater has gone into a coma. As soon as we hear any more, we will update you.'

'Fuck.'

The two of them said it together. Rick punched the dashboard, and Hunter banged on the window.

Finally, the three of them were a team.

*

Calix sat watching the TV news. Toose lay on his bunk chewing a pen and scowling at a kid's bumper book of puzzles.

'Migrant workers are still dying in Qatar. They're building the football stadiums for the 2022 World Cup. In June the Qatari government postponed a vote to reform the kafala sponsorship system. This vote has still not taken place, and FIFA are being heavily criticised.'

The newsreader took a breath. 'This is now a scandal. A local government official who didn't want to be named told us that, last year, 183 Nepalese workers died, and estimated that by 2022 the total will exceed four thousand.'

The screen switched from the studio to a reporter

waiting outside a large house. The door opened, and a man stepped out. *Terry Williams, FIFA vice president* flashed up on the screen.

Barney's father. By kidnapping Barney and Spencer, Khetan had tried to force him to change FIFA policy. Tried, and failed.

'Four thousand dead workers building your football stadiums, Mr Williams. Is that fair? Is it justifiable?' The camera panned across the road to the River Thames, and back to the house. Three storeys. *River View.* Terry Williams started walking down the road. 'I've got no comment.' The reporter fired more questions as he followed him. On the corner, a street sign. Calderdale Road.

Calix switched off the TV. It was possible Khetan might have another go – target Williams' wife or even Terry Williams himself – while he was in the UK.

Unlikely, but conceivable.

He looked up at Toose, lying on his bunk. 'I need the phone.'

'Now!'

Toose nodded, swivelled his legs over the side and jumped down. At the door Calix looked out obliquely through the re-inforced glass. The smell of Spice percolated through the air holes. He looked along the landing the other way, and raised a thumb at Toose.

His cellmate dropped to his hands and knees at the side of the bog. He pressed down with his fingers and eased up a tile. Calix checked the landing again, then back over his shoulder. Toose pulled out the phone.

They swapped places.

Calix pulled down his jeans and shorts and squatted. He removed the bag, rinsed it, then inserted the SIM in the phone.

'Guard,' said Toose. 'Aen the stairs.' Calix put the phone in a pocket and sat on his bunk. He could hear footsteps on the metal corridor. He picked up a newspaper and pretended to read. The metal hatch dropped down.

'Stand back from the door.'

Toose spat through the hatch. The hatch was slammed back up. 'Sweep team,' he shouted over his shoulder. He kicked the door. 'Gonna take more than twos of yer.'

A guard blew a whistle and moments later a klaxon sounded. More footsteps clanged along the landing. Along the wing, like falling dominoes, cons began to shout and clink the pipes.

Calix turned on the phone. Toose stamped down on a plastic chair, snapping it into pieces. He grabbed a leg and struck the door. Calix made the call.

Engaged.

Outside the cell a guard spoke with a loudhailer. 'Stand away from the door.' A dog barked. Toose broke the second chair and flung the pieces at the door. The klaxon kept wailing.

Calix tried the number a second time. It started ringing.

'Stand back from the door.'

'Entry teams,' shouted Toose. He picked up the TV, ripping out the leads. A buzzer sounded and the cell door rolled open. A tortoise of shields entered – three guards in a triangle, two men with shields at the front and one man behind them without a shield who controlled the two in front.

Toose hurled the TV at the guards. It bounced off the shields and hit the floor. The screen shattered and sprayed glass. The three guards hugged tighter, stepped forward and over the TV. They retreated, pulling it back. Well drilled, not panicked. Calix's old man would have approved.

Toose rearmed himself with chair legs.

The phone kept ringing, and Calix retreated into the furthest corner.

A second triangle of guards entered, and the first advanced. Toose flailed at the shields with his plastic daggers. One guard struck him with a long baton. Toose chucked the chair legs. They hit the shields and bounced away. He picked up the microwave, feinted a throw. The guards stepped back, braced their shields.

'Capeman?' said Darren on the phone.

'Tell your man: BARNES.'

The second tortoise stepped forward. Toose hurled the microwave. They stepped backwards, the microwave hit the floor, bounced, and clattered to a standstill.

'Tell him CALDERDALE ROAD. CAL–DURR–DALE. As it sounds. CAL–DURR–DALE. ROAD.'

The second tortoise advanced again, stepped over the microwave and pushed it backwards. A guard in the doorway removed it.

More guards in riot gear arrived. One held a fire extinguisher, a second the leash of a slathering Alsatian. The alarm continued ringing. Boots clanged on the metal stairs and landings. Cons yelled and whooped, and barked at the dog.

'Tell him, a house called RIVER VIEW.'

'Barnes, Cal–durr–dale Road. River View House. Got it.'

Calix slid the back off the phone, then dropped it as he pushed out the SIM card. No time to stuff it, so he swallowed. The second tortoise came towards him and for an instant he felt he was on the set of a prehistoric film, fighting some ancient multi-limbed monster. A limb rose from amongst the shields and struck his hand holding the phone. The screen broke, and his fingers throbbed with pain. The second strike was to his face, and blood poured from his nose. 'Resisting arrest,' shouted a guard.

They held him down while next to him on the floor guards thrashed around with Toose.

The alarm was clamouring. The dog was snarling. Toose was roaring in Scots. Cons were shouting and jeering and whooping and laughing and bellowing.

Calix spat blood on the floor.

Now he could only hope.

Rick switched off the radio. The newsreader hadn't mentioned the link between the second item and the last item. Nepal – obvious, but it made him rewind all the way to the beginning. He'd reread the files at the hospital.

The year before, Khetan had kidnapped the twin sons of a FIFA vice president, Terry Williams. Motivated by honour – *Dharma* – Khetan had wanted to pressurise FIFA into changing its policy in respect of Nepalese workers building stadiums for the Qatari World Cup. Spencer Williams had died as a result. But Barney Williams and Mrs Williams were still alive. And Terry Williams was the only FIFA official living in the UK. Rick had been to their flat overlooking the river. The perfect place to watch the Boat Race, Mrs Williams had told him.

Khetan had failed to influence FIFA, but while he was in the country there was a chance he might have another go. A final headline-grabbing flourish.

While Rick was pondering, the DI from Hounslow phoned back. He sounded upbeat. 'There's been another LOS near the dump site, an almost identical car. It's a red Honda Jazz. I'll ping you the reg.'

Khetan, on the move again? Not the airport. A change of plan, or the FBI target's plan all along?

Even if it wasn't Khetan, it didn't matter: it was the nudge Rick needed.

'U-turn, Gary.'

'Frimley Hospital?'

'Barnes, we're going to Barnes.'

Hunter pulled off at the next junction, turned right and

right again, and accelerated hard. Rick grabbed the handle on the roof to steady himself and, praying he was right, gripped so hard the colour drained from his knuckles.

52

Hunter drove at a hundred miles an hour in the overtaking lane. He drove with the headlights on and ignored the hooting and hand signs from other drivers. Rick fingered his phone while watching the road.

There were four calls to make, and Rick started with the most pressing: the FIFA vice president. He hugged the phone to his ear and waited, hoping he'd be able to hear above the scream of the car. They overtook an Italian sports car, the driver on the phone, a young blond woman furious about something. Lawyer? Banker? Two things he knew for certain: she wasn't police, and she might as well sell her wing mirrors.

The phone rang out. Rick dialled again. In the opposite carriageway an accident had brought the traffic to a standstill. A lorry had jack-knifed and a campervan lay on its side.

'Terry Williams.'

'Sir, it's DCI Rick Castle, Manchester CID. I investigated your sons' disappearance last year. I came to your house on the river.' Rick paused. 'And I met you again when we brought Barney home.'

'Yes. Detective Castle?'

Rick explained the risk of Khetan targeting their family for a second time. They were still passing stationary vehicles on the other carriageway. Some of the occupants wandering about next to their cars.

'You think moving to temporary accommodation is absolutely necessary?'

'Yes, sir. You need to phone your wife and tell her not to go back home. Then phone Barney and tell him the same thing. Pick them up and go to friends or a hotel and phone me when it's done.'

'You're sure?'

'I'm sure.' He ended the call and watched two ambulances speed up the opposite hard shoulder. Risk was risk: he was damned if he was right and damned if he wasn't. One down.

'Hope you know what you're doing,' said Hunter.

'You, too.' Rick watched the needle creep up to 110. The car began to shudder. Rick plugged his phone into the cigarette lighter and pressed for the second number: the duty officer at Barnes police station. He put the phone on speaker, rested it in the cradle, and waited. 'Did you—'

'Course I did. Done all the courses except dogs, horses, and underwater dive.'

The engaged tone filled the car.

'Try Russell,' said Hunter.

Rick phoned the hospital, and as they waited for the call to be put through they passed a car stopped under a bridge. A man held a young girl over a potty.

'Are you family?' said a female voice.

'Police, darling,' said Hunter.

'Don't darling me.'

Rick backtracked and elaborated.

'Hold on,' said the woman.

They waited. They drove under a succession of footbridges.

Sheep were being chased by a dog. A waving family stood with their bicycles. The third was devoid of life.

'I'm sorry to have to tell you this,' said the woman, 'but the infection's serious. Fifty-fifty if you want a number. So many people do.'

Hunter drove faster. He scratched his wrist, his neck, then behind his ears, folding them down as if they were sun visors. One of his ears started bleeding.

'Russell's alright,' said Hunter.

Rick dialled again, staring out into fields of stubble. A jumble of old farm machinery lay abandoned in a corner.

The number was engaged.

Hunter braked hard, swerved into the middle lane. He undertook an estate car doing ninety, swerved back.

Rick texted Maggie. *Can you get into work, need you to run some intel checks. Start with an LOS from Hounslow. Red Honda Jazz F63PEG. Flag it with my name, and upload onto ANPR.*

She messaged straight back.

Leaving now

He dialled again.

'Duty Officer,' said a woman on the phone. 'Sorry if you've been trying. It's been one of those mornings. How can I help?'

Rick pictured her in the inspectors' office writing up the morning's incidents, her radio chuntering away on the desk. It was early afternoon, and at the same time as talking to him she'd be thinking through her handover to the next shift and listing the number of things she still had to do before she could go home. But his investigation had been running for nearly two years and it felt like he was about to squeeze a book into a text message.

He took a deep breath. 'DCI Castle, South Manchester CID.'

'Inspector Cummins.'

'You know about the shooting in Aldershot?'

'Yes, sir.'

'I'm investigating it.' Traffic slowed behind an oversized transporter with a mobile home. They passed a lorry with steel rods and dangling yellow flags, a farmyard truck with squealing pigs, and two minibuses on a school trip.

'Okay.'

'I think the suspect – Hant Khetan – is heading to an address in Barnes.'

'You *think?*'

'I'd like an OP and firearms teams ready for when he turns up.'

'*If* he turns up.'

'If he turns up.'

'So just to be clear, Khetan is not there now?'

'No.'

'If he's not there now, you're looking at a pre-planned firearms operation.'

Hunter accelerated hard, away from the slow vehicles. The road descended in a huge sweeping curve, woods on one side, houses on the other. The needle touched 120 and the car shook with effort.

She was right procedurally and legally, but Rick had hoped she'd bend the rules for a suspect who'd shot one of the police family. A colleague who was deemed alright by Hunter, and a mountaineer who'd become Rick's friend. And he didn't have many.

'It'll need a full risk assessment by one of our superintendents, but you'll need one of yours to sign it off first.'

Hunter braked sharply and the bonnet dipped. Three lorries jostling for position on the slow and middle lanes had forced a white van into the overtaking lane. The van driver hadn't looked let alone indicated. Their car juddered as the brakes took effect. Hunter released the brake pedal, then pushed down again hard. The car lost speed, enough to match the accelerating van. He shook his head.

'What's the intel?' said the inspector.

As the van reached ninety Hunter double de-clutched into fourth gear. The car sounded like a racing car.

'Sir, are *you* driving?'

Using a finger Hunter drew large capital letters in the air above the steering wheel.

L

I

D

Rick didn't disagree: uniform officers were obsessed with traffic offences, even when there was serious crime at stake.

'No.'

'But you're heading to Barnes?'

'I think Khetan'll be there.'

'Tell me about the address.'

'Terry Williams – the UK vice president to FIFA – lives there with his family.'

'Where are they now?'

'I've moved them.'

'So there's no actual threat to anyone?'

'No.'

'If they're not there, what can Khetan actually do?'

'Burn the place down.'

'If you can arrange access I'll get a fireproof letterbox fitted. And a patrol car to be parked outside.'

'Inspector, I assume you know who Hant Khetan is? He's the FBI's number one target in South Asia, and one of Manchester's Most Wanted – our deputy chief has taken an interest. And now he's shot a police officer.

This is a golden opportunity to arrest—'

'Rules must be rules, sir, even in Manchester.' She paused. 'I have to go now. If you don't want a box or a car, then the best I can do is update my relief, Inspector Whitaker. He'll contact Trojan who'll provide armed response if Khetan turns up. Inspector Whitaker will also brief the afternoon shift and get patrols to pay passing attention. I'll tell him to expect your risk assessment later on. Good luck.'

Hoping Cummins would drown in the pool or have a heart attack on the golf course, Rick thumped the phone back in its cradle.

'Lids are like migrating birds,' said Hunter. 'Eat, shit, and go home.'

Rick watched the traffic streaming past. *Oxford 10 miles, 10 minutes* flashed up on an overhead gantry. They were still an hour from Barnes.

'Sometimes they mate in the back of the area car.'

Rick tapped the phone until he heard a dialling tone. Before mobile phones, policing had been slower but simpler – one enquiry at a time. 'Last call.' As he waited, he stared at his reflection in the window – it looked like him, but he felt like he'd lived three lifetimes.

'I wondered when you were going to grace me with a call,' said Robbo. 'Where are you?'

Rick explained his thinking on Barnes, then summarised his conversation with Inspector Cummins. He finished with the 50/50 update on Russell.

'I'm sorry to hear that.' The superintendent waited a few seconds. 'Rick, you astound me. You're currently under investigation for gross misconduct, and yet here you go again. On an operational level, I agree with the Barnes duty officer: you've averted the risk by removing the family and you've briefed the local units just in case. Yes, it's an opportunity to arrest Khetan, but it's not very likely and you're not the right man to do it. Update the Aldershot SIO, and then you're done.'

Hunter slowed to the speed limit.

'You and DS Hunter need to turn round, and get back up here. You hear me?'

Rick dumped the phone back in the cradle. They sped past a farm lorry on the inside lane. Bullocks stared out through the slats with glassy eyes. Written in faded gold lettering on the cab door: *Andrews Abattoirs*.

'You get that?'

'The gist.'

'I'm going to Barnes, Gary, but, I can drop you at the nearest train station.'

'Okay,' said Hunter, reaching down to scratch his shin.

They reached the outskirts of London. The M4 became the A4, and the traffic slowed. It was warmer and hazier. Houses and light industry and high rise as far as the eye could see.

They waited at a junction. Two men on ladders were unscrewing an advertising hoarding.

'What would you do in Barnes if you were Khetan?'

'Wait somewhere nearby,' said Hunter. 'Probably in a vehicle. Maybe the Hounslow LOS. Maybe a different one.'

At a set of red traffic lights, Rick opened his window. The other side of the barrier a man ran along the path behind a boy on a bicycle with stabilisers.

The lights turned green and Hunter took off. He slammed through the gears as he took a short cut through an industrial estate.

'Five minutes 'til landing.'

Rick reached behind the driver's seat and hauled Hunter's kit bag closer. It was time to dress up.

53

They drove across Hammersmith Bridge. Below them, the Thames gleamed emerald. On the Barnes side of the river, a dredger swung across a barge and dumped a bucket of sludge. A large sailing boat with a horizontal mast motored seawards.

One hundred metres after the bridge they turned right into Calderdale Road.

'The Williams family live at the far end, Gary, about a mile. Their house is called River View. Drive past it, U-turn at the roundabout and drive back this way. See what we see.'

Hunter opened the window and rubbed his elbow along the protruding edge of glass. Rick pulled down the visor. He angled his head for a side view of the flat cap and tortoiseshell glasses.

'Maggie might like them,' said Hunter.

They drove past detached houses with small front gardens. Then a nature reserve on the river side of the road.

Rick felt cold as a body in the water. This was it: their last chance.

His last chance.

At the end of the reserve, the road ran alongside the river. Grating seagulls trailed the pearl-grey sky. Two sculls glided past, and a speedboat bumped along by the far bank.

Rick turned to the houses and the vehicles parked outside. If Khetan arrived by boat, Rick would leave the Job and become a full-time beekeeper. If he was wrong about Khetan, maybe he would have no choice.

'Slowly, Gary!'

'Seen him.'

An Asian man stood by himself at a bus stop. He wore thick glasses, held a newspaper. Shirt and tie. Anorak.

Rick tensed, even though the man was too fat. Khetan could have put on weight. Rick peered through the back seats. Not only was the man dumpy, but he was too short. Not by much but enough.

'It's not him.'

'Still, don't imagine there are too many ethnics in Barnes.'

Rick let the word go. Hunter probably had a name for people like Maggie.

They were getting close to the Williamses' house. No sign of the red Honda Jazz, but three vans were parked in a line, the nearest one thirty metres before the house. No police officer liked vans. Criminals moved stolen goods in them; pretended to be window cleaners or engineers; surveilled from the back like police. The public didn't give them a second glance.

'River View is coming up. The one with the shiny black gate.'

'Got it.'

The pavement on the river side of the road widened. There was a series of benches and a telescope to observe whatever spectacle was being offered. An elderly couple sat sharing an ice-cream.

No one resembling Khetan.

In the back of a van?

The Williamses' house was a grand affair over three storeys, commanding panoramic views of the river. Each of the upper floors had a set of French windows and a small terrace. They drove past. The gate was shut, the doorstep clear. Upstairs, one open window. In the tiny front yard, a covered area for two dustbins was large enough to conceal a person.

'Pull in, Gary, just before the roundabout. Have a wander, become part of the scenery, maybe sit on a bench. And don't forget your phone. I'll drive back around the roundabout and try to park in the space beyond the three vans.'

Hunter stopped in a loading bay, and climbed out alongside a baker's. The smell of bread wafted into the car. Next door was a chip shop, a queue of people stretching into the street, then a pub with a blackboard offering Sunday roast for £9.99.

Rick shuffled across to the driver's seat. He pulled into the traffic and drove around the roundabout with the seatbelt sensor beeping. Already, he'd lost sight of Hunter.

He drove back up the road, glancing at River View. The gate was still shut, the window still open. Sunday strollers on the pavements on both sides of the road: parents with kids, rollerbladers, single men with newspapers under one arm, a man with binoculars. The space beyond the vans was still there. He reversed in.

He turned off the ignition and set the mirrors, unable to resist a double-take in the rearview. A selfie would amuse Mum and Becky, but Dad wouldn't get it – wouldn't get there was anything to get.

If Rick was found guilty of gross misconduct, at least Dad wouldn't suffer.

In the glovebox he found an old bag of Werthers, and sucking on a sweet, took stock. The driver's wing mirror showed the pavement and the Williamses' gate. A family walked by with a pushchair, two balloons attached to the handle. The three vans were parked behind him: blue, white with red lettering, and grey. The rearview showed the road and the pavement opposite the Williamses' house. The elderly couple had gone, and two backpackers were sitting down.

Rick adjusted the rearview and inspected the blue van directly behind the car. *Hammersmith Vehicle Rentals* – and a phone number. He texted Maggie the registration plate. All three vans were possible hiding places for Khetan. He imagined the FBI nominal sitting on a crate in the back, watching the Williamses' front door through a DIY surveillance hole. Next to him a bottle of chloroform and a pair of plastic cuffs.

Hunter reappeared, crossing the road and eating a pastry. He stopped at an information signboard. A seagull flew down and hopped around at his feet.

Rick unwrapped another sweet. His phone beeped.

Hes got worse now 75/25 + poss of brain damage thought youd wanna know Velvet x

Rick closed his eyes. He hoped Russell wasn't in pain. The end was nothing, and nothing was nothing.

He crunched the sweet to pieces and opened another. Russell had climbed Everest five times, he'd set up a successful trekking company. He'd married, brought up a child, and was having an affair with a nineteen-year-old. He'd done more than most.

More than Rick. A detective who'd made DCI, and kept bees. But he'd not yet married, not had children, wasn't even living with his girlfriend. His front fence needed fixing, his car hadn't been serviced for three years, and dirty plates had been sitting in his dishwasher for a fortnight.

His phone beeped with a message from Maggie. He forwarded Velvet's text to Hunter, and opened the email.

No reports on PNC. HVR told me it's been hired for a week by Ashok Suma – 1982 DOB (same as Khetan – coincidence?),

*address in East Ham. The employee who dealt with Suma
described him as 'brown, not black, not fat, not small and not
tall'. Wouldn't recognise again. They don't have CCTV and
didn't photocopy his driving licence. DVLA computers are down
so I can't check the dl number (which HVR did write down –
probably wrongly). No intel on his home address. Do you want
me to send a unit to the Ham address? M*

He checked the mirrors. The gate still closed, the front yard
still empty. The backpackers were eating crisps on the bench.
He put another sweet into his mouth, rolled up the wrapper
and made a knot.

Russell was 75/25. There was still 25. Russell was a strong
man, a fit man, a determined man. He was a mountaineer. Rick
texted Maggie, then Velvet.

Yes
Thanks for update 25 for normal people or for Russell?

Two texts arrived in quick succession from Hunter.

Fuck
No windows in back of hvr van 2 other vans empty

Rick stared up at the house alongside the car. A leaking
gutter had caused a green stain down the first storey of
brickwork. There were too many variables. Khetan could be
Suma. Or he might be coming later, or the next day. Or not at
all. Or he might be sitting in another van or the Honda Jazz
further away. Or staked out at the rear of the Williamses'
address, or on the other side of the river near the boathouses,
armed with a telescopic sight.

He could send Hunter to have a look, scout around the back

of the house. Or he could go himself. He needed a team of people, fifteen or twenty, and armed, to do things properly. Maybe Khetan was back in Nepal and had recruited someone else. Maybe Rick had put two and two together and made four thousand.

Maybe they should call it a day and drive across to Aldershot and wait at the hospital with Velvet.

A rough sleeper dragging a sleeping bag shuffled along the pavement. Following behind, a scruffy dog sniffed a litter bin.

Even in Barnes.

Rick switched mirrors and searched for Hunter. He found him: he'd walked further down the far pavement and sat on a bench. Nearby, a couple sat on the wall eating fish and chips. Three young boys ran along the pavement and stopped by a bin. They pulled out an umbrella, and the tallest boy hurled it over the wall and into the river.

He checked on the HVR van.

An Asian man was unlocking the driver's door. The man climbed in and drove away. He could have been Suma, but he definitely wasn't Khetan.

Rick checked his watch: five already. Was Russell getting better or worse? 74/26 or 76/24. He texted Velvet a second time.

A new queue had formed outside the chip shop. Seagulls flapped above the waiting crowd, and next door people were drifting into the pub. A different man would call it off, grab a take-out from the chip shop, and drive to the hospital.

He wasn't a different man. He checked the mirrors. A man on crutches and his leg in plaster worked his way along the pavement outside the target address. It only made him think of the Jackal. On the opposite pavement the benches had filled up with people and their greaseproof wrappers. No sign of Hunter.

He unwrapped another sweet. His phone beeped.

No change Velvet x

Another white van parked up behind him and on the far side of the two parked vans, the cab facing the roundabout. No one got out. No markings he could see.

He spotted Hunter crossing the road again. Then lost him in the crowd outside the chip shop. Possible he was inside, or in the pub. Although it seemed unlikely Khetan was waiting there, maybe he was doing the unexpected. Intuition and counter-intuition had been a paper on his last CPD refresher.

He texted Hunter: *Can you check on new white van, and text Maggie the reg.*

The queue outside the chip shop moved aside as a dogwalker with half a dozen dogs walked by. The queue swayed back.

Hunter reappeared with a bag of chips.

Both pavements were busy now. Couples, families, two joggers, a gang of young boys on skateboards. Cars were starting up and driving away, and new cars were parking. An ambulance flashed past on blues and twos, and a helicopter throbbed up the river.

The three vans sat there, no one getting in or out. Which meant there was at least the driver of the white van sitting within thirty metres of Rick. And within thirty metres of the Williamses' front gate. Plus countless other cars within striking distance, and dozens of pedestrians.

It was hopeless.

But what choice did he have? Russell was 75/25. Rick would wait all week. He'd wait until Robbo got off his ever-larger backside and drove down to reassign him in person.

Rick felt in the bag for another Werthers. There was only one left. He unwrapped it, and tried to make it last.

A clock struck six. He pictured his mum in the kitchen listening to the headlines and preparing her supper for one.

Dad would have already eaten. Dad ate at five, like a child.

An email arrived from Maggie in respect of the white van.

No current keeper. Last keeper in Staines. One report: three days ago the driver was seen in Wythenshawe B&Q buying overalls, boltcroppers, disposable gloves, rubble sacks, and ropes.

Rick swallowed his sweet.

The van was connected to Manchester, and recently. Khetan? Or someone he'd hired preparing for a different job. Or even this one. A coincidence seemed unlikely.

Hunter strolled up the near pavement eating his chips. He stopped to look at his phone. Reading the info from Maggie, Rick hoped.

He phoned him. A pincer move might work, he thought.

A motorbike blatted past.

When Rick looked back at the pavement, Hunter had disappeared. His phone was still ringing, but his sergeant didn't answer. Surely he didn't have it on si—

Hunter started shouting.

Rick ripped off his cap and glasses, and shoved open the door. He jumped out, ran across the front of the car and into the road. The driver's door of the white van was wide open. Hunter was hauling someone out. Rick drew his baton and extended it.

Hunter bundled the man to the tarmac and booted him in the stomach. The man rolled over. An Asian man: about five foot six, about the right age, about the right build.

They had him.

The FBI's Most Wanted in South Asia, the man responsible for the death of David Coniston, and countless others. Everything was going to be okay.

Rick would make peace with Robbo.

One day he'd marry Maggie.

Russell would recover and be his best man.

He'd invite Hunter to the stag.

Dad would call him Rick again.

Rick sprinted down the vehicles until he reached them. Traffic halted in both directions, people on the pavement stopped and stared.

Hunter bent to apply a handcuff. Khetan swivelled on the floor and scissor-kicked the detective, the handcuffs clattering to the road. Khetan dug around in his waistbelt, revealing the butt of a pistol.

Rick struck Khetan's forearm with his baton as hard as he could. Khetan retracted his hand.

'Firearm!'

A woman on the pavement screamed. A whirl of running, screaming, shouting.

Khetan felt for his weapon a second time. Rick struck him again on the arm. It caught his elbow. There was a crack, and a gasp of pain.

'Hands.'

Khetan held his arms out to the sides, and stopped moving. Rick could hear his laboured breathing. Hunter's, too. All three of them were sweating and blowing like racehorses.

Hunter retrieved his handcuffs and secured Khetan's wrists behind his back. He ratcheted them tight. Rick plucked the handgun from Khetan's waistband and slid it under the van for safekeeping. The crowd edged forward, and there was a round of applause. Car horns sounded, a motorbike slalomed around them.

They really did have him.

'Time,' said Hunter, gasping.

'For.

'A.

'Beer.'

'I'll buy you a whole barrel.' Rick wanted to dance the fandango, get drunk, go up in a space rocket and look back at the earth.

He retracted his baton on the road, and stood up. Slotted it away. A blur of voices all around. He glanced at the halted traffic, the driver leaning out of a cement mixer, the crowds of people, a wheeling seagull. He glanced over the cars at the queue outside the chip shop, heads all turned in one direction, then along the pavement towards River View.

A man he recognised was opening its front gate.

54

Terry Williams wore a suit and carried a briefcase. He closed the gate, looked back at the commotion on the road, and hurried towards his front door.

Rick pulled out his phone and tapped 999 to request a van on the hurry up. Vehicles restarted, and some of the crowd began to move away. They had no idea who they'd seen being arrested. Later, they'd be watching it on the news.

'Search him, Gary.'

Hunter patted Khetan down. Their prisoner's breathing had eased and he wasn't going to die. Nor was Hunter.

The 999 call connected. Rick gave his location, his name and rank, and asked for urgent backup.

At River View's front door, Terry Williams fumbled in his pocket. Rick had told the FIFA vice president to stay away, and he wondered why he had ignored his advice. He was in two minds: wait with Hunter and help ward off the crowd and the traffic, or speak to Terry Williams. He could catch up with him later, after Khetan had been taken away, but something made him pause and reconsider. Arresting Khetan felt too easy.

'Clean,' said Hunter, standing up.

Rick walked around the van and onto the pavement. 'Going

to have a word with Williams.' He took a couple of steps towards River View. 'Backup's on the way.'

He walked on, past a house with green shutters. He glanced diagonally back through the parked vehicles at the road, at Hunter standing over Khetan.

Rick speeded up. Williams was still standing on the doorstep of River View, now making a phone call.

An Asian man stopped at the gate. About five feet six, about the right age, about the right build.

Rick's stomach lurched, and he started running.

Was it Khetan opening the gate? But Khetan was in handcuffs, wasn't he? If it wasn't Khetan, then who had Hunter dragged out of the van? And why did he have a handgun?

The Asian man ran at the FIFA VP.

'Terry,' yelled Rick.

Terry Williams gasped, and slumped to the ground. The Asian man dived back to the gate, glancing to his right – at Rick.

Their eyes met.

Khetan had dark brown eyes, wells of conspiracy and otherness – language, religion, culture. Last time they'd met was on a swaying ropebridge miles from anywhere. The Nepalese man had been composed but this time Rick was on home turf. Last time, Khetan had prevailed, but this time. This time.

The FBI's Most Wanted in South Asia turned left and ran towards the crowd outside the chip shop.

'Stop!' shouted Rick. 'Police.'

He had a decision to make. One decision with two options and four outcomes: chase Khetan or help Terry Williams? Best case was that he arrested Khetan and Terry Williams was okay without his help. Worst that he chased but lost Khetan, and Terry Williams died. One decision, four possible outcomes, but at the time he didn't think about any of them. So he did what was instinctive, and didn't stop: he ran past River

View, glancing only briefly at the prostrate Williams.

He sprinted towards the roundabout, jinking round the clusters of people. Knocked over a rack of postcards. Clipped a woman's handbag. Jumped over a dog. The line of parked vehicles ended at the zig-zags for the roundabout. He stepped into the road gutter, and ran past the pub. The doors were open, and groups of men stared out.

He lost sight of Khetan.

'Turned left, governor,' shouted an old man by the post box.

Rick turned left at the roundabout, his shoes skidding slightly. His speed dropped and he wondered if he should go back to help Terry. It was the right thing to do, the human thing. But he'd been investigating Khetan for over a year, the FBI for far longer. He'd sacrificed his friendship with Robbo, and risked his career taking Coniston to Nepal. He was under investigation. Russell had been shot and was 75/25.

He spotted Khetan. Squeezing between two parked cars. The Nepalese man darted into the road, cars hooting. Ran diagonally, towards the village pond.

Rick dashed past a fishing tackle shop, and a bookies, the silhouettes of two punters sitting on high stools in the window.

Khetan turned into a ginnel.

Rick ran across the road, cars slowing and one driver frantically waving at the alley.

At the ginnel he couldn't see Khetan. A stone wall on one side, wire fence on the other. Ahead of him, a dog started barking. Khetan was close. Rick bowled forward, the alley bending round. Hoping every second, every metre, to catch another glimpse.

From nowhere, a dog hit the fence. Barking and pawing the wire, it followed him until the end of its territory. Still there was no sign of Khetan. He came to a junction. Stopped, listened, heard nothing and took a left. Thinking, please, God, if you're up there, let it be left. And if you're not, still let it be left. If there'd been a set of prayer-wheels, he'd have spun every one.

Bonfire smoke drifted across the alley. He ran on, and emerged onto a road. He checked both ways.

No one.

He ran into the middle of the road, looking all around.

'Fuck!'

A car screeched away from the kerb.

Rick gave chase along the central white line. A blue Vauxhall Astra hatchback. Ornate box on the parcel shelf. Rear wind deflectors. The driver accelerated quickly, the engine moaning and the vehicle jerking with the gear changes.

The car turned a corner.

'Nooo.' Rick yelled. Cursed. Screamed. Scrawled the registration on his hand.

He reached the corner and followed the road around the curve.

A straight stretch, an electricity substation on one side and scrub on the other. No cars. Only a parked telecoms van. He slowed to a halt. It still had roofbars but the telecoms signage had been painted over, and a breathing vent fitted.

Rick heard something. Perhaps a bird, foraging in the roadside scrub, perhaps not. He dropped down onto his hands, then to his stomach.

No one under the van.

He stood up, looked through the driver's window, and into the dark cab. He shielded his eyes. The glovebox was open, wrappers and old coffee cups in the passenger footwell. A pair of socks on the dash. In the bottom of the window, there was a bead of condensation. It ran along the bottom of the windscreen. Something was breathing in the back.

Someone?

A screen with a peep hole blocked the rear of the van.

Rick edged away from the window, and down the side of the van. He listened by the rear doors, and slowly, very slowly, tried the handle. Locked. The van hung down on its suspension. It wasn't empty. A large dog, or a person.

He crept along the far side of the van. The passenger door wasn't flush with the sill.

He should circulate the blue Astra, and call for backup on the van. Probably there was only a dog inside. But a dogwalker would hardly leave their pet. Maybe they had two dogs, and walked them separately.

Maybe not.

Rick flicked his baton out. He prised the passenger door open. Listened. He pulled the door wider. There was no smell of wet dog, no growl or bark. He eased up onto the passenger seat.

There was the sound of a lock opening. Doors opening.

Rick slid back out of the van onto the scrubby kerb.

Footsteps on the road.

Running.

Pell-mell.

Rick started chasing, slipping in the mud, veering onto the road.

Khetan was twenty metres ahead. No hills or snow, only flat tarmac, and woody scrub to the sides.

Rick breathed harder as they ran on. They were evenly matched, the distance between them staying constant. He could slow, aim to get him but not as quickly. Or speed up but risk burning out. A chase not a race, like his pursuit of Coniston from Mosom Kharka.

They reached the corner, and for a second, Rick lost sight of his fugitive. His heart was beating like a stampeding elephant's. He put on a spurt, and Khetan came back into view. Beyond him, houses with occupants who could call for backup.

Khetan would be fit as a Sherpa, except he had a ketamine

problem which levelled things out. Rick began to catch him.
Ten metres.

Five metres.

A final effort, then he hurled himself forward, part rugby-
tackle, part bear-hug. Khetan hit the ground like a sack of
potatoes, Rick landing on top and magnifying the impact. He
knelt on the winded man's back, and handcuffed him to the rear.
Patted him down. He sat him up and backed away. Textbook.

Stood, gasping.

In front of him, also gasping, sat Hant Khetan, Special K, an
international Wanted. Handcuffed, his face gashed with road
grit, his trousers ripped from the struggle.

'You're under arrest,' said Rick, and cautioned him – in
sections, as his breathing dictated. Still holding his baton.

He phoned for a van and requested two escort vehicles.
Didn't he know there'd been a stabbing? He did. Explained who
he was, who he'd arrested. He asked about Terry Williams, and
was told it was touch and go.

The nearest house remained in shadow, and no one appeared
from along the road.

Khetan was still breathing hard, his face shiny with exertion.
His eyes now hard black dots. They were staring at Rick,
reflecting, and no doubt, calculating.

'I no a bad person. I believe *Dharma*.'

'You just stabbed a defenceless man,' said Rick. 'And you shot
my friend.' Engaging a suspect in conversation was good
practice, building rapport for the custody suite and interview,
and distracting from thoughts of fighting back or escaping. With
one proviso: staying in control. Otherwise, distracter could
become distracted.

'Williams work FIFA. Your friend abuse Hari.'

'You've killed—' Rick shook his head. So many.

'I save hundreds, Castle.'

354

Basic Carnegie, using the word people liked to hear more than any other. But it backfired, again reminding Rick of the suspension bridge the last time they'd spoken. Of David Coniston.

He strained his ears for the police van.

'Don't you want revenge, Manchester policeman?'

Coniston wanted revenge, but Rick didn't. It was what made them different. Or perhaps they weren't different. He also wanted revenge, but he could stop at justice. He was a police officer, he'd signed up for thirty, hoped to do thirty-five or forty. Keel over on the last day of the Job.

'See you tempted.'

Rick looked up and down the road, listened again. He swapped his baton from his right hand to his left, wiped his sweaty fingers on his trousers, swapped back.

'Break arm,' said Khetan, presenting a shoulder. 'Or leg.' He kicked out with his foot. The sudden vicious movement revealing as a window.

Rick *was* tempted. Perhaps he wasn't so different to Coniston. But he'd been a detective for a decade and suspected Khetan was laying the seeds for a miscarriage of justice: a brutal arrest followed by an unjustifiable assault; blatant flouting of police procedure; total disregard for the criminal law. Case dismissed and Khetan released.

'Hey, Castle.' Khetan followed up with a scissor-kick, moving his whole body along with the effort.

Rick stepped back, and smashed his baton down onto the road. It retracted. He extended it, and crashed it down a second time. Then flicked it out again, glancing at the circular dents in the tarmac.

Resisting arrest. Easy to effect, and easy to write up. Many people, if they knew, would thank him. But he would be the one left with purple-black dreams, night and day.

He could hear sirens.

Two more minutes.

He wiped his hands.

The cavalry arrived. A van and two patrol cars, sirens wailing, and lights flashing like the Blackpool promenade. PCs jumped out, batons and yellow tazers at the ready.

Rick nodded at Khetan.

The FBI's Most Wanted Man in South Asia looked away, looked away at the leafy sycamores, looked away at the sturdy English oaks from which Peelers had cut their truncheons and English longbowmen had fashioned their arrows.

The PCs loaded Khetan into the cage in the back of the van, and locked it. Rick slammed the van door.

And, after almost two years of setbacks and seemingly insurmountable hurdles, he allowed himself a moment. He balanced his baton on his finger so it was upright, and tottered around trying to keep it there. He threw the baton into the air and snatched it back. Threw it, caught it, twirled it as if he was a majorette.

Then he climbed into the front of the van, and sat there with blue flicker revolving around him.

'Quite pleased, then, sir?' said the van driver.

'You've got the makings of a very fine detective,' said Rick.

The van started off, and the disbelief and shock and relief and increasing apprehension for Terry Williams began to flood into him like bathwater.

55

The sky was dirty grey and a downpour looked likely. Rain would halt garden time, the cons forced to troop back indoors like children at primary school.

Calix snipped spinach leaves and collected them in an old washing up bowl. He squashed a few caterpillars, and after wiping off the green sludge, took the bowl over to the three cons sitting on the bench.

'You're learning, son,' said the man in the middle. A fetcher. His face scarred as a colander. 'Courgettes next.'

The courgette plants had filled one raised bed, and like the Chinese in the South China Sea, colonised all the available land. They'd grown across the paths and into the old runner bean bed. According to Calix's old man, the United States Air Force flew a reconnaissance sortie over the Spratly Islands every day, photographing and documenting. Calix hauled up the dying plants and stuffed them in the dustbin. Their umbrella-sized leaves brown and shrivelled.

He stopped work and just stood there. The Chinese had reclaimed two thousand acres for military purposes. Runways and missile silos and ammunition stockpiles. Always thinking ahead, the Chinese. And his old man.

'Son,' shouted the fetcher. Cigarette burns all over his face. 'What goes?'

Calix knelt down in the earth where he'd buried Girl. He ran a hand through the soil, and broke up clods with his fingers. He removed the sprouting weeds and smoothed the bed with the trowel. He'd done his best for her.

'Son.' The fetcher stood up from the bench and hobbled over.

The rain had moved closer and the temperature had dropped. Less than a block away the sky was fuzzy with movement.

'Son, we're sorry about Girl.' The fetcher looked up at the approaching rain, and glanced back at the guard.

The first of the drops reached the bench and the other two cons stood up, one holding an umbrella.

'We heard about Barnes,' said the fetcher, lowering his voice. 'You impressed The Big Red with your—' He paused, his face contorted with the effort to find the right word. 'With your *in-gen-uity*. With your *cre-at-ivity*.'

Raindrops struck Calix on his head and face. He didn't smile at TBR's envoy: it wasn't a day for smiling. But he was pleased, and later, or tomorrow, he would think of ways to finish the mission.

And after Khetan, he'd start on Rod Stokes.

He'd track them down.

And then, as if they were foxes—

The fetcher turned around, and the other two men walked forward, one opening the umbrella. He held it over the fetcher and together they eased towards the guard waiting by the gate, motionless and at home, like a sentry at Buck Pal.

Calix stole a last glance at Girl's final resting place, and then followed the three men, his cheap plimsolls squelching in the soft earth.

56

Interview room three still smelt of wet trainers. Rick sat alone, thinking about his decision at Terry Williams' front gate. The paramedics and the hospital staff had told him that the FIFA vice president would have died whatever Rick had done, but he didn't believe them.

The door was opened by a guard, and Coniston walked in. He didn't smile, but he didn't scowl.

'As it's just two of you,' said the guard, 'I have to stay.'

Rick glanced at Coniston who shook his head. They agreed. 'Ten minutes, that's all.' Rick pushed a packet of cigarettes across the table.

The guard swept them up, and went out. Practicalities were easier without Hunter, but the task more difficult. His sergeant always made Rick look like the reasonable one. Always distracted from the underlying purpose.

Coniston scraped a chair back and sat down. He had a fresh cut above his eye.

'I got him,' said Rick.

'*We* got him.'

'I got him. You led me on a merry dance.'

'I'll blab.'

Rick glanced at the perspex window in the door, at the outline of the guard. Everyone had their price. Most people. 'No you won't.'

Coniston said nothing. He knew it was the truth. He knew that if he did tell, he'd risk worse than a cut eye. No one liked a grass, and cons weren't caught up on the details. Grassing was grassing.

'I've written to the judge.'

'Really?'

'I asked you for help twice, before and after the operation in Nepal. The first time was annulled by your merry dance. The second time you supplied details on Khetan's associate Agasti and the K2. Your information was true, but didn't lead to the arrest of Khetan. That's what I set out in my letter.'

'I won't get much off my sentence with that.'

'You should have thought about that. You also thought Khetan might go to Barnes, and you could have told me.'

'You're fishing.'

Rick smiled. 'Maybe.' There was nothing – evidence or intel – to connect the gunman at Barnes to Coniston, but Rick had applied to bug the gunman's cell. He wasn't hopeful, less so of Coniston making a slip. But he hadn't been able to resist. He was end-of-case high. 'Great minds think alike.'

Coniston's turn to smile. 'You wanted justice.'

'Yes, for your father David, for Spencer and Terry Williams, for the tens, maybe hundreds of others.'

'I won't be in here for ever.'

Rick stood up. He pushed in his chair, in two minds whether to say what he'd just thought. Or whether it would show a weakness, a chink to be exploited by Coniston in the future. He walked to the door, feeling David Coniston watching him. His moral arbiter.

'If you were, it would be a waste.'

361

The guard opened the door, his keys rattling on a long chain. He smirked at nothing.

'When I get out, I'm thinking of keeping bees,' said Coniston.

Rick turned round. 'I *am* keeping bees.'

The Fox and Hounds was a small dark pub on a corner three minutes' walk from South Manchester. They did good-value buffets with chips, had a not-so-hard quiz machine, and the landlord was clean. Most weeks, there was a police social with vague attribution.

Friday afternoon, the majority of the team working the Khetan case were there, including Louise from the CPS, Robbo, and Elaine, DS Khan, Maggie, Hunter. Plus the uniform early turn, half of the support staff, Kate, and the crime scene manager. The CID office was all present except for two trainees left behind to answer the phone. The only notable person absent was Russell. The chief super arrived, said a few words, and went again. Hunter told a joke about three nuns in a hot-air balloon.

Rick stood by himself, wondering how soon he could leave. He'd bought a round at the bar, avoided Khan, and chatted to a couple of typists about the effect of global warming on honeybees.

His phone buzzed.

He's turned it round, now 25/75. Docs going try wake him tomorrow. Vx

Rick climbed onto a chair and shared the news. He gave a toast to Russell, and Hunter led three cheers. Kate was in tears.

He stepped down, and plucked a chip from the buffet. It was all over. One final appointment with Emma, and then he could move forward again. Return to his day job. Attend rather than delegate the case con for the three-handed student rape. He went to find Maggie.

She was talking to Kate about Russell, and he whispered in

her ear. 'How about dinner and an early night?'

'What about—?'

'Her first.'

She nodded, squeezed his hand. 'Meet you outside.'

Rick moved towards the door, avoiding eye contact. He went outside, into the metallic-tasting air.

Footsteps behind him. 'DCI Castle.'

Robbo's voice.

Rick waited. 'Yes, sir?'

'I won't beat about the bush: further to your reg fifteen notice for taking Coniston to Nepal, there's going to be an internal investigation into what went on at Aldershot and at Barnes. In the meantime you're suspended. I'll need your warrant card.'

'Now?'

His boss nodded.

Rick tossed it over, and Robbo waddled off towards the police station.

Maggie appeared.

'What did he want?'

Rick told her.

'That man!'

Not wanting to breathe the same air, they waited five minutes, then followed the superintendent back to the police station.

At the shopping mall, Rick removed Maggie's wheelchair from the car boot and waited while she transferred. A cold wind blew a pile of abandoned leaflets among the parked vehicles.

They made their way across the car park, and waited at the pedestrian crossing, the road heavy with traffic.

'Thanks for coming.'

'I said I would.'

The traffic lights turned red, and they crossed and headed up

Kestrel Street. Rick stepped into the road so he could walk alongside Maggie. Train announcements carried from Piccadilly Station. Cranes poked upward, like candles on a cake, and behind them a rust-coloured haze clogged the sky.

They took the second right into Opal Street. Labourers in fluorescent jackets streamed out of the building site on the corner. One hoiked and spat. It reminded Rick of Nepal.

At Magenta House he pressed the intercom. 'Rick Castle.' He felt naked without his warrant card.

The door buzzed open and they entered. They waited for the lift. The foyer was spartan: no artwork or plants, not even a name board. In the lift his stomach jumped and fell.

Outside room E12 Maggie looked across at Rick. 'There'll be more time for your bees and to visit your dad.'

The door opened. 'Maggie,' said Emma, surprise in her voice.

Rick felt the fingers of his hand being uncurled, and another smaller, warmer, hand fitting into it. He could feel Maggie's ring, his favourite one.

'Hello, Rick.'

'Hello, Emma.'

Arresting Khetan had to be progress. He followed the two women inside, and closed the door.

Lexicon

Nepali	English
aamaa	mother
aath	eight
aba	now
baliyo	strong
bhok	hungry
biyara	beer
bujhe	understand
buwaa	father
camdai	soon
chaar	four
chaina	no
chha	six
chhora	son
chirpi	toilet
chito	quick
chiyaa	tea
chorachori	children

chorten	Buddhist temple
daai	(elder) brother
dal baht	rice and lentils, Nepalese staple meal
das	ten
dhanyabaad	thank you
Dharma	moral code (Hinduism); teachings (Buddhism)
didi	elder sister (lit.); friendly term for women of same generation
dui	two
ek	one
gaaunko	village
gompa	Buddhist monastery
haptaa	week
ho	yes
javaphaharu	answers
Kaha chha?	Where?
Kahile?	When?
Kati bajyo?	What's the time?
Kati din laagchha?	How many days?
kera	banana
khalti	pocket
Kina?	Why?
kinabhane	because
kukri	curved knife – carried by Nepalese men
kukur	dog
maaph garnuhos	sorry
madal	hand drum; the national instrument of Nepal and the foundation of most of the country's folk music

mama	(maternal) uncle
mani	wall or stone carved with prayers
momo	similar to dumplings, contain meat or vegetables
naam	name
naan	a flat round or oval bread
najika	nearby
namaste	hello / goodbye
naramro	bad
nau	nine
nayaka	hero
paanch	five
paani	water
pachaas	fifty
piro	spicy
prahari	police
prasnaharu	questions
purano	old
rakshi	whisky (local)
ramro	good, pretty
roti	a flat round bread
rupas	Buddha postures
saat	seven
sahib	sir
Sangha	the Buddhist community
sano; Sano Nepali.	small; I speak little Nepali.
sirdar	chief guide
sodhnu	ask
sumgura	pigs
Sunko Keta	Golden Boy
Thaahaa chha.	I know.

Thaahaa chhaina.	I don't know.
Thik chha? / Thik chha.	Are you okay? / Yes, I'm okay.
thulo	big
Timro naam ke ho?	What is your name?
tin	three
topi	traditional Nepalese hat
upahara	gift

Acknowledgements

I would like to thank my critiquing partners, Michael Greenwood and Dan O'Sullivan. Also, Joe Stretch, my inspirational creative writing tutor at Manchester Metropolitan University. Finally, I've stopped tinkering with the old car!

Thanks again to Dr Rachel Bray and Lakpa Doma Sherpa for checking the Nepali. Thanks to Derbyshire beekeeper Graham Roberton for the wonderful comb honey.

I would also like to thank the very long list of supporters who made the first edition of the book possible at Unbound. In addition, John Mitchinson and the team at Unbound, the cover designer Mark Ecob, and my brilliant editors Eve Seymour and Mary Chesshyre.

Finally, I would like to thank Andrew Chapman (Prepare to Publish) for his great help with the second edition.

*If you enjoyed this book, please take a few moments
to write a review. Thank you!*